AXE
and
GRIND

I0823967

ALSO BY TAYLOR HUTTON

Strike and Burn

AXE *and* GRIND

TAYLOR HUTTON

BERKLEY ROMANCE
NEW YORK

BERKLEY ROMANCE
Published by Berkley
An imprint of Penguin Random House LLC
1745 Broadway, New York, NY 10019
penguinrandomhouse.com

Copyright © 2026 by Julie R. Buxbaum, Inc., and Adele Griffin
Readers Guide copyright © 2026 by Julie R. Buxbaum, Inc., and Adele Griffin
Penguin Random House values and supports copyright. Copyright fuels creativity, encourages diverse voices, promotes free speech, and creates a vibrant culture. Thank you for buying an authorized edition of this book and for complying with copyright laws by not reproducing, scanning, or distributing any part of it in any form without permission. You are supporting writers and allowing Penguin Random House to continue to publish books for every reader. Please note that no part of this book may be used or reproduced in any manner for the purpose of training artificial intelligence technologies or systems.

BERKLEY and the BERKLEY & B colophon are registered trademarks of Penguin Random House LLC.

Library of Congress Cataloging-in-Publication Data

Names: Hutton, Taylor author
Title: Axe and grind / Taylor Hutton.
Description: First edition. | New York : Berkley Romance, 2026.
Identifiers: LCCN 2025018485 (print) | LCCN 2025018486 (ebook) |
ISBN 9780593817773 trade paperback | ISBN 9780593817780 ebook
Subjects: LCGFT: Romance fiction | Thrillers (Fiction) | Novels
Classification: LCC PS3608.U93 A98 2026 (print) |
LCC PS3608.U93 (ebook) | DDC 813/.6—dc23/eng/20250423
LC record available at https://lccn.loc.gov/2025018485
LC ebook record available at https://lccn.loc.gov/2025018486

First Edition: January 2026

Printed in the United States of America
1st Printing

The authorized representative in the EU for product safety and compliance is
Penguin Random House Ireland, Morrison Chambers, 32 Nassau Street,
Dublin D02 YH68, Ireland, https://eu-contact.penguin.ie.

To all the readers who also seek solace in dark romance,
we see you.

“They fuck you up, your mum and dad.”

—“This Be the Verse,” Philip Larkin

“Every psycho I’ve ever dated was a Leo.”

—@OverheardLA on Instagram

AUTHOR'S NOTE

This book contains a variety of topics that may be difficult for some readers, including adult themes, stalking, violence, child abuse, domestic abuse, suicide, and explicit sexual content. Please exercise your own discretion.

AXE
and
GRIND

ONE

JOSIE

It's a truth universally acknowledged that on your first Saturday night after breaking up with a lying scumbag, you probably shouldn't be wandering through the crumbling halls of the Ravenswood Mental Asylum for the Disturbed. Officially, it was renamed the Ravenswood Institute for Mental Health years ago, but everyone in town still calls it the Asylum, especially now that it's been bought and turned into a haunted film set slash party venue. So here I am, after four long years of coupledom, pretending not to be brokenhearted at this bizarre party. The good news is I'm rocking a kickass DIY mummy dress made with rolls of gauze, safety pins, and just the right amount of bedazzle. At least I look good, even if I feel terrible.

When I pulled the Wheel of Fortune card from my deck this morning, I took it at face value: a promise that everything was going to change today. The tarot sure has a wicked sense of humor.

Fortune, you tricky bitch.

It's been three hours since I called off my wedding with my now former fiancé, Bryan, after a fight that could have made me a viral sensation. Cue my dramatic exit from the diner, all tears and snot right after throwing my engagement ring on top of Bryan's plate of chicken-fried steak.

"I'd like to wrap *you* around my finger," slurs some random Franken-dude, plucking at my costume as I dart into what I hope is a less packed room.

"Go fuck yourself," I say sweetly.

If this is what "getting back out there" looks like, I should have stayed in.

The cards don't lie, but they didn't predict this, either.

For a moment I wish I'd kept that ring to ward off leering pricks. I'd love to say I'm here to celebrate my freedom, but really, I'm just trying to be a good friend. Weeks ago, I promised my best friend, Honor, I'd be her date for the joint corporate bash her boyfriend, Strike, and his best friend, Axe, throw every year. (Axe? That name makes me think of Vikingcore.) Of course Strike (*his* name makes me think of target practice and tactical drones) is here, too, but Honor knew he'd be too busy tech schmoozing, so she begged me to keep her company.

When I agreed to come, I had no idea the last thing I'd want to do tonight would be to dress up and plaster on a fake smile. But if there's one thing I've always believed, it's that the most important rule of friendship is to show up.

So here I am, concealing the tears and snot with cleavage and glitter.

The theme of this year's SynthoTech/Dark Matter Entertainment party is "Our House of Horrors," even though it is February and not Halloween. Axe is the CEO of SynthoTech, which makes me wonder if Strike is only friends with other uber-rich, uber-hot CEOs. Their teams have pulled out all the stops and transformed this space from low-key creepy into something truly terrifying.

This is my first time inside the Ravenswood facility, though I have seen it on television. Apparently, after the asylum closed down, the landowner had the brilliant idea to reimagine it as a film set, and it's managed to continually bring in business for all kinds of different projects, from local productions to Hollywood studios, all in middle-of-nowhere Shelton, Pennsylvania. Since it has that whole creepy old Victorian mansion vibe, it's been a boarding school for mutants on a teen drama series, a "country estate" for a terrible American *Downton Abbey* rip-off, and the home of the Addams Family in the most recent reboot.

Tonight they've dressed the place with flickering lights and broken antique furniture, and they even hired actors dressed to look like zombies or axe murderers.

Come to think of it, why are axe murderers the only murderers defined by their weapon? Why aren't there gun murderers and car murderers? Why axes specifically? Also, for real, who names their kid Axe? Does he have a brother named Hammer? A dog called Nail?

Man, I can't stand that guy. His full name sounds like a rejected perfume. *Axe MacKenzie for Men, available at a select retailer near you.* And listen, I'm usually chill—I'm the rare person who actually defended *Cats* the movie, if that tells you anything.

Fog hangs low over this decrepit building, and the night is lit only by old-fashioned gas lamps. Every few minutes, a scream slices through the party noise, probably someone caught offguard by a wannabe horror-movie actor lurking in the dark. I've been jump-scared twice already, and each time, I've spilled the mysterious red drink a waitress dressed as a sexy nurse gave me down my front. On the plus side, the fake blood splatter has improved my costume.

Guess Honor's right that I'm a glass-half-full type of girl.

Even when the full half of the glass lands on my dress.

"Here you go. Madness Elixirs! Aka, your basic vodka cranberries," Honor says when she appears with two more martini glasses filled to the brim. "I told Strike he could have done better with the drink names. Like maybe something about blood? But he shot me down." She hands me one of the glasses just as another guest catches my eye. He's dressed as Freddy Krueger from *A Nightmare on Elm Street*. Striped sweater, brimmed hat.

Could the cards have meant I'd break up with Bryan and meet my soulmate tonight? Is my destiny someone with razor fingers? Did he just wink at me?

"Let's hit the lobotomy lab," I tell Honor as I turn away from Freddy. There's a fine line between a glass half-full and desperate optimism.

She wrinkles her nose. "I don't know about that room."

"I think they've got some kind of tableau going on? Could be cool."

"I have to hand it to Axe and Strike," says Honor as I thread my arm through hers to lead her through the hallway. "This place is pretty epic."

I don't think I need to hand Axe anything, but I'm starting to enjoy this party. For one thing, it's getting my mind off Bryan. Also, I might look like rainbows and unicorns on the outside, but I love horror almost as much as I love romance. Scary movies and Stephen King novels are good reminders that things could be worse. Sure, I nearly tied the knot with the world's biggest douche canoe—but at least I'm not being stalked by a psycho clown with a knife collection.

See? That's what I call a glass-full attitude.

Right now, for example, Honor and I stumble upon what I can only assume is the lobotomy lab, and I consider that instead of rocking this sexy mummy costume, I could be that poor actor strung up on a rack, his arms shackled to a steel post. I wonder if they hired some artists from that mutant show, because whoever did his makeup deserves an Oscar.

The guy has fake blood streaming down his face, soaking his ripped T-shirt. He groans in agony when Axe fake kicks him in the gut. The scene is so realistic I can smell the metallic tang of blood.

Axe has clearly gone deep in the act. His knuckles look raw and bloodied, and he bounces on his feet like a pro boxer ready for the next round. Strike stands beside him, his head whipping around at the sound of the door swinging open.

Two things about Axe MacKenzie: He's hot and he sucks. There was a minute last spring when Honor introduced us when she thought her best friend and her man's best friend would automatically hit it off. Unfortunately, the opposite happened.

Yes, he's gorgeous: tall, broad-shouldered, with shaggy chestnut-brown hair and piercing denim-blue eyes. And yes, he has that delicious Scottish brogue that makes women melt. But he's also an asshole, and I'm done with assholes. Life is too short to let some guy ruin my hard-earned happiness just because he sounds sexy calling me a *dear lass.*

The first time I met Axe, he laughed in my face because I happen to be a believer in astrology and the occult. I've got no problem with nonbelievers. I get that it can seem a little kooky to think the stars and planets are out here plotting our lives or that the tarot can tell our future—though in my opinion, it's no kookier than any traditional religion.

But what I can't abide, what made me want to clock him in the face—much like he's pretending to do with that poor actor strapped to a pole—was the disrespect he showed my beliefs.

Don't agree? Totally fine.

Try to make me feel small? We've got a problem.

Also, and yeah, I know how this sounds, but there's something about his aura that puts me on edge. Like he just rolled into town from some Highland Games where he won Most Likely to Hunt You for Sport and you can't shake the feeling you might be next. Maybe it's his unpredictability and contradictions that set me off-kilter—he's all raw masculinity and untamed spirit, but every so often, a sliver of vulnerability cuts through, just enough to mess with my head.

As Axe steps closer now, the dim light casts shadows across his face, and his eyes bolt to mine with an intensity that feels almost predatory.

The air crackles with tension. I shiver.

The man on the rack lets out a cry so loud that it makes my bones ache.

If I didn't know any better, I'd think Axe was actually trying to kill the guy.

TWO

AXE

"You've got to be joking!" I mutter under my breath at Strike, my eyes darting to his lass, Honor, who's standing with her pal pretty Josie the Rosie—that's what I call her on account of her wild tangle of strawberry-blonde hair and the way her cheeks lit up like a bonfire the first time we met, right after I said astrology was fan fiction for nutters, and she looked at me like I'd just insulted her granny.

We've had a few run-ins since then—the second time, I told her believing in tarot cards is about as sensible as taking life advice from a Go Fish deck. Can't help it. I've got a knack for saying exactly the wrong thing with that lass. Honesty's not always the best policy, but watching Josie's cheeks flame is my guiltiest pleasure.

Even if it means I'm constantly tripping on my own words around her.

Both women's mouths are open like a pair of carps as they take in the scene of our lobotomy lab. Christ, how long have they been here?

"You're the dumbass who didn't lock the door," Strike growls, redirecting the eleven-inch blade that he's been using to slice and dice old Petrov—to get the information we need, but also for being the todger that he is—to the space between my eyes. I laugh. No way Strike would even nick me with that thing. We go way too far back—practically kids when the CIA recruited us. Years of missions and a bond forged in fire have made Strike Madden the closest thing I have to a brother. There's no one I'd rather have watching my back.

Maybe I didn't lock the door, but Petrov has proven to be the true dumbass of the night, crying and confessing names we haven't even asked for. He calls himself a pimp and a daddy, but strip him of his guns and flunkies, and the guy's a fucking wuss. He deserves every last punch I've given him. In fact, he deserves way worse. If I still believed in Heaven and Hell, there'd be no doubt which direction this guy is going—and I'd be thrilled to be the one sending him there early.

"What the fuck?" Honor asks as Josie's green eyes widen like teacups. If I'm ever a lucky enough man to blow Josie's pupils, this is not how I want to do it. "Please tell me you are not this stupid."

"What is . . . happening here?" asks Josie, who's rubbing at the crease in her forehead. She looks like a confused Disney princess, but I remind myself this is not someone who needs rescuing.

We need to get the lasses moving and finish the job. Can't have anyone else stumbling down here and catching a glimpse of this mess. The room is swimming in blood. Lucky for us, the whole venue's a forensic nightmare—too much contamination for them to ID anything.

After all the scheming we did dreaming up our House of Horrors, the last thing I expected was for the girls to stumble into the one room where Strike and I—in the spirit of the old days—decided to get up to some of our more questionable hobbies. We knew it wasn't smart or careful, not our usual way. But once the idea was out there, neither of us could back down from the challenge. Who'd notice a bit more gore in an asylum already swimming in the stuff? The party planners painted the walls with buckets of bovine blood, so why not add a dash of human splatter to the mix? The DNA here is more mixed-up than a Scot on a six-pub crawl.

Strike smiles sheepishly at Honor. She's known about our independent investigations since Strike took down her sister's killer six months ago, and it's obvious that we're definitely not fooling her.

"Firefly, don't worry. We got this all under control," he says, and even though he's literally holding a wet knife, Honor melts like butter on a hot scone. Now, I don't believe in soulmates—that's as daft as astrology, or Heaven and Hell for that matter. But when I see Strike and Honor together, the way they just accept each other's darkest bits without flinching, I can't help but wonder if maybe someday I'll find someone who'll love me like that—madness and all.

I shut that thinking down. The last bloody thing I need, the last thing I *want,* is a lady mucking up my life. I've got my ducks lined up exactly as I like them, and I do just fine on my own, thanks. Besides, there's not a soul broken enough in this world to put up with the real me. What's that famous expression? *I'd never want to join a club that would have me as a member.*

"We thought we'd put on a show for the guests," Strike says.

"Maybe *too* real, guys, if you want my opinion," says Honor.

"All part of the fun." I smile at Josie a bit wolfishly. I can feel my canines. She doesn't smile back. I turn to Petrov, hanging by his wrists like a sad sack. His front tooth's dangling by the root, and he fucking stinks—he's gone and pissed himself. Amateur hour.

In the CIA, they taught us how to hold it in even when you're getting the shit kicked out of you. But this guy's a pure novice. Low-hanging fruit. Just the first step in a bigger plan. "Right, Petrov?"

Last thing I need is for Josie to think the CEO of SynthoTech tortures sex traffickers at the annual corporate party. Even if, ah, that's exactly what I'm doing.

"Still gross," Honor says, but I catch her wink for Strike. I wonder if she's got half a mind to drop-kick Petrov square in the stones. She definitely would if Strike showed her his file and the pictures we've seen of Petrov's victims. Some were just wee ones. Twelve, thirteen years old.

Josie grips her sparkly little bag as she surveys the whole grim scene—the blood, the lacerations, even the knife—and shrugs. I don't know her that well, but there's something different about her today. Reflexively, I give her the once-over from head to toe, stealth-like, the way I used to scan a perimeter, on high alert, ready for anything. But I'm never ready for just how stunning she is, luminous even, though tonight her eyes look troubled.

"You okay?" Honor asks Josie as she gives her hand a squeeze and they head toward the door. Both women are dressed to kill—Honor in black velvet like a vampire queen, Josie wrapped in layers of tissue-thin fabric, a mummy costume for a goddess.

"Yeah," Josie says quietly. "Let's get out of here."

Now Honor turns back, her eyes daggers that land first on Strike, then me, then back on Strike.

"Later, boys," Honor says, keeping her voice light and flirty.

I steal one last, long look at Josie, not even bothering to be subtle this time, but she's too busy studying the floor. Funny thing about boar's blood—it looks just like human, but for a split second, I'd swear she knows the difference.

There's something about her. Like she's got a sixth sense or some kind of spooky insight. Her all-knowing act rattles me, not that I'd admit it out loud. So, naturally, I just end up ripping on her astrology as nonsense instead, trying to knock her off that high horse.

That, and to watch her cheeks go pink, of course.

THREE

JOSIE

We get out of there so fast my heel slips on the sticky, wet floor—how'd they get real blood for this party, anyhow? Did they rob a Red Cross? Honor catches my elbow, and we both start giggling nervously as we head down the dark hallway.

"Fucking Axe MacKenzie," I breathe. "He scared the living shit out of me."

"Oh, it was all so fake," says Honor. "Scary, but fake."

"Yeah." I exhale. I press my palms against my cheeks, trying to cool the burning heat spreading across my face—an unfortunate side effect of any encounter with Axe. Why can't the dude just be, I don't know, normal for once? Or at least as normal as a smokin'-hot multimillionaire tech wunderkind with an ego the size of his bank account can manage to be.

"The energy of this place is strange. Do you feel it, too?" I ask. Honor shrugs.

"I don't have your powers, oh young one," Honor says. I'm only a year younger than Honor, but as my boss and a fiercely independent woman, she's always felt like an authority figure. Once she told me she suspects I might have a touch of extrasensory perception. Which is hilarious, because I don't think I have

ESP—I just think I'm open to the universe's weird possibilities, and sometimes that means I pick up on things others miss. It's more like a learned skill than a superpower. Like finding the perfect minidress in the clearance section at T.J. Maxx.

"I'm serious! Maybe it's because so many sad stories happened here. The pain is in the walls, you know?" Just saying it out loud, my arm hairs stand on end. It's like muscle memory. I've spent a lifetime in hospitals—still do, thanks to endless health struggles—and every time I step into a doctor's office, even for a checkup, I get this same prickly feeling.

"They used that room for actual lobotomies," Honor says. "Though Strike and Axe didn't have to be so extra."

Extra is the understatement of the year. I can still hear echoes of that poor guy's screaming, but whatever. Tech bros are into weird shit. Strike runs a feminist erotic-gaming empire, and Honor's one of his best artists. Axe is doing something revolutionary with AI. No surprise, they're horror fans.

"I'm glad I got to see the inside of this place in person finally—but it's freaky to be here. Very different from seeing it on TV," I say. We're back out in the main party area, and the crowd is a slight comfort.

Honor agrees with a nod. "When we were kids, Gracie and I would hold our breath when we rode our bikes past this place. Like whatever was happening was contagious and we would catch it if we breathed in the air." Her eyes look so sad, the way they always do when she talks about Gracie, her twin sister, who was murdered last year.

I don't know much about Honor and Grace Stone's lives before we met. When Honor hired me to help in their store, aptly called Grace & Honor, my impression was they'd had a tough childhood. Honor's focus, her ability to find a way to thrive despite her grief, leaves me in constant awe. I know she's not into tarot, but she reminds me of the Star card—her strength is in her resilience.

"My mom won't even drive by this building. She always cuts across Oak Street to avoid Ravenswood." I shiver, feeling that chill again. As Nonna would say, it's like someone is walking over my grave. I wish this bandage dress had more yardage. I rub my arms to get warm.

"Let me grab you some water, Jos," Honor says. "You look a little pale."

"Yeah, thanks. They make fake blood way too real these days," I joke. But it's not the blood that bothers me. It's something else. Regret about ending my engagement? Doubtful. Did I ever really love Bryan, or was he just my ticket out of Mom's garage apartment? Leaving that diner, packing his things, all I felt was relief—like the choice whether to marry him was finally obvious.

Clearly, the doubts had been there all along; I just hadn't been ready to face them.

That Wheel of Fortune card spins in my head: Everything is going to change.

"Okay, hang on. Be right back." Honor gives a warning look to the random dude dressed as Freddy Krueger, who has reappeared and is circling us a little too close for comfort. Could be he's being paid by Axe to scare us, too.

Honor's held on to her big-sister energy for me, even though I'm an only child, and she's always fussing over my diabetes. She'll probably come back with a drink and snacks—and yeah, I probably do need something. I've got my insulin pump stashed in my purse, ready for any emergency, but honestly, I've hit my drama quota for the night.

I find a chair that's not too coated in spiderwebs—likely

bought in bulk from a Spirit Halloween—away from the party ruckus. I sit and steady myself.

While I'm alone with my thoughts, Bryan resurfaces like the smell of bad milk.

The red flags were all there. For starters, he's a Libra with a Cancer rising, and I'm a Cancer with a Scorpio moon—astrologically doomed from day one. We never should have moved in together, gotten engaged, or dropped a five-figure deposit we didn't have on a wedding. Plus, he always loved his Xbox and the Philly Flyers way more than me. Every once in a while, when I went down on him, he'd pat my head and say, "Achievement unlocked," and when he came, he'd throw his hands up and shout, "Score!"

How did I ever think any of that was cute?

It shouldn't have taken a "boys' weekend" to Atlantic City—where Bryan gambled away our Honeyfund—for me to figure out who he really is. I should've dumped him ages ago, like after our first date, when he took me through the McDonald's drive-through for two Happy Meals.

Honor says my "dreamy" nature is her favorite thing about me. But is *dreamy* just code for *totally clueless*? Maybe it's not so charming to look at the world through rose-colored glasses, assuming everyone's doing their best. Or to say yes when your boyfriend proposes with a "temporary" ring shaped like the fuzzy Philly Flyers mascot.

"Hey, Red. Haunt here often?"

I can feel Freddy's creepy gaze on me before I even look up. His beat-up hat dangles from his razor fingers. He's objectively unattractive, but it's his eyes that really make me shrink into my seat. Why does being a woman alone at a party feel like being a sitting duck? My arms are crossed, legs are crossed—I'm practically screaming *leave me the fuck alone.* Yet somehow, this guy still thinks he's got a shot. That, or he wants to fillet me.

"My date is coming back any minute," I tell Freddy. "So yeah, no. Not doing much haunting."

"Is your 'date' the hottie in the black velvet? Because, damn, I'd happily be the third."

Ugh. "Sorry, dude. I'm just really not feeling it," I say. Freddy is way too tall, especially now that he's looming over me while I sit.

I decide to stand up, which creates a whole other weird vibe in our body language standoff.

"Oh, come on," he continues, stepping closer. His breath is as strong as it is bad. Pickles and mustard and a hard blast of cheap rum. I can't step back, because the chair is already pressing against my calves. I could sit down again, but that feels like defeat. "We both know you don't have a boyfriend. Girls who have boyfriends don't dress like that."

What the fuck is that supposed to mean? I look around, hoping for eye contact with anyone who can rescue me in case this guy gets handsy. Zero people.

"I . . . I do have a boyfriend. A fiancé, actually. Sorry," I say. My second *sorry* in two minutes. Also, I'm deeply wishing I could pluck my engagement ring out of Bryan's chicken-fried steak. A ring on my finger would have hinted that there was a large, buff man coming to my rescue—when in reality, Bryan was a delicate five feet five and got winded carrying groceries. That sensitive topic is also why I haven't bought a pair of high heels in years. I can't believe I let that guy dictate my shoe game.

"Come on. We could find better ways to entertain each other somewhere private. Be my partner in crime, Red?"

He's too physically intimidating to be funny. He has at least fifty pounds on me and a knife hand that's rubber but could probably still do some damage if he's provoked.

"Look," I say firmly. "I'm not feeling great." I'm not kidding—my sudden shakiness and prickling sweat make me even more nervous. Am I having a diabetic emergency?

Please, God, not now.

He smirks like he hasn't heard a word I said. I start to move, quick and unsteady, toward the first door I spot—not sure if I'm shaky from low blood sugar or straight-up fear—but he cuts me off, his body starfishing to fill the entire door, blocking me from reaching the handle. *Fuuuuuck.*

"Let's not play games," he says.

"Agree. Game over," I tell him. Then I knee him in the balls as I yank open the door, enjoying his baby squeal of pain as I slam it behind me. I find myself in the small stairwell that leads to the back exit of the asylum, where the noise outside tells me it's packed. Good way to lose this loser. I'll need to tell Honor where to meet me. Last thing I want is for her to end up alone with this jerk. He knows we're together, and I'm sure he'll be out for revenge.

Breathing deep—*you are okay, Josie, no attack*—I step out into the cold air and am surprised to find a total vibe change in the yard.

It's less horror, more horrible Halloween party.

Morticia the DJ is enthroned on an LED-embedded platform stage, and the writhing bodies below all seem connected in one pulsating disco delirium on a temporary dance floor. I blink, dazed. It's a futuristic fantasy; gamers and coders and techies are either dancing or lounging on giant pillows. I push my way past a group of neon-painted dancers and a couple making out on a beanbag. The air feels thick and hazy and weirdly warm, probably thanks to the fog machines and outdoor heaters and not an indication I'm about to faint. Right?

I should really find something to eat.

I feel Freddy's rubbery grip on my arm before I see his face. Panic floods my system, and I swing around, but he's quicker this time. His expression is a twisted mask of rage.

"You think you can just walk away from me like that, you bitch?" His voice is a low growl, and he yanks me closer, causing me to lose my balance. I try to scream, but the sound is swallowed by the pounding music. I struggle against his hold.

"I'll do worse," I gasp, pulling away and making a frantic dash toward the bar. Honor and I were supposed to take a self-defense class at the Y last month, but we kept flaking. Too late for that now. I stumble through the crowd, my heart beating double time. Everything around me warps—neon lights cast twisted shadows that feel like old, half-forgotten nightmares.

Suddenly, I'm back in Miracle Solutions Hospital, small and vulnerable. Dr. Don looms over me, his face obscured by bright lights and a surgical mask, a witness to all my worst trauma. Antiseptic fills my nose, there's a distant beeping of heart monitors. I'm a child, terrified and alone, each shadow a potential threat. The overwhelming fear from those days surges through me, blurring my vision, making it hard to breathe.

I reach the bar and grasp its edge, the cool surface grounding me momentarily in the present. The bartender shoots me a concerned look, but before I can ask for help, a rough hand clamps down on my shoulder. I whip around, and Freddy's furious face is right there, inches from mine.

For a split second, in my dazed state, past and present blur together, and he morphs into Dr. Don, with his pale eyes, greasy shoulder-length gray hair, sweaty hands, and pitying smile. Dr.

Don was the stuff of my nightmares—perfect for this House of Horrors—but he was one hundred percent real.

For a second, I can't tell where I am—and then Freddy's voice jolts me back to the present.

"Let's find somewhere we can talk, babe." His hand roughly grabs my wrist, his fingers locking me in like a vise, and I feel my bag drop. To anyone in the crowd, it might look like we're dancing—the way he's got his arm around my waist, his smile wide like it's all in good fun as he swiftly hauls me toward the asylum.

But nobody's looking, not even the bartender.

"Stop!" My words are swallowed by the pounding dance music and oblivious crowd. My heels scrape against the floor, my entire body resists, but Freddy is stronger.

He pulls me back inside through the door and down a dark hallway, pinning me against the wall hard enough to knock the wind out of me.

"Finally, some privacy," his says, and the fact that his voice is so calm, almost relaxed, is somehow worse. "All I want to do is get to know you better."

When I open my mouth to scream, his hand clamps down on it. And that's when it hits me—this may be a fake House of Horrors, but I'm in real danger.

FOUR

AXE

Back in my CIA days, when I was neck-deep in code cracking, and later in private security gigs across every sketchy corner of the world, I could practically smell trouble before it hit. I had a knack for sensing when a cover was about to be blown, when an ambush was lurking, or when a mission was going straight to hell. But that talent doesn't seem to carry over to the tech world—aye, I can spot a mole from eighty meters, but my radar for office drama is completely useless.

Maybe it's because the stakes just aren't as high.

But here, at this ridiculous party, that old instinct is kicking in again.

I'm not the only one. Plenty of agents talk about this sixth sense. I imagine it's a Darwinian survival instinct, honed by experience.

The annual SynthoTech/Dark Matter Entertainment bash is my least favorite night of the year. The only upside is that once it's done, I'm free from this nonsense for another 364 days. The party committee, in their infinite wisdom, picked the Ravenswood Asylum as the venue. Despite the way I tend to do things, I'm no fan of horror.

Life is dirty, and I often have blood on my hands. Why mess about with the fake stuff when the real thing is never far away?

"I'm going to find Honor," Strike says from behind me. Petrov's sorted—he'll be chucked out with the rest of the night's rubbish. Our business is done here, even if things didn't go exactly to plan. "I'm not too worried. She'll do damage control with Josie."

"Aye," I say, but I'm barely paying attention. I'm already halfway down the hall, following the alarm bells blaring in my head—or, more precisely, in my nose.

Something's happened to Josie. I can smell it.

I take the stairs to the back patio, party central. I've purposely been avoiding this area—too many hands to shake, too many people who want to either pull me to the dance floor or chat AI. These aren't my mates—I only have one of those—and I can think of a thousand better ways to spend this evening. Billiards or boxing or on my boat with Strike. Home with a whiskey neat, in front of my computer, untangling a difficult piece of code. Working out in my gym, burning off my rage with weights. This is a spectacle of forced merriment, but for me, it's an introvert's nightmare. The real action is in the shadows, where blood and secrets flow thicker than whiskey.

And tonight the scent of trouble is strong. Josie is somewhere out there, and I need to find her before the night takes an even darker turn.

I thread through the crowd, dodging people shouting hellos and "Hey, Axe!" and even one lass who brazenly slips her hands into my pockets and tries to whisper in my ear. I grab her wrists and push them away. Out of the corner of my eye, I clock that she's beautiful, in that TikTok filter way that has flattened so many women—tight skin, lip implants, jaw contouring, fake lashes.

Not my type, even if she wasn't so handsy.

I glance around, desperate now. It's not Petrov's men; I'd know if they were here. But something's off. Josie's no damsel, even with those big doe eyes. She could kill me with a look. Still, I know she needs help.

I dodge yet another bloke trying to chat about AI, not bothering to slow down—seriously, can't they take a hint? I'm stumbling through fake smiles and masked faces. The dance floor's heaving, and the music's so loud it's rattling in my skull. How this noise became part of my job, I'll never know. Tech used to be about the product, not the image.

My eyes scan the crowd around the bar, teeming with people. No sign of her. Then I see it.

Her sparkly bag is lying on the floor near a side entrance to the building. Instinct kicks in and my pulse kicks up. I was right. She's in trouble. I move through the crowd, quickly kneeling to pick up the bag, keeping it in my grip as I scan the edges of the room one last time. Nothing.

I head through the door into the darkness of a service corridor, the cool air a faint relief from the smoke and haze. Immediately, I see them down the hall—a nasty-looking bloke I don't recognize has Josie up against the wall.

"Oi!" I yell, already moving toward them.

"Axe!" Josie shouts.

"Walk away, asshole," he snarls. "This doesn't—"

"—end well for you," I finish as my hand shoots out and grabs him by his scrawny neck, flipping him before slamming him hard against the wall. He falls to the ground and then scrambles to his feet and runs away like a chickenshit. I turn to Josie. She's a deer in headlights, her breathing quick and shallow.

"Did he hurt you?" I ask, my eyes roaming all over her. If he left a single mark, I'll kill the fucker. "Are you okay?"

"I'm fine," she says, though her voice trembles. But then her eyes catch what's tucked under my arm, and she smiles faintly. "My purse? How'd you know—"

"It's all sparkly. It had to be yours."

This earns me a proper smile. "Thanks, Axe. For real."

"We definitely need a stricter invite list," I say, annoyed that security let in whoever that guy was. I shrug off her gratitude. I did the bare minimum. Josie should not be thanking me.

"How about next year you pick a better theme," says Josie. "Like unicorns or *Care Bears*." Then she shakes out her arms and does a shimmy as if to reset her body or energy or some nonsense like that. She's ridiculously adorable.

"I pushed for narwhals, but I got overruled."

"Hmm, maybe *Peppa Pig*?"

"Or the Loch Ness monster. A proper Scottish beast," I say.

"One Scottish beast per party is enough," she says, poking me in the chest.

"Harsh but fair," I say, and crook my arm for her to take so I can lead her back out into the safety of the crowd.

"Josie, I've been looking for you all over!" Honor's on us as soon as we're back to the dance floor. Her gaze flits nervously from Josie to me and then the door. "What happened?"

"Axe rescued me from the party pervert," says Josie weakly. Her curls have gone wild, and they're somehow as expressive as her face. "It's not a big deal. Freddy Krueger wasn't so thrilled that I kneed him in the balls."

"You kneed him in the balls?" I ask, unable to keep the admiration out of my voice. This lass is full of surprises.

"Have you got your inhaler? Do you need a snack for your blood sugar?" Honor asks, ignoring me completely.

"Actually," says Josie. "I think what I need is a drink."

Now, that's an order I can get behind.

I steer us toward one of the heat lamps—Josie's mummy getup is flimsy at best, and I don't want her to freeze—and I flag the bartender. Within a minute, a tray of lemon drops appears. Josie throws back one, then another, and is about to go for a third before Honor intercepts.

"You'll thank me tomorrow," she says, but I'm glad to see the color back in Josie's cheeks.

"Yes, ma'am," Josie says, and salutes Honor, but Honor still looks worried. "Seriously, I'm fine! I promise! Go find Strike and dance and be disgustingly in love. I'm leaving in a minute anyway."

"Will you make sure she gets straight into an Uber?" Honor asks me, as if there was any way I'd let Josie out of my sight until I knew she was safely on her way home.

"Of course."

Honor cups Josie's face, searching her eyes one last time to make sure she's really okay, before finally walking away.

"So this whole party is weirdly rock 'n' roll," Josie says, breaking the awkward silence Honor leaves in her wake. "And also gross. Really, really gross."

"Can't argue with that." I chuckle. "If I had my way, we'd all be home right now in our finest flannel jammies, curled up with a book."

"I bet your pj's are tartan," Josie says.

"Aye, of course. Finest sheep's wool in the Highlands. But I won't ask about your sleeping costume, mind you. Wouldn't be proper."

She gives me a look, half-amused, half-exasperated. As if she knows I don't usually use the words *sleeping costume*, and that

I'm laying the Scottish on a little thick for her benefit. She's not wrong. I'll use every tool in my arsenal to soften this one.

"Being proper has never stopped you before," she says. Is she . . . flirting? Usually, Josie makes it clear she'd rather clean dog poo off her shoe than talk to me.

"You've got me there." Josie looks like she's trying not to smile, which only makes me grin bigger. "All right, then, what do you sleep in? A sparkly nightie to match your purse? I bet you dream in glitter."

Josie laughs, a full, real laugh, and now I do want to know what she wears to bed—and what she looks like waking up. I bet her hair is a right mess, her face warm and sleepy and open.

"I think I should go," Josie says, looking up at me through those impossibly long lashes. "I've had a rough day. And that was even before Freddy Krueger."

"Let me call you a company car," I say.

"Uber is just fine for me, Mr. Fancypants."

"Mr. Fancypants? Ach, never mind. I've heard worse. Let me walk you out. It's the least I can do after that gobshite attacked you at my 'really, really gross' party."

We walk slowly around the place and toward the front gates, Ravenswood lit up behind us. The din of the party feels muffled, and it suddenly makes sense to me why this building has been used in so many films. The effect of the space transforms completely depending on your angle. A minute ago, we were trapped in horror Hell—now it feels all grand and majestic, and Josie looks like a heroine who should be properly kissed by a soldier returning from war.

Once we reach the end of the driveway, she turns to face me, and I can't help it. I reach out to cradle her jaw. My touch is light, careful as I brush my thumb against her cheekbone.

"You sure you're okay, lass?" Josie looks up at me with surprise, like she's seeing me for the very first time. She's so close I can feel the warmth radiating from her skin. She's magnetic, and it's taking every ounce of self-control I have in my body not to pull her against me.

"Honestly, I'm not sure what I would have done if you hadn't come along."

"You would have been just fine. You're strong and scrappy."

"Right," she says, her voice full of doubt. I don't like this impulse I've noticed other folks have around Josie. They treat her like she's a wee delicate thing, like she's fragile when it's clear she's anything but.

"Honestly, that guy was lucky I intervened. Otherwise, I bet you'd be carrying his dick around in your handbag right now."

She laughs, and then my eyes drop to her lips. I wonder if she's feeling this undeniable pull. But I step back. I will not take advantage of this moment, no matter what my body is telling me. But then, to my shock, she's the one who takes another step forward, and wraps her arms around my neck. And then, like magic, her lips are on mine. Her kiss is tentative at first, the slowest, barest of brushes, and I'm too stunned to move, my every nerve crackling with the realization of what's happening. I feel the blood rush warm through my body, and I savor this whisper of a kiss—warm like honey and tasting of strawberries. She pulls away to look up at me with round eyes, as if she's just as stunned as I am at what she's done.

I assume she's going to step away—she's still the same Josie who has made it very clear she despises me—and I feel inexplicably bereft at the thought.

"One more kiss," she says under her breath, as if she's negotiating with herself. I don't know if she even realizes she said the words out loud. "Just one."

She leans in, and this time all her tentativeness is gone. Her teeth nip at my bottom lip, and I respond hungrily. I pull her against me and feel the wind knocked out of my lungs. I wonder if she can feel my heart knocking against hers. We taste each other eagerly, all tongues and hot mouths and that desperate chase for more, more, more.

And then Josie pulls away.

"Sorry," she says, and I laugh, because I'm obviously not complaining. "I don't know what happened just now."

"I do," I say, feeling the corners of my mouth tug up. I want to pull her back. I'm not done with that mouth.

"I plead temporary insanity," Josie says, and though disappointment floods through me, I try to not let it show on my face.

"Well, we are at the Asylum. You were just going with the theme." An Uber pulls up to the curb in front of us—an old Honda Civic driven by a pimply teenager—and I want to scream with frustration at the timing. I don't want her to leave.

"Good night, Axe," she says, hopping into the back seat. She looks a little smudged and confused, and is that regret I see on her beautiful face? Please, anything but regret.

"Good night, Josie," I say, fists in my pockets. I stand on the curb, watching until the car's taillights disappear into the night, wondering how soon I can see her again.

FIVE

JOSIE

In the Uber on the way home, I take a minute to think about that foolish, ridiculous, delicious, impulsive kiss. Savor it a little before the embarrassment inevitably swoops in. My cheeks flush, remembering how I was the one to reach for Axe. Twice!

I bring my fingertips to my swollen lips. I left for this party thinking about the Wheel of Fortune card, and now I'm coming home wondering if it had a certain blue-eyed Scotsman written all over it.

No. No. Absolutely not. This is Axe MacKenzie we're talking about. Even if he did rescue me from that deranged creep, one sweetly heroic moment doesn't wipe out a whole year of his premium-grade dickishness. I'm not about to let myself get sucked in by his superhero rescue or his hot-guy magic and cheeky banter.

I'm usually smarter than mistaking temporary lust for something more. What was I thinking? This has got to be some leftover Bryan-breakup nonsense. Me grasping for a shiny new distraction.

Pathetic.

As the Uber turns the corner onto my street, the bottom drops out of my stomach with a nauseating thud. Crap. All the lights are on at my parents' house. What did I expect? I'm almost never out past midnight. Still, I hope if I'm stealthy enough I can sneak up to my above-the-garage apartment without anyone noticing me.

"Oh, thank God!" Mom says, scaring the shit out of me as she practically tackles me the moment I open my front door.

She pulls back, eyes wide as teacups.

"What are you doing in here?" I ask, and then immediately temper my tone. My mother has full access to my tiny apartment because she owns it. I might be twenty-six years old, but that doesn't stop her from monitoring my entire life. And maybe that's my fault, because I can't seem to officially launch.

I can tell by the look on her face that MamaBearSharon is ready for the Spanish Inquisition.

"Sweetheart, you look off. Is that lipstick on your chin? What happened? Are you okay? What's your blood sugar?"

Time to code switch into JosieFightsOn mode. That was the social media handle Mom made up when they first found my childhood leukemia. She was a total warrior back then, launching GoFundMe campaigns, organizing bake sales, silent auctions, charity runs—our house was Fundraiser Central. She made me feel protected with her endless research and updates on clinical trials. We used to joke that she should have a medical degree from WebMD.

With her support, my fight felt communal.

I wasn't—have never been—alone.

So I get why she can't sleep until I'm safely home. Why she needs to actually see my face before heading off to her own bed. When you've faced too many close calls with your only child, you don't just turn that worry off.

She always says I won't understand her fear or her fierce, unrelenting love until I'm a mother myself. That being a mom is like having your heart walk around outside your body. And in my case, it's even harder, because that heart's already been strained by so much stress.

"Mom, I'm fine." She puts the back of her hand to my forehead, like she's certain I'm running a fever. "Long night, that's all." I force myself to channel my best JosieFightsOn energy. I used that same chirpy tone in the weekly video updates during chemo, keeping the followers fed with positivity. I've mastered smiling through pain and playing the perfect patient.

And on the flip side, Mom knows how to be the perfect caretaker. As MamaBearSharon, she became known on social media, offering guidance and support, in person and online, to her thousands of followers facing their own children's grim diagnoses. Having been through the worst with me, she was determined to pay it forward.

But tonight, despite how weird the evening has been—the terrifying lobotomy lab, my encounter with the handsy psycho Freddy Krueger, that unexpected moment with Axe—I don't need to pretend that I'm all right; I actually am.

"You look like you could use a bath. Upstairs into the tub, young lady! I'll meet you up there."

"Okay, okay." I roll my eyes but head upstairs, peeling away the scraps of my mummy outfit as I go. My mother and I don't always have that much in common, but we both love nothing more than a good, long soak. As I reach the bathroom, I can hear her clattering around, likely getting fresh towels and dry clothes.

Privacy and boundaries have never been Mom's strong suit, and I've only been relaxing for five minutes when she bursts in. She holds a fluffy towel and an old T-shirt I thought I'd given away to the Salvation Army years ago, along with my soft cotton Minnie Mouse underpants.

Where in the world does she store these things? And why?

"Mom, you really don't need to . . ." I start, but she's already putting down the lid on the toilet, sitting so she can give my naked body the up-and-down. She methodically checks for unexplained dark bruises, for little lesions, for new lumps. I can't blame her. My body has always been like a terrible science experiment. She's had to call 911 for me too many times to count—because of anaphylactic shock, a sudden plummet in blood pressure, fainting, etc., etc.

As a patient, I was consistently "atypical," always experiencing the sort of unlikely, terrible side effects you hear about in that low, quick voice in drug commercials.

Mom's checks are responsible, reasonable, and a hard habit to break. Even if they feel dehumanizing. Ironically, this "healthy" stretch has been tougher for my mom and me to navigate. Sometimes, it feels like we don't know how to talk unless it's about medicine, doctors, supplements, blood test results, or—her favorite topic—my recovery. She celebrates my yearly scans like other moms celebrate birthdays.

I sigh but give her a small smile as I sink farther into the tub.

"When you're ready to come down, I'll make some tea. I want to hear all about the party." Mom sounds overly bright, and her voice is the hearing equivalent of looking into terrible fluorescent lighting.

Once she's gone, I let the tension ease out. This isn't so bad. Bryan never took care of me like this. I spent years being homeschooled because of my weak immune system, so my mom was my best—and only—friend for most of my childhood. After this hellish day, maybe some old-school Mom TLC is just what I need, even if it means wearing threadbare Minnie Mouse panties.

Downstairs, over mugs of Mom's bitter medicinal tea that I

can't quite stomach tonight, I break the news about Bryan and the engagement. I always thought she liked him, so I'm shocked when she leans back, folds her arms, and says, "Good riddance."

"It's so much money down the drain," I say. "There's no way I can get back the hotel deposit."

She flutters her fingers. "Oh, we'll find a way."

My skin goes cold. I know that gleam in her eyes.

"Mom, I'm not doing a fundraiser. I'm not playing the sick card if I'm not sick." Last year, Mom suggested a GoFundMe for my diabetes when insulin prices skyrocketed. For complicated reasons, I need my meds shipped from Germany, and just the dry-ice shipping costs thousands. It wasn't a terrible idea, just one that makes me feel like more of a charity case than a person.

Now, as long as I can work and cover my own meds—even if it means running up my credit cards—I will. And I'm sure as hell not asking for help to bail me out for being dumb enough to almost marry Bryan.

"A fundraiser? *I* didn't say that," she says, her eyes twinkling. "You did."

"Well, anyway, Honor just gave me a raise. So I'm not totally going broke," I tell her. "But it does look like I'll be staying in the apartment for the next month."

"Josie, you can stay here as long as you like," she says. "Alan and I love having you so close . . ." She holds up her hands as I start to protest. I'm old enough that I should not have to rely on my mom and stepdad. She reaches her hand across the table to clasp mine, and she looks at me like I'm made of glass.

"But FYI, we were planning on Airbnb-ing the guesthouse when you left . . . so this does mean our expenses will go up." Again, that icy feeling. Mom, who knows me too well, sees it written across my face. “No, no, no. I’m not saying we should do a fundraiser! Sheesh!”

“Good,” I say.

“But I do think you should check in on your socials. Maybe post an update to your followers, let them know how you’re doing, sweetheart? They care about you.”

Do they care about me? It’s true that many of them have been invested in my recovery for years, and maybe even more so in my mom’s journey parenting a sick kid. I don’t think of those faceless people as actually knowing me, though. They’ve been exposed to one sliver of who I am.

“Maybe tonight? Post a picture while you’re still looking pale,” she adds.

Gross as it sounds, whenever I post looking too healthy, I get trolled by people who doubt I was ever really that sick or think we exploited my cancer for sympathy.

Mom grabs my phone, quickly types in my password, and snaps a photo. I make a mental note to delete it as soon as she’s gone. No way am I posting anything.

Still, as much as I don’t want anyone’s pity, the trolls have gotten it all wrong.

I’ve been sick my whole damn life. I would give anything—*anything*—to be well.

Later, once I’m in my bed, the nightmares come.

I’m in the lobotomy lab at Ravenswood, bound to a gurney with old leather restraints, my body thrashing against the bonds. In my worst nightmares, I’m always a kid, helpless in the grip of syringe-wielding doctors—a terrifying, messed-up mash-up of memory and fear. But this time, I'm fully grown, and my younger self sits in the corner, clutching my favorite stuffed rabbit, wide-eyed and terrified like a witness to my own horror.

A masked man leans over me, an electric drill poised right at the center of my forehead. The yellow light from above casts a sinister halo around him. Little me is humming the alphabet song, her small voice soft and unaware, like she can't process what's happening right in front of her. Then, just as he squeezes the trigger and the drill roars to life, beginning its awful grinding into bone and brain, the mask slips.

Denim-blue eyes and soft lips. It's Axe MacKenzie.

I jolt awake, screaming, my heart slamming against my ribs. I want to call Nonna, my grandmother Rosa Greene—the only person who's ever made me feel strong and sturdy. But it's late, and she's even more lost at night. I can't bear the thought of her not recognizing my voice. Not tonight, when everything already feels so hostile.

Not tonight, when that House of Horrors has followed me home.

SIX

AXE

"Get a grip, lad," I mutter to myself, glaring at my PowerPoint. It's the ass crack of dawn, my favorite time to work, and I'm hunkered down at Shelton's 24, the only open-all-night diner that's as neutral as its name. A place for truckers to eat a plate of eggs after a long stretch. There're no distractions here. It's not cozy, not charming, not trying to be anything but open. Which is exactly why I like it. I signal the waitress for a refill. Squint at the screen.

Later this morning, I'm introducing She's the One, SynthoTech's newest product, to an important potential investor, and I've been working on the finishing touches. But the usual gritty magic of this place, the kind that sharpens my focus—along with its coffee, strong enough to wake the dead—isn't working.

Maybe because I still can't shake the image of Josie in her mummy-wrapped dress, the surprise in her eyes as she kissed me.

Strike confirmed she's broken off her engagement with that pickle dick Bryan, which ought to be cause for celebration. If we lived in a different world—and not just one where she didn't think I was a fuckwad, but one in which I was a completely different sort of man—I'd take her out, show her how she ought to be treated, how she ought to be kissed and caressed and undressed. Unwrapped . . .

No. Back to work. I'm not going to blow this presentation because a cute woman had one too many lemon drops and a bad night and thought my lips were the answer. I'm smarter, more disciplined—

"Hey, Wolverine! You'll need to mow that lawn before you face your fans." Strike laughs to see me startle; the fucker crept up on me while I was lost in thought. He smacks his hand against the side of his own clean-shaven face as he takes a seat in the booth facing me.

"I've never heard a single complaint about my stubble," I tell him. "Not even after I've chafed some thighs. But I really do think it might be time I staged an intervention about those silly matching cashmere sweatsuits." Strike has a great flair for fashion, but his high-end choices would not cut it on the heath, and a few of our old colleagues from our private security days would laugh their arses off if they saw him. I consider it my duty to give him shite.

"Honor likes me in these," Strike says. He's not even slightly shy about the fact that Honor has him wrapped around her finger; I'd argue he's proud of it. The good news is my best friend is now about 25 percent less grouchy post–falling in love. He signals the waitress for our usuals, plus more coffee. "Thought I'd find you here. Big day, especially for a complete workaholic who wouldn't know anything about pleasing a woman, what with you living like a monk and jerking off to . . . Christ, I don't even want to think about what or who you jerk off to. Haggis and spreadsheets, maybe? Is that what gets your bagpipe working?"

"All right. Enough. We've got bigger issues than my social life."

"Or lack thereof."

"Fuck off," I say, flipping him the finger for good measure. An image of Josie's mouth flashes before my eyes again, but I let it float away. "The deal deck's just about ready."

"That's why I'm here, my friend. Thought you'd want me to take a look."

"I would. Appreciate it."

She's the One is my baby, though given how long I've been working on her code, she'd be more like a kindergartener by now. I had a paradoxical childhood—both deafeningly loud and crushingly lonely. It was during my brief attendance at the thousand-year-old dungeon that was Queen Victoria School in Scotland that I first started dreaming about a world where someone could explore meaningful relationships in an absence of real-life human interactions.

Bunking on my narrow cot in the all-boys dormitory, lining up for drills, or even walking those vaulted stone halls of QVS, I felt completely abandoned. No mum. An absent dad. Wind-chapped cheeks. A sore arse from the cane.

Misery breeds ingenuity. The memory left its mark, but it also planted the seeds of my life's work. My hope is that She's the One will grow into something more (He's the One, They're the One, A Friend for One) for anyone struggling to find connection in a world full of mostly disappointing humans. If I can create something virtual that offers comfort and companionship to those who need it most, when they need it most, it could actually make a real difference.

And make me a fortune.

Strike clicks through the presentation, his face unreadable. I match his impassivity, but this project strikes deeper than I'd ever admit. I don't care about building gadgets that replace workers—I want to redefine human connection. I want to create the perfect virtual partner and stand at the forefront of the coming AI revolution. I want to solve loneliness.

Bold? Indeed. Revolutionary? Absolutely.

Near impossible? Depends on who you're asking.

Strike stops clicking, then shuts the laptop just as his coffee arrives. His face is neutral as he takes a sip. My nerves are raw as I wait for what's coming.

"It's solid," he finally says. "Presentation's tight. Coding's outstanding. Concept's impressive—always was. But . . ."

I lean back, my arms folded. "Spit it out."

"There's no life in her," he says. "No spark." He leans forward. "No *specificity*."

"That's the point," I say. "The algorithm adjusts itself depending on the user."

"But you need a baseline," says Strike. "A prototype. You need to find the *She* in your initial model for She's the One." As if I haven't already thought of that. As if I haven't been looking for years for the perfect woman to be the model on which I craft the ideal AI girlfriend to demonstrate the product. But perfect people are hard to find. Scratch that. Impossible.

"I don't need to tell you we've been researching this for years. We've data-mapped hundreds of desirable women. Thousands of prototypes later, we decided to create her based on an aggregate—"

"And it feels like an aggregate," Strike interrupts. We're both silent a moment. "Maybe what it needs," he finally says, "is a muse. But look. It's polished, it's professional. Beta test it. I think he'll bite."

He meaning my potential investor, Niles von Grafenhagen, a man as ridiculous as his name.

No, *ridiculous* is giving him too much credit. He's human excrement. He's filthier than Petrov. Not a foot soldier but a mastermind. I will sleep better when the world is wiped clean of him.

Niles will have his reasons for investing. She's the One is in his wheelhouse—a tech start-up that's as risky as it is potentially lucrative. If this deck gets him on board, not only will I get financial backing—though we have plenty of cash, a newish company like SynthoTech could use his eight-figure investment—but in turn, I'll get access to his books. And his books will tell me a story he has no intention of sharing.

Because he doesn't know I know what to look for.

Just then the diner's front-door bell jingles, and in Josie steps, all buttoned up in a heavy coat and boots, shaking off the cold. My body locks up. It's as if I've conjured her from the ether.

Strike doesn't say a word, but his eyes follow mine.

When Josie sees us, she comes right over.

"Of all the all-night greasy spoons in this town—oh, wait, there's only one," she says. "So maybe it's not such a coincidence."

"What are you doing up this early?" I ask. "Or is it *out this late*?"

I doubt it's the latter—I saw her get into an Uber last night. Though she could have ended up at Bryan's. The thought makes my stomach curdle.

I glance at her ring finger. Still bare.

"Couldn't sleep." She says this cheerfully, sunshine in a cup, but she also looks tired. "Everyone knows this is the best coffee in Shelton—thanks, Jill." She smiles as the waitress glides past and hands Josie a to-go cup from her tray. Like they're old friends. I've been here at least a hundred times and never once thought to ask the waitress's name.

"Dark roast with milk and honey, just how you like it," she tells Josie, and she then sets down our breakfast specials.

"And by *best*, I mean *most caffeinated*. I have no idea what they put in here, but it should be illegal," Josie says once the waitress is gone. "Anyway. What's your excuse? Secret mogul takeover of Shelton?"

"Moguls always meet at midnight," says Strike, as he digs into his scrambled eggs and hash browns.

"It's closer to morning," I say, sticking a fork into my pancake stack. "This is clearly a straight-up, heroes-who-make-shit-happen-in-Shelton breakfast."

"Well, I know you're both more into world domination," she says, "but if you want something local, I wouldn't mind if you solved Shelton's three-minute-stoplight problem."

"Consider it done," I say. "Though it will be classified, as with all of Shelton's darkest secrets. So we must never speak of it."

"Never," she says, and her eyes linger on me a moment. Is she thinking about last night and our kiss? It's probably only me replaying it over and over like my new favorite song. She clears her throat, breaking the moment. "Anyway. Time to catch the worm, I guess."

She heads toward the door, her hand up and waving goodbye. As she goes, I remember the feel of her waist, the way her soft curls brushed my cheek.

"You're staring," Strike says, and I whip my head back to him. I shovel food into my mouth to buy some time. It's embarrassing to be caught ogling Josie.

"I wasn't," I lie, which is a waste of breath. We've been friends for too long not to know exactly what the other one is thinking.

"You gonna make me say it?" Strike asks.

"Say what?" Even if he can read my face, there's no way he knows about the kiss. I'll continue to play dumb.

"Josie! The answer is right in front of you."

"What are you talking about?" I look at Strike, and this time I'm not actually playing. I have no idea what he's going on about.

“She’s adorable. Funny. Unique. She’s perfect.” He ticks off each point on his fingers.

“And she hates me,” I mutter. I don’t add that regardless of how lovely she is, there’s no way I’d ever date Josie. I don’t do relationships. Never have. Never will.

“Who cares? She doesn’t need to like you to work for you. Hate to tell you, but not everyone at SynthoTech is an Axe stan.” Oh, of course. He’s talking about She’s the One. I take another sip of my coffee, because clearly I’m not on my game today. I let his words soak in.

“I don’t think so. She’d be an amazing prototype, but . . .” I think about how Josie is one of a kind, hilariously weird, and cute and sexy as hell.

“But?”

“She’d be impossible to work with.”

“Bullshit. You want Niles von Grafenhagen to bite? Call Josie. Now.”

SEVEN

JOSIE

I sit in my car with my coffee. The engine's off, the heater's off—and I've never been so on. My heart is hammering; I do not need the burst of caffeine that's coursing through me. If only I'd just stayed in bed and ignored the internal alarm that always tells me to jump out of my apartment the minute I'm awake. Since I never go down to my mom's kitchen for my morning cup—too big a risk of running into my parents—a quick run to Shelton's 24 has been my new solve.

This is what I get for leaving the house before dawn.

Fate is truly messing with me lately. It's way too soon for another dose of Axe MacKenzie. Especially with his overnight scruff and the way he raised his eyebrow when he said, *Consider it done.* Thank God my coat is buttoned and I wore my boots. The humiliation of Axe seeing me in my pj's—a too-small Walk for Josie cancer fundraiser T-shirt plus glitter-heart sweatpants—makes me shiver. I have no idea why my mother keeps all my old donation swag—like sports award ribbons, only make it illness.

Axe was perfectly friendly, but he didn't bring up any of what happened last night. Clearly it hasn't been on auto-replay for him these past hours. I can still feel the heat of his huge hands around my waist when he steadied me after I kissed him.

The whole thing couldn't have lasted more than a minute, and now I wonder if I imagined the energy crackling between us. Maybe it was just the lemon drop shots and the adrenaline from escaping Freddy Krueger, and Axe wasn't on board at all. His eyes—those ridiculously intense blue eyes—locked on me with a look that could only have been . . . what?

I thought it was desire, but seeing him again, all casual friendly and maybe even a tiny bit startled, I'm not so sure. It might have been concern? Or, on second thought, *pity*? Yeah. Pity feels right. He probably thought I'd lost my mind. What the hell was I thinking, drunkenly kissing him like that? No matter how head-spinningly attracted to him I felt in that moment, it was so messy and dumb.

Anyway, I don't even like Axe, so I shouldn't care what he thinks. I don't care. I *don't.*

The sun's just up by the time I'm back in the apartment, where I see Mom's already been, and the reason is soon clear. She's left a Post-it note on the lampshade next to my bed: *Don't forget! Post to socials this morning!*

Ugh. Please, Mom. Posting to socials—even if it's to celebrate that I'm in remission—is just another way to get people to feel sorry for me. After the childhood I had, there is no feeling worse than imagining someone pitying me. I know the pity face too well—it's the one people get when they see a small, frail child with her head wrapped in a chemotherapy scarf. It's a mix of *Thank God that's not my kid* paired with a mouth pulled down just enough to suggest they've tasted something sour.

People used to stop me and my mother in the grocery store

with that exact face. The more aggressive do-gooders might press a hand to our shoulders and tell us how "strong" we were and how they were "praying for us."

Strong. Which, if you think about it, makes no sense.

Like I had a choice whether to keep living or not?

My mom always responded with a warm smile and her card—pastel pink with a tiny rainbow in the corner, which included a link to our GoFundMe page.

My head aches. Today is going to suck. My unwedding to-do list is a mile long: return the gifts piled in the corner, cancel the florist and the venue, inform our guest list. Worst of all, I need to come to terms with the fact that I'm stuck living with Mom and my stepdad, Alan, for at least another few months.

Shit, the stable future I briefly envisioned has not only gone up in smoke but might have been a cruel little hallucination all along.

I've hit bottom.

Then I check my phone and realize there's farther to fall.

Fifteen messages from Bryan. The first voicemails are sweet and contrite—*I'm sorrys, I love yous.* But as he got progressively drunker or higher last night, the messages turned flat-out mean. *You ungrateful bitch, good fucking luck finding someone who will put up with your sick ass, enjoy your life without me, you'll never get anyone better.*

I block him. Not that I ever had a shred of doubt about ending our engagement, but this makes it even clearer I made the right call. Meanwhile, I've got four texts from my mother, sent exactly twenty minutes apart, like she set a timer: Sweetheart, when you have a moment, please show some love to JosieFightsOn! Your fans are waiting to hear from you; people worry when you're quiet; you owe them at least a picture!

Obviously, I don't block Mom, despite a secret, tiny voice inside me that sort of wants to. I remind myself of the many times she literally saved my life. Even today she's saving me.

I'm living in her damn guest apartment. I cannot be ungrateful.

Alan's the only dad I've known since my own father died when I was about a year old, and he's never gotten to do normal husband things with Mom, like go out to dinners and movies and take beach vacations. Not with his stepdaughter in the hospital half her life and medical bills crowding the mailbox. There's no love lost between Alan and me. We've never quite connected, and I'll never be interested in hearing about his passion for fishing, his obsessive love of Yuengling paired with smelly foods, and his penchant for too-tight T-shirts tucked into cargo shorts.

But I do get why he'd resent the burden I've always been.

I delete the photo my mom took last night and put a Focus setting on my phone that blocks me from logging in to any social media accounts.

Then I send Mom back a heartfelt I love you.

I take a quick shower, change into jeans and a soft, plain sweatshirt, and make my bed, and now I feel refreshed enough to pull out my tarot deck from where it's edged into my bookcase. Nonna gave it to me for my sixteenth birthday; she used to teach me how to read the cards. This deck originally belonged to my great-grandmother, who taught Nonna and who died about a decade before I was born.

If my whole life went up in flames, this velvet-lined burgundy-leather box is truly the only thing I would make sure to save.

The box's lid is framed around an image of Fortuna, the Roman goddess of luck and fortune. The cards themselves are hand-painted on cardstock with gilded edges. Holding the deck in my hands always makes me miss Nonna. Even though I see her almost every day after work, Nonna has severe dementia now, and she lives in the Golden Leaves Memory Care Facility. The place could desperately use a makeover, but it's the best we can afford. Nonna's care is a patchwork of funding: some state assistance, some from Mom and Alan, and the rest from me.

At least she's safe at Golden Leaves and mostly still remembers me. These are the sort of gifts I will never take for granted.

Maybe I should start a gratitude journal to help me shake off this funk.

I sit on my bed with my legs crossed, shuffle the deck, and deal myself my card of the day:

The Devil.

I drop it like it's a hot tamale.

Last time I pulled this card was the day before my last surgery, five years ago. I hoped to never see it again. I don't even like looking at the damn thing. The Devil's clutching a trident in one hand and a torch in the other, like he's debating between grilling hot dogs or stabbing a lost soul.

Flames, smoke, shadows—it's a whole creepy, disturbing vibe. Beneath him, two miserable human figures are chained to a pedestal, looking like they're regretting every life choice that brought them there.

Come to think, it kind of reminds me of that poor shackled actor from the House of Horrors last night.

I return the card to the deck as my phone vibrates. Unknown caller. I let it go to voicemail because I'm not a sociopath—and when I play it, I get an overly friendly male automated voice. "*Hey, this is AI Jack from SynthoTech looking to schedule a meeting with . . . Josie. Please return our call as soon as possible. Thank you.*"

No sooner have I listened to this voicemail than a text message pops up:

SynthoTech is looking to schedule a consultation with . . . JOSIE.

Sheesh. Someone needs to train SynthoTech Jack to not blow up other people's phones. Seriously, of all the dickhead moves. Axe MacKenzie can't even be bothered to place a call himself? Even when he just saw me an hour ago? I'd rather he just ghosted me than have his digital henchman chase me down for a meeting.

My brain snags for a minute. Wait, a meeting? Does he think we need to formally discuss the kiss? Oh God, no.

I'm still staring at the phone when it starts ringing again. I pick up and begin speaking immediately. I have a lot of useless aggression to get out and best to unleash it on a robot.

"Hi, dumbass Jack-bot from SynthoTech who is stealing jobs from actual human beings, this is all-caps-but-very-flesh-and-blood Josie, who doesn't chat with thirsty computers. Also, learn some manners. My generation doesn't call and text and then call again. That's what we call *rude*. And if you're so interested in scheduling a meeting, maybe you should ask your *boss* to call me personally."

Silence. Then a whistle and a low chuckle and finally a very human voice that sends a blush right to my cheeks.

"Well, then, all-caps Josie, it's lucky that it's me. I'm not sure AI Jack could handle you. You'd have his mainframe smoking like a peat fire."

"Axe?"

"'Course. Have other Scottish friends, do you, lass? I'd assumed

I was the only one." His accent lands hard on the word *one*, and I have no idea why it's so sexy, but it is. Ugh, the music of his brogue is wasted on him.

"Didn't know we were friends," I say, but even I hear the smile in my voice.

"Right," he says. "More passing acquaintances who frequent the same filling station for coffee. Who also sometimes ki—"

"Why are you calling me?" I ask, interrupting.

"Not into small talk, I see. Fair enough," he says. "I'm actually calling with a proposition."

My stomach lurches. The Devil. Of course. Suddenly, it all clicks into place. You don't need to be psychic to figure out when a card points straight to Axe MacKenzie.

And here I was, thinking I'd done battle with all my demons this week.

EIGHT

AXE

"She's been waiting for twenty minutes, sir." My assistant meets me at the door of the SynthoTech offices, handing me a file folder as we walk through the lobby, a place I had a hand in designing. It's a mix of organic—wood beams and rafters, paneled-oak floors—and innovative, with sleek wall touch screens that light up when you approach. Like an ancient ship repurposed for modern times.

"Fuuuuck." I rip off my Bluetooth earpiece as I jab the elevator button.

My meeting with Josie was supposed to start at three sharp, and I'm already screwing it up. It was the one thing I did not want to mess with in a day that started in Miami and feels like it's been a hundred hours long. I should have taken the chopper directly to the office instead of home.

Vanity won out—I wanted to quickly shower and change far away from my colleagues.

Just this week, I had to talk Josie off her high horse about my AI assistant. Convincing her I'm not out to steal human jobs was harder than a Senate hearing, and getting her to commit to today's meeting felt damn near impossible. I have a hunch my twenty-minute delay has gotten her climbing right back into the saddle, even though she now knows I employ hundreds of people. She was all spit and vinegar about AI Jack—apparently, I'm not only bringing on the end of days but doing it with bad manners.

If he weren't AI, I'd have sacked Jack's ass on the spot.

After that start, it's a goddamn miracle that she showed up.

I knew I was cutting it tight this morning, but I didn't have a choice. Petrov was a right brute, keeping his girls in line through sheer force, and his business trafficked women into the country through Miami. With him gone, it was time to move on to the rest of the crew and get the girls transported to safe houses immediately. All I can hope is that now they can cut loose with enough—

The elevator doors pop open, and Josie's standing smack in front of me. Green eyes blazing like two hot pokers. Her hair tumbles loose around her shoulders, and the light from the window catches the red, setting it aglow.

She looks like a character from *The Avengers*.

"I'll have you know," she starts, "that I had to rearrange my whole day around this top secret cloak-and-dagger meeting where, supposedly, you'd present your so-called proposition. Which, by the way, you are now *twenty-two minutes* late for. So forgive me if I fail to grasp whatever bizarre system you use to manage your priorities."

"Easy, lass." I take her gently but firmly by the elbow, but she's stubborn and won't walk, so now she's got me rooted to the spot.

I'm not sure what to do. My reaction to her is ridiculous. She's pure temptation; I want to press myself against her body, revel in every last bit of her curvy, peachy softness. But she's here for a business meeting, and I'm undressing her with my eyes.

Bloody ridiculous, I am. Not to mention unprofessional.

"Also, don't *easy, lass* me," she says in a terrible Scottish accent, which makes me want to laugh. "That's like telling someone who is stressed out to relax. Doesn't work. Never works. Not once. Not ever."

"Are you stressed, lass?" I ask, thinking about how she's always so chummy with everyone else and so feisty with me. I enjoy being the exception. It's like I have a backstage pass to the real Josie. "It was a scrimpy twenty minutes! You should really just relax—"

"Oh my God," she says, her chin up. Still, I sense a ghost of a smile.

We're in a stare-off and I cannot look away. Is this why I always say the wrong thing? Because I can't stop staring at her?

"I'd better go. I don't know why I came in the first place." She breaks eye contact as her finger presses the elevator call button. Her pointy nails are painted a glittery silver and look like cute, tiny knives. The door opens, Josie gets in, and I stride after her. This time, before she can press *down*, I press *up*.

We're off.

"FYI, this is the old freight lift," I say, watching Josie's face twist in confusion. It's a rookie mistake, aye, but a common one—especially if you park in the old lot and come in through the back of SynthoTech. Not like the sleek front lifts, but now we're both stuck in this wheezing old bastard, crawling its way skyward.

"As soon as we get to the top, I'm going right back down," she says, all business. I'd wager that her nipples are a softer, rosier shade of her strawberry-blonde hair—and now all my blood is going to my dick instead of my brain.

I should have more sense than this.

"Sounds lovely," I reply with a grin. "I like the ride both ways."

She presses her lips into a thin line. "I knew this was a bad idea. This is madness."

"Nah, lass. This is Shelton." Ach, another terrible line. No shame, MacKenzie. But I'm too distracted for shame.

"Honor told me to hear you out." She sighs, clearly exasperated. "I was looking for a sign I shouldn't be here—and then you showed up late, so it's pretty clear—"

"Josie. Please," I interrupt, hoping logic will outweigh her superstitions. "My being late isn't a cosmic sign of anything, all right? It just means air traffic control had us stuck on the bloody tarmac, and afterward, I needed a shower."

"Air traffic control?"

"I started my day in Florida. Let me explain," I say.

"You were in Florida? Today?"

"The Everglades, yes."

At that, she looks a bit curious.

"This morning?"

"Aye."

"See any alligators?" she asks.

"Yup, and some flamingos, doing the whole one-leg thing. Goddamn show-offs." Josie feels impossible to read, but when she smiles, I decide to take it as a peace offering. "I saw lizards, too. Should have brought one home for you. I bet you'd make a whole terrarium for it, complete with a sequined nest." Actually, now that I'm thinking about it, I'd love to see what she'd do with a pet lizard. She'd probably make it a bedazzled leash and walk it around town and cuddle with it at night. Jesus, and now I'm jealous of a fictional reptile.

I need another cold shower and a stiff drink.

"You are a ridiculous human being," Josie says, but she's grinning.

With a ping, we're on the SynthoTech roof, and I set the lightest touch of my hand on the small of her back to guide her through the glass doors.

When she sees what's in front of us, she gasps. Just as I hoped she would.

"Wow," she whispers. We're looking at my natural wonderland: a two-thousand-square-foot heated hydroponic garden full of imported trees from all over the world, with an unrivaled view of downtown.

"I love it up here," I admit. "This is where I come to think." She seems struck by the giant vertical green sweep of it all—the citrus trees, the orchids, the vines trailing up the trellises—though there's also a fear in her eyes that I don't understand.

"Are there, um, any bees out here?" she asks.

The dossier on Josie, which I've got seared into my brain, says she did not exactly have the cheeriest childhood. Her hospital records alone are as thick as a brick. I did not read them—just skimmed the summary my assistant pulled together. Digging into all her medical details felt too bloody intrusive, a line I was not ready to cross.

"No bees, I promise. Allergic?"

She nods, relieved.

"One sting could kill me."

"Not on my watch," I say, making a mental note to carry not only snacks but an EpiPen for her, too.

"This rooftop is a secret paradise." Josie slowly circles to get a full view. "I've never seen anything like it. You built this?"

"Aye," I say, and keep my voice blasé, though the truth is I might be prouder of this garden than I am even of SynthoTech. The sun is hitting my big thinking chair just right; if Josie weren't here, I'd treat myself to a lie-down. The air's so fresh up here, and the view of Shelton spread out below shows you the whole city at a glance. "The garden's slower-growing this time of year, even with the hydroponics," I tell her. "But in the summer, when all the roses and the Japanese cherry trees are blossoming, it's like a natural wonderland."

"Incredible." When she stops by the koi pond, she drops down to her knees to get a better look—and I've got to hold back a smile.

I've noticed how easily Josie finds moments of childlike joy, and I'm envious of that. My guess is she didn't get a lot of that, growing up in examination rooms and hospitals, and I'm impressed it's left her curious as opposed to bitter. As she stares into the water's depths, I take advantage of the moment to enjoy her soft reflection wavering on the water's surface—I trace the curve of her neck, and I stop at that sweet little spot at the nape where those reddish-gold curls soften like candy floss. I swallow hard.

"I can't believe something like this exists in the city," she murmurs.

I take a deep breath and shake off my overwhelming and irrational desire. It has no place here. I'm not that sort of boss. "Josie, I mentioned I asked you to come here for business reasons."

At that, she bolts up to stand, smoothing her skirt, her curiosity working against a new suspicion in her face. "Yes. What's up?"

I shift my weight, cross my arms. Glance up at the canopy of trees and the skyline beyond. Get it together so that I can stare her down. Be fucking Axe MacKenzie, CEO, former CIA and all-around arse-kicker, and not Awkward Axe, who spent more time coding and reading books than talking to girls.

Christ, what is it about her that gets me so tongue-tied? I give my head a shake, forcing the thoughts to line up. This pitch is a tightrope—the last thing I need is for Josie to think she's my idea of the perfect prototype. That would be both embarrassing and borderline creepy given the professional context.

"We've been working on a project at SynthoTech. An AI partner." I make sure to sound all-business. Keep my eyes trained on hers. Not a glance south, not a bloody twitch. "We've put years into development so far, and we committed an eight-figure budget to it."

Her brow furrows slightly. "Okay . . . ?"

"I know how you feel about AI. But again, this is not about taking away any paying jobs. At least, not legal ones."

"Wait. Did you say *eight figures*?"

"Aye, I did," I say, rushing the words out. "And we need a source model, a baseline for the simulator. So the team was wondering if you might consider it. The data we've been gathering on you—not in any dodgy way, just, ah, observational—suggests that your, ah, personality, your mannerisms, your . . . your . . . everything would work. You'd be well paid."

Fuck, that couldn't have come out worse if I'd written it down beforehand. Come to think, why didn't I script it? Because I never script anything, most likely. And because I spent the morning chopping Petrov's right-hand man into bite-size pieces. Wasn't lying about the gators. Turns out they're brilliant coconspirators—they love the taste of human flesh, and, of course, they can't talk.

My words are met with a moment of silence.

"You've been gathering data on me?"

Oh, bloody hell. I think of the mountain of files in our Dropbox that my research team dug up on Josie.

Leukemia at age six. Years spent in and out of hospital wards. Her mum scraping together the cash, by hook or by crook, to make sure Josie got the care she needed.

Josie hides her shadows so well. And wears her resilience admirably lightly. Apparently, late at night, she likes to read romance novels or watch old episodes of *Antiques Roadshow* while crafting away—I know this from Honor, not my private investigator. If I had to guess what kind of gun she keeps, glue would be my first bet.

"No, no—it's, it's not like that. Not . . . stalkery," I say, tripping over my words, which is not something I do. "At the party. The team couldn't help but, well . . . notice you."

"I don't think I understand," she says, blinking up at me. "What does it mean to be your source model? Like, you'd borrow my voice or something?"

"Not just your voice. Your . . . countenance. And disposition."

NINE

JOSIE

"My *disposition*?" I ask, completely confused by whatever nonsense Axe is spouting. But this isn't some weird Scottish-to-English translation issue.

I cross my arms and wait. When it comes to handling Axe, silence is my superpower.

"Yes, because I think . . . *the team* thinks you'd be an ideal AI girlfriend. I mean, not *you* you, because, obviously, you're not an AI girlfriend. You're, you know, human." Axe is flustered, and I'm thoroughly enjoying this new side of him. Usually, it's me scrambling to recover from whatever casual insult he's lobbed my way, my face burning red.

"Can you try that again? In English this time?"

"We want to model our prototype AI girlfriend on you," he says. "See, you're an interesting case, Josie. Take the other night—your impulses, your reactions, or even the next morning."

"The next morning?"

"Aye, it's not the usual girl who takes her coffee at five a.m. With milk and honey. These quirks, the little idiosyncrasies, can't be pulled from a thousand women and add up to create one person." He looks me in the eye. "What can I say? You're a curious mix of contradictions, Josie. And the model has advanced to the point where it does better with what it can't predict."

Could I be hearing this correctly? This man, who has made it very clear from the first time we met that he thinks I'm an absolute idiot, believes my *curious mix of contradictions* is worth copying? For a technological advancement that has an eight-figure investment?

I feel a little faint.

"What would that entail, exactly? What would I have to do?" I ask.

"For our research, you'd spend time with me. Date me, but not really date me. My team would then collect data on what you do or say on dates, who you really are—"

"Let me get this straight," I cut him off. He wants to pay me to date him? Does he think I'm a sex worker? (Not that there's anything wrong with being a sex worker, but that is most definitely not my jam.) "You brought me up to this . . . this *man veranda*, which doesn't even have an extra chair, to stand here while I listen to you proposition me to be . . . your fake, paid girlfriend? Like your personal toy?"

He frowns. "*Man veranda?* I prefer *guy grove*."

I can't help it. I laugh.

"And why would I have two chairs up here?" he asks, fuming a little. "This is *my* space. I don't want anyone else to get too comfortable and think about hanging out."

"On your douche deck." I smirk. He is not going to charm his way out of this.

"My bro orchard," he replies.

"You didn't answer my question."

"You wouldn't be my girlfriend, Josie," Axe says. "My team at SynthoTech would have access to any data our interactions produce. And we aren't using you as a toy. We're using you as our model for the prototype."

"This is the most bullshit proposition I've ever heard," I say. Why would Axe want me, of all people, for his dating simulator? I've seen the way women throw themselves at him—he could find an actual model to be his model.

"You'd go on the payroll as a full-time employee of Syntho-Tech. Even though it's at most a quarter-time job."

"Hmm," I say, not biting.

"And there's premium health insurance."

Something inside me takes pause at this, but I'm already shaking my head. "Sorry, hard pass. I don't want to be connected in any way with some sad app for lonely guys. Maybe this is tricky for you to understand, but those dudes can be uber-creepy. I don't want to be someone's digital fantasy, and I'm not your manic pixie tech-bro dream girl. I'm a human being."

"It's not like that," Axe says, raising his hands in protest. "I assure you, we're looking for something genuine. Someone real, kind. Who folks can actually find a proper connection with. And it's not as if anyone would actually know it's you."

"Nope," I snap quicker than a mousetrap. Why does Axe always manage to turn me into such a spiky porcupine? It's like he's my personal drill sergeant for conflict—getting me all this practice in standing up for myself. Which, come to think, I probably need.

"Just hear me out," Axe says.

"I really don't think—"

"Fake dating me couldn't be any worse than actually dating that arsewipe Bryan." It hits like a bomb. And, honestly, he's not wrong. Every day I'm free of my ex-fiancé, it's like a fog lifts further, and I realize just how much time I wasted on a guy who never deserved it.

But here's the thing: *I* get to say that. Not Axe.

I'm not about to make the same mistake twice, and I'm definitely not wasting one more second on another asshole. His one chair up here says it all, really. Axe is just another selfish rich boy who thinks the sun shines out of his ass. Too in love with himself to share even this space with another human being. No wonder he's creating an AI partner to fawn all over him.

"I'm sorry," Axe says. "I didn't mean—"

But he's too late. I'm already in the old freight elevator. I refuse to look back as the doors slowly clunk shut behind me. Not at the ridiculously perfect garden, and definitely not at Axe's shame-filled face.

TEN

AXE

The rejection stings.

More than I thought it would. I want Josie to know how many years of research have gone into this project, how many prior iterations we've created, how many women we've analyzed and data-mapped, and how none of them pop like Josie. How She's the One is so much more than some half-baked fantasy for lonely blokes. All the platforms we want to build off it. How we want to meet the needs of all sorts, not just men. The business side of me is shouting to take my private express elevator and meet Josie in the lobby. Not let her leave until she says yes. More than that, I want to make sure I can put out that blaze in her eyes. She looked at me like I was some kind of heartless bastard.

I've hurt her. Disappointed her, too. The very last things I wanted to do. What an eejit, mentioning Bryan! I don't know why or how, but Josie has this way of stripping me of every last bit of sense I've got. I spent years in the CIA learning to pick my words like they were bullets. Around her, all that training goes straight to shite.

I end up on the express elevator, but instead of heading for the lobby, I shoot straight down to the underground parking, where

I keep my fleet of motorbikes. Among them is my pride and joy, my custom-made Ducati Apollo—a feckin' marvel of engineering, if I do say so myself. It's as smooth and easy driving through the city as it is tearing up the hills, with a 170-horsepower V4 engine and a design that could make grown men weep. The Apollo's the crown jewel of my collection and worth every penny, especially when I need to get out of town and let off some steam.

Like now. Before I do something daft like beg Josie to come back and listen to my pitch again. Boxing and the gym are grand when I'm raging at someone else. Biking, though . . . biking is best when I'm furious with myself.

I exit the city and head up to the ridge, pushing the beast hard, taking the sharp twists and feeling the burn on the steep climbs. When I hit the long stretches, with the snowcapped mountains rising on one side and the bone-dry meadow stretching out on the other, my mind wanders back to that gorgeous lass . . . and how I always manage to fuck it up with her.

Long ago, I figured out how to numb myself to my surroundings, go ice-cold whenever I needed to stay on high alert. That skill not only got me through a rough childhood (Philip Larkin had it right; they fuck you up, your mum and dad), but it also carried me through the CIA and into private contracting without a single close call. Strike used to say it was both terrifying and impressive, the way I could just shut down every emotion and become a warrior robot.

Which is why turning into some tongue-tied, spotty lad with a hard-on every time I'm around Josie is especially confusing. And not exactly ideal, seeing as I need her help with this bloody project.

My meeting with Niles von Grafenhagen is set for Friday. I need to have a legitimate AI prototype in place before presenting.

If I'm going to mix business with pleasure—though *pleasure* may not be the right word; *purpose* is more accurate—then I'm going in with guns blazing. Metaphorically. I'll save the literal ones for later.

I press the pedal, take the turn a bit fast, and hear the tires squeal. No fear, only thrill.

I'm edging over 110 miles an hour when I hear the sirens. *Fuck.* I pull to the side of the road, stomp my boot down on the dusty ground.

At least I'm not in my car.

The last thing I need is for the officer to see what's in the boot.

ELEVEN

JOSIE

Twenty minutes after I've stormed out of SynthoTech, I'm still all worked up, gripping the steering wheel like it's the only thing that's keeping me from flying off the handle. Fucking Axe MacKenzie. I swear to God, I'm *allergic* to that man. My phone rings, and I see Mom's name pop up. I answer even though I'm driving and I don't really feel like chatting. But she'll take my mind, and other blushing body parts, off Axe.

"I hope I'm not overstepping your boundaries," she starts, which is basically her calling card for *I'm definitely about to overstep your boundaries.* Same energy as *I hope you don't mind my saying* and *I'm your mother, so I know.* "Josie, are you listening to me?"

"I'm here, Mom." I try to keep my sigh from becoming a groan, and my foot presses a little harder on the gas. Like going faster might let me outrun this conversation.

"So, since you weren't handling it, I went ahead and posted to your socials—and yes, I know we had an agreement, sweetie pie. But, Josie, this is for Alan and me, too. We're really trying to help you get back on your feet. And you know the medication costs are outrageous. I could show you the stack of bills, all the extra expenses insurance refuses to cover. We were counting on renting out that apartment unit this spring, and since we're not—"

"Shit, okay. I get it," I snap.

I'm now stuck behind a bus coughing exhaust into my AC. My hands are sweaty on the steering wheel as annoyance sweeps through me.

Silence.

Mom hates any kind of "rough language" from me. At some point, my JosieFightsOn personality—the sunshine-and-sunflowers daughter I needed to be for donations and crowdsourcing—seemed to merge, in Mom's head at least, with the real me. Anything outside the margins upsets her.

She'd be literally gobsmacked if she saw how I popped off on Axe.

Come to think of it, I am, too.

To be fair to Mom, even I can't always tell where JosieFightsOn ends and the real Josie begins. You tell a story about who you are long enough, and it starts to feel like the truth.

"It's no big deal, Josie. And don't use profanity with me," she snaps, all frosty. Because obviously the issue here is my use of the word *shit*. Not the fact that she steamrolls over my personal boundaries.

"Dammit!" I yell, but this time my cursing is not actually aimed at my mom.

My car just made a noise. A clunking noise. "Shit! Shit! Shit!"

"Josie! What's wrong?" Of course she goes straight to panic.

"I'm fine. I'm fine. A small car thing. We'll talk later."

I pull the car to the shoulder and get out. Yup. Flat tire. Looking as deflated as I feel. There's no spare in my trunk—Gertrude, my car, is currently being held together with duct tape and optimism. I also don't have AAA, because I'm twenty-six years old, live with my parents, and can barely afford a microwave burrito let alone roadside assistance.

And right on cue—just like my tarot reading warned me—this day takes another turn for the worse. I'm pulling out my phone, debating who to call, when I feel the first raindrop hit my face.

"You have GOT to be kidding me," I mutter to absolutely no one. The highway roars with passing cars, and then, of course, the heavens open up like I've been personally chosen for a cosmic dunk tank.

Within seconds, I'm soaked.

Perfect. Just perfect. Nothing like a surprise rain shower to top off a total shit show of a day. Right now, I'm about as far from JosieFightsOn as I can get.

I feel the rage bubbling up. Rage at Bryan, at Axe, at the universe that decided to swipe my childhood and leave me with debt I can never pay back. Rage at my mom for never getting how humiliating and wrong it is to have your life turned into a crowdfunding campaign.

And then a memory hits me like another sudden storm, but this one's from deep inside, dark and heavy: I'm a kid in a hospital bed, tubes running into my arms. I can't move, can't even turn my head without feeling like razor blades are scraping against my spine and the base of my skull. I'm boiling with anger at the unfairness of it all, at the people who put me here. At the body that betrayed me. At myself, most of all, for not being strong enough to crawl out of that bed and rip the tubes out.

I'll never forget this. I'll never forgive it.

Just as quickly as the rage floods in, it drains away as I give myself a shake and reset. Who can I call for help? Definitely not my parents—I'm not ready for round two with Mom. So . . . who, then? Honor, maybe? She had to borrow my car for months before Strike gifted her that shiny new Audi convertible for her birthday.

If anyone gets it, it's her.

I shoot a text to Honor, and she promises to call a tow truck and swing by to get me ASAP. I climb back into Gertrude, soaked to the bone and shivering like a wet dog. I sit there, staring at my phone, debating whether I'm brave enough to check my socials. It can't be *that* bad, right? Besides, this day—no, this *week*—can't get any worse. I've already sent out 130 emails canceling my wedding. Surely I can handle a quick scroll through Instagram.

I take a cleansing breath, make a wish even though it's not anywhere close to 11:11 and I have no loose eyelashes, and click.

Oh no. No. No. No. No. No. I feel nauseous.

The post from my account is sugary and begging—a straight-up cash grab—and my mom's imitation of my voice makes me sound like I'm fifteen years old.

> Heya Everybody!
>
> It's me again, your one and only lil Josie!
>
> Some of you know me from my childhood battle with my leukemia (thanks for helping me kick cancer's butt!), and others know me from my challenges living with type 1 diabetes since I was eleven years old. Managing the cost of my special U-500 insulin has always been super-duper challenging, since I need to get it imported from Frankfurt, Germany, and lately the prices have, sigh, skyrocketed.
>
> Even though I'm working a full-time job (shout-out to Grace & Honor, visit our web page, where my bedazzled phone cases

are 40% off), and I've cut back on every non-essential cost I can think of (I even took a break this semester from school!), I go to bed every night completely freaked out that I will not be able to afford my next dose. Guys, insulin is my lifeline—and that's why I am launching this GoFundMe campaign.

My goal is to raise enough funds to cover six months' worth of medication, including shipping and storage costs. Every contribution makes a humongous difference and is a major impact in terms of my ability to live my life.

But if you can't make a donation today, please feel free to share my story. It totally sucks to have to choose between finances and health, and I appreciate every last penny you can spare.

Thank you soooo much!!

I love you all times a million.

XO Josie

The photo is of me from about nine years ago, standing in *Powerpuff* pajama bottoms and a Shelton Softball T-shirt without a bra. You can see the bumps of my new breasts and the shadows of my nipples. The ickiest part of all is that I'm holding Bun-Bun, my plushie rabbit, when I'm clearly too old to be clutching a stuffed animal.

Of course Mom said *school* instead of *college*. She wants me to sound like a child! What manipulative bullshit.

My cheeks burn and tears sting my eyes. I can't sit here and look at this—the humiliation actually feels physical—so I jump out of the car again, right into the pouring rain.

I imagine my mother's face when I get home—that very specific, shiny-eyed high as she listens to the *ka-ching* cash register sounds as the donations for her latest fundraiser hit her phone.

I feel so trapped. Nothing in that post is technically a lie. And yet.

I look up to the dark sky, to the universe beyond, and plead for some guidance. Just one sign. The universe, of course, doesn't answer.

As much as Axe thinks I'm a dimwit, I'm not usually the type of person who is desperate enough to yell up at the heavens.

And then I see it, and I can't help myself. I start laughing, then crying, then laugh-crying so hard that my tears mix with the rain.

There it is—a giant billboard, not two hundred feet away.

A *literal* fucking sign that reads: **Take the Exit to a New You.**

It's an ad for a plastic surgeon, but it might as well be mocking me straight to my face. I'm right back to an hour ago, on Axe's rooftop, when he let slip the three magic words: *premium health insurance.*

Nothing would be an easier exit to a whole new me than having my medical costs covered. What's worse than my mom pimping out my sickly adolescent body and asking people to send her money for financial struggles she won't even explain to me?

Premium health insurance.

Take the Exit to a New You.

My mind races, and I wonder, panicking for a second, whether my face looks just like my mom's did when I came home. That same frantic desperation. Because I'll admit it—I want, no, I *need* cash. My budget is so tight, I have no clue how I'll pay for the tow truck and a new tire. I can't even afford to get home.

Besides, what's the difference between the "disposition" that my mom invented for me as a way to shake the money tree for my diabetes-related expenses and the "disposition" that Axe's horny SynthoTech geeks think makes me a good choice of girlfriend for She's the One?

I guess I've always been a curious mix of contradictions—how could I not be? Living under the spotlight as a child with a terminal illness, I've been performing my whole life.

But with Axe's offer, I'd have an active say in the project. Or at least I'd demand one before agreeing to anything. That's the difference. I could shape how the ideal girlfriend gets rolled out. Whereas when it comes to JosieFightsOn, my mom has turned me into a Frankensteinian creation, cooked up by social media's algorithms and a careful study of click metrics, without any consideration for who I might want to be or who I really am.

With Axe's offer, I'd have a real shot at getting off my parents' insurance plan. Getting out of their house. Stopping the constant drain on their finances. Finally, independence. My entire relationship with my family and friends—my entire life—has been dictated by my health needs. I need to take back some control.

I look up at the sky again. Wipe the rain and tears from my face with my sleeve.

A literal sign in front of me. Just the other day, I flipped a Tower card—a hint it was time to take a big swing.

I *am* receiving guidance, if I know how to look for it.

And yeah, the Devil card is still bugging me, but it's possible I got that all wrong, too. Who knows? The Devil may be the anonymous dirtbags who are right now jerking off to JosieFightsOn.

TWELVE

AXE

Three hours later, with a $350 ticket jammed into the pocket of my now-ruined leather jacket (cheers to the pissing rain all the way home), I haul my bike right up to SynthoTech's front door, pull off my helmet, and rake a hand through my hair.

The second I step into the lobby, the place goes dead quiet. You can almost hear the sound of arses clenching as they suddenly remember they have very important work to do. I catch a glimpse of myself reflected in the window. Aye, I'm a dangerous-looking motherfucker after a ride. Like there's hell to pay in the thud of my dirty size-thirteen boots on the tiled floor. The gauntlet gloves, the reflective gear—I'm halfway between *Mad Max* and a Norseman fresh off a pillaging.

I'm rarely a dick at work, but if I said *boo* to any of these MIT kids, they'd likely keel over.

But now it's my turn for an effing heart attack: Josie's sitting in the atrium, and she's staring right at me.

Not a speck of fear in her eyes. Figures.

"Hey," I say as every single other human being melts away.

She's showered, her hair's damp and twisted up in one of those little clips. She smells fresh and clean, and it turns out she's even more beautiful without a speck of makeup. She's also wearing an ugly navy blazer that hides her. Big, shapeless, the kind of thing that says *Don't look at me*. Like she raided her closet for the dullest bit of armor she could find.

"Can we talk in private?" she asks.

Earlier, I'd have gladly traded a pinkie to hear those four words. And now here she is—no blood sacrifice required. Just a little road rash from a rage skid. Maybe I've tracked some grit onto the marble floor—but ach, who cares? Only makes me look more badass.

Two minutes later, we're in a first-floor conference room. I'd prefer my office, but Josie looks skittish enough to bolt, so I play it safe.

"I'd rather eat a ghost pepper stuffed with wasabi and topped with ground-up glass than take this job," she says flat out, and I cough into my hand to smother my spit-laugh. Josie is dead serious.

"What about if I throw in a rubbing alcohol chaser?" I ask, and she smirks. "And a signing bonus bag of dog shite?"

She almost smiles, then reins it in. Not giving an inch. I respect that.

"If you're trying to make the perfect girlfriend, you're off to a terrible start."

"In what way?" I ask, genuinely curious. I am always interested in what Josie has to say, even when it's something ridiculous, like warning me that Mercury is in retrograde.

"You have manipulated my consent," she says.

"How?" I blink, genuinely baffled. Consent is sacred to me. "You said no earlier, and I watched you walk out. Didn't stop you. Now you're back, on your own terms. You haven't consented to anything yet."

She holds my gaze, chin up. "I need this job for your health insurance. There are medications I need that aren't available here, and my life depends on them."

"Ah." I nod and lift my brow as if this is new information. Josie doesn't know that I know about her special insulin. I don't betray even a trace of pity—mostly because I don't feel any. Josie's a tough little cookie, not some sickly hothouse flower. This woman is a true survivor in every sense of the word.

And survivors don't need pity. They deserve respect.

"Aye, we all take jobs for different reasons. Health insurance seems as good as any." She frowns, and I catch myself staring at the way she purses her lips. I shrug. "Sorry, lass, but that's the truth. I didn't create the system. I want you on my team, and if it's my generous insurance that seals the deal, then fine. That's your beautiful American capitalism at work."

I let that hang in the air for a moment. Josie needs to know who she's dealing with—a man who's sharp, calculating, and playing to win. But fair. Always fair. I expect the best from my people, and they get the best in return. High salaries, great benefits.

"We can get you on the health plan today, if that's what it takes," I say. "Contract will be in your inbox in five minutes. Signing bonus wired to you by the end of the day. And I know what you're making at Grace & Honor. Trust me, this is more. A hell of a lot more. And we're not even asking for full-time. Just a few evenings here and there."

She swallows but says nothing. I push on, leaning in to close the deal.

"And I wasn't joking when I said we have a premium insurance plan. I picked the most expensive, top-tier coverage plan for me and my employees. Call me old-fashioned or just plain Scottish, but I believe everyone should have access to the best health care available." I catch myself, wondering if I'm babbling, but she's just sitting there, wielding that silence.

"So you're a bleeding heart? Is that what I'm supposed to believe?" Josie asks, and I bark out a laugh.

"Not even close, lass. Taking care of my employees makes good economic sense. Also, contrary to what you believe about me, I'm not a fecking monster. At least not as a boss."

"What are the goals and expectations for She's the One?" she asks, suddenly businesslike and crisp; this is a Josie I've never met before.

"That'd take a few hours to explain properly. But the short version? You'll be cocreating with us. Nothing gets locked in to the final model without your sign-off and consent." I grin. "I promise it'll be more fun than ghost peppers and wasabi."

Something in my words must hit the mark, because I see her shoulders relax a bit and I feel like I've finally scored a point.

"Sounds reasonable."

"The working contract is a fifty-two-page, single-spaced document," I tell her. "I want you to go into this with your eyes wide open. Take all the time you need to read it line by line. If you want a lawyer, we can refer you to one."

"Send it over."

I get out my phone to do just that, and I email Rita from HR and tell her to add Josie to our plan immediately. All I want to do now is make it official and take her out—maybe something that starts with champagne and ends with her lips on mine, though Josie's navy blazer is not invited. I don't like anything that intentionally tones down or hides her natural sparkle.

But I know better than to push. I will have to wait to see what it's like to fake date Josie Greene.

I deliberately check my watch like I've got places to be. My own eagerness is making me exceptionally uncomfortable. I don't do eager.

"Any other questions?"

She hesitates, then says in a rush, "I drew the Devil card today."

I smirk on instinct but quickly wipe it off my face. I've got to stop mocking what she cares about to make this work. If she's this seriously into tarot, maybe I should pick up *Tarot for Dummies* and learn a thing or two. Even if it's all obvious horseshit.

"The Devil," I repeat.

"And I really hope I'm not making a deal with him."

I nod gravely, though I want to laugh again. If she only knew. "I feel more like a guardian angel."

"Don't push it," she scoffs, but her lips twitch.

"You haven't seen our prescription drug coverage yet," I say, and kiss my fingers.

Every meeting's a game of timing, like poker in Vegas—a balance of knowing when you've won and it's time to stand up and leave before you blow it.

And right now, it's time to go.

I rise, still in my damp gear from the ride, and her eyes flutter like she's staring right at Satan's brother himself. And considering the filthy thoughts all chasing one another round in my head—involving this table, her open thighs, and my tongue—maybe she is.

THIRTEEN

AXE

The girls arrive looking so sleepy. This is always what Axe notices first when he stands waiting for them on the dock, his basket of flowers in his arms, as the boat of new arrivals comes in. He likes to greet them and present each with a bunch of wild Scottish heather and thistles, plus a sprig of Scotch bluebell, all picked himself and tied in a white ribbon, because it puts a smile on their dazed, baffled faces.

They perk right up to thank him, and they ask how old he is (seven) and they tell him in all different languages that his eyes are beautiful, as blue as the ocean they've recently crossed—the water that now separates them from home.

Wherever they're from, they ruffle his hair like he's a lucky charm.

They're collected from all over, these girls, but they always have two things in common. They are very, very pretty, and they are very, very young. Even at seven, he can tell they're bonny lasses. When they step off the boat onto the dock, they look up at the enormous castle looming in the distance, unsure what sort of fairy tale they've found themselves in. Their baffled eyes take in the many outbuildings, the barns and the orchards, the barracks and the keep.

Axe and his brother, Hamish, are responsible for bringing the girls inside.

They've all been lured here because they want to become models or actresses or hoteliers or massage therapists. These are the promises that have been made, what they'll get if they work hard enough. Though Hollywood is so far away from Scotland, it might as well be Mars.

Sometimes the girls end up being babysitters. Or they work as Pa's special friends. Sometimes they end up dead, but as Pa has told him many, many times, we are all going to die eventually. Death is unremarkable, as much a fact of life as eating blueberries off the low, spreading woodland shrubs in the summer and falling asleep under wool blankets to the sound of a crackling fire in the winter.

"Death comes for everyone, Axe," Da says, as if this is something that should make Axe feel better.

Instead, those words make him feel like he swallowed the stones he likes to skip from the bluff.

Mrs. Collins, who takes care of Axe and Hamish but also manages the girls, used to be pretty, but she is old now, with a slash of red lipstick and tall black heels. She is Pa's "right-hand man," but he never kisses Mrs. Collins on the lips like he does the girls when they're dressed up for him in the great hall.

Mrs. Collins wears shirts buttoned all the way to her neck and pleated trousers. Sometimes her sleeves creep up her arm, and Axe can see raised jagged lines along her wrists. He imagines she was once bitten by a shark.

If anyone can survive a tussle with a shark, it's Mrs. Collins.

All the girls call Pa Daddy, and the staff calls Pa Eldy—so Axe simply thought that Eldy *was just another way to say* Da, *too.*

His brother, Hamish, who is five years older than Axe and knows many more things, tells him that it's not Eldy, *ya stupid arse, it's* El D*—short for El Diablo, the Devil.*

Then Axe really does feel like a stupid arse, because he still doesn't understand. So he asks Hamish, the only person on the island willing to field Axe's questions, though he knows he has to dole them out sparingly. He doesn't want to test Hamish's patience: "Why is Da the Devil?"

Hamish shrugs. "Because Da owns everything and everybody in Skara Brae, and if you get in his way, he will make your life so bad, you'll wish you were dead. Now come along, Axe, let's make a fort oot this bramble!"

The boys play forts a lot. Sometimes they're soldiers and sometimes they work for Her Majesty's Royal Air Force. Axe dreams of a day when he will get to fly a real plane. His whole life is Skara Brae, filled with girls who need to work hard for his da, and all Da's friends, who look very happy when their big, fancy boats dock here. Da's friends are rich, with large bellies taut like drums, and they are mostly old and smell like whiskey and tobacco. When they step onto dry land, they pronounce Axe's home Heaven, which is confusing. How does the Devil live in Heaven?

Though sometimes Axe understands that this place is different, especially when he scrambles up rocks on the shore and lets the mist whip his face and talks to the otters that, like him, know how to camouflage. Especially when he prays to God in the chapel and watches the sun move through the stained glass and make rainbows on the dark oak floor.

Sometimes whole days will go by and no one will notice or talk to Axe.

The men are here to sit and drink wine and get massages, and the girls are here to serve them. They rub the men, who lie like large and greasy beached whales on the massage tables. No one can ignore their snapping fingers, the way they grab at everything as if the whole world belongs to them.

The girls wear skimpy see-through T-shirts and tiny thongs, and they bring food and drinks to the lounge chairs around the pool in an endless loop. If the Whales pinch their asses or shove their tongues down their throats, the girls act happy and excited, though Axe can tell from their eyes that they're sad. That they want to be anywhere but here.

Axe gives the girls flowers because he wants to see them smile one last time before they stop smiling altogether. Their job here is to make Da and the Whales happy. They're like teachers or camp counselors or nurses, Da says. They're supposed to take care of people. That's what they signed up for.

But Axe wonders who is supposed to take care of them.

Once, one of the girls offered to massage Axe if he'd help her leave, and he didn't know what to say to that. He didn't want to be massaged, and he had no idea how to leave. He'd been here, on the island, every single day since he was born. He'd taught himself to read by sitting on the cold stone floor of the library, tracing the letters with his fingers.

He'd never watched the telly, though the staff often moaned about missing it most from "the real world." As a child, he hadn't really understood what it was, though Hamish had described it as a screen that tells a story, and at five years old, Axe took that literally, imagining the telly speaking directly to its audience like the old ham radio and the walkie-talkies he and his brother played with.

Now he knows better. Now he understands the telly doesn't talk *to you—it plays out stories performed by beautiful, bonny folk.*

And he wonders if it's anything like the castle, where everyone has a role to play.

Sometimes, late at night, Axe imagines slipping from the rocks into the churning ocean and swimming in the brutal water, pumping his arms until he finds another, better shore.

FOURTEEN

JOSIE

Axe wasn't kidding. The document is fifty-two pages, and there's even an entire section on "intimacy." It's all legalese, a language I don't speak.

Not that it really matters. I'm out of options anyway.

When I got home yesterday, my mom ambushed me in the guesthouse.

"We're already at our goal. Told you that you should have posted," she said, all smug delight, and I was too tired to fight. My car's got a shiny new tire, courtesy of Strike's black Amex. Pocket change to him, but I'll pay him back. I wrote down the exact amount, down to the penny, so I can Venmo him the second Axe's promised signing bonus hits.

Work is work. I've been a store clerk for years, and I once spent a summer doing tarot readings at a fold-out table outside a coffee shop. I've been a waitress, a nanny, a gas station cashier, a barista. This job at SynthoTech is just another gig.

Grace—Honor's twin—used to make extra cash as an escort, not that Honor ever knew. They had a lot of secrets between them, but they kept their own, too. Grace once showed me her personal ad in the back of the *Shelton Free Press* and then put a finger to her lips, like *Don't tell.*

I didn't judge her then, and I'm not judging myself now.

Grace earned her cash, no pity involved. And I'm so fucking done with pity.

I skim the "intimacy" section:

> Both parties agree and acknowledge that solicitation and paying for sexual acts is illegal in the State of Pennsylvania, and is in no way expressly or implied to be part of Josie Greene's employment at SynthoTech.

Okay, cool. No sex. Nice and clear. I keep reading.

> SynthoTech is a technological company developing an AI system designed to sexually satisfy its end user. Both parties acknowledge that this may involve discussing graphic sexual acts and the use of haptic skins. Both parties waive any sexual harassment claims related to these discussions or tech usage and testing . . .

Wait, what? I read it again. I get the sexy talk—that was expected. You can't create an AI girlfriend without some phone sex or sexting.

But a haptic skin?

WTF is a haptic skin? I text Axe. After I hit send, it occurs to me that I didn't have to reach out. I could have googled it. Before I can even open Safari, though, Axe has written back.

I see you're reading the fine print. Good lass

The *good lass* irks me, but I like how fast he wrote back. If I'd texted Bryan, it would've taken him three hours to respond with some nonsense like *whassssup*.

I'm still reeling from the fact that I wasted four years of my life on that garbage human. Just the other day, I got a fraud alert on my credit card because Bryan tried to party at a strip club on my dime. He also bombarded Grace & Honor with one-star reviews, spinning stories of me being rude to customers.

It would be laughable if it wasn't so fucking sad. I'll never understand why it took me so long to see Bryan for what he really is when the truth was staring me in the face the whole time.

WTF is a haptic skin? I text again.

A skin suit that has biometric sensors with feedback systems in place so as to simulate physical touch in the user. Some use electrical muscle stimulation or transcutaneous electrical nerve stimulation and can be used for various purposes

Ugh. Total tech nerd.

In English please, I write. Make that American English, I add.

It's a skintight suit—almost like a wet suit—that, for SynthoTech purposes, can be used with a VR headset to simulate sex

Umm. Is it like the VR headsets you can use in the mall so it tricks your mind into feeling like something is happening, like falling or whatever?

The headsets are similar but more advanced than anything you'd have experienced in a mall. And the suits work simultaneously to stimulate the body with skin sensors, vibrations, and massage etc etc

Huh. I pause and try to imagine it.

I am not a prude. I work at Grace & Honor, which on the surface looks like a typical home goods store but actually has an entire section devoted to state-of-the-art sex toys. I have definitely spent some of my paychecks there. In just a few weeks, I'm going to be helming a booth for the store at Toygasm in Philly, a convention devoted to erotic play.

Why does this feel different? Also, what does *etc etc* actually mean?

So like a full body sex toy? I ask.

Yes and no. It will stimulate in the same way as, say, a dildo, but it will have two distinct advantages. 1. It will involve VR so you will feel fully immersed in the sexual experience and 2. The device will be controlled by either the AI or another consenting partner to create stimulation

I gulp. Axe is keeping it clinical and businesslike, but the words still make me shiver. *Stimulate. Dildo.* My brain is scrambling to keep up with the idea that my new boss looks like Axe (not a big sister, like Honor) and is casually talking about dildos and, um . . . stimulation. We could be talking about anything else—cooking, decorating.

Literally anything but fucking.

I feel a rush of heat between my legs. Is this how Axe is in bed? All nerdy dirty talk? Like *Josie, does this immersive experience of my tongue in your pussy stimulate you?* Somehow, I doubt it. Axe radiates this confident, adventurous vibe, like he'd be up for anything. And that Scottish accent . . . the way his eyes flashed when he stormed through SynthoTech's doors like a Scottish king in badass motorcycle gear—okay, Josie, time to shut down Imagination Central.

But now I'm too turned on to turn off. Is this the breakup talking? Sex with Bryan was a chore—like packing a lunch or scrubbing the toilet. Borderline unpleasant but necessary.

Maybe now that my life is free, my libido's finally free, too.

I think about my first (and favorite) little toy from Grace & Honor: the Buzzlet. It's stashed safely in my epinephrine kit, a tiny two-inch wonder, pink as a rose, with eight different settings. I've got thirty minutes before work, so I lock myself in the bathroom, grab it, and sit with my back against the tub, legs spread. I set it to my favorite pulse: a long, slow throb. I close my eyes, and immediately, something much bigger than two inches pops into my mind.

Good lass . . .

No, no, no. Girl, do *not* think about him. Focus on the pleasure. Think about that thing Bryan could do with his tongue . . . one of the few times I didn't have to fake it. Nope, I hate Bryan. How about the actor on the cover of the *People* magazine that's getting splashed on the side of the tub? Nah, too young and scrawny and delicate.

And there he is again. Axe. The way he looked at me, that sharp glint in his dark blue eyes. Those rugged, weathered features, like he's seen things, lived in different worlds before Shelton. That accent, holy fuck, the accent. *No, Josie, you cannot let Axe bring you to climax. He did his job; find someone else. Literally anyone.*

Aye, don't slow down, lass! I hear the lilt of his Scottish brogue in my imagination, as soft and teasing as I imagine his tongue would be.

And then it's too late. I'm gone.

FIFTEEN

AXE

Niles von Grafenhagen has been out of pocket for three weeks, and looking at him as he strides into my corner office tells me why.

He's had another nose job, plus a new hair transplant.

I don't know what looks worse, a nose like a Barbie doll or a head of baby hair sprouting from his scalp like pickleweed after a Highland gale. But I do know that he fully expects me to tell him how smashing he looks.

His smile is as hopeful as an eighth-grade girl with her braces just off.

"Let's get to it," I say. I'm a good liar, but even I can't compliment that face without wincing. He should sue the doctor who let him go under the knife. Again. God, the poor man is an addict. I'd feel bad for him, if I didn't hate him so fecking much.

Von Graf's smile fades, but he didn't become a billionaire because he gave a shite about winning fans.

"Time is money," he agrees, his voice edged with impatience. He smooths down his new hair. Despite his troll-like stature and his daft plasticky, mismatched face, von Graf exudes his own jarring sort of Napoleonic power. His desperate attempts to cling to his youth have turned his face into a freakish blend of stretched skin and eerily smooth features.

These, along with the obvious lifts in his shoes, make him look like some odd wee man who's gone through Willie Wonka's taffy-pulling machine and come out on the other side a bit over-stretched.

But he wears a hundred-thousand-dollar watch and a suit so perfectly pressed, I wonder if he keeps a steam iron in the back of his chauffeured car. I happen to know his sneakers are 1985 Air Jordan 1s—possibly worn by Jordan himself, now specially shrunk to von Graf's elf-man feet.

To each his own, I think, but my mouth is closed for no more than ten seconds before it just pops out. "How's that new nose treating ya, laddie?" I ask.

Von Graf takes the jab with a shrug.

"If it helps me smell bullshit, then it's a success." But he's pissed. Me and my big yawp—ach, it's just how I am. He's such a shithead. No way I can put sugar on it.

"No bullshit here. She's the One is going to make us a fortune," I assure him, and then we're off to the races as I lower the lights and unveil the wall screen to reveal a full presentation on the project.

Von Graf is a formidable businessman, and his calculating eyes and shrewd, me-first questions got him the nickname von Grab. The tabloids also love to highlight the fact von Graf shuffles houses, cars, and women like a croupier, so when the first photo of AI Josie splashes across the deck, I'm surprised he reacts with such hawkish intensity.

"Who's this?" His eyes narrow as if she's a challenge I've thrown him. A dog about to pounce on a T-bone.

"We're beta testing this prototype. We call her Gemini." Bit of an inside joke, because even though I'm not an expert in astrology, I do know that *Gemini* means *twins* in Latin. Two different Josies. I've not told her about the code name yet. I wonder if she'll find it funny or just plain insulting. Maybe both. Either way, it helps protect her identity. No way would I ever let von Graf know her real name.

"I mean, who is she really?" he snaps. "What woman are you basing her on?"

Something about his tone puts me well on my guard. This presentation is bait, aye, but Josie most definitely is not. "Don't get your knickers in a knot. She's nobody," I say. "It doesn't matter. She's been hired to add finishing details. That's all."

Von Graf nods, and as I carry on with the presentation, he takes tiny sips from whatever special antiaging tonic he's got in that sleek, futuristic silver thermos of his. Another bit of gossip I'd love to unlearn about this wanker is his obsession with dodging death. He's convinced he'll live to be three hundred or some such notion.

Time's the one thing a billionaire can't buy, so naturally, he's throwing millions at the idea of cheating fate. I'd happily be the first to give this man a leg up into his time machine or whatever fever dream he thinks will grant him immortality. Wherever his earthly body ends up rotting for eternity, his soul will be burning in Hell.

But I've got to dot my *i*'s and cross my *t*'s first. I don't take anyone down until everything is proved beyond a shadow of a doubt.

I have rules. My own nonnegotiable code of ethics.

I've been following von Graf long enough to have a solid lead that he's behind a sex-trafficking ring that could involve up to a thousand women. My source says the lasses are mostly

Ukrainian—the wives, sisters, or daughters of men killed in the war—kidnapped by Russian militia and sold to the highest international bidder.

Von Graf "buys" in bulk—sickening, unconscionable, but that's the way of it—and then he "rents" the women out to his fellow billionaires at exclusive parties held across the globe. It's a side hustle for him—one I reckon he does for the power, the control, and the sex just as much as for the money he doesn't need.

If I can get him to invest in She's the One, I'll get to set him and his team up with access to our computer system. Which will really provide me with a backdoor channel to his network and, I hope, his files.

A win-win. Funding for my most important SynthoTech project and fodder to take down one of the biggest pieces of scum on the planet.

I fully intend to break that dainty, sculpted little nose again, this time not via some overpriced plastic surgeon but with my fist.

But first, as with all things, patience.

SIXTEEN

JOSIE

"And now that my first paycheck just hit my account, I can finally say it—I'm moving out!" I announce, doing a little happy dance with my shoulders. But Mom and Alan just stare at me, stone-faced, across the kitchen table. Not exactly the reaction I was expecting. "This is good news, folks! This is what you wanted?"

I don't know why I phrase it like a question. They've been *super* clear about wanting to turn my little garage apartment into an Airbnb for extra cash. Which is fair. I've been mooching for way too long.

The microwave pings, and, as if awoken by a trance, Alan stands up. "Who's up for chili-cheese waffles?"

"No, thanks," Mom and I say at the same time.

"More for me," he grunts, which I think might be his love language. Not chili-cheese waffles, of course, but grunting. Both Mom and I are words-of-affirmation people, so it seems strange that she ended up with someone so uncommunicative.

"I don't understand, Josephine," says Mom, which is what she says when she fully understands something but doesn't like it.

"Mom, you've been hinting for *months* that you wanted me out of the guesthouse! I thought you'd be thrilled to finally rent it out for real money. You could use that cash to pay off the new dishwasher or these kitchen chairs you just bought . . . and whatever else is on your list," I say.

"But we're doing the fundraiser!" she says, her lips pressed so tightly they've disappeared, and I feel something ignite inside me. Like one of those feverish nights in the hospital, when my temp was 104 and I was begging for blankets, sure I'd never feel warm again.

The memory slams fiercely, dragging up that old helplessness.

I try to shake it off, but it grips me like a fucking vise. Anger burns too hot in my chest. Rage at this memory, at them, at everything that kept me trapped in that bed, shivering, while they looked on like my life was some kind of tear-jerking Netflix drama.

"Nope. I returned all the payments and took it down. I don't want to take fundraising money that I don't need. Sorry, Mommy." I can hear my voice turning little-girlish, and I hate it. "It was the first thing I did when I got paid."

Actually, it was the second thing I did. As soon as Axe's signing bonus hit my account yesterday, I went apartment hunting. Found a studio perfectly equidistant between Grace & Honor and SynthoTech and just ten minutes from Golden Leaves, where Nonna lives. I took it on the spot—it's basically a shoebox with a corner kitchen that fits a bed, a love seat, and *maybe* a tiny desk if I'm lucky.

But like Nonna always said, *The bigger the house, the smaller the home.*

Which means this place is gonna be *all* home. I don't need a lot of stuff. Fairy lights, some framed photos of me and Nonna, a dash of sparkle, and it'll feel like mine in no time. The best part, Mom and Alan don't know about it. I plan to keep my new address on the down-low for as long as possible.

I need some breathing room from them.

Mom's face reddens as her eyes narrow. "How could you do that without telling us? We've been working so hard on updates!"

Alan steps back into the conversation, clutching his Yuengling plus a plate of chili-cheese waffles, while their cat, Buster, follows behind him, hoping for dropped scraps. When Alan's angry—and he looks pretty angry now—his whole face darkens so that I can see every splintering capillary vein like a road map to nowhere across his face.

"You're always so ungrateful, you know that, Josie? After everything we've done for you, you go behind our backs like this," he says.

"You won't have to do anything for me anymore. That's the whole point," I say. The smell of Alan's food hits me like a brick, and I try not to gag. Why is he always snarfing down the rankest stuff—tuna casseroles, blue cheese toasties, salmon steaks? At least he's talking in whole sentences for once, since his preferred language is caveman. Like right now, when he pauses his berating of me and looks at my mother and grunts, "Salt."

"Sure thing, honey," she says.

No wonder I got engaged to Bryan. This is the blueprint I had for marriage.

"I'm collecting my things. I'll be packed and out in a couple of hours," I say.

Mom's eyes well up immediately, while Alan looks like he's about to pop a vein.

"You're leaving us *today*?" Mom asks, and her voice is dangerously quiet. She blinks a few times, her fake lashes catching her tears. "This is how you repay me?"

"Mom, no. This is a *good* thing. This is me saving myself. I don't want to be JosieFightsOn forever. I want to just be . . . me.

Grown up, on my own. I'm done with the pity party. I have to start living for myself. I can't keep living . . ." My voice trails off. I can't say it. I can't tell her I can't keep living for *her*. For whatever weird thrill she gets from the endless drama of my medical mess.

Even if this is exactly how I feel. But I learned a long time ago, you can't tell people exactly how you feel. That's the quickest way to lose everything.

Mom shoots a look at Alan, who's chewing like a chipmunk. He nods at her like I'm some bratty teen who needs her phone confiscated.

"Josie, you can't do this," Mom says, blinking hard as the tears start their usual slide down her cheeks, mascara running while she keeps wiping at it, making it worse. It's all so over-the-top and absurdly dramatic, like her old live streams when she'd bawl for donations. I bet it's muscle memory by now. An uncharitable thought, and yet I wish she wasn't so quick with the waterworks. It's not like I'm moving to Australia. Just out of their sad guesthouse.

"Nope," grunts Alan for emphasis. "Can't. Not now."

"What is going on here?" I ask, glancing between them. They've clearly had a whole conversation I'm not in on.

Alan nods again, and grunts, "Tell."

"We knew money was coming in, so we already spent it," she says, her voice flat.

"The GoFundMe money? Are you kidding?" My mind races. Is Mom sick? Does Buster need surgery? Some kind of emergency I don't know about? But Alan just wipes his mouth with his arm, smearing chili over his skin, while Mom looks at me, defiant.

"No, of course I'm not kidding. Why would we give the money back?" she says. Her knuckles are white against the table. "We *earned* it."

"Earned it?" I repeat, stunned.

"You can get off that high horse anytime, missy. We used the money. Same as always," Mom says. Her tears dry up as fast as they came.

"Except this isn't the same as always. I'm not sick. I do not need money from strangers." I take a breath, glaring at my stepdad. "What did you buy, Alan?"

He looks slightly sheepish.

"Boat," he says.

"Bryan convinced us to buy that old pontoon boat of his," says Mom. "He said he had unexpected expenses after you canceled your wedding, and I felt bad for him. Plus, we love to fish, honey."

"Oh my God." I feel sick. Bryan? They used the money to buy a boat from *Bryan*? "And you didn't think I should know? Or that it would matter to me?"

Alan lifts his chin stubbornly. Grunts.

"After everything we've sacrificed for you, don't you think we deserve something fun for just the two of us? Alan's naming the boat *Ship Faced*." Mom smiles at me. "Isn't that funny? I already bought the stencil. You can come on board anytime."

"I don't care how you feel about Bryan or your boat," I say, my voice shaking with rage. "If we had to keep it, that money should have gone toward paying for my diabetes meds."

"And since you're buying your own meds now, with your fancy new job, then you shouldn't tell us how to spend our money," Alan says, suddenly fluent in full sentences. I'd clap if I wasn't so furious.

"The GoFundMe fund is not *your* money, Alan!"

These two have controlled my life for way too long, and they've been absolute crap at it. I didn't have a choice before, but now I do. Alan's clueless about finances—actually, Alan's clueless about *everything*. And he's always loved Bryan. They'd get drunk on the porch, and then he'd tell me I was lucky to have a guy like Bryan since I was so *challenging*.

I've never liked a single thing Alan has liked—other than my mom, and I'm not even sure about her right now. His fart hits like clockwork. What if *Alan* is the Devil card? His gas alone opens a portal to Hell.

I stand up from my chair so fast, it falls backward with a clatter.

"I've got to get out of here," I say, and I leave the house and am in my car before they can say another word.

For the first time ever, I'm rooting for JosieFightsOn to die. That's the only way for me, the real Josie, to live.

An hour later, I find Nonna in the common room of Golden Leaves. She's in a circle of silver-headed seniors in wheelchairs, all of them hanging on every word of their favorite rock star, Judge Judy, who is laying down the law from the television screen.

"Josie, my butterfly!" Nonna's eyes crinkle in recognition. The nurses have told me she mixes up the names of nearly all the staff and residents and can spend days not knowing quite where she is, but she never gets my name wrong.

I know this miracle will not last forever, but for now, I lap it up every time.

"Nonna!" I bend down and give her tiny body a gentle squeeze. I kiss her on the top of her puff of white hair. She smells like she always does—rose water and my warmest memories of home.

"Hard day for your gran," whispers one of the nurses. "She got one of her 'visions.' Why don't you take her outside?"

I arrange a blanket on Nonna's lap and push the heavy, creaky wheelchair down the narrow hall and out onto the back patio. A horrible stench seems to cling to this whole place, indoors and out, even worse than any of Alan's meal disasters. It's like the smell of death and decay is baked into the walls. I lean forward and sniff Grandma's head again, like she's a newborn baby, and feel comforted. She may not be in the most beautiful facility, but she's well taken care of. I think. I hope. Though I did see that nurse back there roll her eyes when she mentioned my nonna's visions.

For the millionth time, I wish I had the money to give Nonna the comfort she deserves in her final years. I can't imagine who I'd be without her always in my corner, cheering me on, reminding me I'm stronger than anyone else thinks.

Come to think of it, for all his flaws, and there are *many*, Axe also looks at me in a similar way. Like I'm formidable. Not a pushover. Like I'm a force to be reckoned with. A worthy opponent to him and a worthy ally to Nonna.

"Nonna," I say, taking a seat and reaching for her hands. I can't wait to tell her my good news. She's probably the only one who'll be genuinely happy for me other than Honor. Nonna's been telling me for years to move out of my mom's house, though I always thought that was more about how she couldn't stand my mother than her believing I needed independence. But maybe I got that wrong. "Guess what? I got a new job!"

But Nonna doesn't smile.

"Cards," she says, and so I dig out my deck from my bag.

Normally, I love a reading from Nonna, but I don't want anything else to dampen my good mood. Before I know it, three cards are laid out before me, and my heart plummets.

"You're in danger, Josie," she whispers, her voice shaky but urgent as her fingers clamp around my wrists tight enough to make the veins on the backs of her hands bulge. Her eyes are wide, full of a fear I haven't seen in years. The hairs on the back of my neck stand up. I glance around at the weed-choked garden and cracked patio tiles, anything not to stare at the cards.

"No, Nonna," I say, brushing her off. "We're misreading them. Everything is great. I got a new place, I'm getting paid—"

"Someone wants to harm you." Nonna starts muttering in Italian, low and fast, and while I don't know the words she's saying, it's disturbing. "You must do all the things I have taught you, my Josie. Burn sage. Tie a red ribbon. Watch your back—"

My grandmother is superstitious, and I've always heeded her warnings, even when they felt silly. But this is next-level. Sure, the cards . . . aren't great, but there are plenty of other reasonable ways to interpret them. Dementia really is the worst.

"Nonna!" I cut in. "You're scaring me."

After her last MRI, the doctor showed me the dark spots on Nonna's brain. Another sort of tarot altogether. The cards no one ever wants to be dealt.

"Trust your instincts," she presses. "Promise me."

"Of course I will. I promise. I always do." A lie, of course. I haven't always trusted my instincts (case in point: getting engaged to Bryan), but starting today, I'm working on a new policy.

"Are you reading your deck? Every day?" Nonna asks.

"'Course, Nonna," I say, dodging the truth about my recent pulls. No need to fuel her paranoia. "Everything is good. I'm good."

"You're healthy, butterfly. You're so strong and healthy," she says, and a faint smile plays across her lips. I've heard this mantra a hundred times, and it always soothes me like a lullaby.

"I am. I am strong and healthy, Nonna," I echo back, just like she used to make me do when I was little.

"Don't drink the Devil's brew," she says, and though I feel a sharp pang of trepidation at the mention of my recent pull—that damn Devil card, twice now—I have no idea what she means. What's the Devil's brew?

Nonna's grip tightens around my hand, her eyes going wide and unblinking—like she's seeing something just over my shoulder. Something I can't.

SEVENTEEN

AXE

I suppose there are worse ways to spend a Sunday in February than testing out my new snowboard on a double black diamond. Would be a hell of a lot better if I wasn't stuck beside Niles von Grab, but what can you do? Hard to turn down a helicopter ride up north and a day at Nemacolin Woodlands Resort. Even if it means suffering his company.

A bit of bonding before we seal the deal, or whatever bollocks he thinks we're doing.

"I don't like handing over money until I understand who I'm handing it over to," Niles said, and while I can't stand the bastard, he's got a point. And truth be told, I'm just as eager to suss him out as he is to size me up.

Strike couldn't tag along—he had plans with Honor, which, of course, made me think of Josie, who I've decided I'm not allowed to think about unless it's at the office and strictly about She's the One. No imagining her in ski pants. No replaying the cringe-worthy moment when I tried to explain haptic suits to her and ended up sounding like a gadget-happy bawbag.

"You sure about this?" I ask Niles now as we look down the steep precipice. I'm an expert snowboarder—I have shredded slopes across the world from Alaska to Zermatt—but I'm not so confident about Niles, especially if the shininess of his boots is any indication of his experience. I do not want this nip-tuck junkie to die falling off a mountain. To let him save face, I pretend I'm the one having second thoughts. "I don't know, mate. This is no bunny slope."

Niles smiles up at me, his grin so tight you could bounce a dime off his cheek. Fortunately, his eyes are hidden by goggles, so I'm spared the full horror of his botched, desperate face, just the peaks of his laminated eyebrows poking over the top like they're trying to escape.

Botulism bandit. Facelift fanatic. The insults invent themselves.

I just hope I can hold my tongue.

Implant imp.

Ach, I need to stop. But those duck lips are a right laugh. If I get through today without quacking at him, I deserve a medal.

Meanwhile, I'm geared up in my black high-performance jacket—waterproof, breathable, and snug enough to show I'm no amateur—paired with charcoal snow pants made for speed and durability and boots customized for precision control. Mirrored visor down, gloves on tight, I'm ready to shred this slope like I own it.

"Are you scared? Wish you had your mommy?" Niles teases. My fingers clench in my gloves, and I take deep breaths through my nose to quell my anger. I will not let this piece of shite get under my skin. "Need a diaper because you're shitting your pants?" he adds, pushing for a reaction. Then he laughs like a comic book villain—*he-he-he-he.*

He thinks he can handle this slope? Good for him. I'm not his babysitter.

I salute him. *Let's go, Silicone Soldier.* I tip the back of my board and start to fly.

The wind immediately whips up in a sandblasting cold that's more cutting every second as I carve the mountain at the only speed I know: breakneck. I revel in the freeze and the steepness of the slope. The snow is a crisp glide beneath my board, and I am full-on crushing it, in the zone, so it takes a moment to register the scream that pierces the air. A sound as high-pitched and urgent as a granny with her hair on fire.

I turn to see Niles losing control, his shiny reflective-red ski suit and those equally gleaming boots flailing as he tries to offset his course. Somehow he's heading straight for the drop-off, the kind that puts the *double* in this black diamond and why we had to sign thirty pages of waivers before we got up here.

Bloody hell. I pivot hard, the deceleration such a jolt that my breath goes ragged, as my crisis training kicks in like a second language. I reset my center of gravity and assess the situation in a nanosecond. Everything slows to a pinpoint, just like it used to out in the field.

If I do nothing, von Graf's a dead man. Couldn't be a better accident—clean as they come and no one would have any reason to suspect me. I can see the headline now: *BILLIONAIRE INVESTOR LOST IN SKI TRAGEDY*—though the bastard's only a nine-digit millionaire; the superrich always get to round up. The police wouldn't even bother investigating. One look at his shiny red boots, and they'd chalk it up to another cocky, clueless arsewipe who thought he was invincible.

But I take my responsibilities seriously, and I will not let a man die without being one hundred percent sure of his crimes. Tempting as it may be.

What I do might be morally questionable to some, but I've got my own code. And letting this rhinoplasty reptile fly off the hill isn't part of it.

So, in the next split second, I make my move. Lunging forward and up at an angle as fast as I can, I wedge myself between Niles and the edge of the cliff. I'm still a bit off, too low, and I've got no momentum to turn.

New plan.

I lean into the wind, and just as he's about to go over, I stretch my arm out and grab the back of his fancy jacket. My fingers catch the slippery, overpriced fabric—probably made from recycled soda bottles and yak semen.

"Mummy," he whimpers, and it's all I can do not to laugh.

Instead, with every ounce of strength in me, I drag him away from the edge. It's like a scene straight out of *Mission: Impossible*, and I catch myself wishing Josie were here to witness my heroic moment. Though I might've misjudged the force; my efforts send Niles tumbling downhill, arse over teakettle, until he skids to a stop just a few centimeters from what would've been certain death.

I check he's safe, then collapse back in the snow, heart pounding, breath roaring in my ears. The cold cuts through the adrenaline, and I let the wind carry the sound of Niles sobbing like the pathetic wanker he is. I give him a few moments, then jump to my feet, brush the ice off my trousers, and head down to grab my snowboard. When I get back to him, he's mostly pulled himself together, and I hold out a hand to haul him up.

The arsehole better invest in SynthoTech now.

"Damn, Axe MacKenzie. Thanks," Niles mutters, still shaky. He pulls off his goggles, wiping away the tears freezing on his Botoxed face. I resist the urge to make a crack about him soiling his nappy—though I'd bet good money he shat himself—and reckon that earns me two medals.

I'll tell Strike later, when we can have a proper laugh about it.

"No bother," I say, just as the helicopter hovers in to "rescue" us back to the resort. Niles climbs aboard like a man returning from war—never mind the wee baby he was a minute ago. He claps me on the back for the pilot's benefit.

"Nice run, bro. Fun times."

I file that away, too—especially the ridiculous *bro*—Strike will eat it up.

At the bar, Niles orders us martinis, which, since I'm a whiskey man, feels like a waste of the crackling fire in the mammoth stone hearth. But I let it be. I've won a big hand today, and now it's time to let von Wrinklefree play right into it.

Like I said, there are worse ways to spend a Sunday in February. And come March, when I get to slice this bawbag open, I'll make sure to say, *Nice run, bro. Fun times,* before I send him off to his maker.

EIGHTEEN

JOSIE

See you at 7pm.

That's all Axe's text says. No clue where we're going, what we're doing, or what I'm supposed to wear. I knew when I took the job that my hours would be weird—that I wouldn't be sitting in the cool SynthoTech office with a cubicle and a laptop. But I didn't think it'd be *this* random. Just vague texts for vague meet-ups, zero warning.

I'm not okay with this.

I start to type something sassy—WTAF—then hesitate. I look around the new apartment, now officially mine. Mini-lights strung up, my stuff unpacked. Honor even brought over my favorite candle from the store, so it smells like manuka honey in here.

Home, home, home. Like if I say it enough, it'll stick. I'm finally out of my parents' sad little guesthouse.

Nope, not gonna risk pissing Axe off. I need this job. Forget insulin; you'd have to pry this apartment from my cold dead hands before I give it up. I will be a good, eager employee.

Umm, I have questions, I write back.

Work had to start sometime, Ginger Snap

Ginger Snap?

Well, you are a snappy almost ginger.
Suits you

I ignore this.

I'm happy to start work! There. That sounded sufficiently enthusiastic and professional. Just would love to have more details

Wear a dress. And then a beat later: You do own a dress not made out of ace bandages, right?

So no mummy cosplay?

Not tonight. Save that for your days off

Right. This is work. I peek into my closet—a black hole of jeans, T-shirts, and hoodies. I could call Honor—she'll have something I can borrow, right? But then I spot it, shoved in a plastic bag at the very back.

I hid it there on purpose so I wouldn't have to face how epically my plans blew up.

In exactly three weeks, I was supposed to be getting married. Funny how time changes things—now my whole relationship with Bryan feels like some wildly fucked-up fever dream.

If and when I can ever afford therapy, the first questions I'll unpack are: *Why didn't I realize sooner I could leave home on my own? Why did I think I needed a man to save me? How did I miss the truth staring me right in the face?*

The same burst of determination that's kept me going these

past few days kicks in. The same energy that made me sign a new lease and ignore my mom's barrage of calls and texts today—six voicemails, fifteen messages—begging for my new social media passwords. I yank the plastic bag off with one quick pull.

The thing is, I could just . . . wear the dress. If I wanted to. Nobody is stopping me.

It's definitely the most expensive thing I've ever bought in my life. I always planned to resell it on Poshmark after wearing it just once, as long as Bryan didn't spill anything on it. Now, looking at it, it feels like the most unhinged splurge.

And yet . . . it's gorgeous.

I never wanted a big, traditional wedding gown. I skipped right past Here Comes the Bride in downtown Shelton, with all their tulle and lace and crinoline, and found a tiny boutique in Pittsburgh that felt way more like me. No pushy salesladies with cheap champagne and bad advice—just a thirtysomething designer with a sharp eye and a vibe that reminded me of Honor.

The dress itself is simple yet stunning. A lemon-yellow silk slip with spaghetti straps. When my mom first saw it, she begged me to return it for something that looked *less like lingerie Kate Moss would have worn in 1995 and more like a wedding dress.*

But it was already too late. I'd fallen in love.

In the same box where I keep my treasured tarot deck, I also keep my most cherished black-and-white photo of Nonna. In the picture, she's around nineteen, effortlessly glamorous, seated in a plastic backyard lawn chair with a martini glass, either toasting or begging for a refill. She looks so painfully young, so wonderfully alive. Her red curls flow down her back, just like mine. And her dress is practically identical to the one I found in that store—a timeless slip of silk, one strap casually falling off her shoulder.

A dress telegraphing a moment and a feeling: freedom. That

I wanted it for my wedding should have told me something. Subconsciously, I must have known I was trading one prison for another, when all I wanted was to fly.

I pull the dress out now, and grin.

Are you going to tell me what we're doing? I text Axe.

Three guesses.

Haggis eating contest? Kilt twirls on TikTok?

Master the bagpipes in ten minutes?

Nah, dentist appointment. I'll bet you'll be a

right bonny lass in a bib.

Automatically, I cover my mouth with my hand. I'm 75 percent sure he's joking, but wait—could there actually be something wrong with my teeth? I thought I'd done all the SynthoTech workups already—the scans, the physical exams, all that stuff. I was super stressed about it, too. I mean, how does someone with my history of medical drama pass a basic physical?

I kept telling myself I was in remission, my allergies wouldn't be a deal-breaker, and my diabetes was under control. But even after I passed, I kept waiting for a call from the doctor telling me that there had been some mistake.

Okay, sure, I text, trying to keep it light. I'll go floss again!

Ha just windin' you up. No dentist date.

You've got lovely gnashers.

Not funny

Hey, could have said proctologist . . .

!!!!

Sorry. I've never been much of a gentleman

No kidding. Fucking Axe. I can just hear him laughing that low, teasing chuckle, so delighted about his childish joke. I stop texting and toss my phone on the bed. Axe got one thing right—he's no gentleman, despite the fact that he did rescue me from Freddy Krueger and has a generous health insurance policy. Men who look like Vikings and talk like they spent a childhood shearing sheep in the Scottish Highlands and say whatever comes to their minds, no matter how insulting—they aren't gentlemen. Also, he is too big, too strong, too likely to pin a woman against the wall as he grinds into her to be considered a gentleman.

Not that I've ever imagined him pinning me against a wall.

Nope. Never. Not even once.

When my phone buzzes again, Axe still hasn't told me where we're going. Just a message: black car, five minutes. I grab a bag and a wrap, and slip on a pair of cute, comfy sneakers. Then I take them off again. This dress deserves heels. I only own one pair, but they are sky-high and a gorgeous snakeskin. Hopefully wherever we're going doesn't require any actual walking.

The car arrives promptly. I climb into the cavernous leather back seat—no Axe, just a thin-lipped driver. In no time we're zipping down the highway outside Shelton to the more rural Maplehill, where we now wind along country lanes. I've never been here—not with my dust and pollen allergies—and my stomach tightens as I grip the seat. I'm going to fuck up this first date in five minutes when I start sneezing like a trombone. There won't be enough tissues for what I will unleash. My anxiety feels like a runaway train. How did I ever think I could pull off being the ideal girlfriend when I can barely leave the house without a careful plan?

By the time the car stops in front of this ancient covered bridge, I'm practically vibrating with nerves—probably because the sign reads HISTORICALLY PROTECTED BRIDGE. NO CARS ALLOWED. The driver opens my door, and right on cue, a man in a leather jacket pulls up on a motorcycle.

It's so perfectly timed, there's got to be some GPS sorcery involved.

Even before he yanks off his helmet, I know it's Axe. Broad shoulders, leather gloves, thick thighs. How many leather jackets does this guy own? This one's different from the other day—softer, dressier, more "man about town" than Hells Angel. Seriously, someone this annoying shouldn't be allowed to look so hot on a motorcycle.

"I got it from here," Axe says to the driver. To me, he says, "A hop across the bridge to supper, if you don't mind jumping on the back."

"Umm . . ." My heart is skittering. The bike is massive and loud, and I've had enough near-death experiences for one lifetime. Then again, Axe doesn't seem like the type to crash. Plus, I wouldn't mind feeling that smooth leather against my skin. In this dress and Axe's getup, we'd look like a perfume ad.

"Ever ridden on the back of a bike before?" he asks.

"Yes, a couple of times," I lie, trying to subtly dry my sweaty hands on my dress before climbing on. Axe hands me a helmet and helps me buckle it under my chin. My hair—already wild on a good day—is going to be a disaster after this. When his fingers brush my neck, I feel a jolt of electricity. Must be static.

Axe suddenly frowns. "You're shivering. Didn't think about it being this cold," he says, shrugging off his leather jacket and draping it over my shoulders. He's wearing an untucked fitted white button-down shirt and gray jeans, both of which are straining against his muscles. He runs a hugely successful company—when does he have time to go to the gym this much? "Here, take this."

"Thanks," I say. The jacket is warm from his body, and it smells like him—clean, spicy, with a hint of something dangerous and addictive. My cheeks flame up instantly from how stupidly sexy this whole thing is.

"All right, now hop on, Ginger Snap," he says. "Nice shoes. Very practical." He winks, and I can't help but laugh.

"They do the trick." I try to look enigmatic, and use my high heel to jump onto the bike. I surprise myself with my coordination and swing my leg around, landing behind Axe. According to the employment paperwork I signed, my role here is to be the sort of universal date all men would want to have. I have no idea what that actually means in practice. The SynthoTech contract was very clear: be natural, be organic. Trying too hard to be perfect is just going to backfire.

I'm better off not trying at all and just being myself.

I will not think about the fact that there's an entire section on good-night kisses on page eight—paragraph four, section B, to be exact—or how there's a very good chance I'll feel Axe's lips on mine by the end of this evening.

"Hope this date will feel better than a root canal," I tell him.

He laughs, popping on his helmet as I hitch up my dress—thank God I'm not wearing tulle—and clamp my legs around Axe's. The engine revs to life, then softens once we're on the bridge, the roar replaced by the tires clattering over the wide wooden planks.

My arms wrap around his waist as I take in the arched roof and filtered, dimming sunlight. I breathe the smell of old, weathered wood and earth. It's all so beautiful. I cling tighter, feeling the heat of Axe's back through his thin shirt as we emerge from the bridge onto an extremely steep incline.

The shift in momentum makes me press even closer, gripping him to keep from slipping off. It's terrifying, but Axe is steady, effortless, and my fear morphs into something else: exhilaration. The trees above are thick and green, the setting sun looks like an orange lollipop melting into the horizon.

Every turn Axe takes is smooth, like he's done this a million times, and each twist sends my stomach flipping as we climb higher, the valley below shrinking to doll size. And then it hits me—an insane sense of freedom unlike anything I've ever felt. I want to whoop, cheer, let out this weird, buzzing energy building inside me.

At the top of the hill, Axe slows down. My heart is pounding, half from the ride and half from the incredible view. But there are no restaurants for miles. Maybe I shouldn't have assumed we were eating dinner.

That's when I spot it: a table set for two, strategically placed for the best panoramic view, under a canopy of trees strung with fairy lights.

Holy shit.

Red wine, white tablecloth, napkins folded on fine china plates, and two cushioned wooden chairs. Beyond romantic. It all feels so surreal, like a scene from a dream. Or an Instagram ad for a life no one gets to actually live. With the stunning hues of sunset behind us, it's like we're wrapped in a glow of peach and melon.

"Wow," I whisper, mostly to myself, because it all feels too perfect to be real.

"Ready?" Axe asks as he swings off the bike, takes off his helmet, and then runs his fingers through his mussed-up hair. Is he trying to be sexy? Because to be honest, it's one hundred percent working. He steps closer to me, and I have no idea what he's doing. Is he going to kiss me? Surely not yet.

I'm way too confused by the whole vibe—the idyllic backdrop, the fairy lights, all of it—probably because I'm now in the business of other people's fantasies. Axe reaches out and gently unclips the strap under my chin. Another jolt of electricity, straight to my core, and my heart skips a beat.

Suddenly, I realize I'm so not ready for any of this. I, Josie Greene, am officially in over my head.

NINETEEN

AXE

Aye, fuck me. She's wearing the most beautiful dress I've ever seen. A slip of silk, soft as liquid, with thin runaway straps, and her strawberry curls, mussed by the helmet, make a tempestuous riot around her Botticelli face.

I was already rock-hard from having her breasts pressed against my back on the ride. Shite, I'm an idiot. I knew this picnic dinner was a bad idea. Thank God for the thick thermal blankets folded on the chairs. Pretty soon she'll be all wrapped up, and I can do what we came here for. Not be distracted by her details, but instead record and memorialize them for someone else's future pleasure.

This isn't a real date with a real woman. It's a professional exercise in gathering intel. I've always been good at coding human behavior into tech, and just because this happens to be the romantic realm doesn't mean it's any different. The philosophy behind the AI software is simple: engage, observe, and translate the essence of Josie into a template that could genuinely help some poor bastard feel a bit less alone. Or offer some solace to a woman stuck in a life where she can't yet come out of the closet.

Our previous iterations' behavior has always too closely coincided with predictive models, which somehow took the messy, glorious humanity out of the product. Josie, who surprises me at every turn, will no doubt provide that captivating alchemy we're missing.

What we're doing is creating something real from something unreal, a digital companion that feels as close to human as possible, that fills those lonely gaps, gives a person the illusion of connection. Aye, the illusion. That's the rub. Making it seem so lifelike that even the most skeptical soul believes it.

Josie sits in the chair and throws the blanket over her lap. Her wrap is loose around her shoulders, and I'm terrified she's going to freeze. But my team has left nothing to chance. Tiny camping heaters are arranged all around us, creating a cozy bubble of warmth. It's as if we're in our own magic world up here.

"Well, this is . . . something," Josie says, flashing that glorious grin of hers. There's always a hint of a secret tucked away in the corners of her mouth, and yet tonight, she seems to have shed a layer of defensiveness. Like she feels freer, maybe. Like the ride loosened something in her the way it does for me. I always tell Strike that the bike is better than scotch, but he's too much of a pussy about road rash to understand.

"It's just us," I say, though it's plain as day there's no one else around for miles. The team decided there'd be no staff up here tonight—bringing more people into the mix would just screw up the vibe. So I'm serving our supper myself, straight from a wooden chest packed with multiple courses in temperature-controlled containers. Seemed like a grand idea until this very moment—my hand's got the slightest tremble. What the hell? Am I . . . nervous? Not a chance. I never get nervous, but this—the intimacy of sharing a meal, the vulnerability of opening up, even slightly—is a different kind of challenge.

Sort yourself out, Axe. You can handle a pretty woman in a slip dress. Jesus.

The first course is a vegan burrata—Josie has a list of food allergies as long as a Highland winter, so we found all the best alternatives—along with Santa Rosa plums that I had flown in from my small orchard. Their deep purple skins glow by the soft light, and the fragrance is intoxicating.

"When you put the plum in your mouth," I tell her, "you must smell it, too. It brings out the taste."

Josie's eyes go heavy with delight as she tastes everything like it's a treasure. We move through the courses: roasted vegetables artfully arranged and drizzled with citrus reduction, along with a selection of Spanish tapas dishes meant to be shared and savored. Everything on the table is specifically designed to make us lean closer, touch more, and forget the distance between us. My team knows exactly what they're doing. Our software will create curated experiences depending on the whims of the user. Some people will want a cozy night in on the couch. Others will want a more unattainable fairy-tale experience like this one. SynthoTech will make anything possible.

Josie asks me about my childhood in Scotland. I give her the cleaned-up version that I tell everyone, my heart trained to keep forty-two beats per minute. I mention the castle and the idyllic island, the warm rolling greens of the bogs, the glens that grow thick with bluebells come spring. I do not mention my father, my upbringing, my family.

What else is there to tell? It would be like someone yammering on about a nightmare they've just had. Nothing to do about it, and no one wants to hear it.

I can't help but notice that Josie also makes light of her history, focusing on kind nurses and teachers instead of procedures and recoveries. She mentions the steadfastness of her mother, not the isolation of illness.

"More wine?" I ask, and when she nods, I pour carefully from the carafe on the table. I'm less shaky now. The meal might be ending, but the night is just starting. The chemistry between us is sharp enough to cut. I can feel it in the sparkle of her eyes, in the way she's let that strap fall down her shoulder, so sexy I want to put my mouth right against her skin.

Then again, no. This isn't chemistry.

Her sorcery only solidifies my choice. Josie glows and spins all those around her into her web. The connection I'm feeling isn't about us, not at all—which is exactly the point. It's about Josie Greene and her witchy attraction in this perfect setting. It's about how she weaves her spell on the everyman.

"It feels like we're on a different planet up here," Josie says, and her words are tinged with wonder. I like the sound of it. I like being responsible for it. "I haven't traveled much. Or really at all. I was medevaced once, to Philadelphia, and it sort of felt like this when I looked out the window. Like I was somewhere completely out of reach of my normal life. It's a rare moment when . . . actually, never mind."

She looks suddenly embarrassed. Like she's forgotten why she's here and has gone off script. But that's exactly why she's here. I need her off script. I need to get to the heart of the real Josie, not some generic woman. I recognize that's going to be the allure of She's the One—its specificity. The Josie-ness of it all.

"No, please, go on," I say.

"It's not interesting," she says.

"Everything about you is interesting," I say, and now it's my turn to feel embarrassed. "I mean, that's what this is all about. For the project. I need to find everything interesting about you and see how to translate that to code. So, please, finish what you were saying."

She straightens a little, a bit more confident. "I was going to say that it's rare when you get to escape the clutches of your reality, you know? And because you're so far from your day-to-day, you get to sort of be your most real self. Which I realize is a bit of a paradox. But it's real for me." Then Josie looks down, as if she feels she's shared too much. Bites her lip and fiddles with her napkin and then takes a sip of wine.

"I've never thought of it that way, but aye. I suppose I know what you mean," I say. I'm half-tempted to tease her. *Paradox*—that seems a weighty word for the light and breezy Josie she presents to the world. But I don't want to get her back up, not when I'm enjoying this glimpse of the person underneath the polish. I didn't have to read Josie's high school transcript to know that she's sharp as a tack—there's a shrewdness in her eyes that she keeps beneath her sunshine, like a Trojan horse. I wonder where she learned the terrible lesson to keep that part of herself tucked away. "I feel that way on the bike. If I need to clear my head, I go out to the mountains until I feel all those layers fall away."

"Layers," she repeats, and smiles at me again, though this is an altogether different kind of smile from when we first sat down. This one says, *I understand.*

"Like a bloody onion, me," I say.

"Well, you do make people cry," she jokes. I want to tell her that I could make her cry out in pleasure, that I can picture her naked, her dress crumpled at her feet, begging me to touch her. I won't, of course. Though I feel my dick ready to answer that thought—not only because of the vision, but also because I'm imagining her reaction to my saying it. I'd wager she'd go rosy from head to toe and heat up properly from the inside out.

"Fair enough," I say, and clear my throat. Shake away my impure thoughts. "So tell me about you, Josie. What do you normally talk about on a first date?"

"Is that what this is? A first date?" She levels me with a playful glare, and if I didn't know any better, I'd say she was flirting.

"Nah, it's only a sim," I blurt out. I do feel obligated to remind her, and yet suddenly she looks so disappointed, like I punctured the fantasy, which is the opposite of what I intended. I only wanted to make her feel comfortable, to remind her we're here for work, so we don't have to playact. Because that's what dates normally are, aren't they? A show for another person? Though, to be fair, I don't go on many dates. I've had my share of beautiful women, aye, but they've always known the deal—I don't have the time or inclination for romantic wining and dining or commitment.

That's why I'm straight up right from the start, when I tell them I'm only interested in a no-strings-attached bit of fun. No more, no less.

But Josie's eyes have dimmed and her smile has vanished. "Right. Work."

The silence between us stretches, heavy and awkward. I fumble for something to say, but I've soured the moment. Josie takes a sip of wine and shifts back in her chair in a way that creates even more distance.

"All the pencil necks over at SynthoTech are monitoring and data scrubbing," I remind her. "They'll be analyzing everything we do tonight."

It's all there in the contract. Plain as day. Josie already knows that my entire body is wired for responsiveness; that every flicker of emotion, every heartbeat, is feeding their endless algorithms. That our conversations are being recorded. That our time together doesn't really belong to us.

She nods, then places a hand over her mouth and yawns and gives me a smile that's about half-wattage, and I can't shake the feeling that I've lost something more precious than I even fully understood I wanted.

"It's been a really fantastic date, too. Good job. But I think if I stay out another hour, I'll turn into a pumpkin," Josie says.

The lass does look tired, and I'm quick on my feet, trying not to look as hugely disappointed as I feel.

TWENTY

JOSIE

I'm not tired at all, but I can't stand sitting here staring at Axe any longer. The setting is so *extra* extra—the hilltop view of the starlit sky, the cool evening breeze, the candlelit dinner. I get that it's the whole SynthoTech *thing*—hyper-curated romantic experiences. But holding the line between reality and fantasy is starting to feel like a second job. Tonight's Axe feels so different from the one I knew before. The whole scene was enlivening my senses in the best way until I was reminded it's all a setup. Then everything turned artificial and too sweet, like I chugged a bottle of corn syrup.

"Is that okay? I know this is a job and I'm not trying to shirk. I just think if this was a real date, this is where I'd bow out, you know?" I ask. Though, I doubt he does. I can't imagine Axe MacKenzie has ever had a date cut short.

He checks his gadgety watch—like an Apple Watch on steroids.

"Two hours and ten minutes. That's your limit for how long you can stand to be around me," Axe says, and I think, but I'm not certain, that he's joking. "Not too bad. If you'd asked me when we first met, I'd have guessed your limit was about two minutes, so this is an exponential improvement."

"In fairness, the first time we met, you insulted me to my face." I smile at him, even though I wish I wouldn't. I've done enough flirting for one night.

"Would you rather I insulted you behind your back?" he teases.

"Um, I'd rather you not insult me at all," I say. He throws his head back and laughs, a deep sound that echoes into the night and lands in my chest with a small jolt.

"Can't argue with that. If it counts for anything, I truly am sorry." He holds my gaze, and he seems sincere. I don't understand this man—my *boss*—who chose me, of all women, to be his AI model. I was too focused on the benefits—my own apartment, independence, finally a path to freedom—to consider how strange this arrangement is. Fake dating. Haptic suits. Bizarre virtual sex. My entire personality being re-created as an AI app.

Later, a team of tech bros, linguists, and social psychologists will gather in some room to replay our conversation—Axe showed me the tiny recording device hidden in the flower vase at the center of the table—and they'll dissect every word, every pause. They'll analyze the readings from Axe's sensors, secretly strapped under his clothes, scoring all our so-called metrics. This whole meal isn't just dinner—it's data.

Axe stands and reaches out his hand. "We're off, then. Door-to-door service."

I take it, my legs feeling like jelly. Oh, right. Ending this date means getting back on his bike, arms around Axe's warm, solid middle. *Fuck.*

Good thing I'm not wearing one of those haptic suits right now, because no way do I want anyone to measure how my heart rate just spiked thinking about my thighs pressed against his. As usual, my body is betraying me, but this time, it's not because of some illness.

Instead of transferring me to a car, Axe takes me all the way home, winding along a route that keeps my heart racing. We finally rumble to a stop in front of my building, and I reluctantly unwrap my arms from his waist, swing my leg over, and plant my feet on the pavement. He pulls off my helmet, then his, and shakes out his hair in a way that is so stupidly hot I'm convinced he must have practiced it in a mirror. He dismounts effortlessly and walks me to my front door.

Guess he's playing the role of gentleman this evening.

I hate that he's pulling it off.

"Listen to me, lass—about that contract," he begins, and then he looks uncharacteristically tongue-tied.

Oh, crap. We're supposed to share a kiss.

"You mean page eight, paragraph four, section B?" I ask. I've read that contract so many times, I've just about memorized it.

He blinks, impressed. "Aye, only if you're feeling up for it. You know how I feel about consent."

I nod. One kiss. Business. I've got this. I have kissed a man before. I have kissed *this* man before. No reason for my legs to be shaking.

"Thank you for tonight," I tell him dutifully as I dig into my bag—past my diabetes kit, inhaler, EpiPen, and pill box—for my keys. Kind of a shock that I didn't need any of my usual meds tonight. Though I feel physically great, I also feel slightly irresponsible that I spent the whole evening not worrying about all the ways I could be taken out—an allergic reaction, a bee sting, a sudden drop in blood sugar.

When was the last time I gave my mind the night off from worrying about my health?

I'm lucky I got away with it.

"It was my pleasure," he says, and for some reason, I think he might actually mean it. Axe MacKenzie doesn't say things he doesn't mean.

I look up, catch his eyes, and then my attention turns to his lips. They're ridiculously tempting. Lips made for kissing. He takes a step closer.

"Ready?" I ask, and then mentally kick myself. I should let this unfold more naturally. But I am so unreasonably nervous.

"Josie, I just want to say," he begins softly, moving even closer. We're inches apart now. The streetlights cast a warm glow on his jawline, highlighting those sharp angles and his ridiculous cobalt-blue eyes. I'm suddenly hyperaware of the sound of the cicadas and my own quickening breath. I want to grab the collar of his leather jacket. "I know this isn't quite real, but some moments—tonight, for me, anyway . . ." He trails off, and before I can overthink it, Axe leans in, his arms wrapping around my waist, and his lips meet mine.

Time stops.

Axe's mouth is warm, demanding, coaxing my response from a deep place. My mind is a sudden scramble—I keep trying to remind myself: *This isn't real. This is part of the sim.* The kiss is so lose-your-damn-mind good that I don't care about the whys. I am only focused on Axe and his warm lips and his grip tightening around me, anchoring me to him. His whole hard body pressed against mine.

My hands slide up his chest and circle his neck, pulling him in. I can smell him: clean, spicy, that Axe scent that's just . . . addictive. His tongue teases my lips, and I let them part, letting him in, and suddenly it's not just a kiss. It's hunger, pure and simple, and every nerve in my body is lit up like fireworks. I'm so mad at myself when an involuntary moan escapes my lips. Where did this man learn to kiss? Seriously, *he* should be the AI model.

My fingers twist and tangle in his thick hair as his hands press their warmth against my back. When we finally pull apart, I notice that I'm not the only one who's breathless. Axe drops his forehead against mine, panting.

We are both panting.

Desire crashes through me in waves. One word pulses through me: *want, want, want.*

"Night, lass." His voice is husky.

"Good night, Axe."

Axe takes a step back, his gaze lingering on me like he can read my thoughts—how could my face not be a full confession that all I'm thinking is *more, more, more*? Does he know how wet he made me with that kiss? Eventually, he turns and walks back to his bike. I watch as he revs the engine and then takes off, disappearing down the block.

My fingertips touch my mouth. It feels scorched and tingling where his lips have consumed mine.

I let myself into my apartment, step inside, then lean against the back of the door. I'm liquid, the heat off my skin could melt a box of Popsicles.

Whatever that was—real or sim—it was the best damn kiss of my life.

TWENTY-ONE

AXE

Rescuing von Graf has left me with a problem and a prize that are actually the same thing: The unwrinkled wanker thinks we're best friends. On one hand, I couldn't believe my luck in terms of how easily he agreed to come on board as a primary investor for She's the One. On the other hand, I'd rather drink a haddock smoothie every day than spend one dram of my free time with his rank crypto-clown ass.

"'Do you have the courage to bring forth the treasures that are hidden within you?'" Strike shouts the quote at me first thing when he steps off the dock and onto the *Loch Legend*, my handcrafted, mahogany-built Spirit yacht, which is this month's meeting place for our book club discussion. We're breaking down *Big Magic*—a book I'd never heard of, but it's another cracking good read. I've enjoyed the author's argument: that your imagination is like fairies floating about, waiting for you to catch 'em (and that even if those ideas are a bit whimsical, they're still worth a chase).

"Aye! I've got thoughts. The book was convincing," I answer. We know better than to talk for real here. I loosen the boat from her moorings and turn her away from the dock. The sun is setting over Lake Erie as I open the throttle and we head out onto the water. I bought this antique beauty after I saw her featured in *Casino Royale*, when Daniel Craig as James Bond drove her along the Grand Canal in Venice.

At the time, the boat belonged to an Italian aristocrat who didn't want to part with it—but everyone has their price.

Is it possible to fall in love with a boat? Because if you can, I'm head over heels with this beauty. It's not just a vehicle, it's a piece of art on water. Six thousand pounds of varnished wood with an iconic wraparound windshield, and it can hit up to fifty knots when I get her going.

Strike sits back in the plush seat, his arms stretched over the decking and one hand casually gripping the guardrail. He's been out with me before. Nobody can get a signal when we're on the water. We'll be discussing more than books, and this conversation is confidential. It's better that our words get lost in the wind.

I rev the engine, the bow lifts, and the boat surges forward with the speed of a panther, skimming the surface of the water. Strike remains impassive, even as I urge the throttle forward just for shits, testing the power of the 45 horsepower engine. The *Loch Legend* responds with a deep growl, and now we're going breakneck, the wind and water stinging our faces as the churning wake leaves a froth of foam. Strike doesn't so much as blink, the fucker, even as my fingers tighten around the teak-rimmed steering wheel, one last push all the way to fifty knots of dead pure reckless exhilaration.

As the air whips around us, I think about the feeling of Josie's arms around me as we raced down the mountain on my bike. How I was more careful on that ride than usual—never would I put Josie in danger—though, for reasons I can't quite explain, the drive felt more perilous. It was risky letting myself get so close. Risky sharing that freedom with someone else. Risky letting that someone else be Josie.

And that insanely delicious kiss? Foolish recklessness.

As soon as I cut the boat's engine, we judder to a stop with enough force to send a wave crashing over the bow, spraying us in a blast of water and nearly sending us both overboard as we hold on for dear life.

For a moment, silence.

Then we both detonate with laughter. Strike leans forward and opens the cooler. "'Your fear . . . '"

"'Is the most boring thing about you,'" I finish.

"I think that was my favorite quote in Gilbert's book. Fucking genius."

"Brilliant," I agree. "Though, let's be honest. We both could probably use a touch more fear."

"Fear's overrated, as you know," Strike says, reaching for the large silver cocktail shaker. "Keeps people small." He pours himself a martini into a frosted V-shaped glass, the only drink I allow on 007's boat. Shaken, not stirred. Some classics are classics for a reason. He finishes it in one gulp, then sets it aside. "Speaking of the truly fearless, talk to me about everyone's favorite cyborg ghoul, von Graf."

"Von Graf is all in. But there's a catch." I give Strike the bullet points about this morning's meeting. "He's agreed to become one of our angel investors, but he thinks he's got a seat on the board when we take the company public. As you know, this arrangement now allows me to gain access to his company and investigate his financial practices."

"Nice."

"It would take the CIA and FBI years to get this sort of access.

I can do it in weeks. I just need to uncover and dismantle his potential trafficking empire as quickly as possible—if that is, in fact, what I find." Bile cuts my throat when I remember the randy expression on von Graf's ball sack–smooth face when he clapped eyes on AI Josie/Gemini.

"So what's the catch?"

"He wants to be the first to beta test She's the One."

"Ah." Strike knows damn well why I don't like this glitch. I don't want von Graf's wee bleached hands anywhere near Josie. Even if it's a virtual version of her, even if—through anonymized data and layers of encryption—it's fully removed from her actual, real-life identity. I realize this is irrational, seeing as the whole point is to introduce her as an AI companion to the world at large.

"I suppose von Grab's tiny dickling needs a loyal fake girlfriend more than most blokes," I say, "but the man's a rat bastard. Even thinking about him so much as *breathing* on my sim makes me want to crush his skull."

"Especially when that sim happens to be Josie Greene," says Strike.

Josie's name in the same conversation as von Graf's consumes me with a sudden rage—and Strike must see that, because he reaches back into the cooler and pulls out another martini glass, then pours my drink. I take it with a nod of thanks and savor a sip of top-shelf botanical gin with that bittersweet vermouth kick.

My mind reaches like a starving dog for a memory I have banked and feasted on since it happened—that kiss. Josie's sweet, warm mouth and berry-soft lips felt like the answer to everything I've been searching for, a healing balm for every wound and bruise I've ever been dealt—and there have been many. Despite my attempts at self-control, the second I got home from our "date," my cock found its way into my hand, and with two quick strokes,

I came so hard and so fast thinking about Josie's tongue, I saw stars.

I don't even realize I've tossed back the rest of my martini until I'm blinking down at the empty cone of my glass. Strike pours us both another round, then quirks an eyebrow. Fucking hell. I need to stop being such a simp. "So. What's the counter-play?" he asks.

I lean in, even though nobody's around for miles. You can never be too careful. We even swept the boat for bugs before boarding.

"I've put him off for now. I told him we need more than just his investment. That I require his influence in the market, leveraging his network to secure additional high-profile users. I've also offered him a percentage of early revenue and exclusive insights into the app's performance metrics."

"He must have been panting like a dog."

"Yup. Played right into his fear of missing the next big thing. Von Graf knows She's the One will explode in the apps market. And if he wants a piece of it, he's got to play by our rules."

"Sounds like you've got this wrapped up, my friend."

I nod, but my gut twists, remembering how von Graf's beady eyes lingered over sim Josie's avatar. Feels like we're dangling her as bait—even if it's Gemini, not Josie, and she's just pixels and code. That wasn't the plan, even if, aye, it *was* part of the plan. But it's starting to feel too real. Maybe I'm risking too much, using this stunning virtual woman like a carrot on a stick, knowing what kind of shite lurks in von Graf's world.

There's no way he can link her to the real Josie. *My* Josie. Not that she's mine, not even close. If von Graf does end up beta testing Gemini, it wouldn't put Josie in any danger. Our privacy-preserving technology ensures absolute security. But just the thought of him looking at her makes my skin crawl with rage.

"You can pull back anytime, Axe. Swap out the sim—you have plenty of more generic backups. Do whatever you need," says Strike, who gets me better than a brother. "I know you like her."

"I do not *like* her," I snap, my irritation flaring. Strike knows I'm different from him. I'll never settle down. Also, *like*? What are we—in primary school?

Still, I get his point, but the businessman in me knows there's no choice. This whole operation hinges on getting von Graf's trust, and Gemini had him hooked from the second he saw her. I knew what I was doing when I chose her. If she's intoxicating to me—with my cold, dead heart—she'll be irresistible to every other man on the planet. Our previous sims do not even compare.

If I yank her now, von Graf will think I'm dismissing his stupid fucking opinions. And he might pull his funding.

"He's a coward and shady as fuck," I say. "After he left, I burnt a bundle of sage in my office, and I swear it did the job and got rid of his rank eejit energy. I'm mostly a skeptic about that sort of crap, but—"

"But let me guess: A certain someone mentioned you should give it a try, and she was very convincing." Strike's smile is all-knowing, and I want to knock it clean off. The other night, Josie did tell me that she'd been researching ancient practices around energy shifting and that sage has been used for centuries. Sure, it sounds a bit daft, but science has backed stranger things. Besides, von Graf left behind such a stink of his precious John Varvatos Dark Rebel cologne, I figured it couldn't hurt. And if it gives me something to chat about with Josie on our next "date," well, that doesn't hurt, either.

"Fuck off. My office smells way better now."

"What's next? Healing crystals in the boardroom? Quick psychic consultations before quarterly forecasts?"

Normally, I'd laugh along with Strike—Josie's belief in astrology and the tarot is downright ridiculous—but this feels too much like I'm taking the piss out of her, and I've vowed not to do that anymore. My hackles go up.

"There's actually some science behind the moon's tides impacting emotions and behaviors," I say, remembering a link Josie sent me about this. "Maybe it's not exactly astrology, but it shows there's more to the universe's influence on us than we think. Just because we don't get it doesn't mean it's all bollocks." Strike raises an eyebrow, but I press on. "And who are we to judge? Everyone needs something to hold on to in this mad world."

Strike still looks skeptical, but he lets it go and shifts back to von Graf. "Be careful with our mark. I think he's savvier than he looks."

"I don't trust him as far as I can throw him."

"Don't forget, you almost threw him over a mountain, bro," says Strike, and we roar with laughter.

"What's done is done," I say. "And to quote Liz Gilbert, 'Done is better than good.' We'll just have to see how it all plays out."

"Yeah, but we need to be extra careful with this guy, Axe," says Strike, suddenly serious. "We don't know a damn thing about him. Feels like we're playing some high-risk cat and mouse here."

I give a short laugh. "We're used to people reinventing themselves, covering their tracks. You don't think I know von Graf used to be some small-town bloke, born Norman Harris from Kickapoo, Kansas, or some shite?"

Strike is only half smiling. "But if that's true, then what's a Norman Harris from Kickapoo doing playing in *this* world?"

"We've dealt with these posers before," I remind him. "Always trying to jump into the big leagues, with their fake names and month-old fortunes."

"Every so often, one of those posers has teeth," says Strike.

"Good thing we know how to pull teeth," I say. Strike laughs, but there's an edge to it. "To the hunt," I add, raising my glass.

But when our eyes lock, the air around us goes dead quiet, crackling with the sense that we're already in the thick of it.

TWENTY-TWO

JOSIE

"Do you think I'm a winter?" The strange man has been in the shop for an hour, silently trying on clothes, sniffing candles, reading the humor books, and not buying anything. We close in twenty minutes. Honor's gone home—I shooed her off to enjoy a hot night with Strike, assuming I could ring up the purchase of this lightweight red scarf, which the man tried on and hasn't taken off since he got here.

"A winter?" I repeat, trying to keep my cool. "I don't know what you mean."

"On the color wheel," he explains, like it's the most obvious thing ever. He twines the scarf around his neck tighter, holds it up next to his face, and squints into the mirror on the wall behind my head.

"Right, the color wheel." I try not to roll my eyes. He's not very tall, so we're basically eye to eye. I'd bet money he's a Taurus—obsessed with his material stuff, and ruled by Venus, because he's clearly all about appearances. One of those older guys who's trying way too hard—and spending far too much money—to look young, but instead it has made him look bizarre. His skin is so pale it's practically see-through.

"The scarf suits you," I say, and tilt my body toward the register, hoping it will nudge him in that direction. It doesn't.

"I'm not so sure."

Okay, time to speed this up. I need to head to SynthoTech after work to, well, work. The digital art team wants to sketch me into my avatar version. As much as Honor would be thrilled if we sell that scarf, which customers love to touch but no one wants to buy, I can't stay here late.

"Sir, not to be rude, but are you planning to make a purchase, or are we just going to chat about your seasonal identity crisis all night?" I throw in a smile to soften it, hoping that I didn't just cost Honor a potential repeat customer.

I'm relieved when he bursts out laughing.

"Fair enough. I'll wrap it up, so to speak," he says. His accent reminds me of those 1950s actors trying to sound New England fancy.

"No worries," I reply, feeling a twinge of guilt. It's not his fault I have somewhere else to be. Normally, I'd let a customer wander around as long as they wanted. But now that Bryan is in the rearview mirror, I can admit how much I used to stall before going home. I'd let customers stay well past closing or hang around doing inventory that nobody asked me to do. I even alphabetized the vibrator shelf once. Never thinking that the issue was my relationship.

Amazing how we only notice what we want to notice.

Or maybe what we're ready to notice.

"Let me collect my items," the man says as he flashes me a smile. Whoa, his dimples look so weird, like they were stamped by a machine into each side of his cheeks. He unwinds the scarf from his neck and drops it next to the register. It leaves behind a puff of powerful cologne—definitely a Taurus, going wayyy too strong on the smell—and my mind drifts to the other night, remembering how the subtlety of Axe's scent lingered on my dress after our date—a fresh and woody blend with notes of ambergris and lemon verbena. It's a fragrance I now imagine must be what a Scottish forest smells like. *No, Josie Greene, you will not think about Axe or that kiss or how, if he hadn't broken it off, you might have humiliated yourself by inviting him inside and ruined everything.*

Clearly, my taste in men is a hot mess. Or, as Nonna would say, my picker is broken. Between my VIP status at MS Hospital and my mother's helicopter parenting, I was embarrassingly late to the whole romance and sex scene. Bryan's been the only guy I've ever known in that way, and honestly, sex with Bryan felt a lot like the way he played ice hockey—he was fast, clumsy, and often left me feeling like I should give him a penalty for rough play.

Sometimes I wonder if I even know what sex is supposed to be. When I was stuck in the hospital as a teen, I devoured series like *Highland Heartthrobs* and *Nights at Castle Glenn*, losing myself in tales of hot heroes and sassy heroines. It all felt so thrilling on the page—stolen glances, forbidden kisses, fireworks. Now I can't help but think those romance novels might've set my expectations way too high and filled my head with these grand ideas of love that real life just can't live up to.

Luckily, there's a whole shelf of products here—conveniently alphabetized—that can satisfy me better than any man could. Sure, my kiss with Axe was unlike anything I've ever experienced. It wasn't so much a kiss as it was . . . a revelation. *Stop it! Stop it! Stop it!* I'm over-romanticizing a singular moment.

Now that my engagement is off, I'm clearly desperate for my life to get some spark. To create drama where there is none. Maybe a childhood spent in constant danger has made me addicted to terrible thrills.

The customer roves around the store, picking up random items and dropping them by the register for me to ring up. A few candles, a wicker picnic basket, our best-selling heated massage oil, silky eye masks, and drawer sachets. The way he's grabbing stuff reminds me of the first time Strike came into Grace & Honor and cleared the whole place out. We sold more in that single day than we had in the previous two years. After he left, Honor and I were so excited we blasted "Happy" and jitterbugged all around the empty shelves and racks.

This dude is no Strike. He's not going to buy everything. Still, it looks like a big enough sale that I'll definitely call Honor after he leaves. These days, money is way less tight for Honor and the store. She's killing it not only by working part-time at Strike's company, DME, but also by selling her own art. She's been getting commissions from big collectors, many of them outside Pennsylvania. But Honor never takes success for granted. She'll be thrilled to hear about Mr. Dimples McSpendy.

"One of your creamers is chipped," he says. "Should I bring it over?"

He doesn't wait for me to answer, just comes over and sets the little ceramic pitcher on the counter with a deliberate clink. As I pick it up to inspect the damage, my finger catches on the jagged edge.

"Ouch!" I watch as a dark bead of blood wells up on my finger.

"Sorry," he says. "I should have told you it was the handle."

"It's fine." I bring my finger to my mouth, sucking on it to dull the pain—when I look up, he's watching me with an intensity that's so unnerving I take my finger out of my mouth, rummaging through the drawer by the register until I find a stray Band-Aid. I quickly wrap it around my finger. "Just a nick."

"Anything else you think I should grab?" he asks. I study his selection on the counter. Who is he buying all this stuff for? Is he planning on taking endless rose-scented bubble baths while burning a forest's worth of pine-scented candles and reading *The Essential Tarot Guide*? (I convinced Honor to stock that book because it's life-changing. Trust me.) Is he hosting a bachelor party and that's why he needs a dozen pocket Big Night Out Survival Kits (includes: mini-flask, breath mints, condoms, energy bar)?

Now I look deeply into his face—his skin is like one of those rubbery Halloween masks. Since we sell all sorts of sex toys, we sometimes get fetishists in the store. No judgment—if your kink is licking pickle juice off someone's clamped nipples, go off, girlfriend. Every once in a while, though, a customer will ask all sorts of questions about our products as a way to proposition Honor or me. It's like they assume that, by virtue of our working in a store that sells erotic items, we, too, are for sale.

"Looks like you did a great job. Um, other than . . ." I glance around the store. He's sporting a pair of limited-edition vintage Yeezys, which I know are worth at least a thousand dollars. ". . . our shoe-cleaning kits? You should definitely grab one. Everyone loves them—microfiber cloth, deodorizer, cute little brush. They'll keep those Yeezys looking fresh."

"Done," he says, and adds a few kits to the pile. Sometimes I think Honor orders these things just to test my sales skills. Our customer base rarely crosses over with sneakerheads.

Suddenly, I'm extra aware that he and I are all alone in here. Dude might not be tall, but he's got at least fifty pounds of muscle on me. His thick wrestler's neck contrasts with his delicate wrists and manicured fingernails.

Is he dangerous? Should I be alarmed? Should I press the button under the counter that summons Strike's personal security team?

My finger finds the button, just to feel it. Just in case.

"So, what's your name?"

And there it is. A flirty lilt to his voice. Shit. He's going to ask me out, and I'm going to need to tell him NO without pissing him off. I hate how often I feel vulnerable as a woman in this world. I look around for a weapon. Could I stab him with my EpiPen?

Chill out, Josie. This man has given no indication he wants to do anything except buy random shit and make awkward conversation. Creepy isn't the same as dangerous.

I blame Nonna's disturbing warning. Freddy Krueger. That damn Devil card. And, of course, I'm still haunted by Troy Simpson—the psychopath who killed Honor's sister. That experience has definitely left its mark.

"I'm Josie," I say, my voice as neutral as beige paint. "Cash or credit?"

"Pretty name, Josie," he says as he hands over a black Amex. Ha, Strike has one. I always tease him that I'm going to use it to buy a private plane. Rumor has it these cards have no credit limit. I swipe it and hand it back with my *thank you for shopping in this establishment*—and not a *please ask me for my number*—smile.

Hopefully, this guy can tell the difference.

"I'm Niles," he says. "Niles von Grafenhagen."

"For real?" I blurt out without thinking. What a freaky-ass name. Like a villain in a bad spy movie.

"As far as I know, yes," he says, and he sounds offended. "That is my name."

"Sorry. Long day. I'm a little punchy. It's a great name. Memorable. Great to meet you, Niles von . . ." I mumble a bunch of vowels and hope he doesn't notice. "Thank you for your business. Have a good night."

I need to change before I head to SynthoTech. I probably won't see Axe tonight—but if I do, I don't want to be wearing these old sweatpants and a T-shirt that says *I'M IN MY GLITTER ERA* in sequins.

To my relief, Niles takes the hint. After he scoops up his five shopping bags, he gives me one last, intense look. "Now that I've found this delightful shop, I expect we'll be seeing more of each other, Josie," he says, and the hairs on my arms stand up in alarm. I don't like him saying my name.

"Sure, see you around," I say with false brightness.

After he leaves, I'm so shaky I double-check my blood sugar. Numbers are good. This is a completely irrational reaction to a friendly customer. Maybe some basic Troy Simpson PTSD. Nonna always says people can read energy, that we all have a sixth sense we've been conditioned to ignore, and if we just tuned in, the world would be better for it. But Nonna could be seriously superstitious, probably just looking for ways to make sense of things.

Of course that odd little elf man is harmless.

Still, after I lock up, cash out, and call Honor to give her the day's receipts—which sends her launching into a passionate verse of "Billionaire"—I pull out my singing bowl from under the register. I stroll slowly around the shop, tapping the bowl with my mallet, breaking up Niles's gremlin energy with the calming vibes and chimes of Zen. I remember how the other night Axe almost spit out his champagne when I told him that I keep sage in my bag for these sorts of emergencies. I picture him watching me now.

Laugh all you want, Axe, I think. I'm not sure when I started having imaginary conversations with him in my head, but here I am. *You can never be too careful.*

TWENTY-THREE

AXE

"You really don't need to be here for this, boss," Theo, my head of graphics, says. "We got this handled."

Theo, in his mid-twenties, sporting a rainbow mohawk and ear gauges, lives with his husband, Chuck, on a farm just outside Shelton. When he's not busy revolutionizing AI at SynthoTech, he's out there growing rhubarb and making jam. I don't usually mix with my staff outside the office—except for the annual SynthoTech-DME party, of course. (My team's already hounding me for new theme ideas, because you can never start planning my least favorite day of the year too soon.)

I've been to Theo and Chuck's croft once, when they had me over for their Fall Harvest Festival. I like and trust Theo well enough, but not enough to let him take the lead on re-creating AI Josie without me keeping a watchful eye.

"I know, lad. But I'm going to stick around anyway," I say, casual as you like. I smile. I've no intention of alienating one of my best employees. "Watch the magic happen."

"Suit yourself," Theo says. Josie isn't here yet—she's meant to show up at 7:00 p.m., and it's 6:55—though my dad, rest his bedamned soul, had a strict rule that *on time is late.* One of his many rigid demands, usually backed up with a cold stare or a beating. A memory that feels more like a scar.

Theo busies himself with his kit, setting up cameras, monitors, and iPads. He also has a tablet that he mirror casts onto a screen. I've never really dabbled with the graphics side of SynthoTech, so it makes sense that Theo is surprised to see me here. I'm far more interested in the technical innovation side of things. I usually leave the visuals to the ones who know what they're doing.

I keep my distance as they finish arranging the cameras and lights. The room is buzzing with activity, but my thoughts drift to Josie. I can see her so clearly in my head, from the way she laughs—pure joy—to the way she scrunches her nose in deep thought.

Theo roughly sketches Josie's features with his stylus, using a cache of reference photos. His line is quick and sure, capturing the spirit of her face. I could watch this all day. I've spent enough time with Josie—long before I hired her, I couldn't help but notice every little detail, every nuance. And it's clear Theo's done his homework, too. He even catches the wee freckle on the top of her left cheekbone.

As Theo refines the sketch, layering in saturation and textures with digital brushes, I find myself sharing specific details.

"When she's been in the sun, she gets a smattering of freckles on her nose. She's got an evil-eye anklet that her grandmother gave her that she doesn't take off. It's subtle, but you might want to put that in. She can whistle through her fingers, though I guess that doesn't help much here. Oh, and her favorite flower is the sunflower because they're strong and sturdy and tend not to show up in hospital bouquets."

Theo nods and lets me ramble on, even though I must sound like a pussy-whipped fool.

"The more info, the better. You know, for the data harvest," I say.

"Sure," Theo says, but I can hear the slightest hint of sarcasm in his voice.

"Sorry, sorry!" Josie calls out as she steps off the elevator a few minutes later. She's in another slip dress, this one pale pink cotton, scandalously short, with a frayed hem. She looks as bonny as ever. For just a moment, I wonder what it would be like to have the right to kiss her hello, to feel her lips against mine.

"I got caught up with a customer. Dude refused to leave."

"You should have called me," I say, and the anger that flares up catches me off guard. Strike insists that Grace & Honor has an exceptional security system that links directly to Strike's team, but I hate the idea of Josie working all alone, especially in the early evenings.

"But it's 6:59! I'm not late!" Josie says, holding up her phone to show me the time. Her lock screen is a picture of her with her gran, an olive-skinned, gray-haired woman with her arms around Josie's shoulders. The same evil-eye charm hangs around her gran's neck. Even though I don't believe in that superstitious nonsense, I hope it works. The thought of anything happening to Josie, or anyone she loves, twists my guts.

"Not because of the time. You should have called me about the customer who wouldn't leave! That could've been dangerous," I say. Josie scoffs like I'm being ridiculous, even though she's the one who checked my chakras with her crystal during our "date" and asked me when I was born so she could make a full birth chart.

"Hi, I'm Theo." Theo reaches out a hand to shake Josie's.

"Nice to meet you," she says, smiling at Theo like he's already a kindred spirit. He even gets her amazing left dimple. The bastard is lucky he's gay, or I might rip his feckin' head off. "Love your mohawk!"

"Love your curls," he says. "Now, you go get comfortable in that chair over there. I promise this will be painless and fun."

"Will you be watching the whole time?" Josie asks, turning to face me directly. I know she doesn't mean it that way, but I can't help myself. My cock twitches.

"Axe has been really helpful," says Theo, clearly thinking I might need a wingman, but it only makes me feel daft. "He's helping with the visual input."

"Is that right?" Josie quirks an eyebrow as she studies her avatar. "Aw, you put me in sunflower-print shorts? Cutest! I'd totally wear that!"

"Let's start with you giving us a variety of expressions," says Theo.

"Sure." Josie laughs. "Does digital Josie do a digital duck face?" She pulls the face, and the corners of my mouth lift. Theo continues making adjustments to his digital sketches, where each new version of the artwork is a separate layer, giving him the ability to focus on specific elements—facial expressions, clothing, background—without affecting the original drawing of Josie. She tries out all sorts of expressions, and I can't turn away.

Josie happy. Josie sad. Josie guilty. Josie disappointed. Josie playful.

I enjoy every version. Theo's also set up a camera that's clicking away, and I wonder if there's a legit way to ask for the images without sounding like a creep. "How about giving me a Superwoman cape, Theo? Or some laser vision? Also, please don't make my hair too insane—I'd like my AI me with ten percent less frizz."

Josie already has Theo under her spell. When I glance at his screen, I'm relieved to see he understands the task: This is about understanding and appreciating the real Josie, every quirk, every bit of charm, and bringing that to life in her virtual avatar. Flesh-and-blood Josie lights up the room, her mood as bright as a sunbeam, and I'm proud and fiercely protective of her. The specificity of Gemini will be next-level.

From an AI standpoint, it's fascinating—we're not just replicating human behavior but going somewhere deeper, distilling the essence of charisma itself. The spark that makes someone unforgettable.

Taking down von Graf has always been the top priority, but it's clear now we're onto something big—this lass is going to make us a bloody fortune.

Time always seems to warp around Josie—so when Theo nods to the team that he's calling it a night, I'm shocked to see that it's almost ten.

"Did you drive here in your old Volkswagen rust bucket?" I ask her. "Or do you need a ride home?"

"Her name is Gertrude, and I'll have you know she's aging gracefully," Josie says, her eyes shimmering. I get the impression she enjoyed tonight, that it was fun for her to ham it up for the cameras and showcase all her sides.

"Please apologize to Dame Gertrude for me. She's a fine old lass, with a bumper to match."

"Hey, you have to buy Gertrude dinner before you start talking about her bumper." She smiles at me. "Actually, SynthoTech picked me up in a company car."

"Ah, right. Page fourteen, last paragraph, subsection C."

"Exactly."

"Well, there's nothing in the contract that says I can't take you home myself. I didn't bring the bike, though," I add.

"Oh dear, no cool bike?" she teases, raising an eyebrow as she plucks a chocolate-covered pretzel from the bowl of snacks set out on a table. As she takes a bite, a tiny morsel sticks to her lips. I want to lick it off. "How will I ever survive?"

"At least this way, you won't be holding on to me for dear life," I say.

She laughs. "You think I need the bike as an excuse?" Then she gives me a look, one I can't quite read, and I can't tell if she's saying it as Josie or as the app, keeping things flirty to stay in Gemini mode.

It's a proper mind fuck that I just can't tell the difference.

"By the way, the date was great, and of course, I took some notes today, but we will need more interaction data from you two in the coming days," Theo cuts in, and I nearly jump. I forgot the lad was still here. Gotta give him credit—he acts like he hasn't noticed a thing between us. Even if what we're doing here is unconventional, it's still a workplace. Josie is still my employee. "We're hoping you might want to do something less fantasyscape and more normal couples-y, like spending a little time in a supermarket or something. We can take one public outing and then map an entire digital world from it."

"What? An isolated picnic on a mountaintop with personal heaters wasn't normal for a first date?" Josie asks, and I feel the beam of her light shift to Theo.

It feels colder now that she's not looking at me anymore.

Theo's just ruined my plan to ask Josie for a proper second date while privately driving her home. Because this is business, not pleasure. Right. I wish I was grateful for the reminder.

"We could go to the farmers market," she suggests.

I blink, a bit lost. "Shelton has a farmers market?" I pretend not to notice Theo stifling a laugh behind his cough.

"You've never been? You're in for a treat. They set it up every Saturday behind the public library. You'll love it. It's super quaint and cute. Small-batch yogurt, hand-pressed olive oil, homemade pies. And . . ." She bites her bottom lip, catches that bit of chocolate. "Then you can see how well you manage a date where you have to do it all on your own, Axe. No drivers, no handlers. No script."

Ach, did she twig that last time, my team printed up a list of questions I could ask if things went sideways? I didn't need to use them, not once—but I must admit, I liked having them in my pocket.

This woman has a way of making me feel off my nut.

"It's been a while since I picked out my own apples," I say.

"See? You can impress me—or at least AI me—with your secret shopping skills."

The air between us is hot as firecrackers until Theo's voice butts in. Again.

"Sounds perfect, mate," he says in a horrendous Scottish accent.

My jaw clenches. I'd like to hook my fingers through those ear gauges and use them to lift him up and throw him into a wall so hard his grandkids will feel it. Instead, though, I nod. It's not Theo's fault Josie has me ass over teakettle.

"It's a plan. Josie, me, and the farmers market," I say.

"Chuck runs a stall there most weekends selling our jam. Maybe I'll come along and bring my sketchbook. See you both live and in action."

"No, mate," I say. "We don't want to make Josie feel like she's being watched. The whole thing needs to feel organic."

"No pun intended," Theo says, but I ignore him. My eyes are on Josie. I want to see if she's on board.

"Sure," she says, flashing me another smile. "Just us." But

there's a twist in her expression now, like she's swallowing down a bit of nausea, and it's unsettling. Is it the thought of spending time with me?

"Aye, just us, then," I say, trying to keep it light. "But if you change your mind, that's fine, too."

TWENTY-FOUR

JOSIE

Even though I've felt sick for the past half hour—waves of nausea rolling through me—somehow I make it home without puking in Axe's fancy sports car. Honestly, it's a miracle. I kept my window down and pretended I was all about the breeze, but really I was just trying to keep my lunch where it belonged.

Axe tried to chat the whole ride through Shelton's winding streets—apparently, Honor told him about me running a booth at the Toygasm sex toy expo coming up: *Are you looking forward to it? Tell me more about your nonna. What do you think of Theo?*

I gave him micro answers (*yes / she's my best person / cool*) without letting on that my stomach was twisting in agony. I'd rather him think I'm rude than sick.

As soon as I'm through my apartment door, I drop my bag and run to the bathroom. I barely make it in time. My body heaves, rejecting and ejecting everything inside. I grip the cool porcelain, my face drenched in sweat, my body trembling. My mind races through what I ate today to see what might have caused this reaction—is this an allergy?

Just thinking about food makes me gag. Lunch was the usual,

so probably not the culprit: my mom's homemade iced tea and leftover veggie lasagna she dropped off at the store as some kind of peace offering, Honor's fudge brownies . . . and a few too many chocolate-covered pretzels at SynthoTech.

I tell myself it's the stomach flu even though it feels so much worse. As weird as that dude at the store was, it's a real leap to assume the cut on my finger has anything to do with it, though for some reason, that's where my mind keeps going. I remember the way he watched me lick off my blood, and it leaves me with the faint prickle of unease that just won't go away. Nah, Nonna just has me freaked out.

When I first started feeling off at SynthoTech, I brushed it off, thinking it would pass. Now, as I lean against the bathroom wall, I can't ignore the growing fear. What if I'm too sick to go to the farmers market? Would Axe fire me?

I've been looking forward to our second "date." Weirdly enough, I'm actually enjoying this new job. I want to get to know Axe as much as he and his developers want to get to know me. I've got a million random questions I'd love to throw at him and hope for more than a one-word answer: What was it like running through the misty moors of Scotland as a kid? Did he dream of something beyond his picture-perfect island? Has he ever taken a risk so wild it made his heart race, like jumping off a cliff into the sea? Gotten swept up in an adventure that spiraled out of control with unexpected consequences?

Has he ever been sick enough that he thought he might die?

I crawl into bed, my eyes locked on the unforgiving numbers of my alarm clock. My 9:00 a.m. date with Axe looms ahead, and every passing minute torches my chances of getting even a shred of sleep. By the time the sun rises, I've spent the night crouched over the toilet, my body racked with dry heaves. Exhaustion settles into my achy bones, but I've spent too much of my life sick in bed. No way am I flaking on Axe.

Dragging myself to my dresser, I catch sight of my tarot deck. I close my eyes and pull: Strength. A lion and a woman face each other, exuding controlled yin-yang balance. I take a deep breath.

You can do it, Josie. Today you need JosieFightsOn energy big-time.

I take a long, hot shower, and afterward look at my haggard face in the mirror. I cover up my dark under-eye circles with concealer.

I chew three more Pepto-Bismol tablets. Then a fourth. I shake out my curls.

I let the cards give me *strength*, just like always.

TWENTY-FIVE

AXE

The island has grown smaller. Now that his height has shot up, Axe feels like he could stretch his arms and reach both the north and south sandy shores, his wingspan wider than a falcon's. But he can't reach. He lives in a literal castle on a hill, with rolling grounds and trees and a ballroom big enough to fit a thousand. Of course, the island hasn't grown smaller, and his life hasn't grown bigger.

Hamish says it's normal for thirteen-year-old boys to want to run away, to dream of getting in a rowboat and leaving everything and everyone you know behind. Axe doesn't feel like he'd be leaving much behind anyway. He doesn't know many people—unless you count the revolving girls, and he doesn't know them, not really—so it wouldn't be too hard to say goodbye. But he doesn't say that to Hamish.

He doesn't want to break his big brother's heart. If he still has one.

Axe has spent his whole life on Skara Brae, except a failed experiment at boarding school. His one chance at escape, and he was home within the year—with two black eyes, a broken rib, a bruise blooming across his back.

The administration said that maybe the school "wasn't the right fit"—what they really meant was they didn't know how to keep this sensitive soul safe from furious little boys playing at being men. Didn't know what to do with a kid who had never watched telly or heard Eminem. Didn't know how to teach a student who knew more about physics and astronomy and history than the faculty.

"Come on, little brother. Put away that book, and let's go watch the girls change," Hamish says on a Monday afternoon like every other—the Whales partying, Axe hiding away in the library. But Axe doesn't want to watch the girls. They look through him like he's a ghost, and he prefers it that way. He'd rather they ignore him than flinch, which is what they do when they see Hamish or Da. Or any other man.

Hamish has never seemed to mind living in the castle, or even his father, though he gets the cane as much as Axe. He admires their da's power, wants to step into his shoes one day. Hamish will be king of the castle for real and not just in the games he used to play with Axe before Hamish outgrew them.

"Nah. Leave them alone. They get enough of that from everyone else," Axe says, turning back to the book in his lap. He now spends all his time tucked away in a corner in a leather armchair facing the window, reading, or outside, identifying trees and plants and flowers to draw in his journal.

"Come on. It's time you learned how to be a man," Hamish says, and knocks Robinson Crusoe, *Axe's favorite novel, out of his hands with a hard swipe. It lands on the floor with a dusty thud, and though it's obvious Hamish is trying to get a rise out of Axe, to make him get to his feet and throw punches, all Axe feels like doing is crying.*

"I don't want to do this, Hamish," Axe says in a tone too weary for thirteen. Lately, he's been learning all about Darwin and wonders if maybe he and his family are of different species or if they've adapted some survival gene that somehow bypassed him. He doesn't want to touch the girls, not with their sad, hollowed eyes, and he doesn't want to bloody Hamish's lip the way Hamish so desperately seems to want to bloody his.

With the girls, the problem is he's seen too much. He knows they swallow pills to stay up late and then more to sleep. Once, Axe walked into a bathroom to find two of them sitting on the edge of the tub, sticking needles in their arms. Once, he came down for breakfast to find a girl passed out in the dining hall in a puddle of her own vomit. Once, he saw the mangled body of a girl who'd thrown herself off the crenellated roof. He wonders what really happened to his own mother, who died when he was ten. How did she go? Was she carted away and buried at sea? No one says. Da never speaks of her. Hamish doesn't know; different mothers, different silences. So Axe did the only thing he could think; he climbed the cliffs and drove a wooden cross into the earth. No name on it—just a way to remind himself not to wait for her return in this world.

"Da's right. You are a pussy," Hamish says, stepping closer, and he sucker punches Axe right in the gut. Axe feels the hit, sharp and fast, but doesn't give Hamish the reaction he wants. Instead, he looks past his shoulder, as if seeing a ghost lurking there that his brother cannot see.

Axe's mum, Lurlene, was a model. She used to live behind a locked door in the keep, the part of the castle that used to be its most heavily guarded building, and it still is—men with rifles stand by its doors all day and night. Lurlene got special privi-

leges because she belonged to Da. She didn't have to go to the parties, didn't even talk to the other girls. Axe wasn't allowed to see her except on special visiting days, when he'd walk past the men with the guns and enter the keep and then sit on his mum's lap while she read to him.

Until one day Da said things were going to change. A lad did not need to be babied by his mother. And then, as if it were of no consequence, he told Axe that there would be no more visiting days; his mum had gone to heaven.

Axe remembers his own mum as warm and Hamish's as cold. Hamish's mom, Ekaterina, was a short, thin woman who flitted around the castle in a bikini even when it was snowing. He remembers her "taking care of the other girls," which seemed to mean yelling at them in a language he didn't recognize when they stepped out of line. Russian, maybe? Axe doesn't know what happened to her, either. She was there before he left for boarding school and was gone by the time he got back. And that's when Hamish changed, too: started noticing the girls, made them look at him and touch him like they did Da and his friends.

"You're just going to stand there, ya daft prick? Come on. Fight me. Show me what you're made of," Hamish says, fists raised like a boxer's. This is what Hamish does when he's bored. He sniffs around for trouble.

"Do we really have to—" Axe says, and before he can finish his question, he hears the crack and then feels the blood gushing from his nose. Hamish punched him right in the face. He is a pussy, he thinks, he must be. Because even now, all Axe wants to do is run.

He understands the girls—the pills and the needles, their unfocused eyes. He understands dreaming about the oblivion of the deep blue sea, of catapulting off this tiny patch of land into the unknown.

Far, far away from the king of the castle. Far, far away from Da.

Axe calmly stops the bleeding with the front of his T-shirt, picks up Robinson Crusoe *from the floor, and lightly brushes past his brother's shoulder as he walks out the door.*

TWENTY-SIX

JOSIE

One hour, two glasses of water, and a handful of antacids later, I roll up to the Shelton Farmers Market right on time. The place is buzzing with activity—vendors coaxing people to try samples, kids on skateboards zigzagging between tote-wielding grandmas—and the air is alive with mingled scents of fresh herbs and baked goods. I spot Axe almost immediately across the bustling fruit stand. Hard not to. He's tall, broad shouldered, and so impossibly good-looking it's honestly annoying. He's carrying a huge wicker basket piled high with greens, and he looks like the farmers market version of the Brawny Man.

I take a deep breath and walk toward him, my feelings all tangled up between anticipation and doubt. Axe spots me, waves, and flashes a grin that could light up a room, and, ugh, I can't help but grin back. As much as I hate to admit it, there's something about him—an effortless charm that's hard to ignore.

But . . . part of me still resists. I'm hesitant, maybe even a little wary. Sure, we've gotten closer, and the more I find out, the more I like. But I keep reminding myself: He's Axe MacKenzie. Blunt, rough around the edges, and definitely not in my lane.

Honor told me that in all the years Strike's known him, Axe

has never been in love. Strike thinks he might not even *do* love. Like, he might be biologically incapable. Not that any of this should matter to me. I'm just here for a job.

As I approach, his smile widens even more, cranking up my pulse despite the queasiness churning in my stomach.

"A posy for Josie," he teases in his lilting Scottish accent, handing me a big, fat sunflower from his basket. "Something to brighten your day."

"Aw, thanks, Axe. It's beautiful." I pop it in my canvas tote. It feels like I'm carrying a smile.

"Did you manage all right last night? You were a bit crabbit when I dropped you off."

"Crabbit?" I snort. "What the hell does *crabbit* mean?"

"You know, a little bit . . . um . . ."

"Bitchy?" I ask.

"I didn't say that!" Axe gasps, feigning innocence.

"Wouldn't blame you if you did. I wasn't my normal happy self. My stomach was feeling off, but I'm better now."

"We could do this another day," he offers. "And, for the record, not always being happy doesn't make you a bitch."

"I'm fine," I say, and instead of continuing to push, like Mom would, he drops it. Trusts me. No fuss, no fight. It's weirdly . . . refreshing.

"So the tech wonks want this whole thing to feel 'light and casual,'" he says, making air quotes. "And they've got me wired for physiological reactions, and the mic will pick up both of our voices. They wanted to wire you, too—but I nixed it. I reckon we can build up to that. Bad enough that I feel like I'm part of a sting operation. I thought my CIA days were well behind me."

"I thought the CIA was like the first rule of Fight Club. You don't talk about it." The corners of his mouth tick up, and I love that I can do that to him.

"Aye," he says, his grin widening. "I guess you make me break the rules."

I start to relax as we stroll through the market. Having Axe by my side is definitely distracting me from my queasiness, and the easy flow of our conversation helps melt away some of the anxiety. I know this isn't my real life (my real life involves late-night praying to the porcelain gods and a cursed to-do list that never gets shorter), but this is close enough. For a moment, I let myself imagine it: Saturday mornings like this, cool air on my face, filling a tote with fresh veggies and overpriced artisan soaps, a hot guy next to me, the world spinning just right. Like the messy parts don't exist.

Not that it's Axe in my little daydream, of course. When his face pops up in my mind, I push it aside.

When we pause at Chuck and Theo's stand selling homemade jams, Axe holds up a jar of preserves, and his eyes twinkle with pure mischief.

"If I had to describe you with one of these jams, I might go with this one," Axe says, showing me the label.

"'Spiced peach,'" I read aloud as a hot blush creeps up my cheeks. I shake my head. Fortunately, the man who must be Chuck—he, too, has a mohawk, like his husband, but instead of rainbow, his is somehow leopard—isn't paying any attention to us. "Actually, I'm more of a strawberry jam kind of girl," I tell him. "But for me, a good jam is less about the flavor."

"Agree. All about the bread," he says. "A fresh-baked, thick-sliced country white loaf, medium toasted."

"That does sound delicious," I admit with a shrug. "But I'm

actually happy with any style of bread-shaped carb. Because, see, for *me*, it's about the spread."

"The *spread*?" He wiggles his eyebrows, and I laugh. His accent inflects everything with innuendo.

"The jam's got to be as even as a bedsheet, right to the edges of the toast." I blush again, this time at my use of the word *bedsheet*. Probably didn't need to bring beds into this. Much like he didn't need to bring peaches.

Axe grins. "Ah, yes. I'll bet you spread a mean toast, Josie."

I manage to meet his gaze, and I can't help myself but flirt back. After all, it's my job, right?

"Oh, you have no idea," I say.

"Josie Marie! What are you doing out here in the sun?! And without a hat?! You know better than that!"

Oh shit, shit, shit.

I freeze, the color draining from my face as my mother appears, weaving her way through the throngs of marketgoers. She's clutching a large canvas @MAMABEARSHARON bag—swag from some ancient GoFundMe, printed with a photo of eight-year-old me with my bald head, Mom smiling behind me, looking a lot younger and cuter. As her eyes zombie-lock onto mine, it strikes me that she looks like she's aged a century.

Axe seems to grasp the situation.

"You must be Josie's mum," he says, his smile as warm as apple pie as he extends his hand. "I've heard a fair bit about you."

Mom takes Axe's hand with limp fingers, but she doesn't bother with so much as a hello, her eyes narrowing as she looks up and scrutinizes him for only a moment before turning her attention to me.

"Josie, why didn't you tell me you were seeing someone new? Poor Bryan is going to be devastated."

Poor Bryan? What is she talking about? It would be funny if my mother didn't look so bananas. Somehow, seeing her out in public, with Axe right here next to me, I can take her in as everyone else might. Her clown-red hair matches her clown-red lips, a terrible one-two punch. Her floral silk blouse with way too many ruffles paired with a pencil skirt one size too tight. A thick layer of jewelry—chunky gold bangles, oversized hoop earrings—completes the look, making her appear like she's trying too hard to dress for a life she doesn't have. But the worst is her bag—*with my sick face on it.* Like it's cute. Like my misery is her fashion statement.

Strength, Josie. But I can also feel my courage buckling along with my stomach. The powerful urge to bolt—to leave Axe here with this live-action hot mess that happens to be my mother—nearly overwhelms me.

"Mom, I'm fine," I say softly. "I'm actually working right now. Can you please leave us alone?"

"Working?" She sniffs. "You're certainly not in good enough health to work—if that's what this is—in the middle of the day. You look awful! Green at the gills! Are you feeling okay? You should be home in bed. Not gallivanting. What are you thinking?"

"I told you, I'm fine!" My tone is sharp. Even Axe can probably tell I'm teetering on the edge of truly bitchy. My mom looks hurt at first, but then decides to just bulldoze right past that. She forcefully grabs my arm as if she's going to pull me home when Axe's voice growls.

"Mrs. Greene, I'm afraid you'll need to let go of your daughter and step back. We don't want to get security involved."

"My last name isn't Greene. That was Josie's *late father's* last name. I'm Mrs. Groznok. And Josie's coming with me—" One of the fruit stand sellers—*wait, I know that guy, he was my driver from the first date*—steps forward. In a few quick strides, he reaches us and firmly takes Mom's arm, causing her to drop mine.

"Ma'am, we have reason to believe you're causing a disturbance. We need to escort you from the premises. Please come with us."

"Causing a disturbance?" Mom's face is as red as a beet. "I'm hardly—Josie, tell them."

I'm not sure what comes over me, but I decide not to intervene. I *am* working, and I *am* fine. I'm twenty-six years old. My mother should listen to me when I ask her politely to leave. And so I let Axe's guy whisk her off with such speed and efficiency that it's like she was never here. I know I'll pay for this moment, maybe for the rest of my life, but the breath I exhale after she's gone is one hundred percent worth it.

Axe and I just stand there for a moment, processing the weirdness of her whirlwind. His eyes on me are so full of concern, I feel mortified.

"Was that okay?" Axe asks. "I figured when you didn't speak up, you were fine with security getting involved? In my experience with this sort of thing, moving fast breaks the momentum and de-escalates the drama. But I can call him and bring her back if that's what you want."

"No. No. Sorry," I mumble. "Mom can be . . . intense. But she's not that bad. Not once you get to know her. She is super protective. It comes from a place of . . . love."

Axe doesn't speak, only waits for me to go on. I don't say that sometimes it doesn't actually feel like love. That it feels like something altogether different.

"I know I look reasonably healthy now. But we had some really traumatic years. And she was the one who kept me safe and fed and clothed and dealt with all the gazillion doctors—somehow got all my hospital bills paid, too," I add.

"I'm sure she's a good woman. Just worried about you," says Axe, his voice neutral. As if he himself is unsure if that's true.

But now something sharp and unexpected snaps inside me, and I'm furious. Dragging myself here feeling like absolute shit was hard enough, but now Mom's managed to hunt me down, order me home, and scold me like a damn child—in public, in front of Axe. It's too fucking much.

"Sometimes, I'm not sure that what she does is all out of love," I blurt, surprising myself. I never talk to anyone about this. Not even Nonna. I never wanted to give her more ammunition to dislike my mother. "When I was little, Mom had this twisted way of preparing me for things. If she knew I was getting shots or some kind of procedure the next day at the hospital, she'd actually stick a pin into my arm the night before." I wince at the memory. "She'd say it was to help me get used to what was coming. Like, seriously—a real, two-inch sewing pin! She'd always say, *Now the worst is over! Cry it out here so that you don't cry there.* So when she filmed me getting treatment, I'd be strong. Bonkers, right?" *Oh my God, Josie. No. This is so* not *farmers-market-date banter. Shut the fuck up, girl. Get your shit together.*

Axe's jaw drops. "Please tell me you're taking the piss," he says.

"I wish." I laugh, but it's a brittle sound.

"That's cruel." He puts his hand on my shoulder, so soft and light, squeezes sweetly, and then drops it.

"She'd come into my room all cheerful. Like it was some kind of girlie bonding activity. *Hold still, Josie,* she'd say, and then—*ooof!* She'd smash the point of it, with all her strength, right into my arm. I'd be sitting there in bed, tears rolling down my face, and then she'd make me cocoa and hug me and tell me how brave I was. How much she loved me. How she wished I wasn't sick." My throat locks up. Why am I saying all this? To Axe. My literal boss. I am having a full-scale emotional meltdown *to my boss* in real time.

And, oh yeah, it's being recorded by tech geniuses.

Axe should just fire me now. How could I possibly represent the She's the One ideal? More like She's One Hot Mess.

"That's . . . that's batshit, Josie," Axe growls. His eyes are hard with shock. "That's not preparing you for shit. That's bloody torture."

"Yeah, I see that now. So it was kind of nice to see someone else dealing with her for a change. Just disappearing her, you know?" I wipe my eyes. "Sometimes I think Mom only likes me when I need her. It's like she thrives on my misery."

"There's an old Scottish saying: 'Better a bare foot than a bad parent,'" says Axe. He looks away as a shadow passes over his face. Then, more quietly, he says, "I grew up wealthy, a proper Scottish toff in some ways. But my father was extremely . . . sadistic. As you Americans would say, he was a 'totally fucked-up dude.'"

He puts on an American accent to lighten the mood, but some truths are too heavy to be lightened, no matter how hard we try.

"All the money in the world, but no kindness. No love. He thought he was toughening me up, too—but it was just his cruelty. Sometimes he'd make me do things just to see me struggle. It didn't matter if I had material things. The emotional scars Da left on me were far worse."

It might be the most honest thing Axe has ever said to me. My chest aches at the thought of him as a little boy running through the grounds of a sprawling Scottish estate, unprotected from the harshness of his father's expectations. His eyes glinting with determination and hurt.

Before I can think, I reach out, taking his hand in mine. "I'm sorry you had to go through that. No child should have to prove their worth to their parents. And your mom? What is she like?"

He just shakes his head, like, *Yeah, that's enough sharing for today,* and I know right away, without him even saying it, that she's gone.

Oh, Axe . . . I let him step closer until I can feel his breath on my skin. Axe is so big that just being near him makes it feel like he could block out the whole world. It's like we're both finding this unexpected sense of safety in the space between us, breathing the same air, carrying the same weight. We've just laid out our childhood messes, exposed all the scars, and there's something strangely deep about being this raw with someone.

When he pulls back to look at me, his hand momentarily cradles my cheek, his index finger brushing away the tear that's slipping down my face. Surrounded by the scent of market roses and the faint, fading warmth of the winter sun, as I stare into his eyes, I feel the whole world disappear, leaving only the magic of the here and now.

"I'm sorry to tell you, lass," he says, and now I hear the old Axe again, his voice a tease, "that between your daft mum's antics and our mutual childhood trauma revelations, this date, so far, has been an absolute cock-up. I might rather burn this data than hand it over to the team."

"I won't tell if you won't tell," I say. "Let's start all over, right now."

Axe does a ridiculous moonwalk, as if he's reversing time. I'm charmed. He's not usually goofy.

"Done," he declares, stopping mid-step with a flourish. "Now let's do some strolling, a wee bit of small talk, and maybe buy a few tatties."

"Tatties?" I choke out.

"Potatoes! Get your mind out of the gutter."

"I think you mean *taters,*" I say.

"I mean *tatties,* bonny lass."

"Okay, fine, tatties," I say, giving in with a smirk. "But they sound like boobs."

He smirks. "Maybe that's why they're my favorite."

TWENTY-SEVEN

AXE

I drop her off at her apartment. Back home, I work all afternoon, but the hours drag, and my focus is scattered. I then sit by the fireplace, drinking, my fists flexed like cudgels, moving only to stoke the flames with the poker. The crackle of the fire fills the silence, but it doesn't burn away what's gnawing at me.

Something about Josie's mother was off. She wasn't thinking about Josie the way a mum cares for a child. Nay, it was deeper, something more controlling. Those eyes on Josie were drained of warmth, as if she saw her daughter not as a person but as a possession. A thing.

It's a look I recognize well. I spent a lifetime around people who treated women like disposable objects, like tools for their own gain.

I think about Josie's childhood—the constant scrutiny, the endless tests, the doctors and nurses who poked and prodded without a thought for her comfort or well-being. Will Josie's work for She's the One trigger those old feelings of being a guinea pig?

I'm used to the beast that is SynthoTech, with its relentless demands and prying eyes. Hell, I built that beast. But for Josie, it might bring back haunting memories and make her feel like an experiment again rather than the strong, independent woman she's fought so hard to become.

The last thing I want is for her to relive that nightmare.

To make her relive her worst trauma.

I drain my whiskey and toss the glass into the fire, a proper Scottish tradition, rich with many meanings. Tonight, I decide to let it symbolize my release from dangerous memories.

I pour myself a second glass, drink it down a little too fast.

Toss that glass into the fire, too. This one is for Josie.

I stand up, resolute. Put the bottle back into the cabinet. I am not yet ready to give up having an excuse to see Josie all the time. And yet, tomorrow, while it might fuck things up with Niles von Shitforbrains, I'll tell her it's not too late to pull out of She's the One.

TWENTY-EIGHT

JOSIE

"You look pale," my mother announces the moment she opens the door. Not *Hello* or *Sorry about yesterday.* Not even *I'll never forgive you.*

How could I be pale? I slept for thirteen hours and slathered on enough self-tanner to look borderline orange. Turned out the stomach bug, awful as it was, was nothing. Here one day, gone the next. Mom, on the other hand, looks all bouncy and polished like she just rolled out of a luxury salon, with her "red" hair freshly tinted, and she's sporting fresh nail extensions that are definitely not from Nailed It, where she works, but from one of those upscale spots downtown.

"Well, I promise you, I am *fine,*" I insist, flashing a grin. "Look, I'm so good I made you a lemon cake. When life gives you lemons . . . *ba-dum-bump.*"

She takes the cake with a neutral nod. "Thanks."

"About yesterday, I'm sorry—" I start, but she cuts me off.

"It's just that when I see you out and about when you should be in bed, I worry," she scolds. "I'm a mom, Josie. That's what moms do. And then I was shoved away from you like a criminal."

"I was working, and I asked you politely to leave."

"I don't like this new job of yours. Axe MacKenzie is notorious around here. His takeover of the old Merchants Exchange Building left a lot of people without jobs."

"That place had been closed for years! He *brought* jobs to Shelton, Mom. Lots of them."

"Well, if he's so smart, he should have seen that you were unfit to be working. Even if you're just a personal assistant."

I wince. That's the lie I told her when I got the job. My confidence wavers. Mom has always diagnosed me before the doctors, like some hyper-attuned therapy dog. What does she see that I don't? "How are you doing, Mom?"

She pouts and shrugs. "Fine." It's all I'm going to get. "Come sit and have a cup of tea. It'll put some color in your cheeks. I already made breakfast."

It's a truce, if only a fragile one. I sit before a plate heaped with scrambled eggs and microwaved bacon. Though my stomach's settled, it's too early for such a feast. But I won't show weakness. I pick up my fork. She pours me tea—bitter and medicinal, but at least it's iced. Mom fancies herself an herbalist, and she's always pushing us (unsuccessfully, so far) to sell her teas at Grace & Honor.

"Where's Alan?" I ask.

"Bryan's with him. He likes keeping the old man company. Very sweet of him, don't you think?"

I fight the urge to roll my eyes. "Bryan's an asshole," I say, "and he's probably getting Alan to put money in his fantasy ice hockey league. His main revenue stream these days."

"Language, Josie Marie." Her voice cracks like a whip as if I'm ten again. "Alan took care of you. So did Bryan."

"And now I can take care of myself!" My voice is shrill. Now I sound and feel like a defensive teenager.

"I think you should make a checkup appointment with Dr. Don. Just to be sure."

My rage kicks up a notch, my pulse gone rogue. Dr. Don, my longtime pediatric oncologist. He was the only one who ever understood my medical maze, so he stayed on as my primary care doctor even after I entered adulthood. I owe him for saving my life multiple times, but I can't stand the man. Silver hair, round blue eyes like marbled ice. He delivered bad news with the grin of a clown at a child's birthday party. And then there was his treatment. His "special drink" he called it. Some concoction he'd mix up and serve in a paper cup and watch me swallow "for strength." Though all it ever did was make me groggy. I hated the taste. Hated him more for making me drink it.

No way. I haven't seen that guy in years.

"There's absolutely no reason to book an appointment with Dr. Don."

I make surprisingly good progress on my eggs and bacon—amazing what a desperation to get out of here can do—and sip the tea without gagging.

This kitchen looks different, I realize. There's a throw rug under the table, and is that a new coffee machine?

"Should I tell Bryan you'll call him? It would be nice!" Mom shouts out to me a little while later when I've finally escaped the house and am climbing into my car.

"Nope!" I sing back cheerfully. No reason to engage. I'm not going to go ham on my mother for being so fucking clueless.

"Let me at least make an appointment with Dr. Don."

"Nope!" I sing again in full JosieFightsOn sunshine warmth.

Once I've closed my door, I double-check that Bryan is still blocked on my phone. Then I block Dr. Don's office, too. I feel all the fake goodwill seep from my body as my hands curl into fists.

On the drive home, I let it all out, saying every single thing I swallowed back at breakfast. Poor Gertrude's used to these rants by now. Behind the wheel is one of the few places I can actually drop the whole JosieFightsOn bullshit and just admit that, yeah, everything's not fine. I'm mid–yelling out loud about my mother—*and when will she start treating me like a grown-up?!*—when vertigo hits hard and fast. Up flips to down, down to up. My brain feels like Disney's spinning teacups, only this is real, and I'm in danger.

Are my hands still on the wheel? Why is this happening?

The traffic light ahead blurs into a red halo.

I slam on the brakes, a loud squeal pierces my ears, and I brace for impact.

TWENTY-NINE

AXE

I cancel my kickboxing, ditch my afternoon meetings, and hop on my bike. I can't focus for shite. I don't even realize where I'm headed until I end up on a quiet, semi-residential street in a part of Shelton I never bother with. Of course.

I push open the door to Grace & Honor, and a bell jingles above me. The air's fragrant with the scent of lavender and polished wood. Cozy place, shelves crammed with more candles and homemade soaps than any sane person would ever need.

An arrow points to a corner strung up with chili pepper lights—aye, that'll be the infamous erotic section everyone whispers about. A Snuggle Bunny vibrator stares back at me from the shelf, complete with cheeky bunny ears and a grin to match. I'd be grinning like that, too, if I got to be near Josie every day.

I don't spot the security system Strike's company installed, but I trust it's top-notch. It'll keep Josie safe, or so I hope. Truth is, there's no such thing as a truly safe space in this world, not outside my house or Strike's compound. Still, it's hard to picture anything bad happening here, buried under all this potpourri and these ribbon-tied bundles of sage.

My heart leaps to see Josie behind the counter, her red curls falling forward as she concentrates on the ledger in front of her. When she looks up and sees me, her eyes widen in surprise.

"Axe," she says, and—Christ. That smile. It takes over her face like sunrise, and then it's almost immediately replaced by a worried frown. "What are you doing here? Did I miss an appointment?"

"Nah. I just wanted to see how you were since you were feeling poorly yesterday," I say, stepping closer, keeping my voice easy. "For the record, no body cameras recording. Just us."

She nods her head, and I read a hint of relief.

"Oh, thank you. I'm much better today."

But when she shakes her head, I see there's a faint bruise forming on her cheek. My gut clenches. "For fuck's sake, Josie—what happened to you?"

She shrugs and then almost reflexively lifts a hand to her cheek.

"Oh, that. It's been . . . a morning. It's nothing, really."

Tears glisten in her eyes, and she blinks fast, like she's been trained out of letting people see her cry—who the hell taught her that she never has a right to be upset?

"Josie," I say. I keep my hands clenched at my sides, though I want to cup her jaw and look more closely at that bruise. She should get some ice on it. "Tell me."

She stares down at her finger tracing the edge of the counter, her teeth gnawing her bottom lip. She's full-body trembling now, and it takes all my willpower not to sweep her into a hug. I can tell that's not what she wants, though. She wants to stand on her own two feet. I can't help but admire the heck out of this woman.

"Fender bender," she admits, and shakes out her arms as if to let it all go. "I was coming here from breakfast at my mom's. I wanted to make up. We left things badly yesterday, as you saw."

She looks down and gathers herself. I wait.

"So, the apologies sucked, but whatever. It wasn't terrible. Just Mom being my least favorite version of Mom. Then, on the way home, I don't know how to explain it. There was this red light . . . and this vertigo just seemed to come out of nowhere. I've never had it like that before. And never while driving."

"Vertigo?" I ask, my own mind spinning now, recalling some of my medical training. "That could be an infection or an inflammation. Sometimes stress or anxiety can trigger it, too. Any changes in medication recently? Dehydration can also cause vertigo. We ought to look into it."

"Yeah, I will . . ."

"Sorry. Sorry. I didn't mean to pry." I mentally kick myself for saying *we*. There is no *we* who will be looking into anything. I'm annoyed that I did what everyone else does with Josie—treat her as if she's weak, when she's unbelievably strong.

"I've got to hope it's nothing, even though with me, it's always something. I blacked out, I think?" She blacked out? I have the sudden urge to throw this woman over my shoulder, run out of here, and keep running until she's safely tucked into my bed. "Anyhow, the accident was all my fault. I crashed into a mailbox." She sighs shakily. "It could have been worse. Thank God I didn't hurt anyone."

My heart clenches. "Are you all right? Physically? Mentally?"

She takes a deep breath, then nods. "Yeah, just a bit shaken up. And bruised. When I was a child, I had an ear operation. Something to do with my equilibrium? Vertigo can still happen randomly, apparently." She touches her ear lightly, as if testing it. "I don't have the best health luck. You know when doctors are like, *Well, that only happens to one in a million people*? I'm always that one."

"Makes sense."

"Excuse me?" she asks.

"You are one in a million, Josie."

At that, she smirks at me like I'm taking the piss. I'm not. She's exceptional.

"Anything I can do to help?" I ask, and her smirk softens into a genuine smile.

"No, but thank you. Poor Gertrude, though. It's not looking good for her."

"I was starting to have feelings for Gertrude, the old bird. She's a bit of a grande dame, with her taped-up side mirrors and dented fender."

"She might be ancient, but she's dependable. It'll be very hard to put her out to pasture." Josie shrugs, then smiles with real affection for that clunker.

"When it's time, we'll have to do a proper send-off. A Viking funeral," I add.

"A decent car wash, at least."

We stand there for a moment, our silence filled with all the things I want to tell her. Mostly how much I care. How seeing her like this makes my chest ache. How even the thought of something she loves being hurt also hurts me and that there's part of me that wants to get my team to haul Gertrude into the body shop for a full tune-up. That car is a liability for the precious cargo it's carrying.

Suddenly, the solution hits me. "So it's a good thing we added section eighty-nine, subsection A," I say.

"Huh?"

"The paragraph that says your new position comes with a brand-new car."

"Ha." She rolls her eyes, but that contract was as thick as a footlocker, and I can tell she's not quite sure if I'm telling the truth.

"Gertrude should get me to and from Toygasm tomorrow," she says. "That's my last request. Then, maybe, we can throw her a retirement party. But you are NOT buying me a car, Axe MacKenzie."

THIRTY

JOSIE

Of course Axe MacKenzie got me a car.

Parked right in front of my building is a sleek, shiny, new red electric Mini Cooper, buffed and gleaming, a sunflower tucked under the windshield wiper, along with a note with my name scrawled on the front. I pluck it between my fingers and read:

> Key's in Dame Gertrude's glove box.

My heart does a backflip.

This is wild. I can't accept this gift, of course. It's way too much. But . . . borrowing it for tomorrow's trip to Philly? That's reasonable, right?

Seeing Axe earlier felt like a rush of heat, tension, and something deeper I can't quite name, all igniting at my core. My nerve endings are still tingling, caught in the aftershock of a spark I can't put out.

I retrieve the key, and as much as I want to hop in and take the new car for a spin, I feel a twinge of loyalty to Gertrude. I take a deep breath and begin the solemn task of unloading my trusty old companion. Sliding back into Gertrude's well-worn seat, I inhale deeply, savoring the familiar lavender from the sachets I've stashed all over the place—hugs for my senses.

I tuck one into my pocket to bring into the Mini.

Next, I pull out my overpacked medical kit. "Josie fights on," I mutter sarcastically, transferring the essentials to the Mini's pristine trunk, frustrated that today brought yet another medical incident. *You can never be too careful.* Mom's voice echoes in my head, and I almost chuck the kit out of spite. But then I touch my still-sore cheek. Maybe it is time for a checkup. *Not* with Dr. Don, though.

Right now, I need to get ready for Toygasm, the premier sex toy expo happening in Philly. Grace & Honor's never had a booth there before, but since I took over as manager, I've revamped the website and boosted online sales, and now this expo is the next step in my plan to expand the store's reach. I want to put us on the map for sex toy enthusiasts nationwide.

For a second, I think about inviting Axe. Maybe it could be useful for She's the One . . . but no, I'm just making excuses to see him. A sex toy expo isn't exactly the most appropriate place to bring my hot new boss. Especially when I wouldn't mind playing with some of the toys with him.

As cramped as this apartment is, the hidden gem is my deep bathtub. And tonight, I'm going to make the most of it. I draw a hot bath, rose-scented steam from my bath bomb rising up in misty curls, softening the rough edges of a long day. As I sink deeper into the bath, I find a washcloth, soak it in the warm water, and glide it slowly over my skin.

I close my eyes, letting the heat of the water and even hotter thoughts wash over me as the fantasy takes hold. I can almost feel Axe's presence here, his giant, rough hands brushing softly over my cheek, then sliding lower, over my wet skin, leaving a trail of sparks. My breath catches as I let the washcloth slip lower, stroking myself with a gentle rhythm, imagining it's Axe's tongue instead. Down my thighs, over the soft swell of my belly, and then finally between my legs.

I picture his eyes—their piercing, stormy blue, intense and unrelenting—staring into mine. Those eyes that never miss a single detail. The way they lock onto me, possessive and demanding, like I'm the only thing in the room worth seeing.

As if he's the only one who gets to call me his.

I have no doubt he'd be able to read my body and play me like an instrument.

My breath hitches as I let go of the washcloth and my finger finds a steady rhythm on my clit, circling, building tension. The warm water feels cool compared to the heat building in my body, each stroke notching me higher than the last, and I can actually feel the heat of his breath against my skin. In my mind, Axe is devouring me, lapping at my pussy, enjoying my desperate moans. My heartbeat quickens, my skin prickling as I imagine him scooping up my ass to get a better angle with his tongue.

A small yelp escapes my lips as the pleasure builds, the tension winding tighter and tighter. I can almost hear his voice—*Come for me with that pretty pussy, Josie*—imaginary Axe is a dirty talker and I like it.

I feel his hands gliding along my hips, guiding me closer and closer to the edge.

My mind is lost in him—and I don't want to come back.

My finger sweeps desperately now, each circle bringing me closer, until finally, with a shudder, I'm there, and I don't care if

I'm loud as I scream in pleasure, because the release is so, so good. My body trembles, my breath ragged as I sink back into the bath, warm bliss flooding through me.

Thanks for that, Axe MacKenzie, I tell him in my mind, ignoring the nagging voice that tells me I just crossed some invisible line.

THIRTY-ONE

AXE

After I leave the real Josie, I spend the evening with AI Josie—or at least the most basic, bare-bones version of her avatar, which Theo sent me. She doesn't talk yet, nor has she been transferred to an operating system. Right now she's nothing more than a series of illustrations showing different emotional scenarios.

All the Josies are right here in front of me.

So close I could reach out and touch her.

I load the pictures onto my three massive computer screens and let myself be surrounded from every angle. I try to stay objective—I am evaluating a SynthoTech product, not gazing at a lass I can't deny I have very strong feelings for.

But it's bullshit, isn't it?

I like Josie. More than I should. I want to protect her. I want to spend more time with her. Every time I touch myself, she's right there. Right at the center of my mind.

But that's as far as I can or will go. She's my employee. Not only would I be setting myself up for a lawsuit, but I only do casual, and Josie doesn't seem the type for casual.

A sharp knock on the door makes me damn near jump. Perched high above the street, my loft—once an old grain warehouse—now offers sweeping views of the city skyline. It's sleek. Modern. Divided into sections: bedroom, office, kitchen, dining room, library.

The library's where I've got my massive custom fireplace, my only nod to Scotland. Even with that small concession, the loft's a far cry from some ancient castle; it's more like a big contemporary studio.

Which is just the way I like it.

"Axe! It's me!" Strike lets himself in, and I immediately regret giving him a key, which was meant for emergencies only.

As in, if I got arrested. Not for random pop-ins.

I scramble to close all the Josies on my screens, but I'm not fast enough. He comes up behind me, takes one look, and bursts out laughing. "Dude, and I thought *I* had it bad."

"I'm working. This is for work. They're the first mock-ups from Theo."

"Sure," he says. "You keep telling yourself that."

"Also, next time, use the fucking doorbell. Why are you here?" I ask. Strike walks over to the bar set up in the corner and pours himself a drink.

"Want one?" he asks, and I shake my head. And then I change my mind.

"Throw me a beer," I say. Strike's the one person I trust to get into my Scotch or raid the mini-fridge. Aside from the staff—who I keep as scarce as possible—he's the only one who's ever set foot in here.

Strike sinks into the cracked brown leather couch, pops his feet up on the coffee table, and tosses me a bottle of Imperial Stag lager.

"So," he says.

"So," I say, and lift an eyebrow.

"So I walk in, and you're staring at three different pictures of Josie. One of which was zoomed in."

"Nope. Not happening. We are not discussing this," I say, because we are not. "It is literally my job to look at pictures of Josie."

"Can I see your notepad? Did you write her name and draw little hearts around it? Did you write *Mrs. Josie MacKenzie* over and over again?"

"Fuck off and give me my fucking key and get the fuck out of my house and stop drinking my best fucking scotch."

"It is delicious."

"I'm going to ask you one more time: Why are you here? Book club isn't till next week."

"Couldn't wait to discuss *The Adventures of Captain Underpants*."

"Motherfucker, get to the point."

"Okay, okay. I looked through those von Graf files you gave me." Last week, I cracked into Primogen Capital's indoor server and pulled ledgers that were hidden behind one hell of an impressive firewall in the Botox Baron's system. Handed them straight over to Strike—he's better with the money trail, while I handle the tech. We're both deadly-as-hell assassins, and a damn good team when he's not too busy taking the piss.

"And . . ." I get to my feet. This is the moment I've been waiting for. Confirmation that von Graffenplastique is, in fact, a sex trafficker. That I can finally take him down. My fingers are itchy to grab a knife right now.

"I'm closing in. No doubt he has a ton of shady money that I haven't yet been able to fully trace. And he's deep in association with all the known buyers, as well as plenty of—as you Scots like to call them—unsavories. We're seventy-five percent of the way there."

"And the other twenty-five percent?" I'm feeling restless, ready to dispatch this guy. The way von Graf's had access to Gemini, even though it's just Josie's avatar or sketches, makes my skin crawl. The sooner the bastard's dead, the sooner I can be sure he'll never get near her—virtually or, God forbid, in real life.

"I'm working on it."

"Work faster," I say, and Strike barks out a laugh. Fair enough. He does not work for me.

"I'm giving you a pass because I know the unique torture of being head over heels in love with someone and feeling certain you can't have that person."

I grab my letter opener—I know fifteen ways to kill a man with it. Strike just laughs, standing up and knocking back the rest of his drink. "Cheers for the scotch, mate."

He salutes me, walks out my front door, and slips into the night. I click, and Josie's back up on my computer screen. I stare at the three smiling images. *Bonny lass.* One word echoes over and over and over again in my head: *love, love, love.*

THIRTY-TWO

JOSIE

You know I'm not keeping the Mini Cooper. I'm driving it to Toygasm, and then bringing it right back to the dealer.

Feel guilty cheating on Gertrude?

Yup. I'm a car monogamist

I hit send and stare at the phone. Is this flirting? Am I flirting? Thankfully, our texts will not be part of data collection for She's the One. Still, I'd be embarrassed if it wasn't so much fun. We've been texting off and on since six this morning. (Does the man sleep? I have no idea what his house looks like, but for some reason, I think of Batman's underground lair—all sorts of tech gadgets under one long concrete roof.)

I'd expect nothing less from you. And I bet Gertrude respects your loyalty. Though I do think she needs a little help on the safety front

You ride a motorcycle and you're worried about safety?

My motorcycle is held together with more than duct tape and good vibes

Right, it's held together with magic and machismo

There's a pause, and then Axe calls me on FaceTime—and even though I'm in the bathroom, trying to wrangle my hair into something that looks less like a hot mess, my desire to see his face is an irresistible gravitational pull.

"Heyyy!"

"Morning." His eyes crinkle with a quick smile, but then he's all business. "I wanted to give you this news in person before you hear it from the crew."

"I'm listening."

"She's the One wants to data map us for a weekend away. Somewhere cozy, not too fancy, and maybe up near Shimmy Beach."

"Oh cool." I sound casual, but I'm squealing inside. I've wanted to go to Shimmy Beach practically my whole life. It's always in Shelton's top-ten nearby romantic destinations, and my Instagram feed is filled with high school friends flaunting engagement rings with Lake Erie shimmering in the background.

Of course, Bryan never wanted to go.

But then it hits me—my first time at Shimmy Beach and I'm not going there for romance. I'm going there for faux-mance, something even less real than all those staged Instagram photo shoots I've long outgrown believing in. In the next moment, I can feel my smile fade, and then I can't help but dive into the awkwardness of it all.

"So, are they going to map out everything? Like, even how I take my coffee and whether I wake up with bedhead?"

Axe laughs, a sound that eases some of my nerves. "I doubt they'll care about the coffee metrics. Also, for your information, you've got resting bedhead."

"Hey!" I pull out my messy bun, trying now to tame it into a high ponytail, even though my hair doesn't do sleek unless I spend hours burning my fingers and singeing my strands on a flat iron.

"Not to worry. I've got a thing for lasses with resting bedhead."

"I'm not blushing, you're blushing," I shoot back with the kind of sarcasm that fools nobody, hoping Axe can't see the red in my cheeks through FaceTime. Compliments and I go together like toothpaste and orange juice, especially when they come from Axe, who never says anything he doesn't mean.

"But, aye, to answer your question, it's pretty comprehensive. There's a whole haptic suit plan. Section twenty-three of the contract."

"Subsection A, and if I remember correctly, there are additional sub-subsections one and two," I say. I keep my voice calm, though I remember *that* part of our agreement very clearly. I have done plenty of haptic suit googling. I feel my pulse skitter at my throat.

"You should have been a lawyer," Axe says with a grin.

"Instead of my lifelong dream of being an AI avatar? Please," I say, smirking. "Look, it'll be fine, as long as the man in the haptic suit knows how to use his controls."

"That I can promise," he says. "I'm actually looking forward to this weekend. We'll take in the sunset and toast with glasses of perfectly chilled, sweating champagne."

"And write each other's names in the sand," I add.

"Only after I sprinkle the hotel bed with rose petals." His voice is laced with teasing. Now my face is full-on tomato as I imagine Axe and me. In the same hotel room. Sharing a bed. No. The contract was specific about two separate rooms, but still, there aren't enough toys at Toygasm to quench the thirst this image has inspired. Not to mention the fact that my escapades last night have only heightened my wanting. Shit.

"Though we'll have separate suites, of course, in our separate haptic suits. Sorry, I didn't mean to imply . . ." Axe trails off. Now Axe MacKenzie is flustered—and Axe MacKenzie doesn't get flustered. Could this be my favorite version of Axe? A little ruffled? His hand pulls through his thick hair, making it stand on end like it's rebelling against him. Him off-kilter is as outrageously sexy as when he's cool and confident.

"Oooh, can you do that thing where I look off into the distance and say, *The view is beautiful,* and instead of looking at the view, you look at me and say, *It* is *beautiful.*" Oh, no—I've gone and accidentally shared my favorite romance trope of all time. "And it's obvious you mean me and not the view?"

"Sounds easy enough. I won't even have to fake it."

My stomach does a giant swoop, and I bite my lip trying not to grin into the camera. "I'm dreading the analytics team reviewing our hand-holding technique. I can already see the feedback: *Fingers were awkwardly entwined. Zero romantic energy.*"

"We wouldn't want to fail hand-holding. Maybe we should practice before, just to make sure we get good scores. Shimmy Beach looks pretty crap—the truth is, if we're going for a lake view, I prefer the Amalfi Coast. Plus, you get Italian food."

When I'm quiet—does this guy know I don't even have a passport?—Axe adds in a lower voice, almost a shy whisper, "Though

I'd rather take awkward, data-mapped Shimmy Beach walks with you than go anywhere else in the world without you."

Does he realize he's not wired? That he doesn't have to say all this nice stuff when we aren't actually on a She's the One date? Certainly, the butterflies in my chest can't tell the difference between real and fake flattery at this point.

Axe and I chat about all the places he's been—and all the places I'm dying to go—until I realize that if I don't leave now, I'm going to be late for the expo.

"Talk later!" I tell him. "Got to get to Toygasm!"

"Bye, luv."

Luv? Another tease? But he's already left the call.

I blink at my phone, then pop it into my bag, wrangle my hair into a messy bun, and run out the door.

The new car is a dream—*sorry, Gertrude, guess we're ethically nonmonogamous now*—and after ninety minutes on I-76, I zip through the doors of the Philadelphia convention center with only a little time to spare.

Life is one wild ride. I spent the better part of my childhood in hospitals. Now, here I am, smack in the middle of Toygasm, the most unhinged sex toy and game expo on the East Coast. Talk about a total one-eighty. I'm still buzzing from my morning cup of Axe, and I'm running on pure adrenaline while I set up the Grace & Honor pop-up before the crowds flood in. I look around and see every kind of sex merch imaginable, and I'm all in on how bright and loud this world is, so different from a sterile treatment facility like MS Hospital.

God, I still remember the pediatric wing with that stupid *Snow White* mural—every night those dwarfs turned into creepy doctors, ready to poke or prod me. Suddenly, I feel the anger trapped in my chest like a fire. I shut my eyes, willing myself to breathe.

Years—*years* under their control. Their pitying eyes. Their needles. Not once did anyone ask me what I needed. Not once did I have a say in my own treatment. I was just some glorified science project so they could feel like heroes. The irony is almost laughable—it's enough to make me want to smash something. But I'm not that helpless kid anymore. And if this job lets me take back even an ounce of power from those assholes who stole my childhood, I'm taking it.

Fuck. Them. All.

Half an hour later, I've turned my fury into focus. I step back to take in my booth, admiring my handiwork. It's a full-on sensory explosion: slick, shiny silicone toys, lots of plush and fuzzy handcuffs, and some of the store's most popular silky lingerie. The whole setup pops against a pale blush backdrop with a giant Grace & Honor logo blazing in fluorescent pink over it.

We've also got some of the more PG stuff we sell at the shop—like scented candles and oils to set that fun, sexy vibe. I snap a quick pic and text it to Honor to show off my work. Then, on a whim, I send it to Axe. Before I can second-guess myself, he texts back: Pure brilliant, Ginger Snap! Well done, you!

I feel a tingle of anticipation. The booth feels like a candy store for grown-ups—and I get to be the candy lady.

The crowd starts pouring in right at 10:00 a.m., and it's game on. I'm all about pitching our sexy stuff, from the basic to the bougie. It's a skill I didn't even know I had until I started working for Honor. She taught me that there's freedom in pleasure, that embracing desire is basically feminist AF, and that selling vibrators should feel as easy as selling a cozy sweatshirt. Turns out, people love talking about what gets them going as much as they love turning on gadgets that buzz, swirl, light up, or heat up in their hands. I don't blame them.

Life is hard—adults gotta play, too. No shame in that.

The vibe here is electric, and there are many other wacky pop-ups that I'm already planning my lunch break around. The Munch Bunch, which is giving out free samples of edible undies; Fifty Shades of Gay, since G&H needs to make sure we stay inclusive; Blow and Tell—I think they sell flavored lubricants?—and lastly, Lord of the Cock Rings, which is self-explanatory. I'm also eyeing Star Whores—looks like they have fun lightsabers—

"Josie! What a surprise to see you here!"

Oh, crapsticks! I blink, staring into the face of that weird Niles von Redscarf, from the other night in the shop. Mr. Amex Black Card is dressed to the nines; from his chinos to his forehead, there's not a wrinkle in sight. His face is so rigid, it kind of looks . . . dead. Ew.

"Hey. Here to explore, or are you on a mission for something specific?" I keep my tone light, aiming for breezy and nonchalant. Like I'm not at all creeped out that the guy who spent hours lurking around Grace & Honor, a good two-hour drive from here, is somehow standing in front of me now. As if it's a coincidence. I shove away the memory of the chipped creamer—the way the sharp edge sliced my skin.

The way Niles just stood looking at me with his plastic, unreadable face and nineties hair when I instinctively brought the cut to my lips.

My finger throbs, like it knows I'm thinking about it.

The bandage is gone, but the thought won't leave: *Did he poison me somehow?*

I take a deep breath and let it out slowly. *Chill out, girl. It's entirely possible this is a coincidence.*

"Actually, I came for the pleasure of your company. You mentioned this event, remember."

"Oh, right." No bell rings in my memory. Did I really mention *Toygasm* to *this guy*? I can't imagine that I did. For the last few months, saying the word *Toygasm* has made me giggle so hard that Honor made me practice it in the mirror like a mantra: *I am serious. I can say* Toygasm *without laughing.* I can't imagine I offered it voluntarily to Frozen Face. "It's going to be a busy day, though," I say, trying desperately to sound like I have better things to do. "Lots of customers so far." Of course, for the first time since we opened, my booth is empty.

Niles leans in way too close, his eyes locking onto mine with this intense stare that cranks the awkwardness up another level. Which is impressive, honestly, because I didn't think I could feel more awkward than I already did, standing here, holding a remote-control butt plug in the curlicue shape of a pig's tail.

"I'd always go the extra *Niles* for a moment with you," he says softly.

I laugh while stepping back from his bad wordplay like a fart.

"Well, good thing you've got the whole expo to dazzle you. Anything catch your eye?" I gesture vaguely toward the colorful displays behind me, hoping he gets the hint and takes his weird energy somewhere else. Wouldn't he rather hit on the lady working over at the Spank Bank? She looks ready for anything. "Everything is Beatles-themed at the Cum Together booth."

Niles shrugs, and now we fall into one of those bizarre prolonged silences—like he's buffering. "This whole scene is quite a . . . carnal carnival," he says finally, his face lit up with pride at his latest bit of wordplay.

"Right," I say awkwardly. "There's lots of funny names here. There's the Friction Fiction booth over there. I think that's some kind of audiobook app with . . . sensors? And I might grab lunch later at the Tickle My Pickle sandwich booth, or—" but now I stop, watching his eyes go wide.

"We could go together," he says flirtatiously. "A bite to eat, on me? Dildonuts looks good."

"Um." I make a face of pretend regret. "I actually have to work all day, so—"

"Of course. You're busy," he says, smooth as butter. "Actually, I came here to find out when you could have dinner." He takes out his phone. "And I won't take no for an answer. Tonight, or whenever you're free this week. I have a standing reservation at Le Palais Gastronomique. I know the chef quite well—he's a magician. There's a truffle-infused snail tartare that might sound peculiar, but is . . ." He makes a little chef's kiss with his fingers, which makes his plumped lips wobble. Then he leans in, dropping his voice in a way that I guess is supposed to be sexy. "Come on, Josie. Try me. For something new and different."

My stomach turns in disgust.

"I . . . I can't. I'm sorry. I . . ." Does this man not sense that he is kind of the human version of snail tartare—slimy, niche, and definitely not to everyone's taste? But he's also a Grace & Honor customer. I need to let him down gently. "Listen, Niles, I think you're cool, and I hope we can be friends. But I can't date you. I just got out of a very serious relationship, and, yeah." I sigh as if it's beyond my powers. "Not dating at the moment."

"Okay, okay. You don't have to tell me twice." He smiles and lifts his hands in the air, as if to say no harm, no foul. "Not interested, no problem."

I relax my shoulders. Phew.

"By the way," he says, "I read my tarot this morning, and I pulled the Tower. I noticed your shop sold tarot cards. Do you know anything about how to interpret that?"

Seriously? He's asking me about tarot? I feel myself perk up. The only thing more fun than talking to people about sex toys is talking to them about tarot. Maybe Niles is more interesting than I realized.

"I do! My nonna taught me when I was young. I never miss a day."

"Me, either, though I'm still a beginner," he says. "I have many decks, but my favorite is one I found in Prague. I was there for work and stumbled upon this antiquities auction, and it called to me. I knew it was meant to be mine."

Okay, that's . . . unexpectedly cool. His veneers, though—so blindingly white, like the grille of a Cadillac, headlights on. But he means to be friendly, I think.

"Drawing the Tower usually means change is on the horizon," I tell him. "It can be unsettling, but it's a chance for renewal."

He nods. "Thanks—that makes sense." He reaches forward and clasps my hand, his touch warm but a little too lingering. "I really appreciate the insight. Finding you feels like picking up a private conversation with a dear old friend." Now he looks so wistful and sad, and my heart tugs with pity. "I don't have that many close friends."

I nod, not sure what to say to that.

"Oh, I almost forgot. I have something for you. One of my clients owns Spa-la-la in Shelton, and they gave me this gift card. I think it's good for at least a couple of treatments. I'll never use it—I'm pretty picky with who gets to touch my body—so figured you might like it?"

"Oh, wow! Thank you!" I take the card, genuinely grateful,

trying to ignore the ick factor of him talking about people touching his body. Mom loves spas; we can do a girls' day. It's a way fancier olive branch than a lemon cake.

And maybe we'll be able to reconnect after we've relaxed.

"Enjoy," he says.

Then I watch him turn and beeline toward a booth called Cock, Paper, Scissors, which looks very BDSM. Well, whatever gets you off.

THIRTY-THREE

AXE

The day has finally arrived. I'm grinning like a Cheshire cat as I settle into the driver's seat of my cherry-red convertible McLaren 720S Spider.

The roar of the engine is pure music.

All week, when I wasn't working with the tech team, tinkering with our haptic suits, or thinking about Josie—who am I kidding? I'm Axe MacKenzie, I can do both at the same time—I've been digging deeper into von Graf. Cracking his password-protected files delivered me a treasure trove of gruesome information about Primogen Capital's dealings—if not a peep about his family or personal life.

I shift gears, blow past a clown car full of teenagers and a station wagon with a **COEXIST** bumper sticker. The top is down, and I can feel the wind ruffling my hair. I can't deny that I felt an urge to wear driving gloves—the McLaren practically begs you to go ninety—but I settled for badass sunglasses instead.

My mind spins through von Graf's files as I drive, a grim catalog of evil. There's no doubt from the nature of his businesses—import/export, private security firms—that von Graf is a sex trafficker. But I'm surprised by the extent of his operations—this man is truly the Devil incarnate. This bastard has recruiters in twenty different countries and buyers from everywhere. He holds monthly in-person, high-end parties for the world's richest and most debased men at remote locations. (I have not been able to nail down where yet.) He even has a dark web auction site, where he sells off his girls to the highest bidders.

Once Strike and I identify each and every person involved with his enterprise, we'll dismantle his rotten operation piece by rotten piece. As much as I want to—and believe me, my mouth is watering at the idea of carving out this wanker's heart—we never move fast. We are deliberate, careful, sure not to leave any stone unturned.

The last thing I did before I slung my bag into the trunk was send over the newest files to Strike so he can cross-reference them with the names that popped up with Petrov. One common point of interest—Petrov's wife, Veronica. Just as dangerous as him but in a completely different way. She keeps herself planted in the public eye, all smiles and charity events, using her good works to cover the quiet deals and favors she hands out behind the scenes. And if her name keeps springing up, it means this mess is bigger and nastier than we thought.

Good. I am ready for it. Hell, I was born for it.

Then, like the pop of a champagne cork, Josie's text pings on my screen.

> Bikini might be overly optimistic, but it's
> packed—I hope you're bringing an umbrella?
> The official forecast is rain.

We've been texting all week, pretending it's about work, but veering wildly off topic, revealing bits of ourselves that neither of us expected to share. It's madness how easily I can talk to her about everything—except, of course, what's really on my mind.

I picture Josie wearing a bikini, and my thoughts spiral. Not just at the idea of seeing her in that way but at the possibility of this weekend taking us somewhere new. I'm truly unsure of where this will lead. I've imagined so many scenarios, each more distracting than the last, and it's becoming difficult to focus on anything else—and now my dick is pushing up against my zipper.

I dictate a text to my phone: Be there in five. If it rains, I've got a whole plan B. And a playlist that will blow your mind

She responds almost instantaneously: I hope T. Swift is on there

I can't help but grin as I Voice to Text: I've got the full Eras experience

She shoots back an immediate reply: Wait, like—you know all the words?

Quickly I dictate: Every bridge and key change, lass. She's a great storyteller. I could practically go on tour

Her reply makes me snort: I'm so on for us belting All Too Well for the data minions

I hit back with: Try for a She's the One—popstar experience?

Josie: Go big or go home . . .

The light turns green and I step on the gas. My speed climbs, and it takes all my willpower not to push a hundred. I'll be there soon enough.

Need to hide at least a bit of my eagerness.

A weekend of pretending to fall in love—what a daft idea. And yet the only reason I've not swapped myself out with someone else is because this has been the most fun I've had in . . . hell, longer than I care to admit. Christ, I'm in trouble.

The real Josie, smiling when she sees me, stands outside her apartment building with a sprig of jasmine blossoms tucked in her curls. She's casually dressed, in a formfitting sweater and tight jeans that hug her hips and do exactly nothing to cool me down. I am ridiculous. This woman makes me ridiculous. When this project is done, I'm going to have to settle for getting my Josie fix from an AI approximation. Which is also ridiculous.

"Wow, this car!" But the minute she hops in, the rain clouds decide to sprinkle a light drizzle over us.

"Should I pop up the top?" I ask. "I think we're going to drive through it."

"No, keep it open. It's just a mist," she says, smoothing her hair. But then, in the next minute, I've got to work to keep from laughing.

"What's so funny?" she asks, but she knows, as her fingers work to tame those wild ringlets.

"Is that what the rain does to your hair, lass? It looks like it doubled in size."

"Not funny."

"I'm just imagining you in the Scottish Highlands. It's all mist all the time. You'd be pure Medusa."

"Watch your mouth, or I might turn you to stone right now," she jokes, but her cheeks are red.

Now I roar with pent-up laughter as I press the button to close the roof. "Ach, look at that. We managed to wrestle all those curls under one roof."

She rolls her eyes. "You're just jealous you can't pull off this look."

"Only teasing, mind," I say. I've been looking forward to this weekend so long, and as good a sport as she is, I don't want to ruin it with my smart mouth. If she only knew how much I've dreamed of seeing her hair spread out on my pillow, of letting my hands cup the back of her neck. How badly I'd like to be responsible for that untamed bedhead.

Josie shifts. "I think I'm sitting on your phone—here—" She's about to give it back, but then it dings with a new text message that plays across the car's screen. Dammit. I'm usually more careful about my privacy but I've never had anyone in my passenger seat before.

> Strike: Got the file. Nice work. Now have fun, and don't forget to grab your Magnum XLs for if it goes one way 🍆 and a spare room key in case it goes another.

Josie's eyes narrow when she reads the message. She looks up at me, horrified.

"Ah, that's just . . . give me that." I paw for my phone and then jab at the screen to make it go away. Fucking Strike. I am going to destroy him. It will be a miracle if she doesn't make me turn this car around and go right back to Shelton.

"Seriously. What the hell, Axe? He used an eggplant emoji!"

"I'm sorry, luv. Strike is just being an arsehole. Since before we even met, he's been trying to set us up," I admit. This is true. Long before I first clapped eyes on Josie at Honor's art show—when she rightly put me in my place—Strike was telling me how he'd found my soulmate and couldn't wait for us to meet.

Soulmate was not a word I'd ever heard Strike use, even when he'd proposed to his deceased wife. I'd put his new romantic streak down to Strike suddenly finding himself madly, stupidly in love and then madly, stupidly heartbroken when, for a while there, it looked like he and Honor were going to crash and burn.

Josie softens a bit. I pick up speed again, like if I get us to

Shimmy Beach fast enough, she'll be less likely to make me turn the car around.

"Honor wanted to set us up, too. She was so bummed when I . . ." Josie stops, embarrassed.

"When you *hated me* on sight?" I say.

"I did not *hate* you," she says, crossing her arms. "I found you . . . insufferable."

"And now?" I ask.

"You're still insufferable," she says, but there's a smile sneaking into her voice. "And also kind of great."

I try to keep a straight face, but I can feel a grin breaking through.

"Magnum XLs . . . ?" she asks.

"I didn't say it. Strike did," I say and wait a beat. "But . . . he's not stretching the truth."

Josie's jaw drops, and as I'm about to lean over and close it, we both jump as a zap of lightning breaks in front of us, followed by a thunderclap that rattles the car. The sky opens up and the rain pours down in buckets.

Reckon we're going to plan B.

THIRTY-FOUR

JOSIE

Axe pulls over to the side of the road. The storm has hit hard and fast, and it's impossible to see more than one foot in front of the windshield.

"The rain can't keep up like this. Let's wait it out for a few minutes," he says.

I appreciate that he's not going all macho and putting us in a dangerous situation. Bryan once drove us through a blizzard so he could grab a jalapeño double cheeseburger from a Carl's Jr. drive-through. He couldn't even be convinced to stop at the closer KFC, because to him, my life was worth less than a Big Angus El Diablo.

The car smells like new leather and Axe's cologne—it reminds me of woodsmoke and Christmas morning. We are cocooned in here, rain pounding on the roof like background music, with the windows all fogged up. Axe turns in his seat to face me, and I feel his look all down my body, especially between my legs.

"So now what?" he asks.

"You totally planned this, didn't you? Getting trapped in a storm is like a perfect fantasy scenario." I meet his gaze, but it's intense—too intense. His blue eyes are burning holes right through me. I have to look away.

The moment feels electric. My heart's racing and my stomach's in knots in the worst best way.

"I do not control the weather, Josie Greene." There's something about him saying my full name that makes me go weak in the knees. He reaches out his hand, and he traces my jaw with his fingertip until he reaches my chin. He tilts my head the slightest bit up so I have no choice but to look at him again. My chest burns, but I shiver. "Are you cold, lass?"

Is he wired already? Are we being live streamed for some corporate control room so that data crunchers can pore over and parse every charged moment between us? I picture a white van not too far away, like something out of an FBI sting operation. A mismatched pair of cops laughing at me for falling for this man's every line. I shake away the thought. This may be a job, but I was wrong about Axe. He'd never make me the butt of the joke.

"I'm fine. It's toasty." Though the heat I'm feeling has nothing to do with the temperature.

"Thanks for coming with me. For doing all this," he says, his voice low and sincere.

I shrug, trying to play it cool. "I needed a health insurance plan."

"True, but this whole thing—the dates, the haptic suits, us using you as a model—isn't easy. And you've been so open and game. I appreciate it." Axe pauses and then seems to make a decision. "The whole team does."

The team. Of course. Two steps forward and one step back.

"Well, it hasn't all been torture. I bet Shimmy Beach will be cool." I lean back, trying to sound breezy. "Even though it's no Toygasm."

Then Axe drops his gaze to my lips, and electricity zings between us again—*oh God, I desperately want him to kiss me*—but

I see him change his mind. He turns to look out the windshield. "Rain's letting up a little. We can still make up for some time."

Carefully, he maneuvers us back onto the highway. The rhythmic sound of the windshield wipers slows, and I watch as patches of blue sky peek through the heavy clouds. Anticipation fizzes up inside me.

"You know, I've never been so far north," I tell him, "although my mom drove me to Long Island once. But that was just because they had to run some diagnostic tests. I was only at the blood lab."

Axe frowns, his hands tightening around the steering wheel as he returns his focus to the rain-slicked road. "Nobody can accuse you of having a carefree childhood, can they, lass?" he asks, but it's not a question. Not really.

"Maybe not—but this morning I pulled a tarot card," I tell him. "Got the Fool, so I knew today was gonna be a good one."

Axe shoots me a look, intrigued. "All right. I'm listening."

"Well, the Fool's all about unexpected stuff—like crazy, funny adventures," I explain. "Which is basically what we're doing, right? Every day with you is a whole wild card situation. To be honest, I'm gonna miss these wacky fake dates."

Axe smiles, but then suddenly seems to sink deep in thought. I go quiet, too. I wonder if he's thinking what I'm thinking—that, yes, soon this will all be over. The She's the One team will have their info, and my ongoing work will involve tweaks with the tech guys and some voice-over instead of these elaborate dates.

At least he'll be left with an AI Josie. I'll be left with nothing at all.

Scratch that. I'm getting health insurance, keeping my cute new apartment, and starting a whole new life thanks to this opportunity. And right now, I'm sitting in a sexy sports car in the middle of a rainstorm next to the hottest guy I've ever seen. Might as well soak it all up while I can. And if I literally have to sit on my hands for the rest of this trip just to stop myself from grabbing Axe and kissing him . . . welp, that's just part of the job, I guess.

By the time we pull up to the Nautical Nook, the rain has calmed down to a gentle mist. The air feels clean and cool, and I'm feeling oddly good, despite the fact that I've been snacking on Sour Patch Kids and Bugles for the last forty miles. No sugar crash, no headache, and miraculously, no asthma attack from the humidity—Mom would be stunned. Axe, on the other hand, is out of the car like a shot. "What the fuck?" he snaps, looking hugely pissed, though clearly not at me. I have no clue why he's mad. The storm cleared. We made good time.

Presumably, we're back on track, even if I don't know what that track entails.

"What's wrong?" I ask. He looks around, wide-eyed.

"What's wrong? Look at the place! It's a shithole! The team told me it had five stars. Josie, I'm so sorry." I glance at the hotel, then back at Axe, then back at the hotel. Honestly, I think it looks pretty adorable. The building is wrapped in a fishing net, there is a giant anchor statue out front, and a hand-painted sign reads **AHOY MATEYS**.

"Maybe it went *overboard* on theme, but I'm kind of into it," I say truthfully as I get out of the car and join him. "Check out that anchor. It's a pirate's dream vacation—I should have brought my waders. Hey, and I bet we find some buried treasure in the minibar."

"We'll be lucky if we find clean sheets." Axe rolls his eyes, but I can tell my treasure joke has landed. "Unbelievable."

“I literally do not get why you’re so stressed.”

He drags his hands through his rain-dampened hair. “I was expecting something with a touch more class and a bit less . . . Jack Sparrow,” he mutters.

“As long as we don’t have to swab decks, I’m all in.”

Axe is still unconvinced. “Look, I can call the team now, and we’ll reroute. I’m sure I can get a suite at the Ritz or the Four Seasons in Philly. I think they’ve booked us dinner at some local French bistro—but it’s cancellable.”

“Nope. We’re in this together. Come on,” I say, slipping my hand through his, feeling the warmth of his skin against mine. A little thrill shoots up my arm as I tug him toward the door, which is designed to look like the entrance to an old ship, complete with a fake wooden wheel affixed to one side as a doorknob. “Remember the tarot? Embrace the unpredictable. This is supposed to be authentic, so we’ll roll with it. Besides, pirates never stay at the Ritz.”

He hesitates, but the heat between our clasped hands seems to sway him. I lead him up the steps, and it’s only after we step inside and approach the check-in desk, which is in the shape of a ship’s bow and manned by a sixteen-year-old in an oversized pirate hat, that I reluctantly drop his hand—just as one of those plastic singing-bass wall plaques starts bellowing “What Shall We Do with a Drunken Sailor?” “See?” I laugh. “You can’t get that kind of entertainment at the Four Seasons.”

“No,” Axe says, and he starts to turn around. “Not happening.”

“You’re a wuss,” I say.

“Ginger Snap, I spent years in private security. I am not a wuss. I refuse.”

“You can’t refuse. The ship has already sailed.”

He levels me with a look. “You did *not* just say that.”

"Oh, but I did." I gesture at the lavish decor. "You need to embrace the theme. Let go, be free."

Axe closes his eyes. "This is my nightmare."

"And follow orders or I'll make you walk the plank." I bump my hip against his and grin up at him. "No joke, I truly love this place and am psyched to be here with you."

"You're a menace, you know that?" But he's smiling a little.

"And you're my first mate. So let's do this."

I turn my attention to the teenager behind the desk. He's dressed in a striped shirt, wears an eye patch, and is clearly deeply embarrassed by this whole setup.

As we approach, he mutters an unenthusiastic "Um, ahoy . . . mateys," his voice barely above a whisper, as if he's hoping we don't hear him. "Checking in?"

"Yup. MacKenzie. Two rooms," Axe says. He's polite but carrying an edge of authority that, along with the half a foot of height he's got over this poor kid, only seems to make the clerk shrink even smaller.

"Yes, sir." The boy, whose on-brand name tag reads SKIP, fumbles with his one eye to type on an ancient computer that's draped in fishing net with a starfish dangling precariously off the side. "Umm, your first name is Axe? Like, for real?"

"For real," Axe says.

"Cool name, bro," he says.

"Is *your* name for real?" I ask with a smile.

Skip blushes as he grins back. "When I'm on the clock, it is. Ma likes a nautical theme."

Now *that's* an understatement. The corner of Axe's mouth quirks up, and I have to hold in my laughter.

After a long minute, Skip looks up. "But I only see a reservation here for one room?" he says, his voice rising at the end like it's a question, and I almost feel sorry for him. Skip suddenly looks like he's staring down the barrel of a cannon.

"Nope, it should be for two. Either way, we need two rooms," Axe says. He keeps his voice firm but kind, a combination that makes people straighten up without realizing why. It reminds me of something Theo once said about him when we were talking through his most recent sketches—that Axe is the type of guy who can lead his team through a storm without ever raising his voice, earning all the respect by just being himself.

Ironic, actually, that he led me safely through a literal storm to this . . . erm . . . ship.

"I'm sorry, sir, but we're all booked."

At that, Axe laughs, as if it's silly to think that anyone would willingly stay at this hotel. I notice that we're back to him calling Axe *sir* instead of *bro*. "Impossible."

Skip is scrambling to make it right. "Uh, okay, let me just, uh, fix that for you. Sorry, uh, sir."

"Come on. I'll pay double the rate. Triple. I'll rent out the whole place. I don't care. We just need two rooms."

Skip looks truly seasick now. He glances over his shoulder, hoping someone might swoop in to save him, like a lifeboat on the horizon. "The thing is, it's my cousin's wedding. Ma will kill me if I give up the rooms. And then with this weather—it's supposed to get bad again—and we're already double-booked." Skip's words come spilling out in a mess, his voice getting higher with every excuse, like a kid trying to talk his way out of detention.

Axe turns to me, and for the first time, he actually looks kind of freaked-out. "I swear I didn't plan this," he whispers, eyes wide with worry.

The idea of Axe plotting something like this is straight-up hilarious. The Axe MacKenzie I know is painfully honest with me. Sure, I've heard he can be a ruthless shark in business, but he's not sneaky. If he wanted us to share a room, he'd have just asked—and probably would have written it into section thirty-nine, subsection C of our contract.

I press my lips together, but the giggle is hard to hold in.

"What's so funny?" Axe looks at me, completely flummoxed.

"It's just that it's the classic one-bed, one-room trope," I say, grinning.

Axe looks blank. "I have no idea what you're talking about."

"You know, in movies or books, when the almost-couple checks into a hotel, and there's *supposed* to be two rooms, but *whoops!*, there's only one, and *surprise!*, there's only one bed? It's iconic. I didn't know this kind of thing actually happened in real life."

He frowns. "That's a thing?"

"Oh, it's a huge thing. Not in my favorite rom-com, *Notting Hill*—but it's all over the genre. Hallmark movies love it. It's practically a rule: one bed, cue sparks! Axe, how do you not *know* this?"

He shrugs, unbothered. "I'm not sure I've ever seen that sort of movie."

I gasp. "Not even *Notting Hill*? But you're *from the UK*!"

"Aye, not even *Notting Hill*."

"No!"

"Aye!"

"We're going to have to fix that," I say, and then blush because I'm making it sound like I assume we'll be hanging out just for fun after the project is over.

Axe turns back to Skip, who's trying to make himself invisible. "What sort of room is available?" Axe asks.

"Umm, it's the Seafarer's Sunrise Suite?" Skip swallows hard. "It's not really a suite, it's just a room. But it does face the sunrise. I think? And I can throw in a free Pirate's Plunder breakfast buffet for two and two complimentary drinks at our excellent downstairs bar, Davey Jones's Lager."

"I mean the bed situation. How many beds?" Axe asks.

"One, sir. There's just one king bed in the room, sir."

"Ha! Of course!" I burst out laughing, already picturing this lone bed that's probably shaped like a boat's hull, with a porthole window looking out on the parking lot. I'm trying *really* hard not to think about the other part—Axe and me stuck together for the whole night—because that thought is making me feel a totally different kind of breathless.

"We'll take it," Axe says tightly.

Skip nods, then hands over a key that is attached to a giant starfish, and all I can think is how much better I could make it with some glitter and a little gold paint.

"Thanks, Skip," I say.

"I'll bring your bags up," he says helpfully.

"No worries, we got it," I say.

"We can still leave right now," Axe says into my ear. I feel a tingle down my spine with his mouth so near. "I didn't drive you here to this blasted, idiotic theme hotel so that you could be uncomfortable."

"I'm happy to be here. I've never been to Shimmy Beach, and I don't think I can live another day without kicking it off my bucket list. So. What can I tell you to get you to stay?"

He thinks, then grins. "You really have a pair of waders?"

"Yep. Green, with the straps and everything."

"You need to promise to wear those waders for me one day."

"Deal." I laugh. "Whatever floats your boat, Axe MacKenzie. If imagining me in waders somehow makes this whole ridiculous situation feel better for you, I'm all in."

But when I catch his eye, the only way to describe how he's

looking at me is smoldering. It's like he's imagining me. Naked. In my waders. And it's the sexiest fucking thing he's ever seen.

He opens the door to the room, and I step in. Axe is right behind me, so close I can feel his breath on my neck. The smile drops from my face, and my entire body heats up. One bed, just like Skip promised.

I am so screwed.

THIRTY-FIVE

AXE

Someone at SynthoTech would be getting the sack if it weren't for Josie's obvious fondness for the Nautical Nook. I shouldn't be surprised, though. She always manages to find the silver lining in any cloud. When the rain stops, we decide to spend the afternoon strolling the boardwalk, and I have to admit, even on a cold, wet day, the charms of Shimmy Beach are growing on me.

The streets are lined with pastel-colored buildings painted with murals of the sea and surfing. The few shops that are open are all the usual kitsch, from the Flamingo Fiesta's dancing flamingos, hula ornaments, and refrigerator magnets to my personal favorite, Bubble & Squeak, a bath and body shop.

The skies are low and dark, and Lake Erie stretches out before us like black glass. It's a moody backdrop that feels familiar.

"Think the Nautical Nook's got a backup generator?" I ask. Josie laughs, and it's fast becoming my new favorite sound. She's been downright giddy since we got here, with just a wee bit of nerves underneath. I'm nervous, too, if I'm honest. She knows that after dinner, we're meant to be putting on those haptic suits. We were supposed to be communicating virtually, from totally separate rooms, as per the contract.

Not real sex, of course, but a simulated approximation.

I cannot fathom how we'll make this work in one king bed.

I know how I'd like to make it work: without haptic suits and data recording and remanufacturing our date into someone else's fantasy. I want my skin on her skin. My lips on her lips. I want to lick the curve of her hip.

I want to hear her gasp my name and then beg for more. I want to *plunder her.*

She's mine, I think. Like a stupid goddamn pirate who thinks he's entitled to treasure he doesn't deserve.

"Yeah, unlikely. But there really is a brass-bound chest at the end of the bed. I wouldn't be surprised if there are flashlights in there," she says. "That or a fake skeleton."

"And here I thought it would be filled with gold coins."

"You have enough gold coins, MacKenzie."

"My work— Watch it," I say as I notice a drunken old man who I clocked stumbling out of a pub a few minutes ago lurching toward us. Although he seems harmless—likely a local who had one too many rainy-day pints—I instinctively pull Josie closer, wrapping my arm tightly around her and guiding her far out of his reach. I firmly clasp her hand in mine and tuck them both into my pocket to keep her fingers warm and safe. "My work has actually never been about money for me," I say, picking up the conversation.

"Then why do it?" she asks, and I feel a flicker of shame. I shrug, wishing I'd kept my mouth shut. She's working for insulin and rent. I've never had to think about either of those things.

Me, I'm working for revenge.

"Tell me something I don't already know about you," she says, sensing I'm pulling back. "Something no one else knows."

"You know a fair bit about me," I say. "Too much, I reckon. We've shared enough text adventures to write a saga."

"True," she says. "But with you, there's always another twist."

"Let me think." She likes my stories about boarding school. "Ah, there was that one time at the Queen Victoria School when I dressed up as Father Christmas, and I gave out pies to all the teachers."

"That's so sweet," she says. "I can totally picture you as Santa."

"Aye, but the kicker is they gave everyone food poisoning!" I throw back my head in a laugh. "Nearly got myself expelled. They thought I had done it on purpose. It took Hamish to bail me out."

"Hamish?" she asks, curious.

I hadn't meant to let that name slip. But there's something about Josie that makes me want to share things I've kept buried. "My half brother," I tell her. "He died. Many years ago."

"Oh," she says gently. "I'm so sorry."

"It's all right. I barely knew him, to be honest. He was a good bit older. But when the headmaster accused me of spiking the pies and making everyone rat-arsed sick, Hamish came down and said he'd been the one who sent the cakes. Got me out of a right mess."

"Nice save. You must have had such a special bond," she says.

"We did," I say. "But then things changed—*he* changed—and we drifted apart. I hadn't seen or even spoken to him in a decade when I heard he'd passed. He was living the fast life. Hard drugs, drinking, you know the type."

Josie nods. Watching me.

I take a breath. "So when I heard he'd crashed his Porsche, it wasn't too much of a surprise."

"Sounds like he was a lot to handle," she says quietly.

"He was." I nod, my mind slipping back to memories I've tried to bury.

"What a loss, though," she says. "I always wanted a sibling." She touches my arm gently. "I'm here anytime if you want to talk about him." Her smile is soft, her eyes full of understanding. I'm still startled that I've spoken Hamish's name—I've not said it once since he died—but I'm even more surprised by how much comfort Josie's words have brought me.

Her gaze locks with mine, and that undeniable electric tension builds between us, drawing us closer together. In this moment, all the words we've shared evaporate, leaving only the heat of connection between us. It feels like we're the only two people on the boardwalk, maybe the only two people in the whole wide world.

I lean in slowly, feeling my heart hammer as she moves closer. I've never wanted to kiss someone so badly in my life. Our lips meet chastely at first, but then our kiss deepens in heat, urgency. I trail kisses along her jawline and softly across her cheeks, savoring the warmth of her skin. Each touch sends a shiver through me, and I can feel her responding with the same intensity—

My phone rings, snapping me out of it.

I groan and pull back, torn between answering it and staying in this perfect moment with Josie.

It's Strike. I've got to take it. I know he's got an answer for me.

THIRTY-SIX

JOSIE

Axe raises a finger and mouths, *One sec,* then steps away down the boardwalk to take the call. I'm just standing there, frozen, my lips still tingling like they've been branded. What is even happening to me? I've never felt like this. Not with Bryan. Not with any of those awkward guys before him.

I'm literally *craving* him. Aching in places I didn't even know could ache, and I have no clue if I can handle this level of . . . whatever this is. I've got a high pain tolerance, but do I have a high enough tolerance for this? The kind of connection where you just hand over your heart and hope they don't drop it?

"Is it done?" Axe asks into his phone, his question carried over with the wind. The call's timing couldn't have been a coincidence. The universe is telling us to cool our jets, to take a step back, not to cross this line. Right?

"Aye, aye," Axe says, and I can't help but smile. He sounds like a pirate. I wish I'd brought a white ruffled blouse for dinner tonight; Axe would have cracked up. Maybe I can scrounge up a parrot for my shoulder.

"We'll move on him as soon as I'm back. Nice work," Axe says, and there's an edge of triumph in his voice. I wonder what happened? Did he secure more funding for his project?

"Everything all right?" I ask when he ends the call.

"Yup. Just our bro Skipper calling to confirm dinner." I look skeptical, but Axe is sticking with his story. "Sure you want to cancel the posh French place?"

"One hundred percent," I say with a laugh, thinking about Niles and his offer of snail tartare. "Let's keep things simple."

We head back to the hotel to shower and change. Axe has been in a good mood since his call—yeah, definitely not Skip—but it's not my place to push. If he's lying, he's probably got his reasons. And judging by that smug smile he keeps trying to hide, I'm assuming it's SynthoTech-related.

We take turns getting ready in the bathroom, both of us pretending not to notice the giant king-size bed right there in the middle of the room, taunting us. I've put on my navy polka-dot sheath; Strike comes out wearing dark blue jeans, a crisp white shirt, and a baby-blue cashmere sweater so soft it makes me want to rub my face against it.

The not-French, not-fancy restaurant Skip picked for us is called the Sock Hop Stop, a cute retro diner a block away from the Nautical Nook.

We slide into a bright red vinyl booth as "Rock Around the Clock" plays from the jukebox in the corner. The walls are plastered with framed classic posters of fifties icons and shiny records, giving the place a cute authentic vibe.

Our waitress (name tag: SALLY) bounces over to us. She's got on a poodle skirt and saddle shoes, and she looks like she just stepped out of a fifties movie. Shimmy Beach sure loves a costume. "Hey there, doll!" she says, her eyes lighting up as she takes in my outfit. "Your dress is the bee's knees! You look like you stepped right out of a vintage magazine."

"Aw, thanks." I smile.

What Sally doesn't know as she slides over our laminated menus and starts hyping up the "classics"—milkshakes ("malt's the best, obvi") and cheeseburgers—is that Axe and I are basically undercover. We've got recording devices strapped under our clothes and little monitor stickers stuck to our chests like we're walking science experiments. Later, each dumb joke and awkward laugh we share will be fed into some AI program, analyzing every tiny heartbeat blip like it's cracking the code to our souls.

This is my first time wearing the tech, and I decide my best bet is to pretend it's not even there. I have no idea how any of it actually works; I've chosen blissful ignorance.

The whole point, I know, is for us to believe this date is real. Sounds great in theory, making our reactions seem genuine, but in practice, it feels risky. I have to keep reminding myself this is a job. Like I'm pinching myself to wake up from a dream. These new feelings I have about Axe are as synthetic as this diner's corny fifties vibe or when someone declares their love on *The Bachelor.* Except . . . there was that kiss.

Even now, the way Axe absently runs a hand through his tousled hair while studying the menu is so distracting that it's becoming way harder to tell what's genuine and what's not. How can anyone look so effortlessly handsome while deciding if he wants cheese fries?

As I sit across from him, every fiber of my being is telling me this is the real thing. Hoo boy. I try to lose myself in the upbeat energy of the Sock Hop Stop and Sally. I'd bet my paycheck she's a romantic, dreamy Pisces. The place is buzzing, packed with tourists all in on the corny, rained-out delights of Shimmy Beach. The jukebox is now blasting "Good Vibrations," and the smell from the grill is a total sensory overload, making it easy to forget that we're being monitored.

I look up from my menu to see Axe staring at me with a smile that could light up Times Square.

"What?"

"You," he replies, his eyes twinkling. "You're glowing. Like you belong right here inside this timeline. I suppose an all-American girl is every Scotsman's fantasy."

I laugh, feeling a blush rise to my cheeks, suddenly remembering those *Highland Heartthrobs* books I used to binge-read as a kid. It was a series about Scottish avengers and the women who loved them. Tartan kilts, manly thighs, even bagpipes made the cut as sexy. Thanks to those books, I now know that real Scots go *regimental*—a fancy way of saying they wear nothing underneath those kilts. Safe to say I never looked at tartan the same way again.

"I'm getting the burger and a Coke Zero," I declare.

"Ah, I thought for certain that you'd fancy a milkshake."

I repress a shiver.

"Nope. Milkshakes were ruined for me forever when I was a kid. They'd tell me barium tasted like a vanilla shake before X-rays. Lies, all lies. Can't touch them now," I say, and I wave my hand like I'm clearing the memory. "So, does Scotland also have theme restaurants?"

"I wouldn't know," Axe replies with a wry smile. "I didn't go to restaurants much as a kid. My upbringing was . . . unorthodox. I grew up on a small island with an estate that looked like it belonged on a postcard. On sunny days, it was breathtaking. On rainy days, it felt like a dungeon."

"Yes, but for this Shelton townie, that sounds like living in a literal fairy tale," I say. "Like weather doesn't even matter, except maybe if there's the occasional dragon lurking around." I pause, then add, "Honestly, it's kinda hard to picture you as a kid. I mean, I can't imagine you as anything but this perfectly polished, in-control CEO daddy." I cover my mouth. I didn't mean to say that last part out loud.

"CEO daddy?" Axe repeats, amusement dancing in his eyes as his mouth twitches with a smirk.

"You know what I mean!"

"Well, but growing up, I was a sensitive lad. I wore specs, and once the internet finally made it to our neck of the woods, I got obsessed with computers and coding. That's how I ended up meeting Strike and eventually joining the CIA. I was desperate to leave home and hopefully do a bit of good in the world."

"No way. You were a nerd?"

"A proper bookworm!" His laughter is a roar. "Ah, you don't believe me. But yes, the library was my hideout. I'd camp out there for days, devouring every book I could lay my hands on." Honor once told me that Strike and Axe have a top secret bro book club, meeting religiously every week, with a patented algorithm to ensure diverse reading. I thought she was pulling my leg, but now I'm not so sure. Good thing they don't allow outsiders; Honor and I would probably get pregnant watching those two gorgeous CEO daddies discuss literature.

"I wish I had known you then," I say as Sally reappears to take our orders, rescuing me from my overshare. There are no more embarrassing childhood confessions for the rest of dinner, though Axe does dive into his casual list of epic adventures, which involve hot-air ballooning over the Serengeti and scuba diving in the Great Barrier Reef.

"The colors of the coral and the fish are unlike anything you can imagine," he says, his eyes soft. "It's a bit like playing inside rainbows."

While I don't have anything exotic to share, I explain my plan to get outside by sunrise tomorrow to look for treasures on the beach. "Believe it or not, I've never actually put my toes near the lake before," I admit, a little sheepishly, though Axe doesn't need to hear it again—how my mother was afraid of everything from riptides to jellyfish to the petri dish of ocean germs, all waiting to pounce.

"You know," says Axe, as if reading my thoughts, "I meant to tell you earlier, but for a bairn as sickly as you supposedly were, you're surprisingly . . . hearty. We've spent an entire day together, and I haven't seen you so much as sneeze."

I nod as my eyes prickle. I've been thinking about this so much lately—how my mother's worries, at least sometimes, might have been more about her own anxieties than my actual health. But it's not a thought that I'm quite ready to share.

"I guess I grew out of some of it," I say, my voice steady. "I still have to be careful, but yeah." I smile. "It's time to take risks and live on my own terms." My hands are sweaty; I take a breath. Not good for the app.

At that moment, Sally returns with the check, placing it on the table with a smile. "Enjoy the rest of your night, kiddos," she says with a knowing smile. Which is funny because I bet that whatever she's thinking doesn't involve haptic suits.

Axe tosses a few bills onto the table without even glancing at the total—Sally's easily getting a 50 percent tip.

It's go time. As we head out of the diner, Axe's eyes lock onto mine, a flame of something exhilarating passing between us. But reality tugs me every bit as hard. What we're about to do isn't just a moment between Axe and me. Every move we make is about to be sliced, diced, and fed into the algorithm. And I really need this job. My medical history means I have no choice but to be on constant lookout, that the threat of expensive treatments always lurks in the shadows. I can't forget that in recent days, I both had the stomach flu and passed out while driving.

Funny how, despite all this, I've never felt more alive.

I let out a small sigh, barely audible over the rain, which has started up again, as I try to ground myself in the here and now. Axe pops open the umbrella—because of course he remembered to bring one—so that it shields us both, and he gives my hand a reassuring squeeze, his touch offering a tiny moment of calm and comfort in the storm of my thoughts.

As we walk back to the hotel, I steal another glance at him, determined to savor this connection before the next-level suits and their high-tech sensors intrude. I want to enjoy this for what it is: something real—almost real?—in a world of simulations.

Even if, soon enough, everyone will have my data in their hands and know just how real it feels to me.

THIRTY-SEVEN

AXE

We're both quiet as we cross the threshold into our room, bringing with us the scent of rain-soaked pavement. As the door clicks shut, I'm keenly aware of the charged atmosphere. I shake off the umbrella, sending droplets scattering across the shag carpet.

When I turn on the light, the theme hits me again like a sugar rush. Walls plastered with cartoon murals of mermaids lounging on rocks, and above the bed dangles a giant starfish light fixture, its limbs spread-eagle.

"Today was perfect," Josie says, flopping onto the bed, which emits an unnerving creak in response. "The rain really adds something magical to this place, doesn't it?"

"It does," I reply, dimming the light and tossing my damp jacket onto a chair. The bedspread is an explosion of glossy seashells, with a plush, sequined mermaid-tail blanket tossed on a treasure chest. The whole room looks like the ocean decided to host Glastonbury and forgot to clean it up, but Josie is genuinely chuffed with it all. She is truly oblivious to the chintzy crap, and I adore her for it. Her enthusiasm might be catching, too—there's something glorious about all this naff kitsch.

Josie kicks off her shoes and stretches out with a sigh, her head sinking into a pillow embroidered with seahorses. "And that cherry pie at the diner . . . heavenly. If we sold those pies at the shop, we'd make a fortune."

"If anyone could do it, you could," I agree, sitting beside her. She giggles as the bed dips with my weight. The way she relaxes into the pillow and peers up at me makes me hard again—yes, the day was perfect, right down to the acute case of blue balls I'm getting just by looking at her. And that kiss earlier . . . Strike called at the perfect time, because I didn't trust myself not to take her right there on the boardwalk if she'd have had me.

"So, do you think we're ready?" she asks, glancing at the corner where the suits hang like two high-tech wet suits. Which feels appropriate, given the whole under-the-sea vibe. It's like we're about to go scuba diving, not have really awkward virtual reality cybersex. "Want to try them out?"

I exhale, pulling my hands through my hair. "I realize this wasn't the plan. The contract was pretty clear about separate rooms, so we can call it. No pressure if this makes you uncomfortable—"

"I'm not uncomfortable," she says, cutting me off. She tucks a rogue curl behind her ear, and it is so fucking cute, I force myself to think unsexy cool-down thoughts.

Gym socks. The outrageously convoluted American tax system. Moldy cheese.

Jesus, it'll be an effort to take it slow. The last thing we need is me coming in my haptic suit too early. I'd never be able to look my team in the eyes again. "I'm sort of looking forward to it," she adds.

Something clenches low in my sternum, and all I want to do is chuck those suits out the window and toss her straight onto the bed. I want to lock her legs around my neck. Screw the data, and to hell with She's the One. I want this woman for myself, but I know as well as anyone, we don't always get what we want.

"Okay, I'm game if you are," I say, clearing my throat and swallowing. "Though I can't promise I won't make a fool of myself. I've never tried these, either. This is not the way I'm normally intimate."

"You mean you don't normally wear head-to-toe latex to fuck?" she asks, and that word, *fuck*, said so casually by Josie—who wears socks with ruffles and tiny hearts on them—as if it rolls right off her tongue, makes me go rock solid. The wanting has turned into something I can't quite control. Every part of my body longs to touch hers—I want to lick her pussy, eat her until her eyes roll back into her head.

I'm already pissed off at these stupid suits and the bloody barrier they'll put between us, and I haven't even zipped mine up yet.

"Nah, lass, I don't need accessories," I say, smug as you like. She's not actually going to feel the real me tonight, so there's no point warning her.

We take turns in the bathroom—me first, then Josie—to wriggle into these ridiculous haptic getups. The material's sleek and tight, with all sorts of compression, massage, and vibrating bits. Makes me feel like some off-brand superhero. I can hear Josie struggling with hers, grunting in frustration.

"You need help?" I call.

"Nope, but I am definitely turning out the lights so you can't see me in this thing," she says. True to her word, an arm shoots out to flick the switch. She fumbles her way to the bed, flopping down beside me. "I look like Catwoman meets Inspector Gadget."

I laugh and make a mental note to google Inspector Gadget later—Josie is always making cultural references that never quite made it to the Hebrides. At least we're both acknowledging how bizarre this whole thing is.

"Ready?" I ask.

"Ready," she says.

We both pull on our VR headsets and press our remotes. The suits start humming softly, springing to life as a virtual image unfolds before each of us, the mirror image of each other's. I see VR Josie and she sees VR Axe. We're in a hotel room, but this one is definitely more high-end than the Nautical Nook. It's sleek and modern and sexy—flickering candles everywhere, a faux-fur rug.

Once the prototypes are done, these suits will have two functions: letting people get busy with their AI girlfriend or letting long-distance lovers have a virtual romp. They're not exactly designed for same-room use, so we skip the provided earbuds. The team—after they heard about our one-bed situation—strictly instructed us not to look at each other in real life while this is going down. Headsets only. We each control our own avatar on the other's screen, so if I reach out a hand, she'll see it in her headset and feel it through the sensors in her suit. Same goes for her with me. Which means rule number one: no touching in real life. We've gotta stay on our sides of this big bed, keep the data clean.

No touching or we'll screw up the test.

So here we are, side by side, each playing in the other's virtual world. Avatar Josie's in that same polka-dot dress from earlier, and it makes me smile. I went with a blue sweater that's a dead ringer for the one I just peeled off.

"Okay, I'm just going to say it. This is weird," she says.

"So bloody weird," I admit, already moving toward her.

"But the back massage feels nice." In the virtual realm, I'm now standing behind her. I've lifted her beautiful bounty of curls to one shoulder, and my hands are moving up and down the back of her neck. The bed behind us is big and impossibly white, its crisp sheets turned down enough to tempt.

"Aye, you like it?"

She groans, and all I want to do is turn my head and look at her for confirmation.

"I do. It's so . . . real." The tech is remarkably advanced, and soon I'm all sensation. "I . . . I, oooh." I lean in closer to her ear and lick the shell of her lobe. I assume I'd look insane if she took off her headset and saw me, my tongue poking out of my mouth, but I trust that she's here with me in this strange bubble we've built. If the little gasp she makes is any indication, she's as turned on as I am.

Christ, I need to slow down. But how? We've barely touched.

Josie turns around and asks, "Can I kiss you?"

I don't answer. I just lean in and grab Josie's avatar, and she meets my mouth in virtual reality. Somehow, though our actual lips are not touching, the kiss feels true and honest. Her arms wrap around my neck, and the kiss gets hotter, desperate. She pushes me back onto a simulated bed—this bed is plush and vast, not a pirate accessory in sight—and I feel the weight of Josie's body on mine. The suit is mirroring her movements—giving me the sensation of her against me—and it's so delicious, I can't even imagine what it would feel like if it were her tangible skin.

"You feel so good," she says on a hard exhale, and I can hear the tightness in her voice. "How? I don't understand—"

But she stops talking when I sit up and start to undress her. I pull her dress over her head, and her breasts are now exposed. Perfect pink nipples pucker under my fingertips. I lean down, take one into my mouth, and suck.

"Yes," she says, arching back. The room around us is falling away, and all I can think and feel is the Josie in front of me, her moans, her desperate hands.

"I'm going to make you come, my bonny lass," I promise.

"Spread your legs for me." She's lying down on the bed, her knees bent, and I'm stretched out next to her. I reach down to touch her, and start with a little teasing. I stroke my fingers along her thighs.

"I'm already so wet," she whispers, and somehow when I reach her center, I actually feel it. I know she's soaking for me, not only on my screen, but definitely in the bed next to me. Fuck. I'm so hard, my dick is pushing against the suit. When she slides her hands down my trousers, the sensors tighten, and I'm wrapped in her grip.

"No," I say, and I pin her hands over her head. "I want to last. I need to see you come first. I want to see that beautiful blush across your cheeks." I trace her lips with her own wetness, push my finger into her mouth, and she moans as she licks her own juices.

"Axe," she says. "Holy shit. Axe. I didn't think it would be like this." I know exactly what she means. I am on fire, desperate to plunge myself inside her. The fiction we have spun with the VR is all-consuming, a multisensory experience that has Josie shaking on the bed next to me. "I'm dripping."

She is feeling my every touch, and I never want to stop.

THIRTY-EIGHT

JOSIE

I am having sex with Axe MacKenzie. Except I'm not.

But I am. And also not. I swear I can feel his fingers trace the skin of my inner thigh and dip between my legs. I can feel my juices trickling down. I can hear him narrating what he wants to do to me, and I have no doubt I will let him.

If these suits go on sale, this man will be a billionaire. I'll never want to leave my house again.

"Oh, you taste so good," Axe says, and I see his head bobbing between my thighs now. I don't understand how any of this works, but his tongue is lapping at me and luxuriating in my pussy. I can see it and feel it, even though my rational brain knows this is not possible. That the shifting weight I feel on the bed next to me is the real Axe and not this phantom in front of me.

And yet his tongue is absolute magic—none of that stupid, basic tracing-the-alphabet shit that Bryan must have learned from TikTok. Axe keeps bringing me to the edge, and then slowing down, as if he's having too much fun to let me climax.

"I could do this all night," Axe says. Soon, his fingers join his tongue and find their way inside me at the perfect angle. One, then two, then three, and I feel myself stretching to accommodate him, feel him touch that impossible-to-reach spot inside.

Damn, he is so good at this.

"I want you to come all over my face. Can you do that for me, luv?"

His dirty talk is working—honestly, before now, I didn't even know I liked dirty talk in real life—and I can't get enough. He swirls his tongue on my clit one last time, and then my entire body tightens, my spine tingles, and suddenly my orgasm hits so hard and fast, I can't help but scream out my pleasure.

I have sampled every toy in Grace & Honor and even a bunch I brought home from Toygasm. Still, I have never come so hard in my entire life. I'm shaking from head to toe, giddy and alive, and all I want is *more, more, more.*

What is this sorcery?

"I need you. Can I take you now? Please, Josie," Axe begs, and I nod, because I'm so wrung out and messy I can't even talk. He pumps his cock with his fist once, twice, and suddenly I'm wondering how accurate a representation this is—he can't be that big, can he? And then I stop thinking at all, because he thrusts himself inside me. I'm filled to the hilt with him, and I reflexively clench around him.

"Jesus," he groans. "So fucking perfect."

He pulls out slowly, gently, and then pushes himself right back in. I gasp.

"Are you okay?" he asks as he cups my face and tucks a hair behind my ear.

"Eh, all right," I joke, and he laughs, and for just a second, he presses his lips against mine, and the moment is so tender I feel tears spring to my eyes. I hope the thin, soft actuator pads on my forehead, cheeks, and lips can't pick up the rush of emotion I suddenly feel.

Axe starts thrusting harder and faster, and I'm gasping now. He feels too good. Too real. Too everything. How can it be like this?

"Shit," he says. "Fuck. So good." And then he picks up the pace, and my eyes roll back in my head with the pleasure of it all. He lifts my legs so they're on his shoulders now, and that changes the angle, and it's exactly right—how did he do that? How does he know? He's not even really touching me. But the thought gets lost as I'm notched higher and higher and his groans grow louder and louder until we both explode within seconds of each other.

I'm so limp and ruined, with the ecstasy of the whole experience etched into my soul. Now that I know sex can be *this*—fucking perfect, as Axe put it, and yeah, those are exactly the right words—how can I go back to normal life? Pay bills, eat vegetables, ring up customers? When I could spend my time doing *this*? With Axe MacKenzie. Or at least virtual Axe MacKenzie.

We slowly return to Earth, and I don't know what the etiquette is here. Do we talk? Do we take off our masks and see each other's faces in all their postcoital glory?

On my screen, Axe reaches for me again, pulling me in, and just like that, virtual me is the small spoon to his big spoon, and we're cuddling. A wave of relaxation and peace floods through me, and I drift off to sleep.

It's only hours later, when I wake up disoriented, my mask having fallen to the floor, that I realize we are mirroring our avatars in real life. Axe's actual body is glued to mine—he's taken off his suit—and his arm is thrown casually over my waist, his maskless face nuzzled into my neck. Soft rain pitter-patters against the window.

I am not going to freak out. Instead, I get up quietly without waking Axe, wiggle out of this magic sex machine, and fold it neatly on the chair. Then I crawl back into bed, and Axe sleepily pulls me up against him again. I sink into the delicious glory of this very real man while I still can.

THIRTY-NINE

AXE

My dreams are rocky and dark, filled with the scent of blood and smoke. Harsh words echo around me, and there's a sense of urgency pounding in my chest. I'm trying to save them, to save them all, but they float away out of reach. Just when the darkness seems overwhelming, a softness breaks through.

"Axe," a woman whispers, her voice a lifeline in the chaos. "Wake up. You're having a nightmare."

I surface into consciousness, shaking off the remnants of the dream. Blinking, I take in my dark surroundings. I'm next to Josie, this beautiful woman whose touch still reverberates through me from last night. Everything is good. More than good. Perfect.

"Nay," I say, turning to face her. "Lass, I'm far too much of a CEO daddy to have nightmares."

She giggles. "Okay, sorry. I must have imagined it."

I reach forward and tug the shade open—we do have a view of the lake. It won't be sunrise for another half hour. I want to lie inside this quiet moment forever, where my shadows haven't slipped fully away. Before we fell asleep, I decided to turn off the haptics. We've also both slipped out of our suits—Josie must have taken hers off while I was sleeping, and now she's in a baby-soft

T-shirt and a wisp of undies. I kicked off mine, too, and pulled on a pair of boxer briefs. Discreetly, I grab a pillow to hide my forklift of a boner that made its appearance as soon as I saw that scrap of lace barely covering Josie's delicious ass.

"When you were having your not-nightmare, you were yelling at someone," she says quietly. "Your dad? Unless there's someone else in your life you call Da."

I shut my eyes as fragments of the dream return. She doesn't press me for details, doesn't push—maybe that's exactly why I want to tell her. She's like a compass magnet, pointing me to her, even in silence. Around her, all my training and instincts that tell me to hold back—to compartmentalize, to say just enough and nothing more—just dissipate. I can't help but tell her the truth.

I turn on my side so I'm facing her. I get a thrill breaking last night's rules in the quiet morning: I will look and I will touch. I count the beautiful freckles that scatter across her cheeks like fallen stars. I smooth her hair back from her forehead. And then, without even meaning to, I start talking.

"Everything I've ever done has been to spite my dad. To show him he was wrong about me. He's been gone for ages, and still he's the reason I push so hard."

"Who did he think you were?" Josie asks. I can tell she's being both curious and careful, like she knows I don't share this stuff with just anyone.

"My dad thought I was weak. Too soft. That I cared too much about other folk, and that I'd never get anywhere with my 'namby-pamby' attitude. He was toxic masculinity on steroids."

"I have no idea what *namby-pamby* means," she says softly, "but if you ask me, being soft and caring about other people are good qualities. And I think you've got both. Weak, though? Not a chance."

"You don't really know me, Josie," I say, my voice low.

"Maybe not. But after dinner yesterday and the date and last night, I feel like I'm starting to." She squeezes my hand. I wonder what she would think if she knew the real me. If she knew that I enjoyed rearranging Petrov's face with my fists, and then later slicing him open. That my way of proving I'm not weak is by ridding the world of trash like my father. And von Graf.

Of course, I know how she'd react. She'd run in the other direction. My life is not a Hallmark movie no matter how wonderful it feels to stand next to Josie. There will be no happy ending for the two of us.

"Anyway," I say, burying my face in those warm, strawberry-blonde curls. "Here's me, Mr. True Confessions, telling you all about the whole lot of my family, and you never told me even one thing I don't know about you. It's your turn, Ginger Snap."

In the silence, she runs her finger up and down my arm. She's taking my request seriously; I know she's not going to give me something empty like her favorite color (periwinkle) or how she takes her coffee (dark roast with milk and honey).

"Sometimes I look back on my whole childhood—all the doctors, all the illness, all the pain—and instead of feeling like a survivor, I just feel *rage*," she starts, her voice shaking. "I had the worst fucking luck. Every side effect, every complication. And this persona—this JosieFightsOn bullshit—wasn't even my idea. It was this fake, shiny avatar my mom created to make everyone feel better about the whole nightmare." She shifts to stare at the window over my shoulder, searching for answers in the silver-dark sky and ocean. "I'm supposed to feel grateful," she says. "I'm alive. I get it. But I'm also fucking *furious*." Josie's voice cracks, and she starts to cry, and reflexively, I pull her into my arms. She buries her face in the crook of my neck, and it feels like she was always meant to be there. "Sorry." She sniffles. "I hate it, but I cry when I'm mad."

"Cry it out, lass." I pull her in tighter. Rub her back and then cup my fingers at her nape. She smells like strawberries and lavender and sex.

"Does it make you angry that SynthoTech—and, let's be honest, that I—am creating another avatar for you?" I ask once she's gone still, her breath shaky but quieter. "Because if it does, we can stop. No strings, no hard feelings. I'll keep you on the health insurance. You're smart as hell and capable, and I'd love to keep you at the company as a consultant or something." I try to keep my voice steady, though I'm genuinely worried I'm about to lose her. She can walk away from She's the One—it would set the project back, but no problem. But what if she also walks away from me? Which she should. Not walk. She should fecking sprint.

I've never felt like more of a selfish bastard in my whole life than I do right now, letting this woman lie here. I should be protecting her from me, not keeping her close.

When I first hired Josie, all I cared about was that she said yes. Now the thought that she's doing this to survive—to stay healthy and keep her head above water—makes me feel sick. I was such a privileged prick with my head jammed so far up my own arse I couldn't see her.

"No! I want to keep going on the project." Josie pulls out of my arms and looks up at me. She wipes her tears with her fingertips. "This work has been so much fun, and you and your team have consulted me every step of the way. So it kind of feels like the opposite of those awful social platforms. It's like my own secret badass alter ego—who hopefully will feel more like the real me than JosieFightsOn ever did."

"You just have to say the word." I swipe my thumb against her cheekbone and then smooth back one of her errant curls. "You have all the power here."

She nods, and I see a soft smile rest on her lips.

"Sun's coming up," she says.

We let the silence stretch out, watching as the sky gradually lightens. The first rays of dawn seep up from the horizon in shades of pink and gold. It's a peaceful, fleeting moment before the world wakes up.

"Thanks for bringing me here," she says, her eyes reflecting the light of the new day. "I guess now it's back to reality."

Reality.

After last night, I've not the faintest idea how to go back to that.

FORTY

JOSIE

The worst part about having the weirdest, most romantic weekend of your life—you still have to wake up, shower, and drag your ass to work on Monday. Worse, you have to see your best friend in the entire universe and pretend like nothing happened.

There's *no way* I'm telling Honor that Axe and I had virtual sex in haptic suits in a mermaid-themed hotel room at Shimmy Beach. Because then I'd accidentally let slip that it was hands down the most erotic experience of my life, and she'd hit me with the world's biggest *I told you so* before running off to tell Strike, who would immediately tell Axe, and . . . yeah, hard pass on that.

Yesterday Axe and I felt so in sync, it felt like we'd invented a new language, but this morning I woke up alone in my very own bed with the uncomfortable realization that it was nothing more than a simulated dream. Not only is Axe still my boss, but our night together was literally just work. Our entire experience was recorded and will be dissected this week by faceless SynthoTech nerds.

All data, no magic. Axe's first text of this morning sealed it:

Brought the haptic suits in for download.

Team was thrilled

Normally, I'd have clapped back with something like *Hope they got dry-cleaned,* but I couldn't bring myself to joke. The words *Team was thrilled* reverberated in my brain during the whole drive here. I'm not shy about the team knowing what I was like in bed. It's more like I'm pissed that something that felt so incredible, so raw and alive, is now reduced to data points. And somehow, that kills the magic. Like it didn't even count.

I drive Gertrude to work because I need the reminder of who I actually am. Josie Greene. Manager of Grace & Honor, part-time SynthoTech guinea pig, and onetime fiancée of Asshole of the Year Bryan. I own a car held together by spit and rubber bands. I'm not the kind of girl who posts Shimmy Beach weekend getaway pics with the hottest man on the planet.

As I pull into the parking lot, my phone buzzes with a text from Alan:

> When you ignore your mother's texts, I'm the one stuck holding her bad mood. At least let her know you're alive. Better yet, do something nice for her. Surprise her, okay?

I add the world's most reluctant thumbs-up emoji to his message. The worst part is he's not wrong—Mom's texts have been piling up like unopened bills, all quotes about gratitude in glittery fonts and sad-eyed kittens and all-caps memes about DAUGHTERS WHO DON'T CALL.

I slam the car door harder than I mean to. Maybe I'll send her flowers.

"You feeling okay? Your energy is . . ." Honor waves her hands like she's swatting at mosquitoes when she comes in from the stockroom and sees me staring into space, absentmindedly folding and refolding blankets in our new front window display.

"That sounds like something I would say," I joke, but even I can hear that I'm giving off buzzkill vibes.

"Seriously, though. Did you check your blood sugar this morning?"

Oh, crap! I totally forgot. Not only did I not check my blood sugar this morning, I realize I didn't check it all weekend. The good news is that if I was going to go into diabetic shock, it would have happened by now. I feel fine, at least physically.

For a second, I let myself imagine that maybe my diabetes is magically regulating itself. I feel the slightest flicker of optimism—because I'm that person who looks on the bright side, crosses my fingers, lights a candle, slips some crystals in my pocket, and hopes—and then remember I've never been the exception to the rule when it comes to medical stuff.

Shit. I really am cranky today.

"I'm good. Really. The new toys I ordered came in, and I put them out. Still not sure how I want to best display them, especially the alien dildos that go with that new alien-sex erotica series," I say.

"That's genius. Cobranding books with sex toys so they can be enjoyed together. I wish I'd thought of that," Honor says.

"I wish I'd thought of haptic suits," I blurt out, then immediately turn so Honor can't see my face.

"What?"

"I said, I wish I had thought of, um . . . Happy Sticks. It's a brand of incense meant to improve your mood," I say, and, thank God, she buys it.

"Speaking of mood, why don't you take the afternoon off and use that massage gift card from Weird-Face Scarf Guy? I'm not needed at DME today, so I'm happy to hold down the fort," Honor offers.

"I'm really fine! Promise!" I say, feeling guilty that Honor thinks I'm so out of it she needs to do my job. I don't like to be the one gunking up someone else's aura.

"Honestly, I kind of miss being here. Please, go to the spa and relax. You've earned it," Honor says, and beams. It's amazing how much happier she's been since having Strike in her life. The two of them are like lovesick teenagers, and it's adorable.

"Thanks, boss," I say, and now a plan forms. I'm gonna surprise my mom at the nail salon. Maybe a bit of girl time will make things less . . . tense. I squeeze Honor in a quick hug and grab my bag. "You're the best."

"Josie?"

"Yeah?" I ask, one foot already out the front door.

"I hope you know that if and when you're ever ready to talk about whatever is bothering you, I'm here."

"I do," I say, and I find that for the first time since Axe's text, I feel a little less alone.

Nailed It is still tucked into the corner of Shelton Mall, exactly like it was when I was a kid. The smell of Auntie Anne's pretzels hits me as soon as I walk in, along with the sight of teenagers flirting over Taco Bell and toddlers clinging to the same old rusty animatronic pony. I haven't been here in years—partially because I'm on a tight budget and malls are temptation central.

But the nostalgia is hitting hard. I had my first kiss at the theater here. Mom bought me my first box of pads at the CVS. And I shaved my head for the first time before chemo right here at Supercuts. Nothing like watching your long curls hit the floor in public to make cancer extra fun. But enough of that. Today is about mother-daughter bonding, maybe even a massage. I walk into Nailed It, and it's like stepping into a time capsule. Same cracked leather chairs, same eye-watering acetone fumes.

"Josie? Is that you?" Barb, my mom's boss, rushes over and pulls me into a bear hug. I've always loved Barb—tall, bosomy, smells like vanilla, and gives hugs like she's trying to absorb you into her ample chest.

"How do you look exactly the same?" I ask. She's gotta be in her sixties but doesn't look a day over forty.

"I'll never tell." She laughs. "But you look fantastic. Healthy and glowing!"

"Thanks! Hey, is Mom here? I wanted to surprise her with a massage."

Barb frowns. "Your mom? She hasn't worked here in years."

"Wait . . . what? She works Mondays. She always has."

Barb gives me a sad look. "Baby girl, she quit about six years ago, after your last relapse."

My stomach drops. What the hell? I rack my brain, trying to remember if she ever mentioned quitting, but no—Mom still tells me work stories. Stories about Barb, even!

"But this makes no sense," I say. "Why didn't she tell me?"

Barb chews the inside of her lip, clearly deciding if she wants to say something. "Well, we had a falling out."

"Oh my God, Barb, I'm so sorry." I feel sick. "What about?"

"This is really difficult, and please know I love you. But I refused to donate money to your GoFundMe. My little one had just started college, and we didn't have much extra to go around. And I'd given so much through the years." Barbs eyes fill with tears. "She threw coffee at me and stormed out. We haven't spoken since."

I knew my mom leaned on friends and family for help during

those treatment years—mediocre health insurance is about as much help as a paper condom—but I had no idea it was that bad. Now I'm stewing in horror and shame.

Did I seriously just . . . *not notice*? Was I so busy being the sad cancer kid I didn't even realize what my mom was really doing?

I think about Axe and how he's spent his entire life living out a middle finger to his dad. Well, if he can do that, I can work my ass off to pay back every single person who ever threw a dime at one of my fundraisers. Hell, I'll start making and selling friendship bracelets if I have to.

"You said that this happened six years ago?" I ask.

Barb nods. "Yeah, back when Penny was a freshman at Penn State and Ollie was a junior. Double college tuition . . . They never tell you to space your kids out better."

I've got to go. I give Barb a quick kiss on her cheek. "Thanks for telling me. I'm sorry that happened. It was so great to see you, Barb."

"Wonderful to see you, baby girl . . ." she starts, but I'm already halfway out the door, waving her off.

I need to find Mom. Now.

FORTY-ONE

AXE

Checking my phone doesn't change the truth. No new messages. So here I am, gloved up and ready to rumble at Strike's place, Ashburn, throwing punches and getting warm in the centerpiece of his massive new state-of-the-art gym—a professional-grade boxing ring tricked out with all the high-tech gear you could imagine. The walls are lined with mirrors and photos of legendary American fights—Ali versus Frazier, Tyson versus Berbick.

The entire space feels like a shrine to people who know how to give and take a beating.

A perfect place to blow off steam.

Usually, I'm all in for my one-on-ones with Strike, but today I'm too fucking distracted, wrapped up in thoughts of Josie. My phone sits on a bench nearby, and I find myself glancing at it over and over, hoping for something. Anything. Earlier, I had my assistant send a test text just to confirm the damn thing's not broken. It's not.

Nah, the phone's not the problem.

The problem is me.

I'm a mug for misreading everything. Josie's participation was purely professional, end of story. I keep telling myself this revelation is for the best—there was never any potential for more. And certainly it's far better that I'm the one who's hurt, not Josie. The idea of causing that lass more pain is almost unbearable.

"Look at that phone again, and I'm chucking it out the window," Strike warns, his words cutting through my thoughts. He throws a hook that I dodge, the motion pulling me back to the moment.

"I was checking the time," I growl.

"Don't you have a watch for that?" Strike dances back, readying another punch.

"Fuck off," I grunt, meeting his jab with one of my own. I wonder if I've ever had a conversation with Strike in which I haven't told him at least once to fuck off. He's having a laugh at my expense. He doesn't know about my weekend with Josie at Shimmy Beach for She's the One and how I came back changed, raw. But the depth of my connection with her—the fire of what's happening inside me—is none of his business.

Since I handed over the project details to my team, I've been *this* close to yanking them back. Every time I immerse myself in the spreadsheets and replay the audio from that night, I want to punch the wall. How did I let the best night of my life get reduced to data points and file transfers for a bunch of coders? Even if Josie herself has been nothing but professional about it, I just can't sort it out right in my head. Should I text her again? Nah, I need things to settle, especially with the app's upcoming beta launch.

"So, I've been thinking we let von Graf go all in financially first, making his estate contractually obligated," I propose, trying to keep my mind on our plans.

"Nice." Strike nods, pausing as we both catch our breath. "And

I'll take point after Honor's art show. She'll be nervous, and I want to be fully there for her, no distractions."

"Right, then," I agree, though a part of me wants to scoff at his pussy-whipped status. But what's wrong with prioritizing someone you care about? My own inability to do the same is eating me alive.

We touch gloves, dive back into the rhythm. As we weave and bob, the ring becomes our whole world.

"What else about von Graf? Found anything new?" Strike asks as we dance around each other, each move calculated. "Anything else on his childhood? His background? My best guys can't dig up shit."

"Aye, he's a ghost. He was born in Kansas and, at some point, totally reinvented himself. Covered his tracks well, especially with the money," I say, throwing a punch that Strike counters with ease. Men like von Graf tend to cut all ties, assume new identities, especially if they've got priors.

But von Graf's done an especially fine job of burying his past and hiding his dirty cash. Gotta hand it to him, the bastard's clever. Shame he didn't use that brain for curing cancer instead.

Strike lowers his voice, his expression turning serious. "We're also getting rumblings that Petrov's old lady is on the warpath. She's not going to let go of what we did quietly."

The news hits like a solid cross punch to the gut, and it fills me with adrenaline and dread. "Yeah, suppose we'll need to watch that closely," I mutter.

We exchange a dark look. Strike knows full well how dangerous Veronica Petrov can be. We both figured that after we took out her man, the missus would lie low, let us focus on von Graf. Clearly we misjudged her. If her late husband was loud and brutal, Veronica's the opposite. Calm, clever, all charity galas and glossy magazines—but beneath it, she's a dagger in a velvet sheath.

We've got a rule: no more than one active target at a time.

But it turns out you can't underestimate the wife of a sociopath. Broken always finds broken, and odds are fair that she's cut from exactly the same cloth.

FORTY-TWO

JOSIE

For the first time in my life, I use the Find My iPhone tracker on my mom. She linked our accounts a while back, and I never gave it a second thought. Suddenly, everything clicks into place. Like why she hasn't been bugging me for my new address. She must already have it. How she knew to find me at the farmers market with Axe that day.

The fact that she could always track me down never felt sinister until right now. Suddenly, it feels downright terrifying.

What else has she been lying about?

I follow the little blue dot and see she's at the Keystone Hotel. Weird.

I hop in Gertrude and speed across town, kicking myself for not taking the Mini. I would've been there way faster if the engine hadn't shorted out three times on the way. Normally, I don't yell at Gertrude—she's been through everything with me—but today, I'm *so* done.

"Goddammit, you have one job, Gertie! One job!" I bang the steering wheel and accidentally knock my turn signal, which somehow falls off into my hand. This morning's card—the Five of Wands—predicted mayhem, but I hoped it'd be the zany variety. Like maybe I'd notice my dress was on inside out, or a butterfly would land in my hair.

I'm starting to get mighty sick of my own baseless optimism. This day has been one big shit sandwich, start to finish.

I pull up to the valet parking at the Keystone and throw my keys at the attendant. He looks at my car, and though he doesn't say it, I see it written all over his face: *Are you sure you're at the right hotel, lady?*

At my dark look, he decides against saying anything.

I've never stepped foot inside this place before. It's a world apart from the rest of Shelton. The lobby is cavernous, its ceiling soaring at least three stories high, supported by white marble columns that gleam under the chandelier's soft light. Low blue velvet couches are arranged with precise symmetry, like something out of a design magazine. Do people even sit here, or is it all just for show?

At the back of the lobby, I spot a sleek rectangular bar, its shelves artfully arranged with glass bottles that seem more decorative than practical, each one placed like an exhibit in a museum. I scan the area but don't see my mother.

Oh shit, could Mom be holed up in one of these guest rooms? Is she cheating on Alan? I mean, I'm not exactly Team Alan, but still, I kind of assumed they were blissfully boring together. I always figured Mom was the faithful type.

Then again, I also thought she was still working at Nailed It, so my Mom radar is clearly out of sync.

There's a restaurant off to the left called Seraphine. Fancy as hell. I glance at the gold-foil menu in a glass case and nearly choke. A $150 tasting menu? Yeah, no. This place is so out of Mom's price range. Alan's retired, and now that I know she's not pulling a paycheck from the salon, I think it's safe to say they're not splashing out on Wagyu.

"May I help you?" the host asks. His suit is tailored like it was made with only him in mind. This whole place is a far cry from Cheesecake Factory–casual.

"I'm looking for someone," I say. I'm dressed for a normal workday at Grace & Honor, an oversized cream sweater, distressed jeans, and a stack of thin bangle bracelets that Nonna bought me a while back. I tighten my ponytail, like that'll make me look more like I blend in here.

"Do you have a reservation?" He raises an eyebrow, and I'm just about to beg him to let me take one quick lap to see if I spot my mom—and then I notice it.

On the ground.

Two tables over.

The fucking tote bag with my printed bald head.

Only now do I realize how insane it was that my cancer—*my cancer!*—had a goddamn merch line.

I storm past the maître d' and walk right up to the table that holds six women, including Mom. Each has a rare steak plated in front of her, and my mother is wielding her knife as she talks. Her back is turned. She hasn't seen me yet, but I recognize her cheetah blouse—it's her date-night top—and her dyed-red hair, pulled up into a claw clip like it's the nineties, anywhere.

"Right, which is why it's so important to give. We know how hard this can be. All of us. Firsthand," she's saying as I approach.

"Mom!" I snap and she drops her knife with a loud clatter.

"Josie? What are you doing here?" She looks up at me through false eyelashes so thick it's a wonder she can see.

"What's going on?" My voice is sharp, fueled by an anger that's been simmering beneath the surface. Six years—six years of lies.

"Nothing, sweetheart," Mom says, her voice as sweet as the glass of sparkling rosé in front of her. Around the table, the middle-aged women exude a polished elegance—diamond-ringed fingers, buttery highlights—like it's a brand-new season of *Real Housewives of Shelton.* Mom, by comparison, looks out of place, her outfit and energy more desperate than glamorous. "Let's talk later. Now is not the time."

"Mom!" I demand, not backing down. Needing answers. Needing truth.

"Josie, this is a support group for mothers whose kids have or have had cancer. Please give us our privacy." She calmly takes a sip of her wine and smiles up at me. "I know you are used to things being about you. But this is about us, for once."

I have no words. It's true that my mom's life has always revolved around my health, and I've always felt guilty about that. Whenever I was given a treatment plan, the doctor would, after delivering the bad news, turn to my mother and ask if she had her own proper support. They'd remind her that caretakers need to take care of themselves, too.

She'd weakly smile up at them, her face streaked with tears, and say, "Yes, Alan is my rock." And I'd think, *Alan? Really?*

"Mrs. Basso's fifteen-year-old, Stacey, is in remission. Isn't that the best news? You remember Mrs. Basso?" Mom nods toward a woman at the end of the booth, and I can't even look. Shame floods me. These women have gone through hell, and here I am, causing drama over . . . what, exactly? My mom's probably got her own trauma from all my near-death experiences.

But standing here, I'm also hit with how deep Mom's secrecy

runs. It feels like a punch to the gut, like I've been shut out of this entire part of her life. She feels like a stranger, someone whose private world I've never been allowed to see. Why did she pretend to keep working at Nailed It? It makes zero sense.

"I'm sorry to bother you all," I say to my feet. I'm wearing sneakers. Sneakers in Seraphine! "Have a great afternoon." I turn on my heel and start to walk away as the women start chattering behind me.

"She looks so healthy!" one woman exclaims.

"That beautiful hair!" another adds.

And just as I reach the door, I swear I hear Mom's voice, faint and smug: "It's a wig."

In a heated daze, I whip Gertrude to my parents' house. Alan's home, and based on the smell wafting through the kitchen, he's making his signature atrocity: salmon mac and cheese.

"Just me!" I yell, stepping inside. "Getting some of my old clothes for Goodwill." I book it up the back stairs, trying not to sound like I'm pulling some *Mission: Impossible*–style snooping. My mother used to tell me spooky ghost stories about this attic, probably to keep me from coming up here. Even now, I'm still a little scared, rubbing my arms with my opposite hands as my eyes search the room.

There it is—the old filing cabinet where Mom kept all the records. My heart pounding, I judder open a drawer and grab as many files and folders as will fit into my envelope bag.

Downstairs, Alan's come out of the kitchen to roadblock me. His eyes are narrowed, and the spatula in his grip looks melted—Alan goes through spatulas like Kleenex.

My face turns bright, guilty red.

"Find what you're looking for?" he asks. "Your mother won't like you messing around up in the attic."

"Yeah, I just needed some of my old W-9 forms. For work."

"I thought you said you were getting clothes?"

Oh, crap. "That, too. But, uh, I couldn't find any, so . . ."

"Your poor mother. Radio silence from you for weeks, then you barge in here—"

I sniff. "What's burning?"

"Oh, for God's sake—hang on a sec." He dives back into the kitchen, and I seize my chance to dash, feeling like a middle schooler caught cheating in class. But I've got a hunch these files might bring me closer to Mom's secrets.

On the drive home, my hands are shaking on the wheel, my stomach twisting. What is my mom hiding from me? Where is she getting extra money to dine out at five-star restaurants for lunch? What else is she not telling me about her life?

I need to understand now.

I run into my apartment and make a beeline for the kitchen, clutching my bag. I'm full-body trembling as I dump the files onto the counter. At least it's a place to start.

What happened to me? Was I even sick six years ago? Do I have my own timeline wrong?

No doubt I've blocked out the worst parts of my childhood. Mostly on purpose, but maybe my unconscious brain did some of it on its own, too. Like, doesn't everyone try to move past their trauma? What's the point of reliving your worst moments just to burn them deeper into your amygdala?

The questions circle like vultures in my head.

I need to understand the real story of my childhood.

This is it. No turning back now.

I flip open the first folder. Mom is notorious for holding on to everything. My fingers brush past birthday cards and childhood drawings and old report cards. Garbage, garbage, and more garbage. Dust puffs into my face, and I cough. Not good for my asthma, but I'm too wound up to care. I reach for a giant accordion folder stuffed with papers. My chest tightens to see it again. Mom used to lug this thing around back when I was little. She'd save every scrap—medical notations, invoices, prescription duplicates. Inside, I find folders labeled with my name and dates spanning several years of my childhood. The records inside chart my roller-coaster health history, and for the first time in my life, I'm ready to face it: I want to see the details of my cancer—the diagnosis, the treatment, the recurrence.

I drop cross-legged on the floor as I spread out the documents around me. I extract a bundle of yellowing papers from the file, and I recognize Nonna's careful, spindly handwriting. A record of doctor visits for the first three years of my life, including immunizations, growth charts, and a few minor illnesses. A typical child's medical history. Ear infections, strep, stomach flu.

My percentiles for height and weight are consistent.

Flipping through the pages, I search for any mention of the word *cancer* or related terms: *malignancies, tumors, atypical masses.* It feels surreal sifting through faded documents to piece together my own health history, like I'm reading about someone else's life. The Josie Greene who, at eighteen months, reportedly knew "far more than the benchmark number of words," according to one doctor's visit.

Still, no evidence of sickness. Of course, I just haven't fast-forwarded far enough into the future. I was six the first time I was diagnosed . . . I think? That's when we went to Supercuts and shaved off all my hair.

So why does it feel like there's a piece of the story missing?

One document catches my eye—a doctor's note that's annotated in red with a sense of urgency, explaining that our health insurance denied further testing and that the doctors had already gone above and beyond the typical protocol for an earache. But it's my mother's familiar handwriting in the margins, anxious and insistent. *I'm sure something is wrong,* she wrote. *Mother's intuition!*

A follow-up letter from the same doctor suggests my mother seek an alternative primary care physician for me. That we were no longer welcome in the practice.

I squeeze my eyes shut and try to remember an earache. When did Mom get in an argument with a doctor about my care? Nothing comes to mind.

I delve deeper, and my cheeks go hot as I follow a trail of my mother's anxiety. Her notes are frantic, desperate, overshadowing the calm reassurances of medical professionals.

A particular report catches my eye, and my stomach tightens. The note details a series of particularly aggressive tests—some of the most painful procedures I can barely allow myself to remember. The word *leukemia* stares out at me from the pages, as if highlighted in neon. Dr. Don, a name that sends a shiver through me, is mentioned frequently throughout the notes. I think of his curdled smile, his dry, papery fingers, his insistence that I take off all my clothes for a checkup.

I pull out my phone and enter his full name into the search engine: Dr. Donald M. Rogers. I didn't know his last name; I only knew him as Dr. D or Dr. Don, like we were pals. And when the results load, I'm not even slightly surprised: a splashy malpractice suit was filed against Dr. Rogers by families accusing him of diagnosing and treating illnesses that were, at best, dubious. I read a formal public notice from the medical board detailing how Dr.

Rogers was stripped of his license due to unethical practices, but by then he'd made millions overdiagnosing his pediatric patients and subjecting them to experimental treatments.

But that's not the part that chills me to my bones. The lawsuit and the revocation of his license happened more than two decades ago.

I was his patient *after* the class action suit was settled.

What the fuck was my mother thinking? Why would she take me to a charlatan? Was I that close to death? Were we so desperately out of options?

I dig deeper into his record. After Dr. Don left the traditional medical world with a badly tarnished reputation, he reinvented himself as an "alternative medicine specialist," slipping through a loophole in FDA regulations through a private practice that he called Miracle Solutions. My blood surges when I find a photograph online of the building I came to know as MS Hospital, where I spent the worst days of my childhood. It was in Pottstown, Pennsylvania—and felt like a thousand miles from home.

I never once thought about what it looked like from the outside—just a squat concrete box—probably because I spent so much time trapped inside. Now it's like a protective barrier has broken down in my mind and I remember it all: the shared room, the revolving door of young roommates, our nighttime cries echoing off the walls, the bedpans filled with puke, and that ever-present smell of sickness.

The more I read about Dr. Don, the worse it gets. My skin is prickling all over now, a million tiny needles on my skin, my legs are shaking, and I have to put my head between my knees to breathe.

As I let the memories flood back, I'm struck by the stark horror of those days. How many gruesome experiences I've suppressed. I remember when a girl in the wing, Isla, just twelve, died in the bed next to mine. Her body lay there through the dark hours of the night, untouched until morning light when there was a shift change. Her parents, unaware until then, arrived and mourned over her still form, their grief echoing down the sterile halls.

How could I have forgotten Isla, with her soulful eyes and bunny teeth? How did I not relive the sheer horror of hearing her mother's keening? How could any of us have accepted this as normal?

I type Miracle Solutions Rogers Pediatric into my phone and learn that in the five years he operated it, Dr. Don marketed the place as a groundbreaking clinic offering alternative and holistic cancer therapies and targeted desperate families who had been failed by conventional medicine. The treatments included unapproved drug regimens, experimental procedures, Reiki, and natural herbal supplements. All untested. Mostly junk science. There's a detailed exposé in *The Philadelphia Inquirer* with a cover image of Dr. Don grinning at the camera in his doctor's coat, a stethoscope looped around his neck.

When I see his face, I have to run to the bathroom to vomit.

Curled over the toilet, I shake as my body relives every nightmarish appointment with the evil man. Dr. Don stabbing a hypodermic needle into my arm. Dr. Don, with a smile, asking me to rate my pain on a scale of one to ten while I was in too much agony to even answer. Dr. Don leaving me to lie in my own piss and shit for hours until the nurses came on shift.

My mother must've still been reeling from my father's death, making her an easy target for a shady doctor promising a miracle when regular medicine failed to immediately cure my leukemia. Dr. Don made it sound like he had the key to something groundbreaking, and in her fear, she believed him. That's the only way I can make sense of it.

I dig back into the files, and this time, I extract a worn envelope caught under the flap of cardboard at the bottom of the file. Brittle with age, addressed to Nonna, it's from the year my father died. Carefully, I open it and pry out the letter tucked inside. The handwriting is familiar—Mom's again. As I unfold the letter, a wave of apprehension washes over me. So far every revelation has been worse than the last.

Dear Mama Rosa,

I know these past months have been hard on us all with Harry's passing. Even though your visits are fewer than I'd like, I've received good care here and I am much better. The doctors think that I will soon finally be ready to come home. I worry what my staying too long at this place will do to the baby.

Come home? When was Mom away from me?

I check the return address on the envelope.

Sharon Goggins Greene
275 Holloway Road
Shelton, PA 19320

Wait, 275 Holloway Road? I know that address. It's the address for Ravenswood. The now-shuttered psychiatric facility—aka the House of Horrors.

What the fuck? When did my mother live at Ravenswood?

No wonder she can't even drive by the place. Numbly, I keep reading:

Nighttime is the hardest. I lie in bed, trapped in my mind and body, thinking about Harry. And Josie. And the life we were supposed to have together.

I am not going to lie to you. I am also very scared to leave, Rosa. But I miss Josie so much. I feel that if we are reunited, I will be better. She will cure me. That is what babies do. They are little miracles. Next Sunday, when you see me, they are going to let you sign for my release. Rosa, you know it is the right thing to do. Harry would want you to do this for me. I should not be kept one more month from my precious little girl, especially with Harry gone. I will love her and keep her so safe and healthy with every cell in my body.

Love,
Sharon

This is all too much.

I need the truth. The real truth.

I need to see Nonna.

FORTY-THREE

AXE

Josie still hasn't answered any of my texts. I've been waiting all Monday, and now it's Tuesday. Forty-nine hours since we said goodbye in person, but who's counting? I've got my ringer cranked up as loud as it'll go, and every time I get a message, I nearly jump out of my skin. All work stuff—folks buzzing about how far the prototype's come, confirmation for the investor launch, final graphics approval.

Never Josie.

I'm stuck in a no-man's-land between giving her space and wanting to just bloody well know what's going on.

How did I get this so wrong? I thought I understood her.

I can't bear it another minute. I need to see her face-to-face. I pick up my phone and call. As it rings and I wait for her to pick up—*please, let her pick up*—my mind flits back to Shimmy Beach. The memory of us side by side in that massive king bed. Every touch, every sensation, every shared moment felt as if it happened outside the boundaries of any sexual or romantic experience I've ever had before. It's as if that night unlocked a door to another dimension in our relationship, and I can't dismiss it as some escapade. As data.

As something less than it was.

How could she?

"Axe?" Her voice, so calm and familiar, grounds me as soon as I've got her on the phone. I suddenly feel completely ridiculous. There's no need for us to be in communication until next week, when she's supposed to come in and give us notes on what we've created. But she doesn't sound surprised to hear from me, either.

"Josie, I need to see you about the app," I say, as the first excuse that pops into my head spills out. "Can we meet? Tonight?"

There's a pause on the other end. Just long enough for me to worry that I've made a right mess, again—but then she answers, her voice soft and filled with something I can't quite place. "Yes, I think . . . we need to talk. Why don't you come by my apartment tonight? At about seven? I'll cook us something."

I thank the God I most certainly don't believe in.

"Sounds grand. I'll bring us something, too."

The rest of the day stretches out like an endless Monday morning. By the time I'm taking the stairs two at a time to stand outside Josie's apartment door, I'm a bundle of nerves.

She opens it before I've even knocked, greeting me with a smile that makes my stomach flip over. She's wearing a simple, silky peach jumpsuit, her curls are pulled back, and her eyes shine with that familiar spark I've become addicted to.

"Come on in," she says brightly, but there's a flicker of something else in her eyes—an uncertainty or worry that she's trying to hide. She looks knackered.

As soon as I walk inside, I'm struck by how perfectly Josie's apartment reflects her personality. The small space is a whimsical haven, alive with color and creativity. Gauzy curtains float at the windows, spilling soft light onto a lilac sofa covered in soft feather pillows. The aroma of something delicious fills the air, along with the sweet scent of jasmine from the vase on her small dining room table, set for two.

On every surface, tiny votive candles flicker.

I take it all in, feeling a smile spread across my face, even as the business side of me now realizes the irony—that without a lot more input about what Josie's very own perfect night would look like, She's the One is destined to fail. We've captured only one-tenth of her magic.

But I don't want to talk about any of that.

"This place is brilliant, Josie," I tell her. "It's so . . . you."

"Tell me the truth," she says. "How many of my apartments would fit in yours? Five? Ten?" I keep the real answer to myself. Josie's place is smaller than my walk-in closet.

"Everyone knows size doesn't matter," I say with a smirk, knowing otherwise.

I follow her into her kitchenette, where the countertops are crammed with bits and bobs from Grace & Honor. A set of floral-printed nested measuring cups and matching spoons. Ceramic salt and pepper shakers shaped like little owls, their eyes wide and watchful as they perch on the counter. Above the stove hangs a decorative tea towel embroidered with stars and moons, adding a touch of Josie's love for astrology to the space. Every item has been lovingly chosen, unlike my loft, which was outfitted years ago by a ferociously overbearing interior designer named Helga who couldn't keep her hands to herself.

"Dinner's almost ready," Josie says, glancing over her shoulder with a smile that doesn't quite reach her eyes. I sense an undercurrent of something she's trying to hide.

"Smells delicious." I lean against the doorframe, watching her work. "You really went all out."

"I drew the Empress card from my deck this morning," she

replies, her hands moving deftly as she slices through a cucumber. "The Empress means nurturing and care. So I figured it was a good day to dig out one of Nonna's recipes. Cooking is kind of therapy for me."

"Well, I'm chuffed to reap the benefits," I say as I spy a loaf of homemade focaccia on the counter, its golden crust speckled with rosemary and sea salt. Her back is to me, but she's tensed, on alert. "Are you sure everything's all right with you?"

She hesitates, the knife pausing in the air before she resumes chopping. "Some family stuff," she says lightly, though her voice is thin with strain. "Nothing I can't handle."

She adds the cucumbers to a wooden bowl, and as she moves around the kitchen, I notice a hen-shaped timer ticking away next to a collection of whimsical hedgehog canisters with tiny acorn handles, labeled Coffee, Tea, and Magic in Josie's round bubble handwriting. Her kitchen feels like a world apart from anywhere I've ever lived—especially during my own childhood. I've never known a sense of comfort quite like this. My father's world was one where children were kept out of sight and meals were eaten alone in my nursery or among strangers.

Rosy-cheeked with triumph, Josie serves us up two heaping plates from the stovetop skillet. "It's called Chickadee Lemon Basil Pasta Delight," she says. "Nonna's recipe. Pasta in a creamy lemon sauce with strips of tender chicken and a sprinkling of fresh basil."

"Fantastic." We bring the plates out, along with the focaccia and a couple of beers from her fridge, and settle down at the dining room table.

"Nonna taught me how to make this dish when I was very young," she says, her voice filled with tenderness. "Sometimes she'd sneak it into the hospital so that she could fatten me up after chemo."

I close my eyes, savoring my first bite of creamy, lemony chicken. When I open them, Josie is watching me with delight.

"Holy Gordon Fecking Ramsay, this is incredible," I tell her. "In my kitchen, things get elevated if I add a splash of chippy sauce."

Josie laughs. "I don't think I have that. Though, I gotta say, Scotland isn't, um, exactly famous for its food. Is it bad to assume the bar's kinda low?"

"Aye, that's my country you're rippin' into. Just you wait till I serve you up my famous boiled cabbage and haggis surprise," I tell her. "You already know we have the best tatties around. And my homemade custard's so thick it doubles as a weapon."

She laughs, and we keep the conversation easy, clinking beers when I finish a plate of seconds. It's not until we've pushed away from the table and resettled on the couch that the lightness fades from her face, and I sense that something is going on and it has nothing to do with me. Josie's mind is elsewhere.

"What's weighing on your heart, lass?" I ask her, smoothing her hair out of her face. No recording devices, haptic suits, or VR headsets between us. Just Josie and me, side by side, talking because we want to. "Has it got anything to do with why I haven't heard from you this week?"

She nods. I watch as she tries to compose herself, her cheerful mask fully slipping away to reveal the vulnerability beneath. She tucks one leg under the other before she turns her full attention to me.

"You can tell me anything, Josie," I say softly, and reach for her hand. Her voice wavers as she begins.

"It's complicated—and I don't even know the whole story. I went to see my nonna earlier to get some answers. But the nurses keep saying she has been having a rough time—a bad stomach flu—and to try again tomorrow."

I nod, remembering the snippets she's told me about her nonna, who sounds like she was the kind of granny I always wished I had.

"It's my mother. I think she's been keeping a secret. Something she's carried for a long time." Her eyes fill with tears, and she looks away, blinking them back as she struggles to find words. "While I was growing up, Mom was *obsessed* with making me healthy. Not her fault. I was ridiculously sick for so long. But she dragged me to all these extreme doctors, including this one guy, Dr. Don. He was a total quack, and I'm pretty sure at least some of his so-called cures did more harm than good."

"There's always someone happy to make a pound off of someone else's pain."

"Yep." Her laugh is short, bitter. "And looking back, I realize my mom might have had her own serious problems," she says, her words tumbling out in a rush. I want to pull her into my lap, shield her from every dark thing she's about to say, but I don't. I let her speak. "In fact, I think she was a patient at Ravenswood back when I was a baby. She never told me, and neither did my nonna. And I'm not sure she ever got fully well."

The mention of Ravenswood hangs in the air between us. I already sensed that Josie's mum was unhinged, sure as a cow loves grass. But I also know that Josie loves her.

"That must have been hard to learn," I say, reaching for her, wishing I could wash away her pain. "I can't imagine."

Except that I can. My own childhood was a proper stew of dysfunction, where the people most dangerous to me were the ones who kept me closest.

"It always felt like her love was wrapping around me too tight, like I couldn't breathe," she confesses, tears streaking in ribbons down her face. I brush them away with the back of my hand, wishing like hell I'd brought a handkerchief. "I just wish I'd known she was fighting her own demons. She was all I had—but maybe deep down I always understood something was off with her? You know how you can know something but also really *not* want to know it at the same time?"

"Aye," I say, and a list unfurls in my mind. Da's business. Hamish's predilections. Even now, sometimes a nonnegotiable truth stares me in the face that's too hard for me to accept. Perhaps . . . the extent of how much I care about Josie.

A molten wave of anger surges through me at the thought of Josie's mother doing anything—no matter how well-intentioned—to bonny little Josie. She dragged that tiny, curly-haired, trusting girl through so much trouble.

Where were the other adults? Where was the law?

"I wish I could have been there for you," I say, and tuck my arm around her shoulders to draw her closer to me. She feels small and delicate, her cheek the lightest whisper on my chest.

"You're here now," she says, but the fury settles in my bones. If the dickless bastard Dr. Don is still breathing, he won't be for long. I imagine storming into his dodgy little office, fueled by righteous fury. I see him sitting there in his leather chair, oblivious. The first punch will wipe the smirk off his face and send him sprawling back. I'll get Strike's knife set to slice him as neatly as deli ham. Fuck him and the empty hope he sold to his victims. Fuck all the physical and psychic pain he inflicted. I will take him out sure as—

"Axe?" Josie has turned to look up at me. "Your heart is pounding. Are you all right?"

I force myself to shake off the fantasy, to focus on the girl in my arms, the only thing that matters.

"Aye," I say gruffly. I can't change what's happened. Can't go back and protect Josie from those people. But I can be here for her now, for whatever comes next. I want to tell her these things and more, but the words catch in my throat. "Of course I'm good, Ginger Snap. And so are you."

Her lips part, but I press on. "You're healthy and strong, Josie, and I believe in you. Getting your answers will hurt, but you'll face it head-on, like you always do. And you won't have to do it alone. I'll be right here by your side."

"Thanks." She lets out a shaky laugh. "This isn't what you bargained for when I said I'd make you dinner."

"What are you talking about? That was the best Chicka-lemon-deedee whatchacallit I've ever had." I pull her onto my lap.

"But I'm not wearing a haptic suit," she says, and she can't hide her vulnerability. She stays rooted to the couch, as if moving those few inches will make her more exposed. "There will be no data to send to *the team*."

"Thank Christ for that." And then the penny drops. "Josie, is that why you didn't text me back at first? Because I said I'd handed in our suits?"

Her silence speaks volumes.

A deep, aching regret unfurls in me. I feel a desperate longing to go back in time and meet Josie under completely different circumstances. And then I remember—I did. And she hated my guts. "I will dismantle this entire thing right now. You are so much more important than this stupid project."

She looks down, unable to meet my gaze.

"Josie, look up at me, lass. I'm serious. I can kill it immediately. I told you that the other day, and it's still true. You've got all the power here." Saying it, I realize I mean it with my full heart.

I want Josie more than any profit I might earn on She's the One.

I can find another way to take down von Graf.

I can find another AI model.

I can't find another Josie.

And the ache I feel for her, even with her sitting right in front of me, is almost unbearable. I want to scoop her up, lay her down, and strip her bare. I want to cover her with my body, shielding her from the cruel world outside. I want to taste every inch of her skin, make her gasp and moan my name until she's trembling beneath me.

"I don't want you to call off the project," Josie says, her cheeks flushing. I wonder if she's thinking what I am. How incredible it felt to be together, even in virtual reality. How we kissed, sucked, touched each other. How the thought of experiencing that in real life seems almost overwhelming, like it might actually undo me. "I just hate being reminded that *this*—whatever it is between us—is all tied to creating my avatar."

And suddenly it clicks. She needs reassurance just as much as I do. The time we've spent together feels so delicate, like it can slip through our fingers at any moment as easily as sand.

"I like you sitting right here." In answer, she wraps her arms around my neck and then nuzzles her lips against my ear.

"Axe," she whispers, and I shiver. My dick stiffens with want.

"Aye, lass."

"We're not . . . I can't . . . not tonight." I grasp her tighter, kiss her forehead, between her brows, her cheeks, her mouth. My kisses are gentle, asking for nothing in return. They are me acquiescing to her boundaries.

"I know, sweetheart. I understand." And I do. I can see the hunger in her eyes, how easy it would be to turn this night into something wholly different. It's so tempting. We could fuck our pain away, lose ourselves in each other's bodies. But that's not what she needs right now.

"I want to. Holy shit, do I want to," she says, her breath hot against my cheek, and she shifts in my lap so she can feel me against her. A slow, deliberate wriggle—and I throw my head back with a low, desperate groan. She must feel how close I am to unraveling, because she hesitates—just for a second—before dragging her tongue in a slow, tantalizing line up my neck, from clavicle to ear. "How can such a bad idea feel so fucking good?"

The energy between us has shifted, the tension strung tight, a taut wire ready to snap. I'm burning up inside, so close to losing control I could explode in my pants just from looking at her. I place my hands on her waist, savoring the heat of that touch for one delicious second before lifting her and gently setting her down on the couch beside me. Thigh to thigh will have to be good enough.

"Not tonight." I lean forward to pick up the remote from her coffee table. It takes every ounce of self-control I learned in the CIA to resist the urge to pull her into my arms, toss her over my shoulder, and make her come until she's screaming my name. I keep my face calm, pretending this isn't the hardest thing I've ever had to do. "How about we watch my very first rom-com instead?"

FORTY-FOUR

JOSIE

My phone buzzes on the nightstand, vibrating so loudly that it nearly falls off the edge. Half asleep, I grope for it in the dark. The bright screen stings my eyes as I squint at the messages. There's a missed call from Mom—the last person I want to hear from—followed by a flurry of frantic texts.

Josie, wake up!

Wake up!

Are you even there?

Why are you ignoring me? This is an EMERGENCY!

Your Nonna is at Shelton General. It's serious. Get here NOW.

The last text, received just moments ago, reads: Please hurry!!! I need you.

I'm out of bed before I can think, my heart racing as I throw on the first clothes I can find. Not Nonna. Not yet. I am not ready.

I yank my jacket off the chair, grab my keys, and head out the door. As I pass through the living room, I pause, caught off guard by last night's wreckage—the empty carton of Ben & Jerry's Half Baked on the coffee table, two spoons still sticking out.

Axe. The warmth of our time together washes over me. How our evening stretched into the small hours, luxurious and slow, the electricity between us reset to a slow burn no matter how badly my body longed for his. At some point, we DoorDashed the ice cream and ate it together on the couch, our legs braided together so innocently, talking about everything and nothing until the night grew soft and still. Eventually, we fell asleep curled against each other, with *Notting Hill* playing on the screen, the strength of Axe's presence wrapping me up like a blanket.

Axe left only after we'd both drifted off. He scooped me up and placed me on my bed, and I can still feel the print of the kiss, gentle and lingering, that he gave me just before he slipped out the door.

Where are you, Josie!? I need you!!

I hurry out the door, the Mini's keys jingling in my hand. No time to take a chance on Gertrude. Shelton General isn't far, but Mom's texts make it sound like every second counts.

The sliding doors whoosh open as I rush into the sterile, brightly lit lobby and then into the elevator to the ICU. A nurse at the desk glances up, clearly expecting me.

"I'm here for Rosa Greene," I say.

"This way," she says, moving fast, as if she already knows I'm running out of time. My feet feel like they're moving underwater.

Down the hall, we stop at a door that's slightly ajar, and the nurse leaves me, gesturing that I should go in.

I gasp when I see Nonna lying in the hospital bed, her skin sallow under the harsh hospital lights. Her breathing is shallow, wheezy. Tubes from her arms connect to machines that beep in steady rhythm.

Mom is perched on a chair beside the bed, her eyelashes clumped together and hanging like crushed spiders, her hair looking as disheveled as I've ever seen it. When she sees me, relief washes over her face.

"Oh, Josie! Thank goodness you're here!" She rushes over, pulling me into a grip like a chokehold. "I didn't know if you'd make it before . . ."

She lets her sentence hang there.

"What happened?" I pull back, trying to get a read on her. Mom is nearly shaking with anxiety, her eyes darting around the room like a startled bird, and as always, there's that edge of manic energy thrumming just beneath the surface.

I think about what I said to Axe last night, how sometimes you can't see what's right in front of you. I did that with Bryan—I was blind to his faults because I was desperate for freedom. And I've done it my whole life with Mom, refusing to notice her rabid, belligerent anxiety because I was taught that it was the same thing as love.

"She's been failing for weeks, not that you'd know," Mom says. Classic passive-aggressive jab. "Last night . . . last night she told me it was her time. She insisted that I bring her a huckleberry pie from Shelton Farms. We shared a slice, just the two of us, just like we used to when I was young and Harry was still alive. She seemed happy when I left. But then, an hour later, I got the call to come back." Her voice breaks, and she dabs her eyes with her sleeve. “I think . . . I think she knew this would be the last time. She wanted to say goodbye to *me.*”

I nod, absorbing my mother’s need to make it all about herself in this moment of extreme crisis, and I shove any reaction aside. Now is not the time to remind my mother that Nonna was never a fan.

I want Mom to go—I need her to go—as far away from Nonna and me as possible. “Mom, why don’t you step out and get some air?” I suggest softly, coaxing her with a press of my hand on her cheek and a reassuring smile. “You’ve been here for hours, holding everything together like you always do. Let me take over for a while.”

“I don’t know. You need me.”

“Remember what the doctors always say? Caretakers need care, too. You’ve been a superhero! Give yourself a break.”

She hesitates, then nods. “Maybe that’s a good idea, sweetie. I’ll be back soon.” She kisses Nonna’s forehead, smoothing back her silver hair, then gives a final, teary glance before leaving the room.

And the Oscar goes to . . . MamaBearSharon. You fucking phony.

The thought is so angry and intrusive it shocks me.

Is that what I really think?

Once the room is quiet, I pull the now-empty chair closer to Nonna’s bed and sit down, gently taking her frail, bony hand in mine. Her eyes are closed, her breathing so light I have to strain to hear it. I sit for a few minutes, listening to the rhythm of the machines, willing her to wake up—will she ever?

When her eyes finally flutter open, I feel a shot of relief that quickly twists into panic.

Nonna’s gaze is unfocused, clouded over, as if she’s staring straight into a void.

“Nonna, it’s me, Josie,” I whisper.

Her lips move, but the words are too soft to make out. I lean in closer.

"The cards," she breathes, and I know exactly what she wants me to do.

Quickly, my heart pounding, I reach into my bag and pull out my deck. I always keep my cards handy, a habit I picked up from Nonna. I spread them out across the bed, and then I grasp her frail hand in mine. There's no time to waste—Mom doesn't like to be alone for long. Nonna needs to tell me something important, and I'm certain it's tied to what I've discovered about Mom and the secrets of my childhood.

Nonna has always been cautious, dropping hints and offering warnings, all while clearly fearing Mom's reaction and her power, the very same way that I do.

But now, with time slipping away, Nonna's urgency is palpable.

I think back to our last visit. Her warning about danger. Was she trying to tell me something? A message that I didn't understand? We've always had a deep connection, so I close my eyes, tuning in to the energy between us, feeling for the slightest shift, the pull of something more. Nonna's fingers twitch slightly, her grip tightening ever so faintly, and I know she's guiding me.

My hands hover over the cards, and I pull one as if drawn by force.

The Moon. I close my eyes. A card of delusions, secrets, hidden truths.

When I pass my hands again, I feel something lighter, and I grab it.

The Star. A card of hope, healing, and renewal. I feel Nonna's silent approval.

Finally, my hand is pulled to a far card that flips over to reveal the Ten of Pentacles. A card of legacy, of wealth.

I look at Nonna and the cards laid out before us, and though her eyes are clouded, I know she's aware. She understands what they mean.

But I don't. Why these cards? There's something she wants me to know. Something I need to figure out. I don't want her to see that I'm struggling, that the cards are eluding me, that I'm terrified that I'm losing my grandmother. All I can sense is that she herself is satisfied with the message.

She murmurs something as she looks at me, but I can only make out one word—*sick*. I feel my heart crack.

Outside, I hear footsteps. I don't need Mom seeing this. I slide the deck back into my bag just as she reappears, Diet Mountain Dew in hand, her hair and makeup fixed but her face pinched with worry.

"My pack of Sun Chips is stuck in the vending machine, and it was my last dollar," she says, her voice so disproportionately upset you'd think someone had run over her puppy. "I pounded on the glass!"

It's clear she's teetering on the edge of meltdown.

"I'll go get them," I say dutifully, and her face softens.

"Thanks, honey bunny."

"Be right back, Nonna," I say with a quick look at Nonna, who appears to be sleeping, before I race down the hall to the lobby.

The vending machines are one floor below—a longer hike than I expected, and it's feeling like some absurd side quest—until I finally find the damn thing. The Sun Chips have fallen, ready for retrieval; they must have dropped after Mom gave up on them.

Great. Crisis averted.

On my way back, I see a commotion outside Nonna's door, and my heart slams against my ribs.

Then I hear my mother scream.

I break into a sprint, but the nurse from earlier steps into my path, blocking me.

Inside, monitors are pinging, a doctor shouts, and another rushes into the room. I lunge forward, but the nurse—unreasonably strong for her size—holds me back.

"Let me in!" I demand, but she doesn't budge.

I hear Mom's voice, shrill and cracking. "Do something! You have to do something!"

And that's when my fear turns to full-blown panic. I crane my neck and catch a glimpse of the monitors. The flat line. A piercing, steady tone that fills the room.

"Get everyone out," a doctor yells, motioning to my hysterical mother. "I can't work like this."

The nurse abandons her attempt to keep me away, and instead heads to Mom. Unlike me, she treats Mom with kid gloves—folds an arm around Mom's shoulders and leads her gently outside. If I wasn't so terrified, I'd be impressed with her ability to intuit the situation—she knows immediately that my mom is chaos.

Inside, the doctor shouts commands: "One, two, three—charge!" The paddles jolt Nonna's body. We wait an interminable minute and watch the heart monitor.

No beat.

The doctor does it again. And again. Time loses all shape. Minutes? Hours? I'm not sure I've taken a single breath.

And then the room goes quiet.

"Time of death 12:25 p.m.," the doctor says in a calm, even tone. Like my entire world hasn't just crumbled to dust. Like I haven't lost the one person who has loved and nurtured me and tried her best to keep me safe since birth.

The doctor turns to leave, her face totally blank, and as she walks away, her foot catches on a pillow—the one that was just cradling Nonna's head minutes ago. I grab it, and a sob rips out of my throat, a sound I didn't even know I could make. The doctor barely even pauses, barely looks back, just slips out the door.

"Nonna?" I whisper, my voice trembling as I finally manage to edge around the machines and reach my grandmother. But when I see her, still and lifeless, the floor beneath me gives way. A tightness wraps around my chest and squeezes until I can't let in the air. The room spins. I grip the bed frame, gasping, but it's no use. Nonna's gone. Her face—*not peaceful. She is not peaceful; in death, her mouth is twisted in rage.*

She looks so different than even how she looked just before I left the room to get Mom her fucking snack. Then, at least, Nonna seemed calm and purposeful.

But this—this is the image that will stay with me, the last one I'll ever have of my nonna, my favorite person in the world. Her tired, gentle face burns itself into my memory as my breath catches. Everything's shrinking, like the whole world's collapsing in on itself and all I can do is cling to scraps of her: the smell of Sunday dinners she'd make from scratch, her laugh when she'd catch me sneaking hard candies from her bag, the way we'd lie on our backs at night, side by side, whispering wishes to the stars through my bedroom window.

Now, though, it's all slipping through my fingers, leaving only the silence where she used to be.

FORTY-FIVE

AXE

When Josie messages me saying she won't be able to come in to work on some She's the One edits because her grandmother has passed, I put SynthoTech on full alert. I send massive bouquets, flowers upon flowers, trying to do *something*—anything, really—but it feels like grasping at air.

There's no funeral to go to, no gathering for closure. Her nonna didn't want any of it, made sure there'd be no fuss. Josie's brief texts are sweet, but there's a lost, numb sadness to them that breaks my heart.

As much as I've wanted to be right there beside her—to take her hand, to hold her close through this—she makes it clear she needs her space.

Josie wants to grieve alone.

In Scotland, with the exception of Skara Brae, when someone has passed, grief is our national sport. Wakes go on for days. Mourners take turns keeping vigil, not leaving the body, not for a moment. The family steps in, helping the caretaker with the burial, all before gathering together for the repast, sharing stories and memories. Grief's not meant to be suffered in silence. It's messy, loud, human, shared, and held up by your kin.

The next time I get to see Josie will be at Saturday's Turning Point Gala—a benefit for the shelter Strike and Honor support, which serves women and children rebuilding after domestic abuse—and anticipation jolts me awake before the sun's even up. I head to the gym for a punishing round of dead lifts, with the reward of a Green God smoothie from the juice bar: spinach, kale, banana, and some shit that tastes like powdered Band-Aids.

Then I sit down, my thumbs hovering over my phone. Josie would be the first to tell me she doesn't need me to coddle her. But . . . I can't help but check in.

Oi, Miss Greene. Still stepping out tonight for Turning Point?

A few seconds pass before her reply: Of course! I wouldn't miss it

Looking forward to seeing you outshine all that fancy art

Ha, flattery will get you everywhere. Looking forward to seeing you, too

My heart expands like a bellows. I'm trying to cook up something just right to send back when my encrypted email sounds off.

To: A. MacKenzie
From: Niles von Grafenhagen

Subject: Final Review NVG Inc. Contribution.

> I'd like to schedule a meeting tonight, 7 pm sharp, to finalize the remaining details of NVG, Inc.'s commitment to the She's the One initiative, specifically regarding the blockchain-secured investments and the cloud-based infrastructure we've allocated for long-term scalability. For convenience, let's meet at the Quarry Lounge, just next door to the Gala. I also intend to make a significant additional contribution to Turning Point this evening.

My phone buzzes again. It's Strike, who has been monitoring all of Niles's communications. "You get the message?"

"Just came through. He's got shit timing. We'll have to step out of the gala."

"It looks like he's planning more than just a casual business meeting tonight," says Strike. "He sent out a coded message earlier today—something about *pressure points* and *timing around the gala.* It's vague, but it doesn't sit right with me. Especially because it pinged near a tower not far from Veronica Petrov's estate. He's got something else going down tonight. Something that involves more than just his contribution."

I rub my hand across my jaw. "So there's more in motion. Let's meet him together and keep things tight."

"Agreed," says Strike.

When I've hung up, I stare at the phone, unhappy. As much as I wanted to spend the whole evening with Josie, it's not an option. If von Fuckwad is up to something shady, especially with Petrov's missus, keeping Josie clear of it is nonnegotiable. Her safety comes above anything else. But it's been three days since I've seen her, and just the thought of Josie walking into that hotel has me grinning like a fool.

Even if this night is about to get a lot more complicated than I thought.

At six-thirty sharp, I'm at the Keystone in a business suit that fits like a second skin, custom-made to perfection. Midnight black, immaculate. The tie's a bit too fancy for my taste, but it'll do the job. No room for half-arsed measures here. I look confident and in charge. I smile to myself, remembering when Josie called me a hot CEO daddy.

As I toss the keys to my McLaren to a teenage valet who looks like he might jizz his pants for the pleasure of parking it, I can already hear the prattle and laughter floating out from the hotel courtyard. I'll write a six-figure check before the night is out, though I would have happily done that without someone serving me canapés on a tiny napkin.

Early as it is, there's already a crowd in the hotel's atrium. I spot Honor, and I step into the ring of fans around her. She's standing in front of her latest piece. It's named *Jaxon's River*—a little boy canoes on a river of red. If you look closely, you can see that the boy's bruised wrists have broken free from fallen zip ties. The painting is as beautiful as it is disturbing—the longer I look at it, the more I see that Honor's message is about how blood needs to be spilled for you to find your way to freedom. Well, I couldn't agree more.

"I love this one," the mayor says. "It's just so . . ."

He stops, looking for a word. I get the impression the mayor knows nothing about art and is scrambling. His husband steps in.

"Happy," he exclaims. "It's just so carefree and happy."

Honor's lips quirk into a smile—she'd never let them know she's laughing at how badly they've misinterpreted her work—

and nods politely. But when Honor catches sight of my mug, she looks downright pissed. "I hear you and Strike have a hot date at seven," she hisses under her breath. "You know I'm all in on what you guys do, but come on. Not tonight. It's super shitty of you to schedule a work meeting in the middle of this event."

I hold up my hands. "Aye, I know, and I'm sorry for it. Truly. Wasn't my call. I'll bring him right back, I swear. But can you keep an eye out for Josie while I'm gone? She's had a brutal week, losing her nonna and all. I want to make sure she's not getting overwhelmed by all this."

At that, Honor's glare melts away, replaced by a knowing smile. It's subtle but unmistakable—like she can see right through me, like she knows how much I care about Josie. Am I that obvious? Is it written all over my face?

"Of course I will."

I nod, glancing at my watch. Time's ticking. Josie's last text said she'd be running late, so I'm hoping I can get to the Quarry, deal with Niles's business, and be back in time to sweep her off her feet for the night.

Still, there's something stuck in the back of my mind. Like there's something I saw and I can't shake, a darkness waiting just outside my peripheral vision.

Six fifty-seven. Right, then. Let's get this over with.

FORTY-SIX

JOSIE

I'm late, but I don't see Axe or Strike anywhere; Honor is on the other side of the room, practically getting mobbed by art groupies, and I'm starting to think coming here was a mistake.

I spent way too long just sitting on my bed, looking at old pictures of Nonna. Now, standing here in this sea of people, sipping a glass of water, I feel overdressed and underqualified—and way too grief-stricken to manage small talk with strangers.

Honor gestures for me to come over, and I make a face that I'm okay right where I am.

I really thought Nonna and I would have more time. How stupid of me—once again, ignoring what was right in front of me until it was gone. But no, no tears. Not here. This is Honor's night. Her art is on display, tagged with prices so high I nearly gasped when I saw them. My best friend is living her wildest dreams, and that's something worth celebrating, even if I feel like refried garbage.

I'm just about to head to the powder room to text Axe when a tiny elegant woman in a glittery dress catches sight of me standing alone. She smiles warmly and approaches.

"You must be Josie Greene," she says with a soft Eastern European accent that adds to her air of sophistication. She reminds me of the women I used to watch on soap operas from my hospital room as a kid; the ones who could order a chic murder without ever raising their voices.

"Yes. That's me."

"Veronica Petrov." She must be in her mid-fifties, her black hair pin-straight and pulled into a low chignon, diamonds flashing around her neck in a double-stranded choker. When I reach out awkwardly to shake her hand, she gently brushes it aside, going straight for the double kiss, and we end up doing a weird bump.

I blush, flustered. "Sorry. I guess I don't know the rules. Not sure I really belong here, to tell you the truth."

She waves it off with a small laugh. "You fit in just fine, dear. I've been collecting art for years, and you meet all manner of people at these events. I've done some work with Strike Madden's various philanthropic funds. Lovely organization, Turning Point. Such meaningful initiatives."

My face lights up. "That's really cool. I've always admired what Strike does. The scholarship fund especially—it's so important."

"Couldn't agree more." Her smile is all warm approval, but she's also eyeing me carefully, as though assessing. "Though, I admit, I didn't just stumble upon you. I sought you out for a reason."

My brows lift in surprise. "Me? Why?"

"Why are you here, Josie?" she asks, her voice taking on a curious tone, but there's an edge beneath the question, like she already knows the answer. I shuffle my feet, trying to collect my thoughts.

"My best friend, Honor—she's Strike's girlfriend—is actually showcasing her art tonight to raise money for Turning Point. I'm here to support her," I say as I gesture toward the pieces scattered around the gallery.

"And that's a noble thing, to support your friend," Veronica agrees.

"I guess . . . If you know Strike, you know Axe MacKenzie, of course," I add. I smile faintly at his name. "It's been a rough week for me. I'm helping him with a project, and I think that seeing him tonight will help me feel focused again."

"Axe MacKenzie, yes." Her tone shifts. "You must be careful, Josie."

"Careful?" My impulse is to laugh, but Veronica looks dead serious. She presses her lips together as if she's about to share something she'd rather not reveal. "I sought you out tonight because you need to know that Axe is . . . complicated. You work for him, yes?"

I nod. "Yes."

"There are things you may not know about him. His business dealings aren't always what they seem. He has a side to him—and his business—that could be very dangerous for a young woman like you."

I step back from her. "What are you talking about? Dangerous how?"

Veronica's expression is calm, almost too calm. "Axe MacKenzie doesn't just run a tech empire, my dear. He's also involved in . . . darker ventures."

"That can't be right," I say. "You're mistaken."

"I'm afraid she's not," a familiar voice cuts in. I turn and find Niles standing there, dressed in an impeccable navy suit with a shirt that's open one button too far, holding out two champagne flutes. I take one gratefully and swallow it down fast. I need some liquid courage. Veronica takes the other and gives Niles the same airy double kiss before he turns back to face me. "Hello, Josie-Jo. I hate to speak out of turn, but it's true that a lot of these ultra-wealthy types have some very, very dark secrets."

"Axe MacKenzie is an animal," Veronica says, her voice firm. It's as if seeing Niles has given her an extra measure of confidence to speak her mind. "He killed one of his rival associates at one of his own corporate events—the House of Horrors, I believe it was called. Beat the man to death in front of a crowd while pretending it was some macabre performance. A twisted joke." She pauses, her eyes dark with knowing. "And, of course, he walked away untouched. Men like Axe MacKenzie always do."

My knees almost buckle as flashes of that night at Ravenswood hit me—the blood and bile, the very real smell of piss, the man hanging by his wrists, barely conscious. A wave of fear and nausea overtakes me when I remember Strike was right next to Axe in that torture room. Does Honor know? She didn't seem particularly scared that night.

"Why are you both telling me this?" I ask. Because this isn't some casual warning—it's more like some kind of weird intervention, like they've both arranged this meeting to deliberately confront me. I feel completely blindsided. Veronica Petrov even knew my name.

Across the room, Honor is signing autographs for all her fans. She might as well be in a different zip code. Shit.

"Josie, you need to listen to me," says Niles, his fingers locking onto my arm, his eyes filled with a seriousness that chills me to the core. "You're deep into something much bigger than you realize." His tone drops to almost a growl. "And I suspect you're in grave danger."

"In what way?" It's all I can do not to shake off his touch.

"She's the One? It's not what it seems. It's a multimillion-dollar front for a sex trafficking empire." He pauses, his eyes narrowing.

"I don't understand." I truly cannot process this. *A sex trafficking empire?* It feels almost comical. "Not Axe. Not my Axe."

Veronica is eyeing me with an expression that feels close to pity. As if she can't quite believe how naive I am. That it was *pathetic* of me to use the word *my*. "We don't have time to spell out the specifics, but you have to trust us on this, Josie. None of this is what you think it is."

"I don't know what I think," I whisper through a flash of panic. Mostly what I'm thinking is that this is even more disturbing than that night at Axe's House of Horrors, when I tricked myself into believing that what I saw with my own eyes wasn't real.

"You are, unfortunately, the perfect choice," says Veronica. "A gorgeous thing like you. Naive and innocent. The perfect pick."

"No, no, I'm not . . . it wasn't . . . that's not what—"

"My team has been surveilling MacKenzie's actions for months," says Niles. "I didn't just stumble into Grace & Honor that day—I was keeping tabs. Trying to protect you. Same reason I was at that convention."

"Team? What *team*?"

"Josie, we're CIA." Niles pulls a sleek black phone from his pocket. He holds it up and, with a swipe, presents a QR code. "Scan it. It'll take you to my credentials, agency-issued."

My hands tremble as I fumble for my phone and force myself to open the camera and hover over the code. The screen blinks, and a government web page pops up. There, in front of me, is a mile-long list of personal details—under a different name; his real name, I guess—with the CIA symbol.

Niles leans in. "We'll need to move fast. You've got to come with us, where we can keep you safe." His words creep through me, unsettling—and yet they make a twisted kind of sense. He's CIA, after all. He's clearly had me under surveillance.

I think of that poor man hanging from shackles—how I watched him die like his murder was a fun show at SeaWorld.

I think of Nonna's face after she died—that rictus rage. All those warnings from her that I chose to ignore. The ones I couldn't understand.

Her last word to me echoes in my head: *sick*.

I think of all the times in my life I've chosen to turn the other cheek and ignore the obvious.

I stare into Niles's eyes, my mind spinning too fast, and let him hold me upright. Tonight, Niles von Niptuck suddenly feels like the only person I can trust.

FORTY-SEVEN

AXE

"He's ten minutes late," I mutter, eyes glued to the clock on my phone. I'm pacing the Quarry like a caged beast, trying not to let my irritation spill over. The bar's got that hazy cocktail-hour light, barely enough to be able to see without getting too cozy, and the hum of the gala next door is making me even more restless. Strike sits across from me, calm as a bloody cucumber, tapping his fingers on the table.

I can feel the impatience grinding in my chest. This was supposed to be quick—a meeting, a handshake, and back to the party.

Strike doesn't flinch. "He'll show. Or he won't. Don't let it get to you."

Easy for him to say. I open my mouth to fire back when my phone buzzes in my hand. I glance down, expecting a message from Niles.

But it's nothing like that.

It's a notification for a bid on the piece of jewelry I contributed to Turning Point. I frown at my phone, confused. The antique MacKenzie brooch, the one with the family coat of arms that I donated just to be rid of it, got a bid for fifty grand at the auction?

My body prickles with unease. Something doesn't feel right.

"What's going on?" Strike asks, glancing up.

"Donation," I mutter, scowling at the screen. I shake my head, trying to make sense of it—when my phone pings again.

This time, it's an email. My guts roil the second I see the message. It's from von Graf.

> Subject: Package Received
>
> I've picked up what I needed from Project Gemini. No further meeting required.
>
> Best regards,
> N.

I stare at the words, feeling like I just took an ice plunge. "Package received?" I repeat, like the words might explain themselves.

My mind races, the realization sinking in fast.

Fuck. He's not coming. Never was.

My gut twists hard, that sixth sense I've learned never to ignore screaming at me. He needed to sideline us to pick up what he wanted.

The only thing he ever wanted.

Gemini.

Josie.

Strike leans over, reading the email with a frown knit between his brows. "What's this shit?"

"Order the chopper," I say. "The takedown happens now."

My mind plunges into a dark, unforgiving place. Rage feels like it's taking me hostage. If I'd known—hell, if I'd even *imagined*—

for one second that bringing von Graf into She's the One would lead him to Josie, I never would've created the damn thing in the first place. But regrets are a luxury I can't afford right now.

I think back to all the safeguards I put in place—the firewalls, the encryptions, the trapdoors meant to shut everything down if anyone got too close. I've never encountered a coder who could get through my traps. Somehow, von Graf slipped in anyway. My precautions weren't enough. Not for him. Who the fuck is he? Where did he come from? Former CIA?

No time to dwell on that now. No time to let the rage boiling inside me take control. The clock's ticking, and every second that slips by is a second Josie's farther out of my reach. No more waiting, no more games. We're burning this entire operation to the ground. Whatever it takes.

I storm into the gala, heart pounding, the noise and lights barely registering as I shove past partygoers. I scan the crowd, even though I already know it; Josie's not answering her texts, and she's nowhere to be found. I push through the throng of people, calling her name, my worst fears confirmed.

Von Graf planned this from the start. And now Josie's in his hands.

"Primogen Capital headquarters," I say.

Strike nods. "Chopper's on the roof."

We're coming for her, and Hell's coming with us.

Five minutes later, we're tearing through the night sky, the helicopter blades slicing the air like a knife through flesh.

Below, the city blurs by; I notice none of it.

Von Graf's office is exactly like the man, a slick front for something far darker. At first glance, it's nothing more than a high-end corporate lair—gleaming steel, polished floors, all sharp lines and cold edges. It wouldn't raise an eyebrow. Which is exactly the point. But beneath the surface, it reeks of something far worse.

Getting in is laughably easy. The security guard at the front desk is already distracted, scrolling videos on his phone, so we pick the lock on a side entrance and slide right in without worrying about the cameras he's definitely not looking at.

Strike drops into the chair behind von Graf's massive desk. His fingers fly across the keyboard as he hacks through the layers of encryption protecting his mainframe.

"Almost there," he mutters, his fingers moving rapid-fire. He's brilliant, but I'm running out of patience. "A few more seconds."

"Seconds we don't have," I snap, my voice tight. My phone buzzes in my hand as I pull in intel from our FBI contacts. "His private jet took off from Blue Bell Airport. No flight plan was filed," I read. "Three passengers—two women, one man. No passports registered."

Fuck. So, for all we know, they could be halfway to Kathmandu by now.

Strike pulls up a series of encrypted files and starts downloading them onto a secure drive. I can hear him muttering under his breath, something about firewalls and proxy servers. He's speaking my language, but it's all white noise to me. My head's already a thousand miles away—or, more accurately, halfway across the Atlantic, assuming they went east. The chopper is on the roof to take us to my G700 the moment we get intel on their direction.

And in the meantime, we're going to crush von Graf's business into dust.

Strike's fingers pause briefly, and he leans back with a satisfied smirk. "Got it," he says, tapping a final key. "The mainframe's cracked. I'm pulling up everything now."

Screens light up all around us, with row upon row of files. Hundreds of names flash by, each belonging to a young woman caught in von Graf's web. I grit my teeth as images appear, showing women of all ages, some as young as fourteen. It's beyond reprehensible, beyond disgusting.

I glance over at Strike; his jaw is tight, eyes burning with the same fury I feel twisting inside me. "Flight coordinates confirmed," he says, indicating a screen on his left.

When I see the coordinates, a howl rips out of my throat before I can stop it. My chest tightens, a flood of rage and desperation surging through me. Of all the places, it had to be there. This is not a coincidence. Niles is fucking toying with me, has been the whole time, like a cat with a mouse.

I am no one's goddamn mouse.

"Are you sure?" My voice comes out sharp, almost desperate. I can feel my heart pounding harder with each beat. My mind spins, flashing back to memories I've kept buried for years. Every corner of that cursed place is filled with ghosts I've tried to outrun my whole life.

And now von Graf is taking Josie there, dragging me right back.

What I don't understand is why.

By the time I've pulled myself together, Strike is already disconnecting the system, wiping our tracks.

I grab my phone and dial a secure number, contacting a private crew that occasionally gives me backup. "This is Axe. Niles von Graf is en route to Skara Brae. I need a tactical team on standby, ready to move."

FORTY-EIGHT

JOSIE

I'm on a private jet flying over the Atlantic, and even with all this ridiculous luxury, I can't stop crying. The leather seats are basically hugging me, the air feels like it's been custom made for rich people, and the engine hum is almost like a lullaby. I've never traveled anywhere before—let alone like *this*. My dreams of seeing the world were always crushed by two things: my fear of getting sick and the fact that my credit cards are maxed out on insulin payments. And now here I am in a space so fancy I didn't even know it existed, and I feel like . . . I'm drowning.

I try to focus on my surroundings, but everything blurs at the edges. Even the bubbles in the champagne glass feel too sharp, too bright. Instead of wonder, a strange heaviness fills my limbs. My thoughts are slipping, scattered like the stars outside the window. I sink deeper into the seat, unable to fight this wave of dizziness that is crashing over me.

Across from me, Niles sits watching me with his usual creepy intensity. He keeps telling me that I'm safe now. His weird calm feels like the opposite of safe.

Time feels wavy; I was at the party, and then Niles said he'd protect me, and within the hour, we were in Blue Bell, Pennsylvania, at a private airport, where Niles's Bombardier Global 7500 was waiting. Apparently, when you are as rich as Niles von Grafenhagen, you can whisk a woman out of the country without even showing a passport. Or I suppose his contacts at the CIA would have helped him with that part. He says where we're going is isolated and secure, and there's no way Axe could reach me there.

I was too overwhelmed and terrified to ask for details. More than that, I feel utterly heartbroken. My mouth has mostly stopped working, and despite the tears flooding my face, I'm almost catatonic. I must be in shock.

It's like I can still hear the screams—the guy trapped in the lobotomy lab, begging for his life. His voice was shredded with fear. The smirk on Axe's and Strike's faces, like they were having . . . fun. It wasn't some prank. The sound is stuck in my head, crawling around in my brain like a tarantula.

Why can't I ever see what's so obvious to everyone else? My mind spirals, looping with the same questions, all snarled up in confusion and regret. How did I not realize She's the One was a front and not the groundbreaking AI innovation I so desperately wanted to believe in? How did I not see Axe for who he really is? I feel like I'm swimming through glue, barely keeping my head above the surface. I fold over, pressing my forehead to my knees, trying to anchor myself in the midst of the overwhelming dizziness.

I love Axe—*loved* him, I keep telling myself—and really believed he was my future. I thought he was different. Kind. That he actually saw me—the real me. Not some weak, easy-to-manipulate Josie like everyone else saw. He saw the version of me

I wanted to be. Strong. Brave. Someone who could hold her own. But now, with tears blurring my vision and this heavy weight in my chest, I finally get it. I had him all wrong. Just like Bryan. Just like my mom.

He didn't see *me*. He saw a mark.

I fell for it. Hook, line, and fucking sinker.

"We'll be there soon," Niles says. "You're safe now, Josie-Jo."

Ugh. *Josie-Jo?* God, I feel like I might vomit. Niles taps my knee with his hand, and it lingers for a second too long. Did I imagine that, too? Why am I having such a hard time thinking straight?

I try to sort through the facts. Axe is a sex trafficker. Is Strike one, too? Where is Honor in all this? Niles is CIA? But he's also a businessman? With a private jet? Does that make sense?

My head feels too heavy to move, but I catch the sound of a woman's voice behind me—a slight Eastern European accent lacing her words.

"Just knock her out already. She's getting on my nerves with all that crying and rambling about tarot cards and her nonna. What the hell even *is* a nonna?"

Am I rambling? I can't even tell anymore. I can't feel my lips.

"Leave her alone," Niles says quietly, brushing a finger across my cheek.

Everything feels just out of my grasp. I lean back and close my eyes, because I don't have the energy to keep them open anymore.

Then I'm in a car, the outside world zooming by in a blur. The road is rough, jolting me with every bump. I feel a hand on my thigh—small but firm. My head feels like it weighs a ton, and my thoughts are all fuzzy, like static on a TV. I try to speak, to ask what's happening, but I'm so tired—*too* tired. Before I can grab on to any clear thought, the darkness pulls me under.

When I wake up again, I find myself in a massive bed, the room around me drafty despite its grandeur. Heavy velvet drapes hang closed, trapping the room in a haze of dust. For a moment, I'm taken in by the beauty of what I can glimpse through the dim light—the majestic canopy bed, the intricately carved wood furnishings adorned with Celtic patterns. But a sinking feeling grips my stomach.

Where the hell am I? Ravenswood? The thought crashes through me. No, I'm really far away from Shelton. I was on a plane. With Niles. Niles, who is creepy but safe, right? And a woman. My mother? No. Nonna? Nonna is dead. *Oh, oh, oh, Nonna is dead.* This memory is like pressing a bruise.

I float in and out of consciousness. The energy in the room suffocates me, thick and dark. I can almost hear Nonna's voice, a warning from the grave. *Rimettiti in sesto, Josie. Il pericolo è dietro l'angolo!—Pull yourself together, Josie! Danger is just around the corner!* No kidding, Nonna.

I try to sit up, but my body won't cooperate. My heart is pounding, my head spinning. Somewhere, faint and far away, I hear screams. Pleading. Desperate. Or maybe that's just in my head? Maybe it's me screaming?

I clutch the heavy blanket around my shoulders, unsure if I'm hearing ghosts of the past or if my own damn mind is unraveling.

Is this how my mother ended up at Ravenswood? One minute she felt rational and sane, and the next her mind felt like a dandelion blowing in the wind?

Nonna, what would you do? She'd certainly have sensed the traumatic, oppressive energy in the walls of this space. I feel dark secrets here, wrongdoings steeped in the history of each brick. I feel pain, anger, and helplessness. A memory slips in—Dr. Don, his eyes scanning the surgery recovery room with sadistic detachment. I was so young then. So trusting. I can still hear his smooth, friendly voice, ordering those of us who were strong enough to get out of bed to stand and line up in a row.

Squats, he would demand, watching as we bent our trembling knees. Then came the jumping jacks, Dr. Don's hand clap keeping the beat as we all moved together. The aerobic exercise was supposed to be good for our phlegm-filled lungs. "Lovely Josie," he always said to me, his voice treacly. "Everything will be fine, my sweet. Drink and rest."

But no—that's not Dr. Don. My eyes snap open.

Niles is perched on the edge of my bed, his face unnervingly close, a mug cradled in his hands. He's staring at me, too calm. As if he's got everything under control.

I grew frightened of Dr. Don's special drink. It always made me sleep heavily and left me with a metallic taste in my mouth. I test my tongue over my gums. Yes, same taste. Same heaviness in my limbs. I've been through this before.

I've been drugged.

The realization settles my brain into a surprising relief; it lets the scattered pieces slowly start to fall back into place.

"Here you go. Another sip," says Niles, offering the mug. "You've had quite a shock. But you're safe with me now."

My heart is racing, pounding so hard I swear he can hear it. I want to scream in Niles's pasty face, tell him I know what's happening. I know I've been drugged, and I am not safe. His CIA "credentials" are just as fake as the concern plastered across his starched face. It's all part of the same twisted pantomime. Just like Dr. Don, he's hiding behind a mask, spinning lies and false comforts for his own sociopathic pleasure.

I knew Axe, my Axe, wasn't the enemy here. Again, the truth was right in front of me; I was just looking the wrong way.

There's got to be an explanation for the shackled man. I just haven't figured it out yet. Maybe I've been jumping to conclusions, or maybe there's something bigger at play. Something I can't see. But I'm not giving up. I refuse to believe that Axe would just suddenly turn into some kind of monster.

Not after everything we've been through. Not after everything he's done for me.

When Niles gently presses the mug toward my lips, I pretend to sip, trying to keep my breathing steady despite my fear.

Because I need to play along.

If Dr. Don taught me anything, it was how to survive.

"After you've slept," he says smoothly, "we'll have a little bite together. I've whipped up some tatties and eggs for breakfast. You must have a lot of questions."

"Sounds good," I say meekly. Tatties? Is Niles Scottish, too? Also, it's time for breakfast? Shit, I must have been out for hours. "No snail tartare," I add with a weak little smile, keeping it all so sweet, my JosieFightsOn persona clicked into play.

"You minx." Niles chuckles. I hold the smile on my face as I close my eyes, pretend to snuggle down in the bed until Niles rises, and suppress a horrible shiver as he runs his finger slowly down the side of my face. When he leaves the room, the door locks gently behind him. I know that sound, too. I am a prisoner here. I've been a prisoner my whole damn life.

No doubt they've got cameras in this room. But I'm used to being watched—years of doctors and caretakers taught me how to blend in under their unsmiling scrutiny. I let my body go limp, keeping up the pretense of sleep. My breathing slows, deepens, while my mind clears and becomes sharp. I can't let on that I know I'm trapped.

Bit by bit, I let my limbs shift around. I keep each move small, making sure I don't give away what I'm really up to. I play it off like I'm just a restless, drugged-out Josie, tossing and turning, trying to get comfy. When, in fact, I'm scouring the room, my eyes sweeping every nook for where they might've hidden a camera.

And then I spot it. Right inside the eye socket of a carved bust perched on the heavy oak wardrobe. *Oh, you clever fuckers.* I keep my face slack, pretending I haven't noticed a damn thing. Instead, I let out a big, exaggerated yawn and stretch as I slide out of bed, making my movements slow and groggy, like I'm still very much under the influence of whatever they dosed me with. Who is *they*? Niles? Niles and Veronica? An entire security team?

Nothing to see here.

I sway toward the bathroom and absently grab my silk scarf, which is hanging over the chair with my dress, and in one sleepy motion, I toss it over my shoulder. It flutters just right, landing over the bust's head and covering that creepy little camera eye. *Perfect.*

There might be other cameras in the room, but I can't risk waiting any longer to look for my escape. I know I've only got a small window—maybe five minutes tops—before they grow suspicious that I'm doing anything other than using the bathroom.

I check the door. Locked. My bag is nowhere to be found. I scan for any other devices, but nothing. Then I tug at the curtains and am greeted with . . . an unending carpet of green against a gray sky.

Bright, glossy fields stretch out as far as I can see.

Great. Where the hell am I? I could be literally anywhere on the planet. I have no idea how long I was on that damn plane.

My mind racing, I go back to the bathroom and stare at the toilet. It's old-fashioned, the kind with a wooden handle and a metal chain. The tile floor is cold, and the air smells musty. I'm not somewhere particularly warm or dry.

I'm just a girl, standing inside of the bathroom, asking for a way to get the fuck outta here.

Almost as an afterthought, I open the old medicine cabinet, and there it is. Tucked behind a few old bottles of aspirin are bandages, a bottle of bright red nail polish . . . and a bobby pin. Bingo.

I don't think whoever is watching will be able to see through my scarf, but I'm not taking any chances. I drop to the floor and army crawl my way to the bedroom door. I slip the pin in the lock and fiddle for about twenty seconds.

Come on, come on, come on.

When I finally hear a click, I almost groan in relief. Thank God. Looks like the locks are as ancient as the toilets. Slowly, I push the door open, and the realization slams into me. No one is coming to save me. Axe would assume I left the party because I was sad about Nonna. And even if he gets suspicious, even if he worries, he'll have no way of knowing where I've been taken.

It's just me against whatever the hell is waiting outside.

I can do this.

I inch forward, craning my neck to get a look—then suck in a sharp gasp.

I don't know what I expected, but it sure as hell wasn't this.

Where. The. Fuck. Am. I?

FORTY-NINE

AXE

I haven't set foot in Scotland since the day I buried my old man.

And even then, I flew in and out the same day, only to see that bastard in the box. Had to make sure that El D—the truest Devil I ever knew—was actually dead.

I spat on his corpse, told him I'd see him in hell, gave the mortician a thousand quid to burn and dispose of his body. Then turned on my heel and headed right to the airport. Nobody would question it. Nobody would ever admit to knowing El D, let alone being close enough to his gruesome business to care what happened to him after death. His whole empire was built on fear and silence.

I swore to myself I'd never come back. Too many ghosts. From across the Atlantic, I sold off Skara Brae and every last stick of furniture in it to a corporate buyer looking to expand its portfolio of fancy destination spas. Since Hamish was dead, I inherited it all, and I donated every bloody cent anonymously to anti–sex trafficking charities. I'd never touch my da's filthy money. Not a penny.

The plane jolts as the landing gear hits the tarmac, yanking me from my thoughts. The G700's engines whine as we slow to a stop. I see the rain-soaked landscape of Scotland outside my window. A few hazy hills loom in the distance, half hidden by mist, but I know this place all too well—its secrets are buried deep in the earth, and its ghosts are waiting for me.

I squeeze my eyes shut and picture Josie's smile, her contagious joy, the way her aura lights up a room. And aye, I know she'd laugh her arse off at me for sounding like her and using the word *aura*.

I imagine the feel of her lips against mine, full and warm, grounding me.

The plane rolls into the private hangar, and I unclip my seat belt with a steady hand. The stakes are too high to give in to fear. As I step off the plane, Scotland's icy breath stirs up every cursed memory I've tried to bury deep.

Dragging me back to *that* moment. The one that broke me beyond repair. The one that made me into who I am now.

I shove it away, disgust curling in my gut.

My eyes lock onto a figure standing beside the SUV, just outside the hangar. He's leaning casually against the door, arms crossed.

The moment he spots me, a slow, confident grin splits his face.

"Look what the wind dragged back across the pond," he says, swaggering over. His grip is firm when he shakes my hand, then he pulls me into a tight bear hug.

"Hawk! It's been too bloody long, brother," I say, slapping him on the back. Hawk isn't just anyone; he's the kind of guy you don't forget—a tall, broad-shouldered, strapping lad, straight out of an action hero summer blockbuster. We met years ago, working as private contractors on some of the nastiest jobs in Eastern Europe. Mutual trust and steady trigger fingers were all that kept us alive.

It's good to see him again, but the grins don't last long. We both know this isn't a reunion. "This one's serious," I say.

Hawk's eyes harden. "Let's get you geared up." He moves to

the back of the SUV and pops the boot. Inside is an arsenal—pistols, assault rifles, the whole bloody works. As soon as I strap on the tactical vest, my heartbeat steadies. Josie's out there, and she's counting on me. And if there's one benefit to being the wrecked version of Axe, it's this: I know I'll stop at nothing, absolutely nothing, to bring her home.

FIFTY

AXE

The morning when Axe's life is cleaved in two begins like any other: rain rattling against the windows, crows cawing in the distance. He hears the faint clatter of a girl's heels echoing on the marble floors as she slips out of one of the Whales' rooms, heading back to her bunk to crash. The hiss of a shower follows—a girl scrubbing away the traces of a filthy man. Downstairs, the clink of breakfast dishes signals that Mrs. Collins is laying out a buffet for the guests.

Axe is sixteen and constantly starving, his body growing so fast his legs throb at night. Hamish has taken off to somewhere in Eastern Europe—likely on another recruiting trip—and Axe is grateful for the break.

"Check out these tits, Axe," Hamish said right before he left, grabbing a bikini-clad breast and giving it a squeeze. The girl let out a small sound of pleasure, but Axe saw the tension in her eyes, the way she held back. He knew if she had the chance, she'd strangle Hamish with her bare hands.

"Go ahead, touch them," Hamish insisted to him. "It's like you're living in Disney World and refusing to ride a single feckin' ride."

Axe didn't know how to respond, still doesn't know how to tell Hamish that he will never touch any girl who has set foot in his father's house. Da talks to others as if Hamish and Axe taking over the business is a foregone conclusion, that Axe will eventually outgrow his childish objections and start sampling the merchandise. That's what Da calls the girls—merchandise.

The moment Axe steps out of his bedroom, panic slices through him. Something is terribly wrong. The morning's usual eerie quiet has been replaced by shrieks and cries and stomping boots, all waning as they move through the hall. The tension hangs in the air like the faintest trace of smoke—acrid and sharp, it clings to everything, like a bitter, burnt scent that stings the back of his throat.

Today, there will be a massacre.

Mrs. Collins is no longer in the dining room, setting out the usual platters of black pudding—thick slices of blood sausage made from pork blood and oats, a staple of the breakfast table. The dining room is empty.

Where is Mrs. Collins? Where are the girls? The Whales? And Da's security team, always roving with automatic weapons and sunglasses despite the endless gray skies—where have they gone?

"It's Interpol," Axe hears as he turns a corner and runs smack into Da. He looks different today. Unshaven, shirt untucked. Normally he's doused in cologne. "My man in Manchester says we have one hour. One fucking goddamn hour. Let's get this done."

Da is shouting at Gallows, a man Axe has gone out of his way to avoid since he arrived on the island five years ago. Gallows is an imposing figure—shaved head and a Special Forces tattoo curling up his neck that reads Nemo Me Impune Lacessit. *Axe once looked it up:* No one provokes me with impunity. *As far as Axe can tell, Gallows is the only one on Da's payroll who doesn't touch the girls—even Mrs. Collins herself is known to indulge now and then. Gallows, though, watches them with cold, calculating eyes, as if he's tallying cattle. Sometimes, just for sport, he'll kick them in the kidneys.*

"Our twelve guests are already on the boat. They'll be in Glasgow before lunchtime. There won't be a trace they were ever here," Gallows reports.

"Good." Da doesn't even flinch when Axe bumps into him. He's too busy barking orders, too laser-focused to spare a glance at his own son. "Mrs. Collins activated protocol C. All files have been incinerated. Now we just need to deal with the merchandise."

Merchandise. *The word sends a chill through Axe, freezing him to his core. Nausea churns in his gut, and he knows the moment his father is out of earshot, he'll lose whatever's left in his stomach. It hits him harder than ever—he was born to the wrong family, the wrong father, maybe even the wrong continent. If it weren't for the same bright blue eyes and sharp, unforgiving jawline, he could believe he'd been switched at birth. This is why he avoids mirrors.*

He tells himself their souls are nothing alike.

"I don't want a single hair left behind. Do you hear me? No fingerprints. No fingers, for that matter. No blood. Bodies dropped offshore, deep in the ocean. Fifteen minutes."

"Sir, I'm not sure we can guarantee no blood. We've got twenty-two girls on the island and less than an hour. How do you expect me to—"

"Just get it done!" Da snaps. "When Interpol arrives, I want to be sitting in the den, drinking Black Label, smoking a cigar. I'm going to serve them tea, smile in their faces, and send them packing with nothing. My lawyer's choppering in just to rattle them a bit. So they understand exactly who the fuck they're dealing with."

"Got it," Gallows says, snapping a salute like Da's some military god. Axe wants to run. He wants to scream at the girls to run, too—

but what would be the point? He wouldn't save them, just terrify them. There's nowhere to go. No safe shore to swim to.

Da and his men have the guns, the power.

If this is really the end for the girls—on this cursed island, miles from anything that feels like home, their final breaths begging for their mammies—better it comes quick and without warning.

"Axe! Go help Gallows. We need you," Da says as Axe tries to slip around the corner.

"No." Axe's voice trembles as bile rises up the back of his throat. He won't do this. He won't.

"Fine," Da says, his voice snapping like a whip. "But when Interpol shows up, I'll hand you over myself. Tell 'em you've been running the whole thing right under my nose. They'll be thrilled to haul in a MacKenzie. You think they give a damn which one? A notch on their belt's a notch either way."

Terror claws at Axe's throat like a beast. Gallows signals for him to follow, and he does, slipping away from Da's watchful eye. But he knows what he's going to do. He'll leg it—he'll be a bloody coward and run. When Interpol shows up by boat, he'll jump aboard and beg for a lift anywhere that's not Skara Brae. He's clever enough, good with computers. Maybe they'll even hire him.

As Axe is about to take off—he's not even wearing proper shoes, but no matter—Gallows grabs him by the back of the neck and jabs a gun into his back.

"This way, lad." Axe grits his teeth, but there's no choice—he's dragged straight toward Hell.

Once they're outside, the trembling kicks in. Axe has already puked three times on the rocky shore; a grim trail of breadcrumbs for Interpol to follow, he tells himself with a bitter laugh, now on his hands and knees, hacking. Gallows has given up on him, eyes full of pure disgust. He's got a job to do, and Axe can either muck in or piss off. He's not their target, not yet. No sense in reminding them of his existence and ending up as another body tossed to the hungry sea.

The women are already lined up along the shoreline, shivering and scattered, in various states of undress—pulled from their beds, by the look of 'em. Barefoot, standing in two feet of freezing water, no more than ten feet from land, they clutch one another's hands like lifelines. They're crying, their voices a mess of languages Axe can't place, though he doesn't need to understand to know they're begging for their lives.

He catches the whisper of "please, please, please" slipping from someone's lips. What they're begging for, he doesn't know. Probably just for it all to end.

Axe has never felt more useless in his life, and his legs give out. Gallows and his men are armed to the teeth with AK-47s, while all he's got is a spiral-bound notebook stuffed in his back pocket, filled with shite poetry. He's reedy, skin and bones, hasn't touched a weight in his life and wouldn't know how to throw a proper punch if his life depended on it.

As Gallows raises his gun and cuts them down one by one, bang-bang-bang, *the girls fall like dominoes. Blood seeps into the sea, only to be dragged back by the tide. The men move in quickly, bagging the slight bodies and tossing them into the speedboat like sacks of rubbish. And there's Axe, still on his knees, praying—praying for their lost souls, and praying for his own damned one, too.*

Hours later, Axe lies curled up on his bed, weeping as hopelessness presses down on him, heavy as a gravestone.

Interpol never came.

There's no rescue, no boat to slip onto, no escape on the horizon. The plan—the only thread of hope he had—was nothing but smoke. The man in Manchester had it wrong. All of it was for nothing. The false alarm shattered the last bit of faith Axe had clung to, the hope that someone, anyone, was coming to save him.

How could it be so easy for the world to look the other way? Why isn't anyone doing something? Surely someone out there is searching for these girls. Rage boils in his chest, but it has nowhere to go, trapped under the crushing truth that nothing will ever change.

"No matter." Da had shrugged, completely unfazed, smoking a celebratory cigar after a bullet dodged. "Hamish will be home soon with fresh, younger merchandise. Won't be long now."

That's what Da has to say about murdering twenty-two girls for no reason at all.

FIFTY-ONE

JOSIE

The warmth of dark chocolate wood paneling and ancient cranberry wallpaper greets me as I step into the hallway, the fabric worn in places, the whole space dripping with old-worldly, haunted mansion–stye opulence. Oil portraits of stern-faced white men, all framed in gaudy gold, line the walls between massive mounted stag heads. I glance left, then right—the hallway stretches endlessly in both directions, a faded green carpet running down its center like a spine connecting the rooms.

The eerie stillness sends a chill down my back. Not a soul in sight, just the cold echo of an empty space too large for comfort. I think for a moment that this might be Niles von Getfucked's hunting lodge, but no—this place is far too grand. The scale is enormous, far more intense than some "lodge."

I glance down at the floor, searching for footprints, hoping for a clue about which direction to take. There's nothing—no sign of anyone. I make a quick decision and turn right, moving as quietly as I can, my footsteps light as I shuffle through this strange . . . palace? Mansion? Hotel? Whatever it is, it's massive and disorienting. If I weren't literally fleeing for my life, I might even be curious enough to explore. After what feels like forever, I stumble upon a spiral staircase and descend three flights. At the bottom, I step into a giant industrial kitchen. It's empty, but the lingering scent of hot oil hangs heavy in the air, a sign that someone was just here.

The place feels recently alive yet completely abandoned.

I feel like I went to sleep at Honor's art show and woke up a prisoner in Downton Abbey.

I slip out the back door, and the wind hits me like a slap—sharp, cold, and drenched in rain. It cuts through my wrinkled, sweat-soaked black dress, and every step sends a raw sting through the soles of my bare feet as they meet the rough concrete. I turn, staring up at the building I just escaped. The dark gray walls seem to shoot into the sky, crowned with turrets that jut out like ridiculous dunce caps.

Okay, this is a motherfucking castle.

Now I break into a run. No plan, no map, just go. I sprint up a grassy hill, hoping for a view—a town, a highway, hell, even a McDonald's. By the time I hit the top, I'm panting hard, but at least my asthma's in check—good thing, too, because my inhaler's God knows where. Probably with my bag. I imagine Niles dumping it out the plane window at thirty thousand feet, laughing like an asshole.

I spin around to see a scattering of buildings and green lawns, which seems to be my best option. My heart leaps out of my body, because beyond that, there's a perimeter of jagged, brutal cliffs and, beyond that, nothing but a churning curtain of black-blue sea.

This is a motherfucking castle . . . on a motherfucking island.

Ten minutes later, I end up in a chapel—a totally random choice of building after a sad, desperate game of Eenie Meenie Miney

Mo. I crawl under a pew and, because I've got no clue what else to do, I start to pray. The last time I did that was at MS Hospital, right after Dr. Don had told me the cancer was back, and he'd hit me with the *you'll be lucky to see the end of the year* speech.

Fuck Dr. Don and double fuck Niles von Grafenhagen.

When the footsteps come, I cover my head and curl into a tiny ball.

"Josie-Jo, I know you're in here. Skara Brae has cameras everywhere. That's how we keep this place safe. Come on out, sweetheart. I'll never hurt you." Niles's voice is soft, like he's trying to coax a scared kitten. In a split second, I change strategies—I will revert to old tried-and-tested battle plans. I will go full JosieFightsOn.

"I'm here," I say, from under the pew. I try to make myself sound small and fragile, though every fiber of me is burning to roar, to leap up and tear Niles apart with my bare hands. "But I'm scared. I know you drugged me, and I don't understand why."

My voice wobbles perfectly. No tears—I'm too pissed for that—but just enough to sell it. I clench my fists so hard I'm surprised I don't break skin.

Niles will not see my fury. I will only show him my faux fragility.

"Oh, sweetheart, I had to do that. You were so scared because you knew Axe was coming to get you, and so I figured that was the best way to get you here. To safety," Niles says. "It was all for you. To protect you."

I slowly come out of my crouch and sit down on a pew. Niles drops down next to me, so close I have to bite back a gag. His thigh presses against mine.

"Where are we? What is this place?" I ask, all wide-eyed wonder. I will play the role of Sleeping Beauty who just woke up into a magical, unexplained world.

"My castle. In Scotland. It's lovely, isn't it?" Niles asks.

I keep my voice soft, like I'm still unsure about him but curious enough to stay. "I've never seen anything like it. But I'm scared, Niles."

If I survived my childhood and Dr. Don and the anxiety force field of my mother, I can survive this. I will not die here today in this ridiculous motherfucking castle on this random motherfucking island.

"Oh no. Don't be scared." He drags one long, creepy finger down my hand, then across my collarbone. Gross. He moves to smooth my hair with his whole palm, like he owns me. "I love you, Josie-Jo. I knew the second I saw you that you were mine. I'll protect you. There's so much evil in the world, and I won't let anyone hurt you."

Gaslighting prick.

"Especially not someone like Axe MacKenzie. Who thinks women are garbage. Playthings to be bought and sold."

I let my mind drift to Axe and block out Niles's words. I will not believe a word this psycho—who spiked my drink and locked me in a room—has to say. Where is Axe right now? Does he care that I left the party? Does he think I'm back in my apartment, in my pajamas, mourning Nonna? Has he decided I'm nothing more than an employee after all—that AI Josie is really all he needs?

I picture his blue eyes, the way they soften when he looks at me, and his messy hair that somehow always suits him perfectly. I remember how he saved me from that drunk guy at the House of Horrors. He's always looking out for me, making sure I'm okay. I saw Axe beat that man at the party, and honestly, I'd be happy to watch him do the same to Niles. Given the chance, I would easily bite off his ear myself, sever a limb, watch him bleed out on the floor in front of me without a whiff of guilt.

The world is full of evil people. I've felt that same fire, that same urge to tear the world apart, to destroy people who deserve it. Maybe that's why I get him. Maybe that's why we make sense. Maybe we're exactly what the other needs. I think about how much I love him—I do; I *love him*—how that feeling alone should be enough to push me through, no matter how he feels about me. That love is what's going to get me the hell out of here.

I will see Axe again. I know it.

Because if there's one thing worth fighting for, it's love. And love sure as hell is something to live for.

"Can you give me a tour of this place?" I ask, putting on my best sugary-sweet I'm-so-pathetic voice. If my mom were here, she'd be snapping a pic for socials with a #fuckcancer #bravegirlJosie caption. I'm scrubbing that identity from my life if I get home—no, *when* I get home. JosieFightsOn is getting wiped from the internet, and I'm taking back my own damn life. But first I need to take this bastard out. "I've never seen the ocean. I want to see the cliffs."

Niles stands up, extending his hand like some kind of twisted wannabe gentleman. I take it, give it a little squeeze for good measure, and let him kiss me on the forehead.

I deserve a fucking Oscar for not punching him right then and there.

FIFTY-TWO

AXE

We arrive by boat—Hawk drops me about thirty meters from shore so I can slip onto the island quiet and undetected.

"I've got a few of the lads on standby not far from here. We're ready to move if things get messy. You just do what you need to do in there."

"Aye, thanks, mate."

"Don't thank me, just get out of there alive."

There's no denying the danger of what lies ahead—though I don't spare a thought for what might happen to me. All that matters is Josie being taken to safety far from this cursed hellhole.

Grabbing my scuba gear, I glance up toward the estate, the dark silhouette of Skara Brae barely visible through the rain and fog. As I jump into the freezing water, my mind's swimming with questions. Why here? There's something I'm missing, something right in front of my eejit face.

In all the time since my father died, and his empire with him, I stopped keeping tabs on Skara Brae. Hamish had already been gone for years by then, so once I sold the island to some luxury developers, I didn't look back. I couldn't bear to even google the place where the worst of my memories fester. Even if they turned it into some posh destination spa as planned, I wasn't keen to know. But clearly, that project never came to be. The castle stands there still, tall and unchanged, looming over the water like a damn ghost. It's a bloody beacon of violence and shame for me, cutting through the Sea of the Hebrides like some ancient wound that refuses to heal.

At the age of seventeen, I caught a ride to the mainland with one of the Whales for what was ostensibly supposed to be my first recruiting trip but was instead my escape from my father's clutches. I cut all ties with Scotland. Moved to America. Joined the CIA. Started a whole new life.

I've never told anyone the full tale of my childhood. Never had the stomach for it. But it's no bloody coincidence that my father's empire was replaced with the same sick, twisted business. Ending sex trafficking's like a game of Whac-A-Mole, aye, but you don't often see the bastards set up shop in the exact same place.

There's got to be a link—von Graf must be tied to one of the Whales, one of my father's so-called guests who came to the castle to "play." The same vile men, playing the same vile games.

This place is cursed. And I know it runs deeper than just business.

I crawl onto the rocky beach—the same one that, when I was sixteen, ran red with blood. In my memory, it still stinks of copper. Each gunshot still vibrates through me. *Bang, bang, bang.* No time to dredge up the past now. I've got a lass to save.

I strip off my wet suit, shove it in my dry bag, and change into my fatigues. Von Graf may have owned this place for years, but there's no way he knows it better than I do. I could map every inch, every hidden passage, every dark tunnel.

And fuck me, it looks exactly the same. I thought it might seem smaller now, but it looms just as massive, just as Gothic.

Beautiful and barbaric, with its cold stone walls, iron-chained drawbridge, and cliffs sharp enough to keep you trapped on the island and keep the rest of the world out.

I assume the cameras are still in the same places, so I take the old route I used to take to sneak to my mother's window at night when she'd sing to me like a princess locked in her tower. No clue if von Graf runs the same kind of security as my father did, but I'm not about to take any chances.

The last thing I need is to set off an alarm.

Josie could be anywhere—locked in one of the castle's endless rooms, stashed away in one of the outbuildings, or maybe hiding in the tall grass. But once she realizes this place is an island with nowhere to run, she'll play it smart. Josie will charm Niles until she can work out an escape. My girl's sharp as hell, and that's the only way through this.

I wonder if she knows I'm coming for her.

Christ, I hope so.

I let myself think *my girl* just this once, knowing damn well that after today, she'll never be mine. If she ever was. Not after she learns the truth—how this is all my fault. Certainly not after she sees me turn von Graf into fish food.

I work my way up from the beach, past the only boat I've seen, squinting into the gray haze of a typical Scottish spring day. The fog's thick as hell, cold air biting at my wet skin. I scan the horizon—not a soul in sight. No armed men, no staff, no guests. Could be they're all holed up inside, but this place feels hollow. Dead.

If Niles, Josie, and maybe Veronica are here, I'd wager they're alone.

Near the old barn, there's a stack of wood, an axe lying next to it. I've got a gun tucked into my waistband, but I pick up the axe, feel its weight. Never killed anyone with an axe before, but there's a first time for everything. Seems fitting—poetic, even.

I tie the weapon to my back and move fast, searching in circles, working my way in. The cliffs on the south side tower higher, and though I've avoided them since my mother died—ever since I assumed my father tossed her body over them—I decide to start there. When I was a lad, I placed a wooden cross with her name on it to mark the spot, but I never had the guts to come back. Too much to face. But the cliffs offer the best view of the land. If Josie's outside, I'll see her from that perch.

When I reach the top, I hear voices carried by the wind. Faint but close.

I push through a thicket of trees, and there they are—Josie and von Graf, facing the ocean and standing too close for my liking. He's pointing out to sea—maybe at an actual whale, the bastard. More irony. Josie's giving him her fake smile, the one she uses when she's holding on by a thread.

I swear, I will do whatever it takes so she never has to show that smile again.

"Get on the ground, now!" I shout, pulling my gun, aiming straight at Niles.

He turns, too calm, as if he's been waiting for this. As if he's been waiting for me. He pulls out a gun of his own, yanking Josie closer, first pressing the barrel of the gun to her temple—just for a second, long enough to make my chest constrict—then aiming it at me.

"Axe," von Graf drawls, almost as if he's bored. "A bit late to the party, wouldn't you say?" He's handling his gun like it's a bloody prop, like he won't actually have to use it. As if we're having some grand misunderstanding and we're on the same team. "Fun game, though, wasn't it? You thought you were baiting me the whole time, but really, it was the other way around."

"Josie was never bait!" I snap. My finger tightens on the trigger. My mind needs to stay sharp, but that gun—*too close to her, too close*—is all I can see. Even if I shoot von Graf, he might have just enough time to pull the trigger. Josie—*my* Josie—could be gone in an instant.

Focus, MacKenzie.

"Oh, not Josie. Though she's been quite the little firecracker, hasn't she? I can't get enough." His hand strokes the side of her cheek slowly, savoring the feel of her skin. Josie gasps, but I don't flinch. I can't look at her, not with von Graf right there, too close to taking everything from me. I need to stay sharp and locked in. "I meant She's the One. You dangled it in front of me like a rotisserie chicken at the market. Did you really think I wouldn't notice you poking through my servers? You're good, Axe, but you're not that good."

I grunt, refusing to bite. I won't let him rattle me.

"You've been targeting your father's clients one by one for years, so after you finally took out Petrov, I knew I was next. So predictable. The CIA trained you well—or was it here at Skara Brae, under your old man's thumb, that you learned to be so methodical?"

Every muscle in me is coiled, waiting for the perfect second to strike. We ran this scenario a million times in CIA training—rule number one: keep your target talking. As long as they're flapping their gums, they're not pulling the trigger. "Looks like you've taken over the old family business smoothly enough," I say, stalling for time. "It's all yours. I want no claim to it. Enjoy the castle, though the heating bill's a right bastard."

Von Graf lets out a long, loud laugh, then fixes me with a look that chills me to the bone. "Aye, the *family* business." His accent changes, thickens to a full-on Scotsman's brogue. "And what a job I've made of it, eh? Have you really forgotten me, wee brother?"

The shock hits like a bullet to the gut—like he's already pulled the trigger on both me and Josie. I almost drop my gun. Almost. It all clicks. How did I not see it? The surgeries, the new teeth—and he's at least seventy pounds heavier than the last time I saw him. His eyes used to be as blue as mine, so he must be wearing brown-colored lenses. But there's no denying it.

"Hamish?" I whisper, though it's not a question.

"Aye, who else would it be?" he sneers. "Missed me, Sing-Song? Da would be rolling in his grave, seeing how straight you've gone, but me? I'm right proud of ya. And that VR shite you're flogging? Bloody genius. Who wouldn't want to screw this fine piece of arse?"

Sing-Song. His old nickname for me is a stab of memory. He used to tease me relentlessly when I was a wee one, listening to Mum's lullabies outside the keep. I swallow the growl rising in my throat, fighting to keep my cool. His brogue is like a ghost from the past, a voice I've been running from for years. He sounds like Da. He sounds like everything I've been trying to escape.

"Now put down the gun. You might like to play hero and save the lasses, but I know you. No way you'd shoot your own brother. Never had that sort of Devil in you, no matter how hard Da and I tried to drum it in."

"How about we both put down the guns, Hamish?" I say, keeping my voice steady.

"Aye, right," he sneers, his eyes flicking to the memorial. "Look at that. A wee shrine to yer poor dead mammie." His boot—heavy, steel-toed—kicks the cross hard, knocking it loose in the dirt.

"Lurlene was a kind soul, though, wasn't she? Soft. Not like mine." He leans in closer, grin twisted. "My mammie was a right fuckin' cunt."

I keep my hands low, nonthreatening. "You win, Hamish. I'm here. You've got me. If this is about your business, I'll walk away. Whatever you're worried about, I'll leave it. Just say the word." I'm praying to Christ he doesn't already know what Strike's done—torn his whole empire to shreds with a few keystrokes.

Hamish steps forward, sneering. "Business? Nah, I don't give a shite about that anymore. Got more money than God himself, and a helluva lot more than you'll ever sniff at, brother. Petrov's girls? They'll all be mine soon enough. I'm untouchable."

"Then what do you want, since you're raised from the dead?" I ask again, my mind still spinning. Hamish. He was burnt to a crisp when he smashed his fancy Porsche into an underpass in Bruges, or so the police said. Now I'm wondering who the poor charred sod in the car actually was. There were remains. I double-checked with the authorities.

Hamish tilts his head, a wicked smile curling his lips. "Mrs. Collins," he says.

"What about her? I have no idea where she is."

"Nah." He chuckles, low and cruel. "That's what's gnawing at you, eh? Who it was in that car if it wasn't me. It was Mrs. Collins." His sneer widens. "Don't fash yerself, brother. The old bitch deserved it."

I don't say a word. Can't. Because he's not wrong. Had I known where she was, I would have killed her myself.

Hamish grins. "Aye, you always were an open book, weren't you? That's why the lasses fawned over you. Such a sweet lad, all moony-eyed and soft. And that face. Look at you, still so fuckin' handsome. Isn't he handsome, Josie-Jo?" His grin twists, mocking. "I'll show you a picture sometime—I was almost as good-looking as Sing-Song, once upon a time."

I keep my jaw clenched tight. I don't trust myself to glance at Josie; her life hangs on me keeping my focus, sticking to my training. But I can feel her eyes on me—burning holes on the side of my skull. I wish I could give her a signal—let her know I'll die before I let my brother hurt her. But right now, words will just get us both killed.

Should have watched von Graf—Hamish—tumble off that bloody ski mountain when I had the chance. Da was right about one thing—my goddamn moral compass always fucks me in the end.

I force a laugh, trying to shift the tension, hoping to throw him off-balance. "Christ, Hamish, I can't believe you're alive," I say. "Back from the dead. It's madness, you standing right here in front of me after all these years. Do you sleep in Da's old room now?"

"Fuck no," says Hamish. "I hated every second I breathed in this shitehole, but, aye, we had our moments, didn't we? Funny how it feels so natural, being here together, you and me. That's why I finally dragged you back. Remember when we used to roll down the hills behind the barn, laughing like eejits?"

I let out a breath, lean into my accent, which tumbles out of my mouth naturally. As if it's attached to the land itself. "Aye, I remember. That's how I broke my arm, and Da told me to man up while I was just lying there, bawling like a wee bairn. Still aches when the rain comes."

Hamish chuckles. "Da was a right bastard. Toughen up or get tossed aside, that was his way. Reckon that's the one thing we both learned, eh?"

"What happens if I put down my gun, Hamish?" I ask, taking a small step closer, keeping my eyes on his. He won't shoot Josie as long as I've got his attention. I crouch down slowly, place my gun down on the ground right in front of him, and stand to hold up my hands in surrender. "Let the lass go sit over there while we talk. You're right, Hamish. I'm a pussy. I can't shoot you, my brother. I just need her for my prototype."

Hamish cocks his head, a flicker of something in his eye as he mulls it over, toying with the idea. "You fancy her, Axe. I can see it. I made this deal with SynthoTech knowing it would all lead to this standoff with you. But now?" Hamish's tone softens, almost sickeningly tender. "I love her. Aye, I have from the second I laid eyes on her. And the problem with you is that you think just 'cause you're the baby—because you're the good one—she should prefer your company, just like every other woman that's stepped foot on this island. But not this time. She . . . she's different. This one is mine. It wasn't my original plan, but you know what they say, best laid plans and all that."

"Well," I say, playing along, "I need this launch. She's my ticket, Ham. We're so close. I just need to do a little more testing with Gemini and then we're finished. Don't make me start over." I'm feeding him just enough of the truth to keep him distracted and distance myself from Josie emotionally, hoping he buys it. My real game is only about getting Josie out of this alive. I'd give away SynthoTech—fuck, I'd let him shoot me—if I thought it would keep her safe.

Hamish's voice is soft. "Josie's the one thing you've got to let go of, brother. You've taken enough from her already, haven't you? She's what I want. I'm not sharing her with lonely lads across the world."

I let out a slow breath. I wish Hamish's feelings gave me even a modicum of comfort. If he loves Josie, surely he wouldn't shoot her. But there's only a twisted logic with men like him. No doubt, he'd rather see his woman die than be with anyone else. "Aye, Hamish," I say, playing along as steady as I can manage. "You're right. She's not mine to keep. Never was. We'll rework She's the One, scrap Gemini, and start with a new avatar. We've collected plenty of other girls' data through the years. No problem."

Hamish nods slowly, his grip on the gun loosening just a bit, the barrel drooping slightly toward me. His hesitation is all I need. My heart pounds in my chest as I let myself risk a quick glance at Josie. Her wild hair catches and curls in the Scottish mist, her green eyes are wide but fierce. My brave girl. I hope to God she understands the unspoken message in my look—back away. Now. If she's the last thing I see in this life, I'll go in peace.

Hamish's gaze wavers, just for a moment.

Then, without warning, Josie moves. Fast. She lunges forward, sinking her teeth into Hamish's hand with a savage growl. He yelps in pain and surprise as she drops from his slackened grip and skitters a few yards away—I'm already moving at Hamish, charging forward like a bullet. Time slows as I close the distance, adrenaline pumping through my veins. The axe—it's in my hands before I even realize I've grabbed for it. Hamish is still reeling from Josie's bite when I swing the axe, hard and precise. The blade sinks deep through his flesh, crunches into bone—*thwack!*—before cutting clean through. A sick, wet pop follows as the severed hand drops to the ground, fingers twitching.

Hamish's scream rips and echoes off the cliffs before his brain even catches up to the pain. He stumbles backward, eyes wide with shock. Blood sprays from the gaping stump, painting his clothes, spattering the rocks.

"Brother . . ." he gasps, near the cliff's edge, his eyes wide with disbelief.

I look at that face—stretched tight and unnatural, like he

thought he could carve away time itself with a fucking scalpel. All those surgeries, all those potions. "Death has a way of catching up to us, doesn't it, brother?" I say. "And it looks like today it wants to collect." I give him a cold smile, walking toward him at the edge of the cliff. And with a swift kick to his stomach, I send him slipping on the slick rocks.

There's a sudden, sickening lurch, and gravity does the rest. He's gone.

I hear Hamish's body crashing against the rocks, then tumbling down the jagged face of the cliff, the dull meaty thud as he lands . . . somewhere.

I peer over the precipice, the salty wind stinging my face.

There is nothing. No sign of Hamish. Just the churning, endless crashing of the waves, that lonely old sound of my youth, a nightmare that drowned everything else. The sea again claiming someone I once loved.

FIFTY-THREE

JOSIE

I'm still standing on a motherfucking island with a motherfucking castle—apparently in Scotland—and Axe just shoved Niles von Grafenhagen right off a motherfucking cliff.

Oh, and his severed hand is still lying somewhere in the dirt.

One second he was here, bleeding and gasping—the next second, gone.

Well, good riddance to that psycho.

"Josie, are you okay? Christ, let me see."

Axe tosses the axe—a literal motherfucking axe—and turns toward me, dropping to one knee like some worried knight. He pulls out an actual handkerchief to dab at my bleeding shin. Who even carries those anymore, especially when wearing head-to-toe fatigues? "Did he touch you?"

His voice is shaking. But not because he just yeeted his own brother off a cliff. Axe is on the verge of tears—for me. Weirdly enough, I've actually never felt better in my life.

Five minutes ago, Niles was holding a gun to my head, but at no point did I actually think I was going to die. Not after everything I've been through.

Not when I've got so much left to live for.

For the first time in . . . forever, I feel strong. Brave. Even ecstatic. Like I could take on anything. And for once, I don't have to fake it with some plastic-ass smile. It's too bad my phone's probably sunk in the sea, because I'd love to delete that stupid JosieFightsOn account right now in a blaze of freedom. And while I'm at it, I'd block my mother, too.

"I'm fine," I say, and Axe gets to his feet, cradling my face in his big, calloused hands like he's checking to see if I'm lying.

Tears are actually falling down his cheeks—he's not even trying to hide them.

This is the real Axe MacKenzie, and I swear, I could not love this man more.

He pulls me into one of his full-body hugs, wrapping his massive arms around me, and I feel my whole body relax. I feel safe enough to finally let go—to hand over some of the broken pieces I've been carrying for way too long.

"You okay?" I ask him.

My question catches him off guard, like no one's ever asked him that before. He's decked out in full camo, looking like a badass action hero, just like that time I saw him in his office—soaked from the rain in his motorcycle gear. But even teary-eyed, he looks invincible.

"That was . . . your brother, Hamish? And this is your dad's island? Both of them were, um, sex traffickers?" I ask, because we kind of need to clear that up.

Axe nods, wiping his face with his sleeve. "I'm so sorry. I'd never forgive myself if he hurt you. I thought I'd lost you, Josie. I thought he might—" His voice cracks, like he can't even say it out loud. He thought Hamish might kill me.

"You think von Frankenface could take me down? Never," I say with a grin. And it feels true now. I'll never be anyone's victim again. I spin around, taking in the huge, awe-inspiring castle behind me. "So . . . you grew up here? That's totally wild. Are you even aware that you have an actual moat?"

"Aye. Stocked with actual eels," says Axe.

I burst out laughing, because it is all so ridiculous and, of course, also terrible.

Axe's phone buzzes. He glances down at it, his shoulders tensing up in a way that makes my heart lurch. He sighs and flips the phone around to show me the text from someone named Hawk.

> Got a live one. Woman trying to make a break for it by sea. What do you want me to do with her?

"Petrov's wife, Veronica. She was here," I say.

Axe nods. "She must have seen Hamish go over and panicked."

Take care of it, he types, then he pockets the phone.

I have to admit I get a little turned on by how quickly he dispatches the problem. Mrs. Petrov does not deserve to live. I don't feel even the slightest moral qualm imagining the life squeezed from her throat.

When Axe looks at me again, there's something in his eyes—an intensity I've never seen before. I ignite—a flare of desire erupts in me, so strong I tremble from it. His breath is shallow, like he's trying to hold himself back. I stare, daring him to be the first to move. We haven't touched, and yet we're both suddenly panting, the want so intense it feels like a magnetic force.

Axe snaps. His lips crash against mine. It's not soft or sweet—it's desperate, hungry, searching. Like he's drowning, and kissing me is the only thing keeping him afloat. My hands are in his hair, tugging him closer, and he lifts me off the ground like I weigh nothing, sweeping me up into his arms. I wrap my legs around him and he spins me around, burying his face in my neck.

He bites and I shriek.

The storm that's been raging all day suddenly breaks, and the sun bursts through the clouds. It's like the universe is giving us this one perfect moment after all the madness. We don't say anything. We just know. He's running, with me wrapped around him, moving with that long, effortless stride of his, like he's got one thing on his mind and nothing's going to stop him.

"Where . . . ?" I ask, but he just grins, that cocky smile that turns my insides as sweet and soft as a marshmallow.

"To the orangery," he says, and though I have no idea what the hell an orangery is, I don't care. I will go wherever this man takes me.

I lick his neck while he runs, taste the salty residue of his tears. And within seconds, Axe sets me down before a building on the edge of the property.

All four walls are made up of arched panes of glass, and inside is a canopy of green. The place is filled with life—trees, plants, and flowers in bloom, set around a stone pond gurgling with fish. Tucked in with the greenery, a large, low bed, built more like a nest, is draped with soft linens and piled with cushions. It feels like it doesn't belong in this sad, broody castle, a mini paradise smack in the middle of all this ancient drama. Kind of like Axe's rooftop garden—a chill spot, totally disconnected from everything.

"I used to come here when I was a lad. Only place I felt like I could escape to on the whole island," Axe says as we walk inside. "Sometimes I'd even sleep here and look up at the stars through the windows and think about all the other people all over the world under the same night sky."

"I used to do the same from my hospital window. I'd feel so alone and wonder if there was anyone else out there who felt as lonely as I did."

He bows his head against mine, forehead to forehead, and the electricity buzzes between us. "Josie, before we . . . before I touch you, I need to tell you something. I can't be one more person who stands before you and isn't who they say they are." He leads me to a cushioned settee in the corner. I sit and wait. My entire focus is on Axe, his body heat, the strength of his arms around me, his thumping heart. I have no idea what he'll say, but I know what *I* want to tell him.

I want to tell Axe MacKenzie that whoever he is, I already know him and love him. I *love* him.

"Remember at the party, that guy Petrov?" Axe asks.

"You mean the one you and Strike were murdering when Honor and I so rudely interrupted?" I ask, and he gasps.

"You knew?" I lean over and close his slack jaw.

"Not then, no. But Petrov's widow told me, and that's the only thing she said that kind of made sense. And once I landed here in this weird-ass sex dungeon castle, all the pieces fell into place."

"Josie." Axe looks at me with panic now, like he thinks I'm about to bolt. Which is hilarious, because all I want to do is climb him like a tree and feel him inside me. Fit our broken pieces together so I can be full of Axe. He is one of the only people in my life who accepts me as is. I've never once shown him the JosieFightsOn version, because I've never had to. Maybe that's what love is—giving someone the grace to be their own messy, chaotic self. And if that self is a vigilante superhero who offs bad guys, well, who am I to judge? "You don't understand. Not really."

"I think I do. You killed Petrov to stop his trafficking ring, and

Niles was next on your list. Glad you managed it without turning the place into a crime scene this time." I grin at him. "The smell of grown men pissing themselves is the worst."

"You can't. You can't possibly want me after knowing that. Knowing what I do. It's not just Petrov and Nil— Hamish. You just saw me throw my brother off a cliff."

"Yup, and I hope the fishies don't choke on his plastic face. And hey, there are worse hobbies than protecting the vulnerable. You're at least doing some good in this world, even if it's . . . creatively violent." I mean it, too. This man in front of me has the biggest heart. "I'd still—"

But I don't even get to finish, because Axe's mouth is on mine again, and any rational thoughts I might have had just fly right out into the Scottish night.

Axe kisses like he rides a motorcycle. Hard, fast, and in complete command. His hand cups the back of my head, and I feel his fingers weave through my hair. I chase his tongue and nip at his lips, and with every kiss, I grow even hungrier for him. Who knew kissing could be like this? He traces kisses up my jaw and then down my neck, and I throw my head back and moan.

"You," he says as his kisses sear my most sensitive skin. "You. You."

Night is falling outside, and the room dims, lit only by the glow of the moon. From our view in this soft nest of a bed in the orangery, a jutting wall of the castle looms up, its Gothic angles a sharp contrast to this paradise of green bowers and citrusy air. I'm too preoccupied even to gaze at the stars, which freckle the spectacular sky.

There is nothing else in the world but me and Axe and this moment.

"Stand up," he says, and I do on wobbly legs.

He gets up behind me, moves my hair to one side, and tugs down the zipper of my dress. It slides straight to the floor, pooling at my feet, leaving me in nothing but a tiny lace thong. He growls, like I'm a steak dinner he can't wait to eat, and in one long lick, I feel his tongue move from the base of my spine all the way back to my neck. He's hard against my ass, and I can't help it—I wiggle against him.

When I turn around, Axe takes me in with a smoldering look from head to toe, like I'm a work of art he wants to absorb.

"You. Are. So. Fecking. Beautiful. Josie. I am the luckiest man alive that I get to touch you." I smile at him, a big, bold, confident shit-eating grin that immediately falls from my face when he drops to his knees in front of me. If he wasn't holding me still—his arms are wrapped around my lower back now—I'd collapse.

Holy shit. I'm about to get tongue-fucked by Axe MacKenzie.

He licks his lips and hooks his fingers into the waistband of my panties and rips them off with one quick pull.

"That was my only pair, you know," I say, fake pouting, but really, I'm stalling. I'm so wet, I'm dripping down my legs, and Axe has barely even touched me. I don't know if I can take much more. I'm already full-body trembling. The way he's looking at me, the things he says—God, that mouth—he could probably make me come with words alone.

"So perfect." He starts with his mouth on my nipples, his tongue circling and then sucking them into his mouth. The sound that comes out of me—somewhere between a pant and a growl—makes him groan in response. "You like that, sweetheart?"

I don't answer—I have no words—especially when I feel his finger trace down my hip, across my lower belly, up the insides of my thighs, around my ass. I should have known he'd be such a fucking tease. Finally, finally, I feel his finger find my slick center, and my entire body tightens.

"Christ, you're soaking." He's breathing hard now—I can see his chest moving up and down—and I want to take off his shirt and his pants; I want all of him, but I'm too overwhelmed. He feels too fucking good. "I have to. I can't wait one more—"

His words get lost as he buries his face in my pussy at the same time as he picks me up, my legs wrapping around his neck, his hands holding me in place by my ass cheeks, and lowers me onto the settee without his tongue breaking contact.

"Axe," I say. "Holy shit. Axe." I have never felt pleasure like this. I feel my eyes leaking—*am I crying? I think I'm crying*—and I shake my head from side to side. I pull at his tousled hair, softly first, and when he moans into my center, I pull harder.

"So delicious. Come for me, bonny lass. Come all over my face." His hands hook behind my knees so I'm spread wide open for him, and he eats me with abandon. His tongue swirls against my clit, lapping back and forth, wet, eager, and then suddenly my whole body is shuddering, and I'm falling, falling, falling. I explode in desperate release.

FIFTY-FOUR

AXE

I could watch Josie come forever—her body arching, eyes fluttering, like she's caught in some perfect storm. I'd never tire of it. I want to study how her body pulses, how her cheeks blush the most delicate pink, how her legs press tight against my ears. I know I will replay this moment—her taste, her smell, her panting; *Christ, that panting*—over and over till my last breath.

She lies back, her arms spread wide, her lips curled at the edges, luxuriating in the glow of her orgasm. I lie down next to her, my fingers drawing hearts on her stomach.

"Stop staring at me," she says, even though her eyes are closed.

"I'm not staring," I say, though of course I am. My dick is pressed hard against my jeans—watching her explode was the sexiest thing I've ever seen in my entire life—but I'm trying to keep my cool.

"Axe MacKenzie, stop getting all moony, because I need you to fuck me right now." Sweet Jesus. Every drop of blood in my body rushes south, and if I don't get inside her soon, I swear I might die. I start to yank off my shirt, but apparently I'm too slow for her, because Josie sits up and takes over. Within seconds, I'm down to my skivvies, and then like magic, I'm on my back as naked as the day I was born.

"Are you kidding me with these muscles?" Josie says, looking at my chest with pure, dead lust. I smirk at her. I spend my fair share of time at the gym—mostly to work out my rage—but those hours have paid off. She licks her lips and trails her hand up and down my abs. "Ridiculous."

She swings her knee over my torso and rubs her wet pussy against me, just once, like a long, languid lick, and I shiver. She takes my cock in her hand, which is now wet from her and my precum, and pumps the shaft.

"You weren't kidding about needing Magnum XLs," she says, eyes as wide as saucers. I can't help but smirk again. "I won't be able to walk for a week."

"Worth it," I say.

"Fuck yeah," she says. "I'm on the pill and clean."

"Me, too," I promise. "Got tested last month."

She starts to rub against me again. If she sinks down onto me with nothing between us, I don't know how much longer I'll be able to hold on. I catch her at the hips, flip her onto her back, and hover over her. I take her hands in one of mine and hold them above her head. Just like the simulation and also nothing like the simulation. Because this is real, and Josie is under me, and I can smell and still taste the salty tang of her, and soon, so soon, I'm going to bury myself inside her pussy.

I catch her eyes, and she looks right back, and all I can think is *love, love, love.* I still for a moment, savoring, my entire body on fire with anticipation. And then slowly, so slowly, because I do not want to hurt her, I push into her. She feels like heaven. Like home. Like the meaning of life.

"Holy shit," Josie says. "You feel like you were made for me."

"How can it be like this? It's never been like this," I'm moaning into her neck as I slowly, slowly pull out. It's the most exquisite torture. I'm desperate for her—to feel that wet pussy strangling my dick. Jesus Fucking Christ, this woman.

"Axe. I need you. Harder. Please."

"Turn over, bonny lass." She rolls over onto her hands and knees and throws a grin over her shoulder. I wrap her loose hair around my fist so I can pull her head back for a kiss. It's sloppy and desperate, and I get lost in it before my cock reminds me it cannot wait another second. I grab her around the middle with my other hand so I can look at her perfect ass while I fuck her.

Then, because she asked for it, I slam into that perfect pussy.

"Holy fuck," Josie says. "So fucking good."

I thrust harder and faster, and as my fingers find her clit, she moans so loud it bounces off the walls of the orangery, filling the air and wrapping around us like music. Pleasure short-circuits my brain, and we're both panting. I continue pumping, the sound of skin slapping against skin, so much slippery wetness. I'm beyond words now, only sensation, lost in her magnificent, dripping cunt, and then, just as she tightens around me and comes in shuddering, gasping relief, I explode.

In the morning, Josie's awake and full of energy, a wild thing I can't quite catch no matter how fast I try to move. I follow her, smiling despite myself, my hands in my pockets as I watch her spin around, teasing me with those bright green eyes of hers.

"Come on, Axe." She laughs, beckoning me. "Show me something interesting."

What she doesn't realize: Josie Greene is the most interesting bloody thing in this whole damn castle. I spent the most unhappy years of my life here, wandering the halls, hiding from monsters, but she's been here five minutes, and it no longer feels like a prison. I'm no good at words, though. Not when it comes to tender things like this. I just shake my head and huff a laugh, trailing behind her.

"All right, lass," I say to her. "If you want something interesting, follow me."

I take her down a side passage, toward the portrait gallery. The door creaks as I push it open, and Josie slips inside, her curiosity vibrating off her. She stops in the center of the room, taking it all in. It's just as I remember it—Hamish didn't change a thing. The portraits stretch from floor to ceiling, grand and intimidating, generations of MacKenzie eyes following our every move.

She doesn't seem to mind, though. She marches right up to the biggest one. The one that's always been hardest for me to look at. Too much truth in those brushstrokes. I stand on the left, frozen in time as a lad of about sixteen, tall and broad-shouldered, but still more scrappy than filled out. There's a tightness to my posture—like I'm not built for sitting and would bolt if I could.

Hamish stands beside me. He's trying to look the part of the older brother, but he holds himself with a false, awkward confidence. His skin is pale, almost sickly, like he hasn't seen the sun in weeks. His frame is frail, and his clothes hang off him in a way that makes him seem smaller than he is. His hair, as dark as mine, is slicked back too tight.

But it's his eyes that give him away; their blue is dull and shadowed, with dark circles beneath them that the artist couldn't paint away. Before I went off to boarding school, before his mum died, Hamish moved with lightness and ease. The portrait captures him in the after, the new Hamish I returned home to from my year away.

"Poor thing," says Josie. As she turns away, the morning light catches her hair, and it glows as bright as a summer strawberry. "Did you ever really get along?" she asks softly.

"When we were young, yeah. And then later, it was like he had given up on being good or kind. He wanted to be like Da," I answer. "He was desperate to be loved."

Josie steps closer to the painting, her fingers ghosting lightly over the frame. "It's so sad," she says. "At first, becoming like your father probably felt so much easier, but then, I bet, once he crossed that line, it must have been hell. Must've stung him even more, watching you manage to keep your decency in this place."

I exhale, crossing my arms. "He always seemed to hate me for not participating. Like my rejecting Da and all the terrible things he did was a betrayal of Hamish, too. I don't know. Maybe he hated me because I couldn't do it and he could. And then he started living so hard and recklessly, there was no reaching him."

Josie's eyes widen. "I guess then it makes even more sense that you thought he died."

"Aye," I say, my voice rougher now. "Drunk driving was the least of it. I could hardly believe he made it to twenty. Him smashing up his car felt fitting. Hamish was always trying to outrun whatever was eating at him."

Josie steps back from the portrait and shakes her head.

"I reckon he eventually pulled himself together and knew there was no way I'd let him turn completely into Da—I'd have immediately reported him or taken him down somehow. So he made his fortune quietly, shuffling it through shell companies, reinventing himself as fucking Niles von Grafenhagen. Bought the castle through small-time brokers and corporations I'd never think to trace."

"I knew that name had to be made up," Josie says.

"I don't know why, after all these years, he wanted to come after me."

"Maybe because he knew it was only a matter of time before you came after him." Josie takes my hand and links our fingers.

"He was sick," I decide, finding a bit of compassion for my brother now that he's dead. Josie's quiet for a long moment, her gaze still on the painting, though I can tell she's not really seeing it anymore. She's somewhere else, far off in that wild mind of hers. I step closer, wanting to touch her, to pull her back, but she speaks before I can say a word.

"The Moon . . . the Star . . . the Ten of Pentacles," she whispers so softly I almost miss it. "She was sick, too."

"What was that?"

"We need to get home," Josie says, a new urgency in her voice. "I have something I need to take care of." She swallows. "It's time."

FIFTY-FIVE

JOSIE

It clicks.

I'm standing there, staring at the painting, and suddenly it feels like the floor has dropped out from under me. Not in a thrilling, fun-house way, either; it's more like I'm in free fall, my stomach churning, my heart racing, everything in me braced for maximum holy-fucking-crap, everything-I-thought-I-knew-is-upside-down impact.

Hamish. Nonna's cards.

I get it now. Related but twisted. A sick person desperate to be loved.

But it's not Hamish I'm thinking about.

It's Mom.

Axe doesn't need telling twice. We're off the island quickly, ushered by a gorgeous man named Hawk—who looks so much like an action hero, I can't quite believe he's a real flesh-and-blood person—and then soon after onto another private jet, and I somehow have acquired a new sundress and underwear. This time, I'm actually awake to enjoy the ride, holding Axe's hand, my head on his strong shoulder as we watch the world pass below.

"Distract me," I say when we've been quiet for a while. So far, Axe hasn't pushed for details or asked why my face looks like I've seen a ghost. Instead, he's just been there—calm, steady, a fortress in strong wind.

"Aye, that shouldn't be hard," he says, grinning. We're sitting next to each other in plush leather seats, and he presses the call button for the flight attendant. She's standing in front of us in fewer than ten seconds.

"We're going to need some privacy," Axe tells her, and she nods, unbothered, and steps forward to draw the curtain.

I don't wait. I'm on him before she even finishes. I need to get lost in his kisses, in his warmth, in the exquisite safety of his arms. Our lips meet, and I immediately turn the kiss desperate. He groans and whispers into my ear.

"Take whatever you need, bonny lass." He knows I desire total obliteration, and he's the only one who can give it to me.

I want him so badly that my pussy feels hollow. I need him inside me right now.

This will not be slow and tender. I don't want foreplay. I don't want to make love, not during this foray into the Mile High Club. I want to fuck.

I pull off his shirt in one single tug and then get frustrated that he's still mostly dressed.

"Stupid, stupid pants," I say, and he laughs. He sets me down on my feet and stands up. He undoes his buckle and drops his trousers. I yank down his underwear, which is tented by that perfect giant cock, which I give one, then two delicious, slow tugs. Then I push him back down onto his seat.

"I shouldn't have bothered to buy you panties," Axe says. "You should go commando for the rest of our lives." I shiver at his casual mention of *the rest of our lives,* relieved that he, too, understands that this new thing between us is going to stick. Somehow, without saying a word, we both know we're forever. Neither of us will ever look up at the night sky alone again.

A slow grin spreads across my face. "Oh, so you want me to go *regimental*? I was wondering if that was actually a Scottish thing or just something that romance novels made up to make kilts extra hot."

He chuckles. "Aye, lass, it's real enough. But I think we both know you don't need a kilt to make things hot."

"True," I say, tilting my hips just enough to make his breath hitch.

Axe pulls the lace of my new underwear down gently this time, so it doesn't rip. I growl my annoyance. Too slow. He laughs again, delighted by my desperation.

I climb onto him. I'm dripping wet, ready before we've even started. Axe doesn't seem to mind—he's also raring to go—and when I center his dick and then lower myself in one quick motion, his groan rumbles through me like thunder.

"Good girl," he says, with his hands gripping my hips and his head thrown back. "Already so fucking good."

I start to ride him, slow for a few beats, just to adjust to the sheer size of him, and then fast, because I'm suddenly so thirsty for his cock, I can't wait. I pant in his ear and set a punishing rhythm. He finds my clit with his fingers and circles while he nibbles and sucks on my breasts.

"Fuck," I say, because he is giving me everything I want and need. That total obliteration. I am lost only in chasing the feel of him, the high of riding him, the shuddering crash that is going to leave me spent. "You were made for me."

"I was made for you," he repeats, and I can tell he, too, is gone. Meeting me in this place of pure pleasure. More than thirty thousand feet from reality. He tilts his hips, and somehow he finds a whole new angle that hits me in the perfect spot.

"Please, please, please," I beg, near tears, though I don't know what I'm begging for. I want nothing more than what he's already giving me.

"Josie, I'm going to—I don't think I can hold on for—"

But he doesn't finish his sentence, because suddenly I'm screaming from the delicious pleasure of release, and I come harder than I've ever come in my whole life. I grip his shoulders so tightly, I'm sure I've broken skin.

He follows me over the edge, and I feel his juddering release inside me. I still, and he holds me there, forehead to forehead, our bodies still joined, both of us a sweaty mess of exhilaration. We breathe each other's air as we pant, and tears spring to my eyes.

Despite the horror of what I have to face when we reach the ground, I'm not sure I've ever felt more at peace than I do right now. A few minutes later, after we're dressed, I curl back up on Axe's lap, and I tuck my head into his neck. And I sleep like that, distracted and satiated, for the rest of the flight.

The moment we land, Axe escorts me off the plane, his grip gentle and yet strong, and guides me to the car that will drop me off at home. Still no questions, no pressure, no demands—just that quiet I've-got-you vibe.

He somehow knows exactly what I need.

At no point do I feel like I have to pretend to be okay. He will not be shaken by the real me.

When we're at my door, Axe finally turns and cups my face in his hands. He's careful. Like I'm precious but not in any way fragile.

"Do you want me to be there with you while you do whatever you have to do, or do you need to do this alone?" he asks.

"Alone," I say. He nods in full understanding.

"I love you, Josie Greene," he says, and I'm overcome with so much joy and gratitude and sadness all at the same time. Axe MacKenzie *loves* me. Nothing else matters, and all I want to do is pull him inside and let him hold me and fuck me and love me till the sun comes up on another day. But there's still business to finish.

He kisses my lips with the softest peck. "I'm going to trust you to let me know when you need me."

Then he walks away and takes my whole heart with him.

Thirty minutes later, I march into Spa-la-la, because according to Alan, my mom is here using my free gift certificate from Axe's dead brother. The irony in this is so obvious, I'd giggle if I wasn't already so overcome with rage.

The air reeks of lemongrass with an undertone of useless rich ladies, and when I blow past the woman at the desk, she hits me with a raised eyebrow but doesn't stop me.

I must look deranged enough that she doesn't want to.

I find Mom in a treatment room, reclined in a plush chair, getting a facial, cucumbers over her eyes like a parody of the good life. Old instincts kick in—some sick, deep-rooted reflex that almost makes me *want* to tell her about my adventures. About how I flew on not one but two private jets in the last three days. About how I saw Scotland. About how I slept in a motherfucking castle.

But I don't, of course.

"Hi, Mom." Something in my tone makes the aesthetician scuttle out the door.

Slowly, my mother pulls the cucumbers off her eyes and looks at me.

Does she know that I know?

Nonna always had a way of speaking through the cards. Like she was weaving together a story from the symbols only she could understand. The Moon, the Star, and the Ten of Pentacles. At the time, they seemed like abstract ideas. Some kind of invisible-ink fortune cookie I couldn't quite read.

But now—oh, Nonna—I so fucking get it.

"What are you doing here, sweetheart? I've tried you a hundred times, and you didn't return my calls!" Her voice is warm, wounded, and so deeply concerned. She has never broken character. Not once. In all these years.

"I lost my phone," I say, and feel a rush of satisfaction knowing I will never have to see her increasingly desperate calls and guilt-trip texts again. Will never have to feel even a shred of obligation to call her back. After today, I won't have a mother.

"You look tired. You should be in bed," Mom says.

And this time, I can't help it. I bark out a bitter laugh.

I think of the Moon card, with its hidden truths and deception, Nonna's way of warning me that something wasn't right. That what I saw wasn't the whole picture.

"I feel great, Mom. Actually, I've been away, and I left my health kit at home. Didn't need it."

"Josie!" She sits up, horror in her eyes.

The Moon card: all her lies.

And next the Star: hope and healing. *Nonna, I hear you loud and clear.*

"I was never sick, was I?" I fire the words like a bullet. No warning.

For a second, she stares at me, her cucumbers dropping from her fingers onto the floor with a plop.

"Don't be ridiculous, Josie. You were *dying*. You lost all of your hair."

"How could I forget? You carry that tote bag with my picture everywhere you go."

The Ten of Pentacles: a symbol of family legacy, wealth, security.

In my case, the longest con. Because this morning, I took Mom's Social Security card and went straight to Shelton Savings and Loan, accessing the accounts tied to the GoFundMe she set up decades ago. No surprise, she's been skimming from the start. Started small, testing the waters. Got bolder as she got comfy. Then greedy. The statements showed it all: regular withdrawals masked as medical expenses. Payments to bullshit companies with names like Hope4Cancer.

Money rerouted right back to her personal account, naturally.

MamaBearSharon's been helping herself to donations from strangers and basically using every grimy trick in the book to keep the cash flowing.

When I closed the account, I vowed to track down every single person who donated, every well-meaning soul who fell for Mom's lies.

I'll start by paying them back. Every cent. One by one. Even if it takes me the rest of my life.

"All these years," I continue, my voice shaking with something between anger and disbelief. "All those illnesses. You made them up, didn't you? Cancer, fake. Asthma, fake. Jesus, Mom. If you'd wanted attention and friends, you could have just joined a Pilates cult like a normal person."

My laugh is empty. My bravado is faltering.

My mother's voice shifts, becomes cold. Flat. Reptilian.

"You were sick, and I took care of you. Everything I did was for you. Do you remember all those nights you spent puking? How you couldn't even stand up in the shower? I thought my baby was going to die!"

She bursts into tears now, shaking her head, clutching her chest. I have to fight every single instinct to comfort her. Because that's what I've been doing my whole damn life.

"If I was sick," I say, my voice steady, lethal, "it was because you *made* me sick. The doctors said I was fine and you—"

"What do doctors know? I had a mother's intuition! I could see you were so ill."

"Tell me about my special insulin from Germany, Mom. Because I haven't touched it since Nonna died, and I'm totally fine. Feeling great, actually. Allergies? Are you fucking kidding me? How did you do it? How did you make me blow up from that bee sting? Did Dr. Don give you something that he knew would make me sick?"

"Josie, stop it! Don't talk to me that way. You're scaring me. Maybe you need a psych eval. I bet Dr. Don can give us a referral—"

I laugh again; I do sound crazy. But I know I've never been saner.

"I feel like such a fucking idiot. But then again, why would I not trust my own mother? The one person who has always told me she would protect me?"

The shoes keep dropping.

"Have you been poisoning me? Your gross tea! That's why I

had the stomach flu. And then, when I blacked out in the car, I had just been to your house! Holy shit, it was you all along."

"What about *me*, Josie? Your father's heart attack was so sudden. So tragic. He was much too young. All our plans, our life together—up in smoke. I was in shock. People kept telling me to stay strong for the baby—how could I? I couldn't eat or sleep, I could barely exist. You needed so much—I couldn't handle it. I started to unravel. But that place . . ." She shivers. "Your grandmother never should have sent me to Ravenswood. The doctors and nurses all saw me as a failure. The pathetic widow who couldn't keep it together for her baby. I was a problem to be managed and medicated. They drugged me into a stupor. Mocked and neglected me and didn't give a shit how miserable I was. When I finally got out and back to you, no thanks to them, I made a vow to myself that my daughter would get the care and attention I'd needed, one way or another. I would find a path to truly heal." She raises her chin defiantly. "And I did."

I feel my stomach twist into a knot as her words sink in.

"So . . . what?" I manage. I think of how many times I slept on the bathroom floor, my cheek pressed to the cold toilet seat. Praying to die because the pain was intolerable. Praying to live because I was told I wouldn't make it beyond the next six months.

"You poisoned your own daughter . . . You made me sick with illnesses I didn't have . . . I got chemotherapy treatments I didn't need so people would feel sorry for *you*? So that people would see you as a martyr instead of a failure, and give you *money*?"

But I see it now. How she kept me sick, kept me dependent. She had to make sure I stayed her perfect little cash cow, fragile and helpless. Every doctor's visit, every panic over my health, they were only ways to keep the donations rolling in, to keep herself in the lifestyle she wanted while making me her meal ticket.

I was never her daughter. I was just her goddamn moneymaker.

And yet now her eyes flash with something like pride.

"I did what I had to do, Josie. No one understood my pain. I was invisible. So I made them see me. And I made them see you, too. My special baby. Everyone loved you. You were so cute with that bald head."

I swallow back bile. "Listen to you! You made me think I was on death's doorstep. So many procedures. I was in agony. You . . . you stole my entire life!"

"You should be thanking me. You were always so ungrateful."

I stare at her, the impact of everything she's done crashing over me in a thousand splintering shards. I can't breathe. I can't think. "You're sick," I whisper, shaking my head. "You're sicker than I ever was. You never loved me."

"Love?" she echoes, her head tilting to the side like she's genuinely puzzled by the accusation. Her eyes glint dangerously. "I gave you love. I gave you *everything*, Josie." Her voice takes on a strange, almost giddy tone. "We had people—*so many people*—taking care of us. Raising money. Fighting for your future! Lifting us up like we were their *saviors*! We were even on the cover of *Parade*." Her eyes gleam with a terrifying mania.

"That wasn't love!" I'm sobbing now, the tears streaming hot down my face. Everything is just *too much*. "That was betrayal. The only real cancer I ever had"—I choke on my words, half gasping, half laughing—"was *MamaBearSharon*. Jesus Christ . . . how does that even happen? How does a mother become *worse* than chemo?!"

My voice cracks, and the sobs take over again, leaving me hiccupping. I can't listen to whatever this woman has to say next. The mother I thought I knew, thought I loved, is gone, if she ever really existed at all. I've got to get out of here. I'm about to slam the door when one last shoe drops.

Nonna.

No, not Nonna, too. Her mysterious stomach flu the last week of her life. The pillow on the floor—I wondered why it wasn't under her head, but that day was such chaos, I figured a doctor tossed it on the floor to use the paddles.

Suddenly I've never been more certain of anything in my life.

"You killed Nonna," I say, my voice sharp with fury, and my mother doesn't even bother to deny it. "You knew I was closing in on the truth. Once I got my hands on some of those files, it was only a matter of time. So you silenced the one person who could confirm everything."

"Nonna was old, Josie," she says, her voice calm, no-nonsense; it makes my skin crawl. "She was in pain. I just . . . helped."

Helped. What a perfectly grotesque word in her mouth. "Helped . . . like you helped me?" I ask. "Like you're helping yourself to this fancy spa day?"

"Josie, don't you see?" she hisses. "Everything I did, I did for us! We were a team—MamaBearSharon and JosieFightsOn!"

"We were not a team. We were an *act*," I spit out. "A sick, twisted, disgusting double act! That's all we ever were because of you."

"People loved us," she says.

"That wasn't love," I say sadly. "That was pity."

I pick up her cell phone, which is resting on top of her clothes on a chair. "Give me your passwords," I tell her, my voice firm.

"What?" Color drains from her face.

"You heard me. Give me your passwords, or I'll call 911 right now and report a murder."

"Josie, don't be silly!"

"Silly is pretty much the last thing I'm feeling right now."

My mother knows me better than to risk it. In a low, furious whisper, she spits out her passwords. I click through to her socials folder and delete MamaBearSharon's accounts on all platforms.

Her entire empire, gone in an instant.

As I step out of the room, I pull out my phone and punch in 911. "I'd like to report a murder," I say as soon as the dispatcher answers. "And I've got all the evidence you'll need."

"Josie!" screeches my mother. "You said—"

"I lied," I interrupt. "Kind of the way you did for my entire life."

FIFTY-SIX

JOSIE

One year later

"Axe, you gonna make it, or did you finally meet your match?" I shout, glancing back to see him doubled over, hands on his knees, gasping. "C'mon! Don't tell me a big, tough Scotsman like you lets a wee hike take him out!"

"Who are you, Wonder Woman?" he wheezes, trying to regain some dignity as I sprint the last mile of our hike up Ralston Mountain. It's a role reversal, to say the least. A year ago, I was the one playing catch-up. But it's amazing how much easier exercise gets when you're not, for example, being slowly poisoned by your own mother.

Life has a dark sense of humor, and I guess so do I. There's not much that's funny about the pasts Axe and I have survived, tangled up with more than our fair share of Devils in disguise. But Axe has taught me that laughter and a healthy dose of optimism are the best armor we've got.

So we've promised to show each other our truest selves, especially when we're the most lost or broken. I've known for a while now what Axe really does, the bloody work he's carried out with

Strike. On some level, I think I always knew. It doesn't change how I see him. What matters is that Axe has never hidden from me, and I've never flinched from him.

Because if we can't be real with each other, then who else is there?

Nine months have passed since my mom died, injected with a strong dose of that custom brew from Germany, which turned out to be . . . well, definitely not insulin. MamaBearSharon was already under the Pennsylvania attorney general's microscope, practically counting down the days to her indictment. Her death was quickly ruled a suicide.

If the police had been even remotely paying attention, they might have questioned the timing.

But I've got to hand it to Axe; he was all in on my plan, no questions asked. Even let me do the honors.

Next, Dr. Don. The guy was napping on his porch when we paid him a little visit. One jab of his own custom cocktail and he was off to dreamland, his farewell letter neatly placed beside him. Poetic justice, delivered.

Killing my two worst childhood monsters was like stepping straight into the sunshine. No more shadows. Just pure, warm light and freedom.

These days, when I'm not at Grace & Honor or overseeing She's the One—we turned the next-gen AI Josie into a brunette named Clementine, who's infinitely less glitchy than Gemini—I'm outdoors, making up for lost time. Axe and I spend hours in his rooftop garden. He bought another chair the day after we got back from that fateful trip to Scotland, like he knew we'd be up there often. Now we sit under the stars, holding hands, wondering how the hell we made it through our messed-up childhoods, grateful that we still managed to find each other.

Hamish's and Petrov's enterprises have both been obliterated, and since he was Niles von Grafenhagen/Hamish MacKenzie's only living relative, Axe quietly inherited everything. Naturally, he donated all the dirty money to the anti–sex trafficking charity that already had half his dad's ill-gotten gains.

But for reasons even he can't articulate, Axe kept Skara Brae.

We've been bouncing around ideas for its future—a sanctuary for women and children fleeing sex slavery tops the list, with one cottage and the orangery reserved just for us. He still rolls his eyes at my woo-woo stuff, but I've convinced him that a little sage and a lot of love can bring peace to any ghosts still lingering in that castle.

When I reach Ralston's summit, I stop, breathless. Not from the hike, but from the view. It's the exact spot where Axe and I had our first date, well over a year ago. But this time, the scene is even more magical—candles flickering, heaters glowing, and blankets laid out just like before, a perfect re-creation of our twilight dinner.

"Whoa. This is like a fairy tale," I tell Axe when he joins me. "You've gone full Nicholas Sparks on me."

"Only, this time, you're not worried about getting anaphylactic shock from something lurking in the food," Axe says as he hands me a glass of champagne.

"Cheers to that." Lately, I've been sampling every cuisine I can get my hands on. Tonight's menu is sushi flown in from Kyoto, because of course Axe doesn't do things by half. "One day, I'm going to tell the world that the tough Mr. Axe MacKenzie is actually romantic AF," I tease as we clink glasses and sip.

"Don't you dare," he says, but he's grinning, and I know he secretly loves it. We sit down, side by side, because apparently sitting across from me is way too far for Axe's liking.

"It's all so beautiful," I say, taking in the sweeping view of the mountains spread out before us in the distance. "Thank you."

"Aye, it is," he says, but he's staring at me like I'm the real view, and I have to laugh because he's always a bit much, though I wouldn't have it any other way. But my smile slips off my face when Axe drops to one knee and pulls out a small velvet box that looks like it's been through its own little adventure—scuffed edges, faded gold trim.

"So, Josie Greene, love of my life, my Ginger Snap, my bonny Cancer with a moon in Scorpio," he says, "will you end our love story the way the best ones do?"

When he opens the box, my breath catches. Nestled inside is an antique ring with a sparkling pink diamond at its center, the band etched with Celtic knots. "Will you marry me, even though I'm a . . ." He pauses, unsure. "Ach, what's my sign again, lass?"

"Leo," I blurt, but I'm already grinning so wide my cheeks hurt. His hand is trembling, and suddenly, it hits me—Axe, my unshakable, confident, tough-as-all-hell man—is actually nervous. Terrified, even.

This isn't just a grand gesture for him; this is everything.

I grab his face and kiss him hard, so hard we nearly tumble over.

"Of course I'll marry you!" I say, laughing as I pull back, and the way Axe's eyes widen, still so stunned—like he can't believe this is real—makes me fall for him all over again. He slips the ring onto my finger like it was always meant to be there.

"It's beautiful," I say softly, staring down at the ring, taking it in.

"I found it in an antiques shop in Edinburgh," says Axe. "It was a bit banged up, but the stone was shining so bright. Waiting for the right person to claim it."

I look up with a laugh. "Like . . . a fixer-upper?"

"Like a hidden treasure," he says. "When I had it appraised, it turns out this is a rare Argyle pink diamond. A color that also reminds me of your blush, rosy Josie."

Even as he says this, I feel the color rise to my cheeks. "Yes, yes, a thousand times yes," I whisper, wanting to stare at Axe but also at the breathtaking ring on my finger. "But you've got one thing wrong."

"Ach, I know this one; it's *Pride and Prejudice*," he says, his own pride showing through in that boyish grin of his. "I don't mind being Darcy. Rich, aloof. So far fucking gone for Elizabeth he'll do anything for her. But I'm curious—what do you think I've got wrong, luv?"

"You said this was the end of our love story, silly," I say. "But it's only the beginning."

Axe squints, trying to place the line like it's a pop quiz. "What book is that from?" he asks, genuinely stumped.

I lean forward and kiss Axe, slow and deep, savoring every deliciously world-spinning moment. It's not like any of the fairy tales I've ever read or any story I've even imagined—including every romance about every shirtless Scottish hunk in a kilt I've ever lusted after.

It's a feeling too big to name, too perfect to script. It's real. It's right. It's . . .

"Ours," I say.

ACKNOWLEDGMENTS

First and foremost, thank you to our fabulous readers, who have gone on this wild ride with us. We could not be more grateful for your support.

A very special thank-you to everyone at Berkley who had a hand in making this book. It truly takes a village, and we are so happy you are part of ours. A huge shout-out to our editor, Liz Sellers—we so appreciate your thoughtful notes and your sense of humor throughout the whole process. You rock!

And finally, thank you to Trudy the dog for your snoring soundtrack. Best music in the world to write to. (Also thank you to Potato, the other dog, who does not snore and was no help in writing this book, but we felt bad leaving her out.)

AXE
and
GRIND

TAYLOR HUTTON

READERS GUIDE

DISCUSSION QUESTIONS

1. Tarot plays a subtle but persistent role in how Josie interprets her world. Why does Josie take comfort in defining her arc through fate? What does the book say about fate versus choice, especially through the lens of tarot?

2. She's the One is marketed as a tech solution to connection—but what does the book suggest about authenticity and intimacy in digital spaces?

3. Axe and Strike come together through their book club. What does this unexpected analog space provide for them that technology and training can't?

4. Josie often mistrusts her own instincts because she's been shaped by a lifetime of medical gaslighting. How does that affect the way she approaches love, desire, and safety?

5. There's a chilling thread in Josie's plotline, in that she has been subjected to many adults weaponizing care. What does *Axe and Grind* suggest about how authority protects abusers?

6. What does MamaBearSharon's online persona say about how digital platforms reward pain?

7. Who do you think is more emotionally guarded: Axe or Josie? What moments cracked each of them open?

8. Does haptic suit technology feel like progress, avoidance, or a little of both?

9. Axe builds dating tech. Josie reads tarot. Who would you trust more to find your soulmate?

10. Design the perfect tarot card for Axe and Josie.

Author photo by Indy Flore

Taylor Hutton is the pseudonym of a pair of writer friends, one of whom has twice been a finalist for the National Book Award and the other of whom is a *New York Times* bestselling author and Edgar Award finalist. Between the two of them, they have written over forty books, including, together, *Strike and Burn*. When they are not passing their latest sexy thriller back and forth on Google Docs, they are browsing bookstores; sending each other ridiculous memes; walking their dogs, Trudy and Potato, around their Los Angeles neighborhood; and making their children cringe with their TikTok videos.

VISIT TAYLOR HUTTON ONLINE

TaylorHuttonBooks

TaylorHuttonBooks

Ready to find
your next great read?

Let us help.

Visit prh.com/nextread

Penguin
Random
House